DARKLANDS

a vampire novel

by

Donna Burgess

NAKED SNAKE PRESS

Darklands: a vampire novel
Published by Naked Snake Press
Pawleys Island, South Carolina

First Edition
ISBN 978-0-9829665-1-8

Printed in the United States

nakedsnakepress.net
donnaburgess.com

"...but we loved with a love that was more than love...
...in a kingdom by the sea."
—*Edgar Allen Poe*

chapter one

November 1.

Someone banged on the door.

Susan Archer woke.   Blinking hard, she shielded her eyes with her open hand against the sun that intruded the flat. When she tried to raise her head, agony seized her and her eyes flooded with tears, blurring her vision. Sobbing softly, she rolled onto her side. Something sticky and cold coated most of her naked body and she looked down at herself. Blood, so dark it was almost black had congealed all over her skin, the floor, the walls, the bed. A scream bubbled behind her trembling lips and she pushed her fist against her mouth to stifle it.

What was left of the apartment's only window was a jagged grin of glass that allowed in the autumn chill like an unwelcome guest. The crimson velvet curtain billowed out like a malicious tongue wagging over Chalmers Street.

Across the room lay Peter, dead in a heap with a splintered baseball bat protruding from the top of his skull.

Her precious brother was gone.

The night before.

"I'm completely wasted," Peter announced, sounding more proud than he should have. He nodded to the server, an old Goth gal dressed as an even older vampire. After a moment, she appeared with yet another pitcher of something too red and too thin to be anything other than watered-down Kool-Aid tainted with a little cheap house rum.

He was already too drunk—he would be sick before the end of the night. Susan considered saying something biting, but instead regarded her brother across the small table, through the gray haze of smoke. It was almost like looking into the mirror, with Peter dressed as a dead and festering Raggedy Andy to her zombiesque Raggedy Ann. They were Dizygotic twins and nearly identical in every sense. With their deep blue eyes and auburn hair, they were stunning, even in make-up that displayed their pretty mouths sewn crooked and their tanned skin grayed to the pallor of death. They fit well with their surroundings, especially on Halloween. The place was a retro-Goth club, patterned after the gloomy death-children of the 1980s, a dark sanctuary where the jocks and preps dared not go. It had no sign out front and most of the kids referred to it as "the hole." An apt title, Susan determined.

Situated so close to the bay, salty condensation perpetually fogged the club's windows. Inside, dark velvet swathed the walls in crimson, violet and inky black. Smoke curled up like ghostly fingers from the glowing ends of cigarettes. The air was a puzzle of odors, both good and bad, depending upon the proximity to the entrance to the restrooms—cloves, tobacco, pot, spilled vodka, a hint of dried vomit. Lights from a small dance floor flashed red, pink and purple in time with the electronic beat of the music. The rules of Halloween were the rules of "the hole" all year around.

The damned costume itched in all the places that Susan would rather not scratch in a crowd—even in the questionable crowd that loomed in the shadows of the hole. She would have been just as happy back to the flat with a fatty and a little wine. But Peter? Peter was "party-guy" since leaving Reading. The rest of their little group of art college social misfits had departed an hour ago, with ideas of sleep or sex in the backs of their tired minds, leaving Susan and Peter at a booth in the back corner.

Susan was about to call it a night when she spotted the guy again. Dunwich was a resort town, with a smattering of small colleges tossed in the mix. Either way, it was a transient city—people came to school or to hide, either way often vanishing overnight. She was not accustomed to seeing the same faces time and again. But this face she did not mind seeing once more.

How many times had she encountered this particular guy in the past few weeks, though? The thought made her bristle. She could not help but wonder if it was more than simple coincidence. In the library, cutting through the park much too late, and even once, heading home long after sunset.

The first time had been nearly two months ago, back in summer. Susan had become drunk with a strange girl named Mary Lei at the pizza parlor near campus and had almost been attacked as she walked home in the middle of the night. This man had intervened.

Her hero.

He looked her way and she wanted to glower at him— that was the darkchild's way, after all, but a drunken college -girl smile was all she could offer.

He seemed to materialize at their table. "May I join you?'

"No," Peter said.

"Ignore him," Susan said, scooting over to make room on

3

the cigarette burned vinyl. She shot Peter the scowl she had not been able to use on the guy.

"I'm Devin McCree," the man said, sliding in next to her. Susan sipped her drink, trying too hard to act casual. She wanted to look at him, to stare, but instead stole glances when she thought she could go unnoticed. Dressed all in black, golden hair, short and messy. Ginger eyelashes framing blue eyes much darker than hers and Peter's. Close up, it was evident he was older than she originally thought.

The idea of an "older man" did strange things to the pit of her stomach. She took another, longer drink and then asked, "So, what are you? It is Halloween, you know."

"What do you think I am?" he asked. He had an accent, British perhaps, but softened to the point it was almost indistinguishable.

Susan considered a moment before answering. "A guardian angel? Or a vampire. I know a girl who says the city is filled with vampires."

He laughed. "Maybe it is." He glanced at Peter. "What do you think?"

"I think it's fairytales and bullshit," Peter said pointedly. "And her friend's a weirdo, anyway."

When Devin suggested Susan take a walk with him, Peter nearly lost his head. "You'll excuse us," he said, climbing awkwardly from the booth.

Glancing at her new friend, she shrugged. Devin stood and let her out, smirking as Peter hooked his arm through hers and dragged her away toward the ladies room. "Don't leave, okay," Susan called over her shoulder.

The bathroom smelled even more like vomit and cigarettes than the bar. Susan shoved the door closed and yanked her arm from her brother's grasp.

"Stupid! What the hell's the matter with you?"

"You can't just leave with some guy," Peter said. "You know better than that."

"He's *the* guy, Peter. The one who saved me."

4

"He's much older than we are. He might be a nut."

Susan leaned over the sink and peered at herself in the mirror. She fingered a stray smudge of mascara from beneath her eye. "Maybe he's the one taking the chance."

Peter rolled his eyes and rested his chin on her shoulder. In the mirror, they appeared like double vision. "Fucking *please!* You're real dangerous."

"A baby-faced killer," Susan said, bearing her teeth at her reflection. "You wouldn't be so concerned if you had met someone tonight, you know."

"Well . . . that's different," Peter argued.

"If he wanted to hurt me, he's already had the chance."

"Still, I don't feel good about it."

"Give us forty-five minutes, okay?" Susan pleaded.

Peter clenched his jaw. "It only takes a minute for a crazy person to kill a girl. Or rape her. You never think about that stuff."

"He's hot, Peter."

"He's too old. And he's weird. Mom and Dad would have a shit-fit—"

"You're gonna tell them?" Susan challenged.

"N-no. But—"

"But what? We came to here to get out from under their thumbs, Peter," Susan said. "I should thank him, anyway, don't you think?"

Peter frowned. "Sounds like you plan to *really* thank him."

"You make me sound like a giant whore." Susan smiled, then pressed her nose to his. "Forty-five. No more."

Peter shrugged. "Forty-five. No more."

Susan planted a kiss on the faux-stitches at the corner of his mouth, then rushed through the door.

"You'd better have your clothes on," Peter called after her.

Susan's Doc Martens clapped dully against the damp street, but her guardian angel or vampire, whichever, made no such sound as he strolled. When he gave Susan his threadbare peacoat, she slipped into and pressed it to her face, breathing in the scent of age.

They reached the flat just as a thin rain began to fall. Susan led Devin inside and up the creaking, slanting stairway to their room.

"Ah, very nice," he said when she opened the door. She stepped aside to allow him to enter first, but he did not move.

"A decent Deathwalker must first be invited into one's home," he told her.

"Please come inside, Mr. McCree." Then she asked, half teasing, "'Deathwalker?' You're not some kind of monster, are you?"

Devin kissed her as gently as she had ever been kissed. "Do I look like a monster?"

"N-no," she stammered, taking a handful of his shirt and pulling him across the threshold.

The place was low rent and even lower square footage. If they were not twins, there was much doubt she would be able to live so amicably with Peter in such a tight space. The wood floors were scratched, the hot water did not always work and the kitchen was a two-burner stove and a refrigerator barely wide enough to accommodate a frozen pizza. Susan had bought a foldout love seat from the Goodwill store for ten dollars and Peter had brought his thirteen-inch black and white television from home. They had painted the walls with murals of monsters, Goths, castles, mystic creatures and lands—the landlord would have a stroke when they moved out. It smelled of cheap patchouli incense and mold.

Susan peeled off the wool coat and draped it on the back of a desk chair. "Sit down. I'll get us something to drink."

Devin plopped on the loveseat. "That can wait. Come here and let me kiss you again."

She did what he said. How could she not?

Devin's warm tongue traced the line of her lips. With a tiny gasp, Susan opened her mouth slightly, eager to meet his tongue with her own. He tasted of marijuana and whiskey and something else—like metal or perhaps even wild—she could not decide—but it was quite lovely. When he pulled back, her make-up had smeared across his lips and chin like a bruise. She thought of Peter. Would he return in half an hour, as agreed? She imagined him still in the bar, or walking around downtown, sulking, and that was just like him, anyway. He was the very reason she seldom went out at all. Part of her hoped he would not return until dawn.

Devin pressed his lips to her neck.

She felt a little strange, as if there was an itch inside her skull. It must have been from the alcohol, she decided. She tried to ignore it.

"I could feel the hot breath on my neck. Then the skin of my throat began to tingle as one's flesh does when the hand that is to tickle it approaches nearer, nearer," Devin whispered against her skin. "Tell me from where that quote comes, or I shall bite you."

"Dracula," she said. "Dracula. And you can bite me, anyway."

"If you insist."

Devin kissed her throat again, and Susan slipped her hand into his thick hair, pulling him to her. He groaned and pressed his hips against hers. She stroked his chest and then his stomach but stopped there, afraid to move lower.

"Here," he said, taking her wrist, guiding her hand to his lap. His eyes were almost closed.

Susan shook her head and a lazy grin spread across Devin's face.

"Yes. I'll not hurt you."

She shook her head again, a little girl gesture, but still she was unable to resist. She leaned forward and kissed him, tasting the saltiness of her own skin on his tongue. Her palm pressed the bulge in his trousers and drew back.

"I've never—" she began. For some reason, she wanted to confess. She had only been as far as *almost* "doing the deed" with Ethan Walker, the boy she dated for two years in high school. She hated to seem so dreadfully young and inexperienced with this man.

"Don't worry. I know," Devin told her, as if he had read her thoughts. He stroked her cheek and her face grew warm where he touched her. She could drown in his dark eyes. He leaned forward, his lips just brushing hers and then more insistent.

"I've imagined this moment since the first time I saw you. I will make you mine."

A pang of fear uncoiled in the pit of Susan's stomach when he said this. She now hoped Peter would indeed remember their pact. She glanced at the Felix the Cat clock that hung beside the refrigerator. Felix grinned back wide and rolled his eyes. Peter was five minutes late.

Devin unbuttoned her ragged costume dress and pushed it off her shoulders, where it fell to the floor in a soft gray heap. Susan unhooked her bra and tossed it to one corner as Devin knelt in front of her. He mouthed her navel, sending tremors of excitement through her belly and groin, then leisurely, he rolled down one leg of her tattered fishnet stockings, then the other. She stepped out of her panties and kicked them away.

Devin tugged his shirt over his head, then taking Susan's hand, he kissed her fingertips and pressed her palm to his chest. "Touch me, Susan. Feel how quickly my heart beats for you?"

Susan wet her lips and ran her hands over the lean muscles of his chest and stomach. She pulled the sparse blond hair there, and moved closer to draw her tongue around first one nipple, then the other. He shuddered and pulled her into his body, his cock pressing into the soft flesh of her stomach, trapped inside the confines of his clothes.

They sank onto the bed together, and she found herself beneath him. The night became a wicked, electric swirl of ecstasy as Devin's hand slipped between her thighs and his warm fingers kneaded the damp folds there. In only a moment, the muscles in her stomach tensed and she felt as if she might explode.

"I promise I will not hurt you," Devin murmured against her ear. He opened his trousers and her hands found his feverish, hard flesh. She stroked him until he trembled and then he pushed into her.

But something did hurt; something she was not expecting—something not down low, but higher, as though the tender flesh of her neck had ripped. She cried out as hot tears burned her eyes. She crushed her face against Devin's shoulder, smelling soap on his skin. He cradled her against him, his movements slow and delicious. Shortly, that wondrous slow building tension settled in her middle once again, and this time she did explode. Driving deeply into her, he groaned and then shuddered.

Afterward, lying in his warm embrace, Susan hovered at the threshold of sleep. Above her, incense smoke swirled and danced in the purple pinpoints of Halloween lights Peter had strung up. Devin's face floated above hers, smeared and out of focus. He kissed her eyelids and then her mouth. She thought she tasted blood.

The stereo played very low, something quite old, Jesus and Mary Chain or maybe it was Echo and the Bunnymen. Sometime in the midst of night, Devin whispered Susan a bedtime story.

"There once was a city built upon a bay. Now, this city was filled with ghosts—they lingered there because this city was built on history. Of all the American cities, this city held Europe in its breasts.

"Inside the walls of this city lived a princess of auburn hair and alabaster skin. Lips like the petals of a rose and thighs like silken pillows in which a rogue placed his sleeping head."

Susan responded, but she was not sure if the words poured from her lips or circled inside the haze of her brain. ". . . but we loved with a love that was more than love . . . in a kingdom by the sea."

"Jesus! What the hell did you do?" Peter.

Susan moved her lips and tried to answer him, but nothing happened. She drifted semi-conscious. It seemed she was looking through a narrow tunnel. Devin stood, pulled on his trousers and moved toward her brother.

"She's fine, Peter," he said. "She's not hurt."

"She must be! There's blood everywhere." Peter sounded hysterical. It was obvious he was very drunk.

Susan rolled onto her side and pushed herself up. The room swirled crazily around her. The voices, the movements sounded hollow. She had no strength. The muscles of her legs trembled and refused her commands.

Blood everywhere?

Peter and Devin appeared as smudged and impressionistic as images from a painting. Devin towered over the scant form of her brother, who was only as tall as she. Susan looked down at herself, her naked body decorated in scarlet ribbons. She touched her throat where Devin's beautiful mouth left a stingy wound and her fingers came away painted red.

Her scream bubbled behind her quivering mouth and poured out like a flood of sound, uncontrolled.

"Hush, now. You're fine," Devin told her. He put his

hand out to her.

In one corner was a wooden baseball bat that was there for protection than sport. Peter snatched it up and wielded it over his shoulder, his face a mixture of terror and determination.

"Wait, son. I don't want to hurt you." Devin held his hands out before himself, a seeming gesture of peace.

"Fuck you," Peter spit. The bat struck first across Devin's hand, the crush of bones sickening, but not as hideous a sound as the dull thud of the bat crashing into his face. Devin's head flew back in a mist of blood. Before he could move, Peter struck again and drove him to his knees. Devin's handsome face became a mask of red wetness on one side. The other side was still perfect and untouched.

He struggled back to his feet, teetering drunkenly.

Peter slammed the bat down on their coffee table. The cheap wood collapsed and the bat splintered. Peter shook the fragmented remains at Devin. A wooden stake.

"You think you're a vampire? Then die like one!" He rushed at Devin with the bat gripped in both fists above his head, but although injured, the big man was too quick. He easily dodged Peter's attack.

Regaining some awareness, Susan stumbled closer to the two men. She was not dying—at least not just yet. "Wait," she said. "I'm okay, Peter. Stop."

Too late. Devin moved aside and shoved Peter from behind. Just a simple opened-handed push—and not very hard. Nevertheless, Peter was drunk and perhaps the man who called himself a "Deathwalker" did not know his own strength.

In a breath, everything in Susan Archer's life changed.

Peter tripped and fell forward. At first Susan was not sure he was even injured. He was still on his knees, after all. But as Devin's expression melted from agitation to one of horror, Susan knew something horrible had happened. She moved to get a closer look at her brother.

"Peter?"

She knelt before him, her mind unable to register exactly what she saw. Somehow he had fallen onto the splintered end of the bat. The jagged wood pierced the soft flesh under his chin. He still looked at her, but no longer saw her. His faux-stitched mouth opened slightly and inside she saw the blood-streaked base of the bat in there. It was only after another excruciating moment that she realized that the end of the bat had exited the top of his head.

He tumbled over onto his side, still bent at the waist, a discarded doll.

"Dear God," muttered Devin. He sounded ill.

He touched Susan's shoulder as if trying to wake her. "Susan? I'm sorry. Do you hear me? I did not mean to hurt him. You have to believe me." His words were slurred, wet -sounding, difficult to understand. His jaw had been broken.

Susan stared at him a moment, this stranger she, only hours ago, had offered herself to. She shuddered. *So cold.* Inky spots bloomed in front of her eyes.

"Listen. You're going into shock. Here, let me cover you up," Devin said. He wiped at his bloody face with the sleeve of his shirt, then snatched the quilt from the bed. Susan shivered again, her teeth clicking together. A shiny red pool flowered from her brother's head.

"You killed him?" she whispered. She stepped backward, rubbing her eyes hard with her fists. "None of this is really happening."

Devin approached, holding up the quilt, but she backed her way into the bedroom area. Franticly searching for a moment, she found her knapsack on the floor under the edge of the bed. Her eyes never left Devin. She knelt and groped around inside the large bag until her fingers wrapped around her small Swiss Army knife she her grandfather had given her. With trembling hands, she took it from the bag and opened it.

"Wait, Susan. Please." Devin blinked fast to clear the

blood from his eye.

Brandishing the knife, she lunged at him. "Now, you are going to get the hell out of here!" she shouted. "Get away from him!"

Instead of moving away, Devin stepped closer. "Listen to me."

"Get back!" Susan waved the little blade.

Devin sprang then and grabbed for her hands.

Susan thrust the knife forward and it sank into Devin's McCree's stomach, just below his sternum, to the hilt. She ripped the blade downward, six inches or more, as if she were drawing open a zipper. Devin gasped and doubled over. He stayed that way for a moment and then straightcncd up, blood flowing from his middle.

"Susan," he said, looking down at himself. With a deep, pain-filled sigh, he slipped the knife from his belly and slung it away.

He approached her again, the blood pouring out of him; his groin and his legs wet with it. He left perfect footprints of it on the wood floor.

"I only wanted you to . . ." His voice wavered.

Out of room, Susan pressed herself against the wall and steeled for whatever he offered. She closed her eyes and balled her hands into fists.

Devin grasped her shoulders. "Shh, Susan. Please." He sounded desperate and as frightened as she felt. Screaming, Susan thrust her hands forward, her hooked fingers sinking deep into the gash in his gut. Her slick fist wrapped around something in there—muscle, flesh, organ—she did not know, but she yanked as hard as she could. Devin's soft cry built into a howl of pain like nothing she had ever heard. He dropped to his knees, Susan's fist still deep inside him. Susan dropped to her knees in front of him, stunned.

Devin's wide, blood-sticky hands grasped her arm and he shoved her away from him as though she were nothing but a ragdoll. She flew backward into the wall, splintering the ornate trim at the base and ceiling, creating a spider's web of cracks up and down the heavy plaster.

But in an instant, Devin's hands were on her, pulling her up. His fingers pressed her throat, checking for a pulse. "S-Susan? I'm so sorry. I never meant to hurt you. I never meant any of this."

Susan faded from consciousness with Devin's agony-filled face hovering like a ghost over hers, and she forgot all she had ever known for a while.

chapter two

T he present.

Susan's shuffling around pulled Michael Matthews from the first moments of decent sleep he had enjoyed in a week. He sat up, rubbed his eyes, then rubbed his hands through his hair. Elvis, the bushy Maine Coon and Susan's familiar, stirred and peered at him, somewhat annoyed, before nestling back down to sleep.

Susan was up already, dressing. She walked by wearing only panties.

"About time, sleepyhead," she said. She leaned over and kissed him, her naked breasts brushing his chest and then gone again. She removed a running bra from the dresser and tugged it over her head. The newly healed incision on her belly, just at the crest of her hip showed like a frown against the smooth, pale skin. Michael was not sure he would ever grow used to seeing that scar, although he was the one who had made the incision and had placed the sutures.

"You're running this morning?" he asked.

"I need to get back to normal sometime." She pulled on a pair of skimpy exercise shorts, then pulled her hair back into a thick ponytail and slipped a small terrycloth band over it to hold it in place.

He loved how she could do that without ever looking into a mirror. It must have been one of those little tricks only beautiful women could pull off.

"I think it's a little soon." He got out of bed and went to her. He wanted to let her not to go. Not yet. It just was not safe. Officer Susan Archer was not a popular woman among certain people in Reading just now.

She picked up her iPod and allowed him to hold her. Michael had the impression she was not really into the affection he offered so freely, but he held her until she relaxed into his embrace. She stroked his hair.

"I'm not going to become a recluse over a bunch of inbred rednecks, she said. "And I'm not going to dwell on the shit that has happened to us, Michael. We'll be fine."

Tears threatened and he blinked hard and sighed, refusing to let them come. Surely, he could hold himself together. After all Susan had.

Susan was glad to be out, away from the house, away from Michael's cloying presence. Sure, he was sweet and he was only doing what he felt necessary because he loved her, but she needed a break. She had gotten her fill of the kicked-dog looks and the annoying questions. "Do you need anything?" What she needed was space, but she could not bring herself to tell Michael that.

Now she just wanted the autumn sunshine beating down on the top of her head and her face, her feet striking the dirt, her breathing deep, rhythmic, almost hypnotic. She wanted to have the music loud and fast in her ears and her mind as blank as she could get it. She was exhausted, but she wanted to push herself. She wanted things to get back to normal, whatever normal was in her world. The world smelled of rain and saltwater. Closer to the docks the stink of fish would become sickening. When she was pregnant, she had quickly learned to avoid that, after a bout of dry heaves she thought she would never shake.

Sleep had not come easy since that day in front of the All Saints Church of Reading. Her mind refused to shut down and allow her a few peaceful hours sleep. Images of blood and the sound of crying laced her dreams.

Susan had fired her service revolver a total of three times, not counting the range, when she killed Owen Lee. Lee had been holding a gun to the temple of his two year-old son outside the church where his ex-wife was remarrying. That was six weeks ago, but much of what had happened was like a dream itself, the faces dull and smeary, the sounds alternately shrill and muted. There had been three squads there, but for some reason, he fired toward Susan first. Someone later mentioned a vendetta toward women, but what did that matter? The bullet entered at an odd angle through the side of Susan's abdomen, beneath the protective shield of her armor and that was that.

The baby had taken most of the impact, her tiny protector.

Susan in turn had blown Lee's face off before she collapsed onto the pavement. Since then, the man's family had been sending threats, thus the reason for the gun. The threats of an ignorant clan of white trash frightened her about as much as the Easter bunny. She only hoped Michael was not around if anything happened. He did not deserve getting caught up in her mess.

Besides, Lee had gotten what he deserved as far as Susan was concerned, and she felt nothing for him or his family. In a breath, he had taken her child, her future. Maybe he had even taken her heart.

Owen Lee's little boy's confused face, splattered with blood his father's blood, buzzed around her mind like an annoying insect. She swatted it away repeatedly and pretended not to feel. But she wondered if she had done the kid any favors, really. Michael assured her the boy was too small to remember, but she was positive there was no hope for him, now. Thanks to her. Scars like that never healed. She should know that better than almost anyone.

She thumbed the volume higher on the iPod and quickened her pace, almost as punishment.

Run, run, until you collapse. Until what little bit of heart you have left explodes.

The waterfront slipped by, such a comfort that its beauty went nearly unnoticed by her—fishing boats docked, big gray pelicans resting at the tops of the masts, smaller more graceful starlings skimming the gold-stained surface of the bay.

Life moved in a circle, she had always heard. Maybe it was true. In the weeks and months immediately following Peter's death, Susan had spent most of her waking hours playing the night over again in her mind. Sleep had offered no escape; Peter's blood filled her dreams. She had lived in a perpetual hell of Halloween night, her brother's last night alive. The doctors had shoved pills at her—pills to forget, pills to sleep without dreams, pills to dull the moments of horrible clarity. She refused pills now, no longer able to rely on the soft, blurry quality they gave everything. Even the softest memories were haunted.

Besides, she deserved the hard edges. If life moved in a circle, perhaps she was finally paying for getting Peter killed.

From the master bedroom window, Michael had a grand view of the bay a quarter-mile east, where shrimp boats docked, tied and ready for unloading, their nets raised on either side like tattered wings. He could watch Susan run from up there, but it made him feel a little perverted—like a voyeur. He knew she wanted to be left alone for a while.

Instead, he peered down on the little house where he

grew up. Squatty and tiny, it had been a poor family's home. A couple, quite young, unmarried and with a new baby rented it now. They looked like throwbacks from 1969, but they kept the place in tiptop shape. The lawn was green and manicured and the girl planted beds of pansies that seemed to stay in perpetual bloom.

Michael's childhood was a good one in that place, despite the lean living at times. A good, *boring childhood.* His father had been a shrimp boat captain. He stayed away for days at a time and before Michael was very old, he came to dislike the ocean very much. Michael blamed the water. He associated the salt small and the briny odor with his missing-in-action dad. In reality, it was not the ocean, but the call of a whiskey bottle that caused his dad to vanish when it was time to go to his baseball games and birthday parties and even his high school graduation.

"I'll only embarrass you, boy," his old man had told him once when he had gathered the nerve to ask why. He thought about that a while and decided it was probably true and never mentioned it again.

Michael knew his mother only from old photos and his dreams. She decided she wanted no part of a fisherman's life and packed her bags when Michael was still in diapers. He got a postcard from her once, when he graduated from med school. It had made his father sad all the way to the bone. Sad and afraid to give love. His dad made no apology for his lack of affection, and in the end, Michael did not blame him. The old man had loved him well enough through the college fund he had put away. He died in his sleep one night just before Michael graduated medical school. An easy death, someone had said at the wake. Michael had seen enough death since and knew there was no such thing.

Maybe he should move. Perhaps he could convince Susan to leave with him. Maybe he could convince her to run away from the nightmares the both of them carried like stones around their necks. They could start over again--new people in new places. No secrets, no hurtful pasts.

He shrugged and turned away from the window. He would never leave Reading. He would grow old here, overlooking his boyhood home and the bay every day until he died. But now it was looking more and more as if he would be doing it alone. He was losing Susan and the more he wanted to give her, the more she seemed to pull away.

chapter three

An hour later, she was at the police station. She had taken a "forced" leave to recover from the bullet wound, but the whole thing reeked of suspension. Nevertheless, she felt more comfortable behind her desk and at home now that she was back on her feet.

The police station was empty, save for Chief Cotton. Cigarette stink lingered, a bit more tolerable now than when Philip, their other investigator was there, chain-smoking away and talking his macho bullshit. She was glad he was out; she was in no mood for his lip this morning. She had been with the police department for fifteen years and a detective, specializing in domestic cases, for more than nine, but Phil, only five years in, treated her as the perpetually rookie. Victimized women and children--that was where her heart was. Maybe somewhere in the back of her mind, saving some helpless woman or child might make up for losing Peter. But the losses just kept coming and she was no closer to redemption now than she had been years ago, when she made her way back to home from Dunwich, all alone with only her mother and father and a secret surrounding her last night with her brother. Both her parents went to their graves using her as a poor substitute for their only son.

Someone asked her once why she had gone into the line of work she had chosen. "Maybe I can help someone find their way," she told them. Sounded noble, but she had been drunk when she said it.

The late morning sun rained dusty through the window over her desk. She removed a stack of photographs from a drawer and slowly thumbed through them. All of her or Peter, or the two of them together. She had taken them and little else when she left her home for the last time, after her parents had died. Little quarterback and little cheerleader, ten years old. She examined others--she and Peter in front of the old Beemer, all packed up and ready to leave for college. The two of them, arm-in-arm at the beach at thirteen. All she had left were those photographs. Both she and Peter had been majoring in art—Peter had aspirations of becoming a commercial artist; she would teach. Over the years, those images were so ingrained in her mind she could draw them from memory, capturing every angle of shadow across their young faces, every fold in their clothes. If she still had the desire to draw.

Memories of Peter's death had staked claim to her dreams lately. Of course, maybe the recent loss of her baby had triggered it, she reasoned. Long ago, sitting alone under the roof of her family home with her parents blaming her for her brother's death, she decided that shame was her burden. She would live up to the name her mother saddled her with—*Susan the Lost.*

Besides, she had done worse things since. Like keeping her pregnancy a secret from her lover, all the while wondering if she even wanted the child at all. Nevertheless, barely two months along, she had already started thinking of the fetus as a child—*her child.* She liked the idea. But still, she had not wanted to share the news with Michael so soon.

There would be time, she thought. She would surprise him with it. At eight weeks along, she began buying things here and there—a hand knitted onesie, a small blue dolphin made of terry. A pair of dainty booties. All of these things she hid away in a box deep in the back of their closet, behind a stack of Michael's medical textbooks.   It was early, but the excitement had already taken hold.

Last night was a parade of memories, in the form of nightmares--surreal, twisted in time and place.   Hateful, confusing things. A beautiful, fair-haired stranger. He took away her virginity and then her brother's life.   Oddly, however, in the dreams, she was always the age she was now—staring at forty and not particularly happy about it. An adult, not a teenager, and everything even more sordid and rotten than it actually had been, if that was possible. Susan had woken with the taste of blood on her tongue. She had bitten the inside of her lip in her sleep.

Later, she stood before the bathroom mirror as she did most every morning, studying her face, searching for her brother there. What would he look like now? Would he still be so beautiful? She tried to imagine him on the downside of youth, with fine lines around his eyes and smile lines at the corners of his mouth. Would he still be an artist? Successful? Would he be a father? Would they still be close?

She then tried to not only see her brother in the mirror, but the girl she had been. Her face was strangely still much the same. The lines had not encroached at all—but her body was not as colt thin and delicate. She had been a distance runner in high school. Back then, her strength lay in her stamina. But things changed on that Halloween night years ago. Determined to never again be powerless, she became fixated with self-defense and cross training and her body grew curvy but strong. She had lost some of that muscle tone as she recovered from the gunshot.

Susan quickly stacked up the photos and shoved them into her purse, hiding them among various scraps of paper and notes and slipped out before anyone ever realized she had been there.

chapter four

Susan lay propped up on one elbow, looking at the same stack of photos she had sorted through earlier at her desk.

"Are you reading?" Michael asked. He removed his glasses, climbed into bed, and snuggled against her warm body. He pressed his chin into the soft curve of her neck and peered over her shoulder.

"No," she answered. She held up one of the pictures— the one of her and Peter just before they made their drive to the college. "Do you think we looked alike?"

Michael laughed softly. "Are you kidding?" Amazingly, she had changed so little since. He teased her about it sometime, the fact she had barely aged in twenty years. *In the genes, she always told him with a shrug.*

She smiled sadly. "Good. I'm glad." She put the photos aside and her mood instantly brightened. "Now, I'm going to get some cake."

"Sounds good to me."

She got out of bed, wearing one of Michael's t-shirts. Shivering, she reached for the robe lying at the foot of the bed and pulled it on.

"But don't wear that," Michael said. He moved to her and pushed the soft velvet back down off her shoulders.

"Well, why on Earth not?" she asked demurely.

"Because you look really good when you are cold," he said. Her nipples stood out hard through the thin cotton of the shirt and he traced his fingers over them.

She let the robe fall to the floor and they groped their way down the hallway in the darkness, giggling like kids. Downstairs, Susan took a small desert plate from the cupboard and cut an enormous wedge of the chocolate cake that one of Michael's patients brought him. Michael poured a tall glass of milk and, together, they headed back to the bedroom.

Michael stretched out on his belly next to Susan. Through the big bedroom window, a thunderstorm approached over the angry waters of the bay. Sometimes, living this close to the Atlantic, the rain came so hard and fast that they could see it moving across the water like a gray veil. Between bites, Susan prattled about her day and about how when she was small, her own grandmother used to make a wicked German chocolate cake. Michael was relived she had moved on from her memories of Peter. He wished she would put all those photos out of sight for good.

He nodded and responded when he should as she went on, his mind more on how much her brother's murder affected her recently. The anniversary of Peter's death loomed like a corpse in the bedroom, although neither of them mentioned it. The shooting and subsequent suspension went the very same way—no mention of it. Was holding so much inside harming her mentally? She was tough, but nobody was *that* tough.

When they finished the cake and milk, Michael took the dishes and placed them on the bedstand. Then he pulled Susan into his arms and nuzzled her neck. Slowly, he slipped her t-shirt up and over her head, then kissed his way down her breasts, awash in the sweet, soapy scent of her skin. His mouth lingered on one nipple, then the other, until they were as hard as little stones against his tongue.

For a moment, something strange and a bit ugly popped

into his head. Had there been more between Susan and her brother? Was there something deeper and uglier that went on that night? Something had sealed her emotions long before he met her. Mystery painted everything surrounding the murder—to the point that she suggested she might have experienced some sort of memory loss. He forced the idea from his mind. This is the woman he loved, after all.

Susan unbuttoned his shirt and then untied the drawstring of his pajama pants. Her warm hand slipped inside and found him already hard. He pressed hungrily against her hand and she encircled him, stroking until he groaned. Michael's impatient mouth traced the line of her body from her neck to the soft triangle of hair between her legs. He nipped her thighs and she giggled and tugged his hair gently.

"Stop!" she cried, but he ignored her and pushed her legs apart and tasted her until her body grew tense, at the threshold of her climax.

He moved back on top of her then and slid inside her with one easy, practiced motion. How he loved feeling her come against him. He remained perfectly motionless on top of her, only his lips moving against her lips, as she trembled in his arms. The contractions of her orgasm drove him quickly toward his own and he could stay still no longer.

The blaring sun yanked Michael from a deep sleep as it peeked through the curtains. Outside, it dried the world from last night's storms. Susan mumbled softly—"Peter, no." Her hand moved and shot forward, as if she were reaching for something. Michael sat up in the too-bright room and rubbed his eyes hard.

He touched Susan's warm shoulder. "Susan? Wake up."

She did not respond. But for him, sleep was over. He got up, pulled on his pajamas and trotted downstairs. Thanks to the harsh sunshine and the cold wood floor against his bare feet, he was already fully awake. He made his way to the kitchen, whistling softly. Something told him to just hang in there and everything would eventually be all right.

chapter five

From the shadows of the oaks, Devin McCree watched the couple through the window of their kitchen as they prepared a meal. It was the very picture of domestic bliss—something he had missed since his life with Evie and the children. The man—Michael—sliced mushrooms as Susan poured two glasses of red wine. Her laugh was like the tinkle of bell. How Devin wished he could trade places with that man.

One of the better parts of becoming something beyond human was the ability to hear others' thoughts. Of course, this neat trick only worked on mere humans of the *living* persuasion. Those who straddled the line of life and death seemed to be shielded from thought stealing. Tonight he plucked Michael's thoughts cleanly from the air. It was as if they were amplified through a radio receiver.

Devin wanted so much to hate Michael for being there, with her, but could not. The man adored Susan. And Susan loved him, although her feelings appeared darker and laced with more random ideas. Anger. Paranoia. If ideas could be colored, Susan's were crimson, brown and grey, in contrast to Michael's brilliant yellows, blues and pinks.

Ah, Susan, beautiful Susan! Not a girl, but a woman now, so confident and strong. There was not a trace of the innocence Devin had once known as her most dominate trait.

So many years of waiting for her. Of wanting her. He had fled Dunwich, so distraught he was over killing the boy, but the time away was brief. But, he could not stay away from Susan. After only weeks, he found himself in Reading. He became shadow, her protector, waiting like a specter for her to become a woman. Now he watched her, ready to make her what he had been for nearly seventy years.

Of course, it sounded easier than it would actually be. There was a time when Susan dwelled in her hatred of him but that had softened with the passing years. What remained was her terror of him. That was the one thought that came through clearly, time and again. She had tried to kill him before, out of fear. It stung, knowing she was frightened of him. Convincing her to go with him would be one hell of a trick.

Still, if she became like him, she would have to relent. She would have no other option.

Susan killed someone recently, but she did not hold any sorrow for that. At least not *outwardly.* Devin had eavesdropped on the sorrow she held for her lost child, however. It was an emptiness inside her as cold as a winter's night. Occasionally, she fretted over what would become of the dead man's child, but had tried to disown that responsibility.

She was hard now, her mind and her body like stone. She trained herself as if she were a fighter. He watched her run sometime, in the falling dusk, legs pumping fast, her face lost in concentration. During those runs her mind became nearly clean of thought, her breath a steady, whispered song. Other times, Devin watched her sprint as if she were running from something until she had to stop and lean against a tree to keep from collapsing; her breathing like agonized gasps and her thoughts like storm clouds, churning and scary as hell. *Kill myself. Better if I had died . . .*

It was those thoughts that made him decide it was time to

come to her. Perhaps he should have approached her one of those times, but he was too afraid of her reaction. Again and again he told himself she might now be strong enough to resist him, but he still doubted that. Strength against a weak -minded criminal was one thing, but against a creature of his abilities was something else. The decades taught him one very important thing—he got what he wanted, no matter the cost.

So many years had passed and she still looked like the girl she had been when he first set eyes on her. She had seen so many ugly things, things that would have left lines on the face of a mortal woman. But because of his bloody kiss, she would never age like a mortal woman. The aging process had slowed drastically. She was a Halfling—part-mortal, part-Deathwalker—but she did not realize it. She would remain a Halfling until she drank from him or one like him. First, he would again need to take her to the cusp of death.

It was her auburn hair that first drew his eyes. When she turned, the resemblance was startling. The first time he had looked into Susan's eyes sent of flood of old memories back, and he had wanted to be sick, wanted to weep. Instead, he hugged her to him and the girl laughed against his shoulder. He had made her uncomfortable, perhaps a little afraid of him, but he had not allowed himself to care at the moment. All that mattered was feeling good, even if it was just for a while. She could have been Evie at twenty, the summer they met. Quickly, it was clear she was nothing like Evie, but by then he knew he loved her, so it made no difference.

After so many decades of loneliness, he wanted only to possess this exquisite creature, to take her back to his home.

To make her like him.

But that was two decades ago. And things had fallen to pieces. Went straight to hell and here he was in the shadows like some phantom, planning to attack the woman he loved.

He would have her, finally.

chapter six

L ondon, November 1940.

They had only been in the city for a year, since Devin returned from fighting. He was a lucky one—injured, but not gravely. A bullet with his name on it, part of which was still embedded in the muscle and flesh of his thigh, it was enough to bring him home for good. That injury and his father-in-law's pocketbook. Evangeline's father was wealthy and knew the right people. And he wanted Devin to come to work at his construction firm. Devin did not know much about numbers and books, but he did know how to run a construction crew. Besides, they could not pass up the money, when it was theirs for the taking. But the bombing had been going on for over a month. His work became a trickle and the city was in shambles. If only they were back out in Lincolnshire, in the safety of the countryside. He mentioned up sending the children away, only for a while, but Evangeline wept at the thought of it. The children were small—David only three and Anna eight, and she could not bear it. Devin could scarcely bear it himself, but he had to think of their well-being.

"How about you go, also. Work is not a factor now. We could all go," he suggested.

But no. She would not consider the move until "Daddy" said it was all right. "When this is over, you will need the work. And there'll be plenty to go around."

"Let's just get through this first," he said.

She was as stubborn her old man and Devin let it go. It did not matter, as long as they were together. Together, huddled under the kitchen table, the four of them. Devin remembered that moment more than any other with Evie— her face in shadow, mouth drawn in worry, shouting over the sirens, her auburn hair falling across her cheek. They had only gotten two gas masks and pushed them onto the children's face despite their protests. David wept beneath his, his sobs sounding as if they were coming from inside a coffin. How Devin had grown to hate the city.

"It's okay," he told them, although he wondered if it really would be. He stroked the boy's soft hair.

Anna had her hand on his leg, her tiny fingers pinching him in time with the explosions. David pressed his tiny hands to his ears, Evie's hands pressed to his hands. Devin kissed her.

"We'll be fine."

chapter seven

Susan liked Yeoman's Seafood Shack very much despite it raggedy appearance. It was a cramped bar and grill down along the waterfront, decorated in fishermen's net, old ships' wheels and shark jaws. Tacky all right, but the seafood came right off the boats and was cooked to perfection. The smell of fried oysters and shrimp filled the tiny place and permeated the cool air outside. The music was always good, the beer always cold and best of all, it was only a short stroll from home. She and Michael could walk there and enjoy the cool of the evening.

They met Gerald and his wife Joanne there this evening, just as they did almost every Friday night. Michael and Gerald Cotton hit it off from the beginning, just as Susan and Joanne had, despite an age difference of almost a decade between the two couples. On Friday nights, Gerald was not Susan's supervisor, but her friend. Still, it was getting late and football had been the subject of discussion for most of the past hour, and Joanne who was pretty in a motherly way, pretended to doze. She propped her elbow up on the table and rested her face on her hand, her eyes closed. After a while, Susan slipped her hand under the table and up the inside of Michael's thigh, a not-so-subtle sign that she was also ready to head home. It worked like a charm.

"Can't get enough, can you?" Michael whispered into her

ear. A sleepy, goofy smile spread across his face.

"I suppose I can't," she agreed. Then she moved her hand even higher, her fingers dancing across his crotch. He jumped a little, and shortly, paid the tab.

"How about a ride?" Gerald asked as Michael pulled on his jacket. "It's chilly out there."

"We'll walk," Michael told him. Clumsy, he helped Susan into her coat. "Maybe it'll sober me up." He wove his warm fingers through Susan's and gave her hand a sweet little squeeze.

"Or give you pneumonia," Joanne said. She was clearly ready to go home, but Gerald had already moved to the other end of the bar, having found another buddy to talk football with.

Susan and Michael stepped out into the crisp October night. The cicadas were like electricity and a light breeze touched their faces and puckered their lips with the saltiness of the ocean. Nobody good traveled the single-lane road that lead back to the bay this late unless they were coming to Yeoman's for a late meal and a drink. The walk should have been a quick one.

The men were on them before they reached the end of the parking lot.

There were two of them and the first one was huge. Not muscular, but massive bulk—meaty arms and a big swaying belly under a dirty flannel shirt that left the bottom edge of his hairy gut exposed. The other was smaller, only as tall as Susan was, but his body was as tight as a wire.

Susan recognized them right away—relatives of the Owen Lee, man she shot in front of the church. The big one was Alton Lee and the smaller one, Charlie Franks. Both were no strangers to the local police. Susan arrested Charlie twice in the past year for beating up his girlfriend.

Charlie went for Susan and grabbed her around the waist with lightning speed. Savagely, he threw her to the ground. The force of the move was so surprising that she laid there a moment, drunkenly trying to catch her breath and gather her wits. Charlie then flopped on top of her, crushing her breath out of her once again. He easily pinned her arms to her chest.

Gravel rained down into the collar of the woolen peacoat—a gift from a handsome killer she often wore like some sort of morbid reminder. Down into her blouse, the pebbles tore like claws into the flesh of her back as she struggled. Then a loud, solid THUD. She needed to get her arms unpinned and grab to the revolver that was holstered against her ribs underneath her coat. Charlie's jagged nails dug into the skin of her wrists. She would see ugly black bruises ringing her arms like mottled bracelets the next morning.

Michael fell, disappearing behind Gerald's police SUV. Susan screamed for help, but it came out hoarse and weak, as though her throat was made of sandpaper. A dirty hand covered her mouth, crushing her lips against her teeth, drawing blood, cutting the sound abruptly before anyone heard. She only hoped that Gerald and Joanne were almost ready to leave.

She wrestled with her attacker, struggling fiercely to find Michael. Finally, Charlie moved just enough for her to pull her leg free of him. She brought her knee up hard, aiming for his groin, but missed and instead struck his sharp hip. The bone cracked dully and Charlie howled with pain and rolled away from her like a wounded animal. Susan's leg went numb from the knee down for a moment, refusing to work right as she tried to stand.

"You fucking bitch! I'll fucking kill you," Charlie yelled.

Susan managed to get on her feet, slipped in the gravel and fought back up. Charlie snatched at her feet with one hand, but she deftly dodged him. Then she reached under her jacket, searching for her revolver. To her horror, it was gone. When she jerked around, Charlie Franks waved it at her, grinning like a shark.

There was a sickening, loud snap as big Alton's boot caught Michael in the ribs. Michael's breath left him in a defeated groan and he fell flat on his belly. That asshole was going to kick him to death if she did not get a move on. Michael scrambled back to his knees, fighting to get off the ground. He almost made it when the big, square workbook drilled him in the ribs once again. Susan wanted to cry, but bit it back—she had to keep it together. She had watched someone she loved die before. She sure as hell was not going to let it happen again.

"Get away from him, you shit!"

Alton Lee was one horrible creature, with a tangled beard that reached the raveling collar of his food stained shirt. What little of his face was visible was ruddy with exertion. Susan's only hope at the moment was he might drop dead of a heart attack. Of course, she could never be that lucky. Rancid body odor, beer and filth enveloped him like a fog. He stopped a moment and his eyes fixed on Susan's.

"Whacha gonna do, babydoll?"

"What the hell do you want? Money? Take it. My wallet? Fucking take it," Michael said.

"Don't worry, asshole, we will."

Alton Lee reached down and grabbed the collar of Michael's field coat and jerked him from the ground, then punched him hard in the face, leaving a nasty gash under his left eye. Blood streamed down Michael's face and his head dropped back. Alton then hauled him upright, and held him out front like a shield.

Charlie moved forward, slightly bent at the waist. He pressed Susan's revolver under Michael's chin and with the other hand, rifled through Michael's pants pockets, taking first his keys, then his wallet. "This is for what your little bitch did to my cousin."

Susan looked at Michael a moment. His eyes drifted—he was out on his feet. Alton hauled him straight up until his loafers barely brushed the gravel parking lot.

"Tell you what," he said. "Come with us and we let him go. Otherwise, we kill him and you still go with us. In the end, it's all gonna be the same."

Michael slowly opened his eyes. "Don't listen to him, Susan."

Then Gerald was there.

"It's about time," she snapped at the police chief.

"You can't seem to stay out of trouble, can you?" he answered. Joanne cowered in the doorway of the restaurant where the sparse late-dinner crowd gathered to watch the show.

Michael came around some, and Susan could not decide if that was a good thing. Everything took on the surreal slow-motion quality of a dream after that. A switchblade came to life in Alton's grimy fist. In a flick of the wrist, blood appeared on Michael's neck, thick and dark, running like slow molasses. Alton bellowed laughter.

From the darkness, someone or something flew by Susan and a flash of memory hit her like a blow to the face. Twenty years ago and a dark walk home. Like déjà vu, the big silhouette plowed into Charlie like a linebacker and sent him flying across the parking lot. The revolver sailed from his hand. Susan leapt for it, skidding on the rocky surface, and she snatched it up, ready.

In a breath, the shape reappeared behind Alton, who blinked stupidly into the darkness, confused and still gripping Michael's jacket collar. The shadow took hold of Alton's ratty hair and yanked his head back. The blade clattered to the ground. Alton let go his hold on Michael, but gave him a hard kick to the back, sending him reeling face first into the rocks, tearing his chin open and ripping his palms as he tried to break his fall.

Because of the darkness, Susan could not see very well, but the sounds were nightmarish as the tall stranger proceeded to beat Alton to a pulp. Blood sprayed upward like black mist in the chilly darkness. He then stood over the wretched heap a moment, his wide shoulders heaving. He turned toward Susan and for an instant, the light touched his face. Susan's heart nearly stopped.

Devin.

As quickly as he appeared, he vanished into the shadows of the oaks and the tall ship masts.

Charlie watched all of this unfold, his stupid, bleeding mouth open and sucking wind. As soon as he saw an opening, he took off as well, his boots crunching the ground as he disappeared into the night.

Michael sat up, glassy-eyed. Susan ran to him as Gerald approached the battered attacker, gun in hand and ready to fire, if necessary.

Susan kneeled in front of Michael and held him in her arms. She kissed him tenderly, still clutching her gun in a death grip. "Baby? Michael, speak to me." She pulled back a little to get a good look at the cut at his throat. The flow of blood was already slowing and the gash did not appear very deep.

Michael nodded slowly. "Yeah, I'm okay," he told her, his fingers trailing first along his jaw and then his throat. The switchblade had not been close to his jugular, thankfully. "Are you?"

"Yeah," she said, although she was not entirely sure.

"Who the hell was that guy? Where did he go?"

"I don't know." The lie came so smoothly that Susan surprised even herself.

"He saved our lives, you know."

"Yeah. I know."

chapter eight

Michael walked unsteadily out of the emergency room with only a few stitches below one eye and a couple of butterfly bandages closing small gashes in his chin and on his neck. Susan felt like crying with relief, but forced a wide, false smile and wrapped her arms around him.

The attending doc prescribed pain medication that made Michael loopy and Susan laughed most of the way home, Michael's head resting on her shoulder in the backseat of Gerald's white police-issue Tahoe. She was stone sober now and perfectly able to drive, but Gerald and Joanne would not hear of it. Michael muttered nonstop about how terribly slow the E.R. was and how vastly inefficient the staff worked, as though he forgot *he worked the E.R.* himself a couple of times a week.

Gerald even offered to have an officer park outside their house, in case Charlie Franks decided to pay another visit. Of course, Alton Lee would not be doing very much visiting for a while, after the beatdown he received at Devin's hands.

Devin. Susan could not stop wondering why he decided to reappear after all this time. Had he been watching her, as he had in Dunwich? He had not aged a day in the last twenty years. In fact, he was exactly the same, except his hair was now cut very short and he wore a stubble of moustache and goatee.

He was the same. Just as she was . . . almost.

Obviously, he had not come with the intention of killing her.

Susan helped Michael undress for the shower. Purring loudly, Elvis wound around and

through their legs, but miraculously, they managed not to fall over him. Susan found a number of ugly, black bruises darkening Michael's back and belly. The x-ray had revealed a couple of fractured ribs, but there was little to be done for that, aside from rest. They stood under the hot water together, washing away the stink of blood. She soaped Michael's face, then neck and chest, gently touching the bruises and cuts. Michael grinned at her, his eyes half-mast. "You know. You should soap me up all over. I'm really, really dirty."

Susan laughed. "I know you are, but we should get some sleep."

"Okay," he said, agreeably. He yawned. "I'm *sooo* messed up."

"I know. But you'll be fine in the morning." She kissed him on the lips, mindful of the cut there. Below their feet, the water swirled pale pink down the drain.

They toweled off and clumsily she helped Michael into a pair of shorts then got him into bed and under the covers. Next, she pulled a loose-fitting t-shirt over her head, slipped into a pair of boy-shorts and collapsed on the bed. It was only then that Susan realized the full extent of her own injuries. Nothing major, but she would be walking slowly, her muscles sore and tender, for a week. Her knee was the color of a grape, swollen and stiff, where she struck the Charlie Frank's hip, but she was too exhausted to go back downstairs for an ice pack.

Just as Michael fell asleep, he whispered to her, his lips grazing the cup of her ear. "I was supposed to take care of *you,* Susan."

She sat up, propped up on one elbow and watched him a

moment. He said nothing else, but she found the slow, soft sound of his breathing comforting. She touched his cheek with her fingertips and then planted a small kiss on his mouth, mindful of his cut lips.

Susan had often wondered whatever became of the man who killed her brother. Any

other man would have been mortally wounded with the gash she had handed Devin. She had assumed he might have disappeared into the night and died. As all things will, memories of the night became soft with time. She no longer hated the man, reasoning that it was indeed an accident that had taken Peter. After all, he had been her protector. He would not have saved her, not once, but twice, only to turn around and kill her.

As sleep finally started to overtake her, Susan recalled the first time she had seen Devin,

in a situation that was not unlike the one that had taken place earlier tonight. It was perhaps three or four months before Peter died as she walked home, having been out too late.

Someone had been following her.

She could have taken the train, but she loathed the notion of being underground.

Underground meant rapists, robbers, druggies, and rats. She had already had enough rat encounters since moving to the city. The city was teeming with them. Besides, at barely twenty years old, Susan relished the time alone, despite the uneasiness. She remembered how her grandmother always told her that the "monsters" came out after midnight, but she was not especially concerned about monsters.

She had gone out with an exchange student from Malaysia named Mary Lei, who carried with her a vast knowledge of the occult and a fake I.D. Susan had not told Peter because he would have wanted to tag along and monitor her every movement. Together she and Mary spent the little money Susan made working evenings as an artist's model for continuing education students on Wednesday afternoons drinking cheap wine in the corner booth of a dank pizza parlor and discussing scary books. Mary, who was far more strange and interesting than any of the other girls Susan knew, spoke cryptically of how the entire city had become infested with something called k'uei, which as it turned out, was some sort of Chinese vampire. However, after she made a drunken pass at Susan, Susan decided it was best to leave. Susan enjoyed Mary's company, but even with her extremely limited sexual experience, she was quite positive that she preferred men.

Because of the wine, her thoughts meandered along roads they typically would not have traveled. Back to "monsters"—*thank you very much Mary, as a long car* moved down the avenue at coasting speed. The broken blacktop crunched beneath its bald tires. It eased passed, leaving Susan with the smelly vapor of exhaust.

When she rounded the corner onto her block, she spotted the man. Stupid with wine, she wondered was he the one who followed her, and if so, how did he get ahead? She carried nothing she could use as an effective weapon—a canvas bag that contained her apartment keys, a sketchpad and two pencils. She reached inside the bag, wrapped her fist around the pencils and picked up her pace.

The man emerged from the piss-yellow rain of the street lamp, his steps quickening, as well.

Fear settled in Susan's chest, cloying inside the pit of her throat. Thoughts of Mary Lei's vampires again, and Susan reasoned she was only buzzed. She scanned the leaning, decrepit houses on the block. Lights off, all but the blue glow of a television set here or there. Most with drapes shut tight and doors sealed against the night. Over her shoulder,

42

a light rail train roared past like a silver and white snake slithering into the night.

The man raised his face to hers, his hair and eyes inky, his skin as pale as the moonlight. She shivered and considered fleeing into the shadows. Silly, though, she decided, determined not to allow her fear to overtake her rational thoughts.

Ten feet away and the man smiled, or was that a smile, at all? Teeth glinting, lips curled back like the maul of a mad dog, the shadows of the old houses falling across him and then away in thick bars. She did turn now, but as if by magic, he sprang, his fingers brushing the back of her blouse as she began to run.

Another shape flashed by and Susan tripped on the uneven, weed-infested sidewalk as she glanced over her shoulder. She fell sprawling, tearing the skin of her palms and knees through her jeans and flash of a six-year old Susan hit her, falling in the schoolyard, tangled in a jump rope. Wincing, she rolled onto her hip as the larger figure hoisted her would-be attacker from the ground and hurled out onto the street. The man landed in a heap with a loud *oomph* and then lay motionless.

From the darkness, Susan's savior appeared, square-shouldered and fair. He stalked the man lying on the street, his fists clenched at his sides. Susan had climbed to her feet and had sprinted up the sidewalk toward her flat before she could witness what happened next.

Sleep threatened more and more as the minutes passed. Sinking into a doze, Susan

watched the sheer white drapes billow out and fall back in the light breeze. The smoothing autumn air cleared away the last of the alcohol haze, but she slipped out of bed and closed the window anyway. She then locked it and drew the drapes. For the first time since moving in with Michael, she was afraid of being in the big house. They often slept with the bedroom window open. The house was old and a bit musty. It played hell on her allergies sometimes. Nevertheless, tonight the open window was nothing short of frightening. Dangerous, as though she was inviting someone, or some*thing in.* She wanted to lock herself and Michael in against the darkness. She blamed the events of the night finally catching up to her, but it did not change the way she felt.

Her eyes finally closed and she eased immediately into a dream where Owen Lee, a huge chunk of his skull missing thanks to her shooting skills, scaled up their outside wall like a huge, hungry fly. He headed for their window, but this time he had pointed white teeth that glinted in the moonlight like the steel of a blade.

He left a long slug's trail of blood and brains behind him on the whitewashed wood veneer of the old house.

Susan jumped awake. "Don't be so stupid," she muttered into the darkness.

She thought of the growing stain of blood on Michael's throat, imagined it changing the front of his white shirt into bright red and that image brought back the memory of Peter staring blankly at her as his blood drained away.

It was a long time before she found sleep again.

chapter nine

A week later, the sound of footsteps on the sandy road out front pulled Susan from a thin, troubled sleep.

Lying awake, she stared into the gray of the bedroom, wanting to tell herself that it is nothing. Just another nightmare. Next to her, Michael lay curled up and warm, sleeping soundly for what must have been the first time in days. His injuries had been rough on him—cracked ribs prevented him finding a comfortable position in bed.

Susan closed her eyes and stayed perfectly still, listening to her heartbeat in her ears, listening to his soft breaths. Listening for more footsteps or even worse, the soft squeak of a door opening.

Silence.

Nevertheless, sleep was not going to happen for her. She sat up, felt beneath the mattress for her gun, and took it out. When she slipped out of bed, the wood floor was like a sheet of ice against the balls of her feet. She pulled on her robe over her t-shirt and panties and padded to the stairs.

He was down there. She *knew* it.

Devin McCree was in her house, blown in like a wintry breeze. Perhaps he sat at the dining room table, prying through her purse. Maybe he was waiting in the dark for her to come to him. In the depths of her mind, Susan saw him, the black shadows falling across his handsome face, hiding the haunted indigo of his eyes. She gripped the gun tighter, her palms growing slick with sweat.

At the top of the stairs, she paused, her heart pounding, her breath hissing through her clenched teeth. As she began down, she felt as though she were descending into a dungeon. The old, curved staircase was pitch black and seemed much longer tonight.

At the bottom of the stairs now and in the foyer, Susan turned toward the living room, her gun thrust out before her. She moved then toward Michael's office. Nothing but shadow.

Her finger stroked the trigger of the Glock.

"Who the hell's there?"

Hot breath on the side of her neck. "You know who."

She whirled around toward the sound of the voice, her gun raised. "I'll blow your stupid head off," she whispered.

Now she saw him standing in a bar of moonlight that fell between the opening in the drapes, illuminated gray and blue like a ghost or a sinister angel. Devin McCree bent and pressed his forehead against the muzzle of the gun, then stretched his arms out to either side like a dancer.

"Be my guest," he said," but make sure you finish the job."

She pushed the gun hard against his skull and bit her lip. She could do this. Her fear of this man was reason enough.

As if reading her mind, he whispered, his tone mocking, "Do it, Susan. If it will make you happy."

"Why are you here?" Susan lowered the gun, but remained on guard. "Why now, after all this time?"

"You know why." Devin caressed the side of her throat. Grimacing, she pulled away from his searing touch.

"I don't."

"You do," Devin said.

"Get away."

"I don't believe that's really what you want." Devin's sharp, white teeth flashed in the moonlight.

"Then what is it I want? You seem to know, so tell me." He was exasperating. "I want to move on with my life. I'm tired of all the wondering about what happened that night. I thought you were dead. *Hoped* it."

"I want to make things up to you. I want to finish what we started that night."

"What we started?" Susan asked, laughing softly. "I can't believe this."

"You know exactly what I'm talking about. Think about it, Susan. Why do you still appear so young? Do you really believe I had nothing to do with that?"

"I don't know what you're talking about," Susan snapped. "And I don't know what the hell you are, or *think* you are, but it's nothing I ever asked to be a part of. All I know is that you killed my brother."

Devin shook his head slowly. "I never meant to hurt either of you, Susan. I've lived with that every single night of my life since."

"You know, I would love to shoot you now," Susan whispered through clenched teeth.

"You've already said that." Devin stepped closer and pushed the gun back down to her side. His nose brushed hers and he wet his lips slowly. "I never meant to hurt you."

"You're lying."

He slipped his big hand behind her neck and cupped her head. "I want you near me, Susan. That's all I ever wanted." He shoved her gently back against the living room wall, pinning her there.

Susan struggled against him, raised the gun and held it to his temple. But he kissed her so deeply, so sweetly, she knew she could not resist. The length of his warm body pressed hard to hers and she met his kiss. She could not help it, just as she could not help herself when she was just a girl.

They entwined their eager bodies together in the shadows of the winding staircase, but in the pit of her mind, she knew

Michael might wake any moment, find her missing, and come looking for her.

Would Devin kill him, if that happened? He had, after all saved Michael from certain death at the hands of Alton Lee.

Devin took the gun from her loose fist and placed it on stairs. He slid his hand under her robe, opening it and the belt fell to the floor, followed by the robe itself. Then he slipped his fingers between her legs, under her panties. It was as if he was inside her head—he knew exactly how she wanted to be touched. She writhed against his hand, her breaths coming in short gasps.

Hurriedly, she tugged at the button on his jeans, then at the zipper. Freeing his enflamed member, she caressed it. At that moment, he moved his mouth down over her throat. He rested his lips there an instant, then he bit into her skin, causing her to gasp at the sudden, yet familiar, pain.

Devin yanked her underwear down and she stepped out of them. Lying back on the stairs, she then opened her legs to him, and allowed him to enter her. Hooking one leg around his waist, she wound the other around his thigh. Silently, they moved in rhythm. Devin flicked his tongue against the small opening in her skin, lapping at the blood pooling there, sending shooting tremors of pain through her.

Susan's mind swirled. The dim house swayed and the shadows danced. She felt she might faint.

What the hell am I doing?

Devin filled her up, almost painfully so. Even then, the agony laced with pleasure and her orgasm caught her off guard. She wrapped her arms around him, her fingers digging into the taunt muscles of his buttocks, and she pulled him even deeper into her. She was then aware of him drawing her blood from her. It was just as it had been that night in Dunwich. Alarmed now, and thinking of all the blood, of their tiny flat painted in blood, she began to fight him.

"Stop, Devin."

"Hush. Let me finish this."

"No—"

Susan struck at him, but it was futile. His lips worked at her throat making the wound sting again. She felt her blood escaping and there was nothing she could do to stop it. Dizzy and confused, she clutched at him to keep from falling. Her breathing grew constricted—it was as though she was having an asthma attack, but then a surge of adrenalin flooded her body and she flailed at Devin once more.

What's happening to me?

Again, as if reading her mind, Devin whispered, "You're dying. Don't worry—it happens to all of us."

She thought she was still fighting him, but her hands had fallen to her sides. She was so thirsty, so very dried-out. A raw, excruciating sensation ripped through her chest.

Devin whispered her name as he came. Afterward, he became motionless and tenderly held her for a few moments.

She no longer saw anything. Her thoughts remained panicked, but now resigned.

"Don't be afraid, Susan. Just listen to me, okay?" Devin's voice became low drone, a vibration against her ear and neck as he spoke. A warm wetness touched her lips.

"If you want to live, open your mouth. Don't worry. I have you."

With what little understanding she had left, she did what he told her to do. Devin pressed the inside of his wrist against her slightly parted lips and silky liquid flooded her mouth. Finally, as strength flowed back to her limbs; she grasped his arm, sucking hard at the open vein. She swallowed and ran her tongue out to trace the edges of an open gash. Awareness slowly returned.

"That's it, Susan," Devin told her. "Yes. You're coming back to me now."

Acutely alert now and greedy for his blood, Susan continued to drink. She held his arm with one hand and a fistful of his shirt with the other, gripping him closely to her.

"Oh, hell," he muttered.

He tried to pull away, but she was amazingly strong now and she was not about to let go just yet. She was far more powerful than she ever had been. She could break him into one thousand pieces, if she wanted. Devin shoved her against the wall and yanked his arm away.

Susan stared at him, but the dark stairwell suddenly seemed well lighted. With the back of her hand, she wiped his blood away from the corner of her mouth.

"What have you done to me, Devin?"

Devin backed away, closing his pants. Then he kneeled, retrieved her lace panties, and handed them to her. Grinning rather devilishly, he picked up her gun and gave it back to her, as well.

Susan quickly pulled on her panties, and then groped around for her robe. She slipped it on. When she was dressed again, she drew her fingers across the tear in her neck, sticky with cooling blood.

"Susan? Where are you?" Michael was on the landing.

The hall light switched on and Susan and Devin moved deeper into the shadows of the stairway. Devin glanced upward toward the voice. She placed one hand on his chest and a finger to her lips.

She pressed her lips to his ear. "Don't hurt him. *Please.*"

Devin frowned. "I'll be back for you, Susan," he whispered. "I'll be back to take you with me home to Dunwich." Then without a sound, he vanished down the stairs.

"I'm here, Michael. I'm coming."

She made it to the top of the stairs and then collapsed. It seemed as though her strength drained from her. Her world spun and white-hot pain shot through her head. Blissful darkness blanketed her and she knew nothing until she woke in Michael's arms.

chapter ten

Michael helped Susan to the bathroom. Examining her throat, his face pulled into a cute little frown of concentration, his glasses sliding down on his nose.

"How the hell did you do this?"

"I don't know," she lied. Still groggy and a bit confused, she wondered if Michael smelled Devin on her skin. She turned back to the sink, twisted on the cold water, and patted some on her face. Michael then handed her a towel and she dried off. Then she had finished, she looked at herself in the mirror. There were bloodstains the collar of her t-shirt and across the swells of her breasts.

Deep, dark pockets had settled under her eyes; she looked as if she has not slept in three days. Her face was pale and sallow and she wondered how much blood Devin had stolen from her.

She turned back to Michael and leaned against the vanity. Michael put some antiseptic on a swatch of gauze and touched it to her skin. She flinched at the sting and hissed softly though her gritted teeth.

"Sorry," he whispered. "You have no idea how close you came to severing your carotid artery, Susan. You might have died." He placed a clean bandage over the little wound and covered it with medical tape. "Funny," he said, more to himself. "It looks like a tear. Or a bite."

Laughing nervously, Susan pulled on her robe and closed it tightly around her neck. "A bite? Must have been one hell of a mosquito."

Michael chuckled softly. "Must have been," he agreed. "Now, we should get you to the hospital."

Susan shook her head. "I'm not going to the hospital for a mosquito bite, Michael. I'm going back to bed."

"The hell you are. Besides, we both know that's not a mosquito bite."

She stiffened and waited for him to tell her he knew everything. "So, what did this, then?" she snapped.

"How should I know?"

Susan pushed passed him, determined to hide the wooziness she felt. She threw off her robe and climbed into bed, then pulled the covers up to her chin. "I'm fine."

Michael switched off the bathroom light with a sigh and followed her. "Why don't I believe you?"

She leaned over and kissed his cheek, then said, "Because you never do. Plus, you enjoy worrying."

Michael removed his glasses and placed them on the nightstand. He switched off the lamp and slid down deeper under the covers. "Maybe so." He sighed and added, "I do feel like there's something you aren't telling me."

"Don't be silly, Michael," she whispered just before she drifted off to an exhausted sleep.

The bang and roar of a garbage truck out front jarred her awake. The sun poured its hateful light through the window and Susan pulled the covers over her head to shield her eyes. Then she laid there a moment longer, gathering the strength to climb out into the stream of yellow light. Her head pounded and when she finally stood, she swayed drunkenly, a wave of nausea hitting her like a punch in the belly. She dashed to the bathroom and kneeled at the toilet. She heaved painfully and then regurgitated a thin drool of undigested blood. Devin's blood.

Michael strolled in and she flushed quickly, then wiped her mouth with a small wad of toilet tissue. She turned, unable to raise her eyes to meet the morning sunshine and saw only his goofy hairy legs poking out of his boxers and his bare feet. Before he had a chance to say anything to her, nausea washed over her again and she hung her face over the bowl, her body wracked with dry heaves.

He kneeled, his hand gentle on her back. "Jesus, Susan." He held her hair from her face and kissed the back of her neck. "What can I do?"

"Help me back to the bed," she whispered when she was finally able to speak. "And please, close the drapes."

chapter eleven

Michael did not understand what was happening to Susan. From the eyes of a physician, she appeared ill, but it was not that she looked *sick*. She looked *different*. Despite appearing tired, strangely it seemed she was stronger, the muscle-loss she had experienced during the recovery from the gunshot miraculously reversed. Maybe he was losing his mind, but he swore her canine teeth were a bit more pronounced. Her teeth were already perfectly even—one of those insanely gorgeous things about like her unlined skin— but lately it seemed those two teeth were very sharp. He felt them against his lips when he kissed her. Her appetite had diminished. He could not make a proper diagnosis without running tests. Of course, Susan refused.

Being with her had become increasingly frustrating. He agonized over her lack of communication and the sudden lack of physical intimacy. Every couple endured those things from time to time, but she acted just plain odd.

She talked in her sleep. Michael desperately wanted to know who the hell Devin McCree was and why the man entered her dreams night after night. He wanted to know why her sudden interest, albeit only in her nightmares, in returning to Dunwich. But as always, he said nothing to her the following morning.

She was jumpy and this was especially strange to him. It

had been more than three weeks since they were attacked at Yeoman's Wharf, but Susan was a cop. She should have gotten over it more quickly, he reasoned. Typically, she moved on from things so easy he sometimes wondered if she was even human. Like the loss of the baby. She had not uttered a word about how she felt over it and when he brought it up, she somehow made him feel he was prying. As if he had no connection to the child at all. It was symptomatic of posttraumatic stress syndrome or even post partum depression, but he was no psychiatrist and she was stubborn as hell.

This morning she was just this side of frantic, her hands shaking, her eyes welling with tears. Sitting at the empty breakfast table, she cradled her head in her hands and wept. Over the kitchen sink, she had pulled the drapes tightly against the morning sunshine. In fact, the blinds over every window in the house were tightly closed. It might as well have been dusk instead of just after dawn.

Maybe it was fear or maybe it was the lack of sound sleep. Whatever, Michael could take it no more. He knelt in front of her. "We need to talk."

"Talk about what, Michael? Should we discuss why I feel nothing? I feel nothing for that guy I killed. I feel nothing for his kid. Fuck! I feel nothing for *our* kid. Maybe you would like talk about how you think I'm losing my mind?"

"I didn't say that," Michael said, stung by her venom.

"What did you say, then?"

"Come on, Susan. You know how strangely you've been acting. This can't go on. You realize that. You're bottling things up and that's not good."

"I could leave," she offered.

"No," Michael cried. "I mean, I want to help you." He took her hands in his, but she pulled them away. He stood up and turned away. "I found all those toys in the trash, Susan. Don't pretend you're not hurt. We're both hurt. But we can get through it."

He removed an orange from the basket in the center of the table and began to slice it. Paying little attention, the blade slipped and nicked the pad of his forefinger. The blood welled there quickly and ran thick and dark onto the white tablecloth.

"Shit," he muttered, popping the bloody tip into his mouth. He tore a paper towel from the roll and pressed it against the wound.

Susan turned away as if she was repulsed by the sight of blood. She had never been one to be grossed out before. She closed her eyes tightly and massaged her temples.

"You okay? You still look sick," Michael asked. He touched her cool cheek, and his own blood turned icy in his veins. Why was she so cold?

"Listen to me. We can go, okay? We can leave here, if that is what you want to do," he said. "Is it the threats? I have money; nobody will find us."

Susan only shook her head. "It's too late, Michael. It's already started."

chapter twelve

"**I**t's already started," Susan had told Michael. That is an understatement, if there had ever been one. She had died that night with Devin. She had died, yet she was alive. More alive than she had ever been.

She felt powerful. When Michael was not around, she examined herself in the mirror, which was becoming increasingly difficult. She needed to stand at a certain angle to see herself clearly, otherwise it was as if she was transparent nearly. A ghost. She blamed the stupid lighting in the old house but in her heart, she knew it was something else. No matter. What did matter was how her muscles were more defined than they had been before, even during her periods of intense training. She squeezed her fists and her biceps tensed, ready to spring beneath her skin. The long quads in her thighs were like those of a professional runner. She was lean, catlike. Confident. Deadly.

The sunlight poured through their windows in the morning and created blaring headaches that rivaled her worst hangovers. She wished she could remain curled up under the covers most of the day. She could not find sleep at night. The sounds that accompanied the darkness were deafening. The soft rush of the tides drove her nearly mad and the muffled footfalls of a cat crossing their lawn drew her to the window, searching for the source of the sound.

She no longer needed her contacts to see. In fact, the other morning she had forgotten to put them in altogether, but did not notice until later when she saw the unopened lens case, the lenses still inside and floating in the transparent solution. Her eyes were now so sharp she could focus on objects as small as an eyelash from across the room. It was slightly disconcerting how she could read the names of the shrimp boats from the bedroom window almost a quarter of a mile out without the aid of her lenses.

She wanted Michael physically and in so many different ways, but she was terrified she might really hurt him. She lay awake at night and smelled his blood through his skin. She wanted to hold him, to *taste* him. Her mouth watered at the thought of the salty, stickiness flooding her mouth. Would his blood be very different from Devin's?

Many time she thought Michael had spoken to her, but it was odd things—things he would never say. Ideas, really. Nothing more. She realized quickly she was either picking his thoughts or else going even crazier. The latter was the most likely choice.

Still, Michael wondered about her sanity and she did not need to be a mind reader to know that. Plus, he was frustrated with what he perceived to be a lack of interest in sex. He was concerned, but also felt neglected.

Michael was a logical person—to explain to him the things she had done in the past few weeks—died, returned to life, drank a man's blood—would not make him understand. It would get a vacation in a padded room.

Susan needed to make things up to him, but she resolved to keep herself in check. She could not give in to her darkest cravings. She stripped down to her bra and panties and knew he was looking at her, wanting her.

"Come here," she told him, as he was getting ready for bed. Her lips found his, her tongue probing, drawing his tongue into her mouth. His cock rose immediately and she pushed him onto the bed, then straddled him, massaging him through his clothes.

"What's gotten into you?" Michael asked.

"Don't you like it?"

"God, yes."

"Then don't ask questions," Susan said. She freed him from the prison of his pants. He sat and tugged his t-shirt over his head and lay back down under her. He was hers now. She could do whatever she wanted.

Susan bent, sucked hard at the skin of his chest and tasted the faint but wonderful hint of blood coursing just beneath the surface. She flicked her tongue around the hard nubs of his nipples and pulled at the hairs of his chest with her teeth. Michael slipped his fingers under the waistband of her panties, nearly tearing them off her he was so eager to have her.

She rode him with abandon. She had never felt so uninhibited, or so selfish, worried only about her own climax and not his. In fact, she did not give a damn if he came or not.

He cried out as he exploded into her, grasping her waist as if he had anything to do with her movements.

She paid no attention to him and continued to rock against him, intent on her own building orgasm. She dipped her head low once again and her teeth nipped his throat. She wanted so much the taste and the warmth of his blood beating quickly in the vein there. Yet, just before she tore into his flesh, she pulled away, gasping.

She watched him as she climaxed, his intelligent face pulled into a deep frown of concentration. His fingers burrowed deep into the flesh of her ass—normally, she would have had wicked bruises later. Michael dropped his head back and a second, violent orgasm overtook him.

Susan fell on top of him and stayed there until their breathing became normal again and their galloping hearts slowed. A sheen of sweat covered the both their bodies, but it was already growing cold. She moved off him and pulled the covers up and around herself. She wanted to be close to him, but realized she could no longer trust anything she did or felt. She was no longer in complete control of her mind or her body.

Michael lay next to her and a surprised smile touched the corners of his mouth.

"Damn," he whispered.

Susan forced a smile. "What?"

"Damn," he repeated, now laughing.

He held her until he fell asleep. When Susan was sure he would not wake, she pulled away, then climbed from the bed and dressed into her nightgown and panties again. She sat down in the reading chair by the window and looked at the moon shimmering over the bumpy surface of the ocean.

She could have killed him. She could have drained him just as Devin had drained her. But she did not yet have the experience to know when to stop. She was unable pinpoint the brink of death in order to bring him back. And did she really want Michael to be anything other than what he already was—a kind, mild-mannered, normal man.

A human. Something she was convinced she no longer was.

It was not worth the risk. She should leave. She only hoped she could last until Devin returned for her. She knew he had planned it this way—so that she had no option but to go with him.

And if he did not return soon, she would have to go to Dunwich and search for him.

Susan dreamed she was inside a closed casket. She reached out in the darkness and her fingers brushed the inside of the lid, rough, splintering. However, as she woke, the dream held fast. Moonlight spilled in through the window, but something was not right.

"You're taking all the cover," Michael complained, asleep.

"Sorry," Susan answered. She reached out again, but that damned casket lid was still there. "Shit," and she shook her head hard, a sad attempt to unclot the cobwebs of sleep from her mind. She thrust her hands out this time, and her palms struck the cool, flat surface again.

Fully awake now, she looked around her. She was floating. No, *hovering.* Her nose brushed the ceiling of their bedroom. Michael's missing covers hung around her like a shroud. She jerked her head around. "Fuck," she whispered. "Oh, fucking fuck."

She moved her arms, kicked her legs, and in her chest, she felt panic rising, which was not good. She never allowed herself to panic. She wanted to scream, but bit it back. What the hell would Michael think, if he woke to find her on the goddamn *ceiling?* She flailed about, thrashed her hips and the sudden motion flipped her over.

Now face down, the covers fell from her and back across Michael's legs. He was on his side, his body tightly curled like a little boy, against the chill of the old house.

Susan clenched her jaw. That stupid Devin. Somehow, he had caused this. She kicked her legs again, almost as if she were swimming in the air. She was so cold. Her hair fell forward, into her face, annoying, and she brushed it behind her ears, and then took a slow, deep breath.

She closed her eyes and thought hard about getting back down to the floor or the bed without waking Michael. After a moment, she opened her eyes and looked around. She had not moved.

She arched her back and again concentrated on dropping downward.

Then she fell, hard. Luckily, she landed mostly on the bed, one flailing arm striking the side of Michael's head.

"What the hell, Susan?" he said, sitting up, rubbing his sore ear.

"Sorry," Susan said. She pulled up the covers and nestled back down into the comfort and warmth of their bed. She caressed his cheek. "I was having a nightmare, I think."

"Oh." He lay back down, planted a kiss on her mouth and closed his eyes. "Okay, now?" he asked.

"Yeah. I think so, anyway." But she did not sleep again until morning, when she was sure he was gone to the office.

chapter thirteen

Susan sat awake watching the slanting rain come down and the lightning paint the low, swollen clouds that hang over the angry bay. The clock glared at her, red-eyed and accusing. She waited and tortured herself with the memory of the taste of Devin's sweet blood on her tongue.

2:19. Michael had been called to the hospital on an emergency an hour ago. Reluctantly, he went. He had not been on E.R. duty since the confrontation with Alton Lee at Yeoman's and did not want to leave her. Susan assured him she was fine and pretended to fall back to sleep as he hurriedly dressed.

At the end of the bed, Elvis woke with a start and darted into the closet, growling low. And then like a dream, Devin was there. In the room beside her. Susan never heard him enter the house.

"Jesus. How did you get in here?"

"One of our little tricks," Devin said. "Remember?"

"You not supposed to trick me." She could not make herself trust him, despite the fact saved both her and Michael's lives at Yeoman's the other night.

"I'm sorry." He came over to her, his face half in shadow and Susan stood, fists balled at her sides, as if she could do anything with him. He was soaked to the bone, his black t-shirt and jeans glued to his body. He detected the tension in her movements. "Don't be afraid of me, Susan."

"How can I help it? What did you do to me, Devin? I woke up on the *ceiling* the other night."

He touched her face and his eyes softened. "Didn't you like it?"

Susan shoved him away. "Like it? Are you kidding me? I feel as if I am dying all over again. I think of draining Michael's blood when we make love—"

Devin winced as she said that. "Don't you talk of making love with him. You no longer belong to him."

"I belong to no one," said Susan.

"You belong to me," Devin told her, teasingly. He moved closer and took her wrists in his big hands. "You are tied to me and you know it as sure as you know that the sun will rise."

"The sun will rise, but I'll not see it. I can't stand the sun. I feel like every nerve is alive tenfold underneath my skin," Susan said. She raked her hands through her hair and turned back to the window. "I can hear mice scurrying across lawn. I can see the very blades of grass wavering in the breeze. I can smell Michael's blood as it rushes through his veins.

"I can't stand it, wish I could shut it off like a light switch." She wanted to cry, but she would not allow this man to see it. Instead, she clenched her jaw tightly. From the darkness of the closet, Elvis growled again, deep and surprisingly loud.

"Elvis hates you," she said.

"Never was a big fan of him, either," Devin answered, grinning.

"Yeah? Well, he was my cat, and now even he doesn't like me."

"Animals can sense the change," Devin told her. "They're much more perceptive than pathetic humans, you realize."

He caressed her boldly, his hands roaming brazenly over

her breasts. She stiffened and before she could stop herself, she balled her fist and slugged him in the mouth.

"Well, you're not especially perceptive, are you?" she snapped, but instantly, she wished she had not hit him.

Devin fell to one knee. "Still a little fighter, are you?" He flicked out his tongue and licked the blood from his bottom lip. Despite the pain, he seemed amused.

"No doubt. Now, I want you to get the hell out of here." Susan flexed her hand and wondered if she had broken her first two fingers.

"I wouldn't want you any other way." He slowly straightened up. "I'll not force you to go with me. In time, and very soon, too, you'll want to go. You'll not only learn that you need me, but you'll grow to love me."

"You're insane," Susan said.

"In fact, I think you already do. A little." Undeterred, he moved toward her again. He bent and kissed her. She did not fight him this time. He was right, but she did not want to let him win so easily. Still, the taste of his blood on his lips and then in her mouth was too delicious.

Gently, he turned her around and pushed her down onto the bed, his mouth barely leaving hers as they struggled out of their clothes.

"I'm sorry if I hurt you," she whispered against his face.

"I'll live."

She ached to have him inside her and when he finally was, she hooked her fingers into claws and clutched his back and his ass and pulled him even deeper into her. "I know what you need," he whispered against her lips. "Do it."

Susan bit into the taunt flesh of his throat, only a small wound but it was enough. Blood began, warm and sticky-sweet over her lips. Devin held her much more gently than she held him, cradling her head in his hands and allowing her to drink, his hips still against hers.

When Susan's thirst was satisfied, she permitted him to drink from her, as well.

Later, they dozed, tangled in the sweat-damp sheets, limbs locked, and Susan's hair spread across Devin's slowly rising chest.

Susan woke, mortified. The rain had stopped and the sky had lightening to a pale purple. Dawn was still two hours away, but the clouds had moved and the moon was bright and almost full through the window. Michael would be home soon. Ashamed of herself, Susan realized she had hardly thought of Michael since Devin arrived. How could she have been taken in so quickly by this crazy person?

She sat up and punched Devin hard in the shoulder. "Wake up."

Devin opened his eyes a little. "Ready for another go?"

"Have you lost your mind? Michael will be home any minute."

Devin rolled over onto his elbow. "So?"

"This doesn't really look good, you realize," she said.

She threw the covers aside and got out of bed. She gathered up her nightshirt and her underwear and dressed quickly.

"Looks okay to me," Devin said, appraising her with a wicked smile.

"Don't be an ass. Get dressed."

She watched him stumbling awkwardly around to find his clothes, his naked body as white as marble in the moonlight. His eyes were still heavy with sleep and his hair stood up in spikes from sweat and rain. He was beautiful, and she bit the inside of her cheek to fight a smile. She felt better than she had in days.

"You've done something to me, Devin. What was it?" she asked. "Hypnosis? Drugs? Vampires aren't real."

Devin frowned deeply as he pulled on his jeans. "I don't

care for that word. It makes me sound like a monster."

"You are a monster. You murdered my brother."

"Christ! You're not going to let that go, are you?" Devin said. "It was an accident and you know it. Think, Susan. Remember everything about that night. For the last twenty years, you've made me into a monster in your head because that was the easiest way for you to deal with it."

"To hell with you," Susan said. She snatched up her cell and scrolled through to see if Michael had phoned. Nothing and she tossed it onto the bed, relived. He usually called as he left the hospital.

"You know it's true, Susan." Devin said. "Now, do I look like a monster?" Taking her hands, he pulled her him.

Susan struggled away and wrapped her arms protectively around herself. "What about crosses?"

Devin laughed loudly. "What? Crosses? I'm not Count-fucking-Dracula. No, crosses will not harm me. I do find them to be a bit superstitious and antiquated."

He sat down on the edge of the bed to pull on his socks and boots.

"Garlic?"

"Unappealing, but certainly not poison."

Susan moved closer, thinking of Peter wielding the broken bat at him. "Wooden stakes through the heart?"

"Painful, but something we can recover from." He stood again and put on his shirt.

"What about the sunlight, then?"

"Sunlight is a deal breaker, I'm afraid."

Susan sighed. For a moment, she thought her heart might explode. "I love the sunshine, Devin," she said. "Why did you do this?"

"You'll learn to love the starlight equally as well."

"Bullshit. Tell me. What will happen if we are exposed to the sunlight?"

"Your eyes will ache from the brightness, at first. You'll feel physically ill. Extremely weak. Too long and your pretty skin will begin to blister." He touched her face. "It will be like being caught in an inferno. You'll feel engulfed in heat. It will be living hell. We cannot heal ourselves adequately from burns, understand?" he said. "I've seen others. They begged for death to come, lying there, hideous and tortured."

"How can we die, then?" Susan asked.

Devin shook his head. "This I will not share with you until I have your complete devotion." He placed a small kiss on the tip of her nose. "That shouldn't take long."

"I'm afraid, Devin," Susan said. "This isn't what I wanted. I just need to be mortal again."

"We don't always know what we want. There was a time when I wanted so to be mortal again. But it wasn't very long before my eyes were opened. Humans are the worst of all creatures and you of all people should know that, Susan. Humans killed my children and my wife," Devin said, his voice rising. "Not Deathwalkers. It was humans who killed your baby. Jesus! Sometimes I hate what I am, but I hate the alternative even more. At least we know what we are. We know we are killers. Why be so hypocritical about it?"

Susan climbed back into bed and pulled her covers tightly around her. She suddenly felt very cold. "You need to leave, Devin. Michael will be back any moment."

Devin pulled on his shirt. "So?"

"Get out."

"As you wish," Devin said. He winked at her and slipped out of the room.

She did not hear his steps on the stairs, but did hear the soft squeak of the front door opening and then closing. She went to the window and watched him stroll across the lawn and up the lane a short ways, to a black Range Rover.

Devin was right. People were shit; at least most of them. They were not truthful to anyone. Hell, most of them could not even be truthful to themselves.

Susan wished he could have stayed with her. For more

than twenty years, she refused to be truthful to herself. She had never hated Devin, despite the fact she thought he had murdered Peter. He had remained in her dreams. He lived inside her mind. Making love with Michael, she sometimes found herself imagining Devin's beautiful face above hers.

For twenty years, she caught herself searching the faces in the crowds for his. Before she met Michael she preferred being alone. She had wondered if there might have been something mentally wrong with her for it. Did she crave pain? She grew to look forward to coming home at night, listening to music, not hearing any voices. She smoked too much pot. She drank too much. She drew and many times, it was Devin's face that grew visible within the soft lines and easy shading.

She burned the sketches in the kitchen sink and washed the ashes down the drain, then drew more. A screwed-up cycle of some kind. Her aloneness defined her and she did not care.

She waited until after dark, and then went out to run the park paths, and felt as though someone was watching. Not every time, no. Only now and again.

She had even called out Devin's name once, her voice shaking like a frightened girl. Devin McCree—the only person she had ever feared and she wanted him. Always wanted him.

She was losing it.

And what was she doing to Michael? He was so different from the pathetic creatures who usually tried to make a play for her. So different from Devin. Sweet-faced and charming—that was Michael.

He was her chance at a normal life and that was something she knew she should want, and what she needed.

So why did she want Devin so badly, instead?

chapter fourteen

Susan had the unsettling sensation that someone was watching her sleep. She squinted into the darkness of the bedroom, again searching for her uninvited guest. Stealthy, she rose from the bed, and then headed downstairs. It had been nearly a week since Devin was there; it was obvious what he was doing. Fine. Point taken. She was not going to make it without him. Not there in Reading. After nearly tearing out Michael's throat the other night, she had not had anything else to do with him. Those glimpses into his head were not helping things, either. He was like a petulant little boy. Things had grown increasingly tense to say the least; they were barely on speaking terms now. She made a pretense of keeping hours similar to his, but it was impossible for her to function in the daylight. Gerald called but she ignored her phone. Work was no longer a consideration.

She smelled Devin before his broad silhouette appeared against the lighter gray of the moon-painted window. That faint odor of blood—it radiated from his very pores, a raw, wild odor that somehow aroused her; and the scent of lilac shampoo. She would later learn that he liked to steal from his victims. Shampoo, cologne, lotion. It might have been humorous, if it were not so horrible.

"Told you I would be back," he whispered.

His hot breath caressed her face.

"Don't worry about waking him," he told her, pointing upward. "We can be as silent as death, when we want to."

He moved behind her. He was so warm, almost burning against her back, her buttocks, her bare legs. What he told her sent chill bumps up and down her legs, despite his fiery touch. Upstairs, the bed creaked slightly and Susan stood motionless one horrible moment, waiting, hoping that Michael had not awakened and discovered her gone.

"Been having some bloody horrible nights, I'll bet," Devin said. He seemed proud of the fact. He pressed himself against her again.

"You bastard," she hissed. "I feel like I am starving. Like I am hollow."

She stepped away, but he slipped his arm around her middle and pulled her back to him. He nuzzled the side of her neck, nipped at her skin, drawing a new dribble of blood to the old wound.

"We are going. Tonight, understand?" He flicked his tongue against the bloody little gash, and she felt the soft thrum of his pulse in time with hers. He was stealing her blood again, and that was what she wanted. She arched her neck, offering herself and only hoped he would return the favor, just as he had before.

He did, taking her head in his large hands and guiding her lips to the hollow of his throat.

"Only a little, now," he said. "We don't have a lot of time before dawn."

After what seemed to be only a taste, Devin led her toward the stairs.

The moon poured in flushing Michael's sleeping face in blue light. She did love him, and had not felt that kind of unconditional adoration since Peter. Until Devin. Her eyes blurred with tears at the thought of leaving Michael and what had been her sweet, somewhat normal life. But she could not even begin entertain the idea of what might happen if she did not leave.

Devin stood over Michael for a moment, watching him sleep and she wondered what might happen if he did wake. Would there be a confrontation? Would Devin kill him?

Panic gripped her and she realized she needed to be away from Michael and the house as fast as she could—for his safety, if not for her own health. She yanked off her police academy t-shirt and pulled on a sports bra, jeans and a blouse that she had to re-button twice because her fingers trembled so badly. Finally, she stepped into a pair of tattered sneakers. She grabbed a small duffle, shoved a few clothes inside. She then removed a small stack of photos from the drawer in her bedside table and put them in, as well.

She straightened up to find Devin now kneeling beside Michael. He slipped his finger across Michael's throat, only a fluttering caress. Michael swatted at his hand, but otherwise did not move. Did not wake. Devin appeared to be amused, but Susan wondered if he wanted to wake Michael, if there was some animalistic part of Devin McCree that craved a battle.

"Just like a little baby," he said. "We could take every bit of his blood right now, you realize. We could drain him. He would never know what hit him."

"Please, Devin. I am going with you. What else do you want?"

"I want you to *want* to go with me, Susan," he said. "Not because you have to."

She could not stand this any longer. "I do. I do want to go." She went to him, stood on her tiptoes and kissed him. "Please don't hurt him," she pleaded. She watched in horrified silence as Devin brushed Michael's hair from his brow. He leaned closer to the sleeping man's face, inhaling his breath, just as a cat might steal the breath of a sleeping child. Michael sighed and shoved his hand beneath his head.

Devin glanced at Susan. "Okay. Let's go."

It was chilly and damp outside. The dew glistened on the grass like slivers of shattered glass, reflecting the round face of the moon a million times. Susan followed Devin a couple of houses up the sandy land to where he had parked his Rover. Away from Michael, he seemed very different. His gestures and his words were again soft, his movements less threatening.

"It will not be as bad as you think, Susan," he said. "In the end, you'll see."

She drew the front of the peacoat that had once belonged to Devin tightly together to fight the cold breeze coming off the ocean. Her mother had asked about that coat sometime after Peter had died and she remembered claiming she had picked it up at a vintage clothing store. Maybe keeping that it had been some kind of weird attachment to a man she thought she had killed. A trophy, perhaps. It swallowed her up, her arms disappearing up the sleeves, but it was toasty warm. She flipped up the collar to block the wind from her neck and imaged she still smelled Devin on it—his musty, sexy scent that reminded her of something entirely naughty.

Devin started the truck and they coasted to the main road, gravel crunching softly under the tires like old bones. Susan looked back over her shoulder at her dark, sleeping home, then leaned over and pressed her face against Devin's shoulder. She was sick to her mind and to her heart, but she had to do what was best for her, and for Michael. This was the only way. Devin stroked her hair gently and planted a small kiss on the crown of her head.

"You will be happy with me, Susan. I promise."

They drove through the flat, inky country and passed familiar landmarks as they chewed up the miles between

Reading and Dunwich. The darkness made everything seem nightmarish, the shadows spilling across the ground overly large and misshaped. Overhead, the sky took on a purplish hue and the clouds grew fat with rain. Far off, lightning painted their low bellies orange for an instant.

After a short while, Susan closed her eyes and fell into a thin sleep.

She dreamed of walking a beach at night and the ocean was as black as the damp road under the Rover's wheels. The sand was like cool shards of glass under her bare feet and nearby, Michael begged to her to come with him. But she could not leave Devin now. She was forever tied to him and to Dunwich.

As quickly as Michael was there, he vanished, leaving nothing but a thick pool of blood in his place. The pebble-sized granules of sand seemed to suck the blood down into it, drinking it up.

Susan woke with a gasp, tears wetting her cheeks. She turned toward the window so Devin could not see and regarded her own hopeless face floating ghostly and transparent in the side mirror. What had she done?

Years ago, she had vowed she would never set foot in Dunwich again, but just ahead, the morning ripped the seam of night at the horizon and the city rose before her, waiting to swallow her up.

chapter fifteen

When Michael woke, Susan's side of the bed was cold. He remained still a moment, blinking hard against the late-morning sun. Then he took several deep breaths and allowed his eyes to adjust to the brightness of the room. He threw back the covers. Sitting up, he scrubbed his hands over his face and rubbed his eyes with his fists, trying to rid them of the residue of sleep.

"Susan?"

He finally gets up and trudges around the bedroom, rubbing his arms vigorously in an attempt to warm himself up.

"Susan?" he called again, his voice hoarse with sleep. No answer. He trudged around the bedroom and rubbed his arms in attempt to warm himself up. He knew Susan was already up—the shirt she wore to bed was on the floor at the end of the bed. She had hardly seen a morning in weeks—perhaps this was sign things were finally returning to normal.

Odd, though. She never left her clothes on the floor, and usually scolded him if he did it. Some bachelor habits were tougher to shake than others. Squinting in the sunlight, he crossed to her side of the bed.

On the bedside table, next to the reading lamp were her revolver and her cell phone. Of course, she never left without either. Beneath them was a slip of paper ripped haphazardly from a notebook.

He picked it up and squinted at it a moment, then found his glasses on his nightstand and put them on. On it was a sketch of a man who looked strangely familiar, but the face was difficult to place. He wondered for a moment how long ago it was done. He knew Susan had been an art student, but he never seen her draw anything. She never even doodled. But this sketch was incredible.

Then it came to him like a slap in the face. This was their hero from Yeoman's the other week. Still, it was odd. They had only seen the guy for a minute or two at the most. This sketch could have been drawn by someone who knew every contour of the man's face. He could have posed for it.

"Susan?" he called again. His voice echoed lonesome in the silence and panic blossomed in his mind. He sprinted from the bedroom, stumbled on the rolled up edge of the rug but caught his shoulder on the doorjamb just before he fell headlong into the hallway.

"Shit," he muttered, rubbing his bruised shoulder.

Everything was too weird. He went downstairs and glanced through the big front picture window. Susan's Jeep was still out there, just where had left it, parked next to his little BMW convertible. Neither car had been touched. Susan's keys were on the little table in the foyer, where she always left them, next to the purse she rarely carried.

Michael's heart pounded in time with the pounding in his head and fresh dread tasted like rust on his tongue. He searched the downstairs rooms, racing from the kitchen to the living room to his office. She would be there; she would be in one of those places and he would end up looking like a complete fool for being so worked up. But that would be all right. He had looked like a fool in front of her before.

Nothing.

He flung open the front door, trying to convince himself that she was simply out for a walk. He sucked in a lungful of the crisp air and that told him all he needed to know about that—Susan was extremely cold natured. She would never go out for a walk in the chill of an October morning. He stood on the front porch and scanned the sandy lane that stretched from his house east toward the bay and west toward the highway that led away from Reading. Deserted, as usual.

Then looking down the sandy lane, he spotted a set of fresh tire tracks. He went to road and found only one set of footprints, small ones and he knew they belonged to Susan. They reached the tracks of the vehicle and then were gone. Anger built now, replacing the panic. Had she left him alone? There had to be another set of footprints.

Still, Michael did not have to wonder where Susan had gone, and whom with. It all made perfect sense. How could he have been so blind? Devin McCree was the man in the sketch, the so-called hero. She had spoken of him in her sleep—he plagued her nightmares. Or were they nightmares at all?

Shivering, he turned back toward the house. He knew exactly what he would have to do next. And he had no time to waste.

chapter sixteen

The miles disappeared beneath the wheels of the BMW. It is just past 7:00 p.m. and completely dark. Rain splattered the windshield and the wipers drum and swish a steady, slow rhythm.

Michael fiddled with the dial and found a modern rock channel. Soundgarden or maybe it was Pearl Jam—he could not remember exactly, but the music was hard and fast. He turned it up and tapped out the beat on his steering wheel more out of anxiety than the enjoyment of the music.

He did not like this stretch of rural road passing through vast stretches of government-protected forests and swampland. Towns so tiny, they did not warrant mention on any map. It was a dreary, boring ride. No traffic—not a single headlight coming, not a single taillight in the distance ahead.

Gerald had told him not to go looking for Susan. Of course, Gerald had all kinds of ideas—that Susan simply might have decided to leave him; that she was unstable as a result of all she had been through recently. Still, unless he had been completely blind for the past year, Michael found it difficult to believe she would have just left, especially in the middle of the night like a coward. She was a lot of things, but weak was not on that list. Besides, she would not have left without her gun.

That gun was now lying in the passenger's seat next to him, loaded. Just in case.

Dunwich was about four hours north of Reading, and he hated that he has gotten such a late start. He should have never met with Gerald and gotten tied up with him in the first place. What a waste of time that had been.

Michael had offered up what he knew, which was not a lot. "She's with someone named Devin. Devin something," he said. "Sounded like McCree." Then he removed the sketch that Susan had done from his jacket pocket and gave it to Gerald. "He's the guy who was at Yeoman's the night we were attacked. The one who beat Alton Lee to a pulp."

Gerald squinted at the drawing. "Devin? Wait." He shook his head. "How do you know?"

"She mentioned him. Something happened between them." It was already too farfetched. He was not about to tell Gerald the acquired this knowledge by listening to Susan talk in her sleep.

"What do you mean, something happened? Like she was screwing around with him?"

Michael shrugged.

"If that's so, why do you even care about finding her?"

"I don't know. I feel like she's in trouble." Michael said. "Look, are you going to help me or not? Otherwise, you're wasting my time." He started toward the door.

Gerald grasped his arm and pulled him back. "Is she even worth it?" Slowly, he let go of Michael, then reached up and patted the side of his head. "Devin. You think it might have something to do with what happened to her before?"

"How the hell should I know?" Michael snapped.

"You can't just run off to Dunwich like this. It's nothing more than a ghost town now, anyway. You have no idea what you might be getting into," Gerald told him. "What you need to do is go back home and wait. I could be a while before we know if we are going to dig up anything on the name. Besides, she might call."

"I'll go crazy just waiting, Gerald. You know that."

"Yeah. Well, that's the best I can offer," Gerald said. He shook his head and ran check on the name. He faxed the sketch, but had turned up nothing by the time Michael had left.

That was hours ago. Since then, checking his phone had become a habit. No calls. He had driven through the rain. Now the big yellow face of the moon followed him, a grapefruit moon, Tom Waits called it, a beacon visible only periodically, most of the time blocked by the gauzy gray clouds. Ahead, the city rose up like manmade mountains and rock faces. Shortly the old blacktop was swallowed in inky shadow. Gerald had not been exaggerating—it seemed everyone had left. Windows were like black squares against the gray granite faces of the buildings. The sidewalks were empty and no cars crawled along the streets. Streetlamps bled pools the color of puss onto the pavement.

Michael passed the mouth of an alley and thought he saw something flash across the pale spray of his headlights. He slowed and looked through the rearview mirror at the road behind him as the shapes sank into hollow black doorways and entrances to buildings long abandoned by normal people.

Probably a stray dog. His eyes were playing tricks on him—he needed to rest.

He needed a fucking drink.

He pushed the gas and brought the car back up to speed. Then he saw it again. Still ahead, but how? Closer now and he jammed on the breaks, his foot crushing the pedal to the mat. The Beemer skidded to a halt, and his foot slipped off the clutch. The car choked and died.

Silence, all but the soft ticking of the engine.

What kind of city was so quiet? But it seemed the very shadows were alive, writhing. The moon slid behind a cloud again and the road became as dark as a cave, the crumbling buildings seeming to close in, to lean over. His headlights cut grooves in the darkness. He reached over and picked up the Glock, his breath and his heartbeat the only sounds in his world.

He wet his lips and clutched the gun in his fist. Squinting into the darkness, he searched for any kind of movement.

Everything was still.

Like a tease, the moon emerged once again from the cover of clouds, brightening the night enough for him to see ahead of him now. What he saw caused his stomach to flip-flop. Silhouetted in the yellow-blue halogen glow of his headlights were possibly a half-dozen figures.

"Oh, shit," he whispered.

He twisted the ignition and the engine reluctantly fired. He threw the car into gear, then gunned it, the tires screeching like a banshee's screams. The slumping, lurking shapes leapt then, heading straight for him.

Michael could see the faces now—ghost-white smears, blurred with speed, mouths like gashes, eyes glowing hot yellow, reflecting the light. He tore through the darkness, gripping the wheel with one hand and changing gears with the other, all the time holding onto the gun.

The shapes jumped away just before he could plow through them. The little convertible skidded sideways and then tipped crazily onto two wheels. When it dropped back down on all four, Michael's foot fell off the clutch again and the engine coughed and died again.

Frantically, he cranked the ignition and it whined back to life, but it did not matter. The car shook as if it had been struck, but from the top, not the sides. Someone or some*thing just landed on the roof and the ragtop sagged with the weight* like an overfilled sack.

Michael took the gun in both his fists, wincing with anticipation of the report, and fired upward at the bulge in the canvas.

A howl of pain or of delight—he could not decide—

pierced the night. The cloth ripped as though made old newspaper and a clawed hand plunged through, dirty nails, grime ground into the palms and the creases of the knuckles.

"Get the hell away," Michael shouted. He fired again, unsure he had hit anything. Either way, the bullets were not slowing this thing down.

Another figure appeared, standing on the hood of the car. His long black coat billowed out behind him like a cape or a pair of wings. He brought a heavy boot up high and then down onto the windshield, shattering it and spraying Michael with diamond shards.

Michael fired a third time, straight ahead and the bullet tore into the man's shoulder, causing him to snap back a half -step. He then knelt down on the hood and thrust his fist through the spider-webbed windshield, grabbing at Michael.

At that same moment, Michael reached between his knees and yanked the lever beneath the seat. The seat flew backward a foot, but that is not nearly enough. The man on the hood growled, exposing an incredible set of teeth, then rammed his arm deeper into the car. He snagged Michael's jacket and pulled him upward through the broken windshield.

Fortunately, Michael was still wearing his seatbelt. He fought the pale, snatching fist as his shirt and jacket ripped under the pointed nails. Those jagged nails gouged the skin of his chest, his neck and then his face, drawing thin lines of blood.

Michael raised the gun again, but this time something tore it from his hand and sent it clattering to the floorboard. The crazed figure then grabbed Michael's shirt again, gaining a better grasp this time. He slammed Michael against the restraint and then the steering wheel, making the airbag deploy like a minor explosion. It rocked Michael backward, throwing him hard against the seat. On the hood of the car, the man shortly lost his footing and released Michael from his brutal hold.

Michael sat there a moment, gasping, his heart lurching along like he had just completed the forty meters. He unbuckled the seatbelt and reached down, groping around for the gun. Relief washed over him when his fingers brushed across the muzzle and he snatched it from the floor.

That gave the creature on the hood of the Beemer enough time to regain his footing. He stretched his arm through the windshield again, then plunged his face through, as well, showing his formidable incisors. His rank, rotting breath whiffed down into Michael's face as his jaws snapped closed, searching to sink his teeth into anything he could.

Screaming, Michael leaned forward and pressed the Glock's barrel against the man's forehead. He closed his eyes and fired.

In an instant, the man or whatever the hell it was somersaulted off the car and onto the shadowy blacktop.

Michael sat in dead silence staring through the serrated opening in his windshield, waiting for another round. What had just happened?

He watched in sick disbelief as the limp body began to twitch. First a finger and then the legs. As if waking from a nap, the man sat up in the middle of the road, a crater-like hole in the center of his forehead.

"Oh, fuck no," Michael said. With one hand, he slapped his face hard enough to bring tears to his eyes. This had to be some kind of nightmare. He needed to wake up.

He fired again, but there was no way he is going to hit anything. His hands trembled too much. Beyond the injured figure ahead, headlights appeared like two gleaming yellow cateyes and an old pickup truck emerged from the dark.

The bastard pickup was really moving and Michael braced for impact, but it screeched to a halt two car-lengths away.

The driver's side door of the truck flew open and a tall, lean man climbed out. The headlights sprayed the road like spilled paint and the driver's breath billowed up and up in a grey vapor from his face. In his hands, he cradled a snub-nosed riot shotgun.

Calm, he stepped toward the man-thing on the pavement and leveled the gun. The injured creature scrambled to his knees and spread his arms out to his sides. At first, it seemed an imploring gesture, but looking up at the truck driver, he began to laugh. Then the laugh grew into a scream and the scream became the terrible howl of an animal.

Michael dropped the revolver. He squeezed his eyes closed and put his hands over his ears. The thundercrack of the shotgun severed gut wrenching sound.

Michael opened his eyes in time to see the creature's head disappear in a fog of blood, bone fragments and brain matter. The pickup driver then aimed the gun in Michael's direction and Michael's mouth went dry. He dropped over, behind the barrier of the dashboard, the gearshift digging into his ribs painfully. He waited, unable to breathe, unable to move.

The creature that had been on top of the car then jumped to his feet, revived. He leapt on top of the Beemer again, and began pawing at the ragtop like a cat scratching at the ground. Determined, he tore through the canvas and the Fiberglas backing. Uneven fingernails scrabbled and snatched at Michael, brushing dirty fingers across Michael's face, snatching at his hair.

BAM! The shape sailed backward off the car, tearing half of the ragtop away with him. Michael straightened up slowly and glanced in the rearview mirror as the creature tumbled away, the piece of the car roof still in one hand.

Michael started turned the key and the car rumbled to life a moment and then stalled out again. "Damn!" He pounded the steering wheel with one fist and snatched the Glock up from the floorboard between his feet with the other.

With a shaking hand, he aimed at the pickup truck driver.

"Don't shoot. Do you hear me?" the stranger called.

Michael snorted, skeptical. "Don't fucking shoot *me,*" he answered. He fingered the trigger, but did not fire.

The driver knelt and placed the riotgun on the road. He then stood up, his arms raised over his head. "More will come." He has a strong eastern European accent. "They'll kill us, if we stay out here."

Michael hesitated another moment, almost as afraid of this tall stranger as he was of the creatures. What has he gotten himself into? Guardedly, he opened the door and climbed from the driver's seat, his knees as weak as pillows.

"Don't kill me," he rasped.

The tall stranger laughed. "*You're* the one holding the gun."

Tentatively, Michael came closer, the gun still trained on the man. The man's face was all shadows and angles in the BMW's headlights, but still Michael could see that he was no monster. Only a man.

Of course, so were the others.

"Quickly. They are on the move."

As if on cue, there was a sharp shriek, carving the oddly still night and echoing along the canyon of buildings. The man snatched up his gun and they sprinted to his waiting pickup.

The first thing that struck Michael about the guy was he seemed damned scary. Maybe not as scary as the things laying headless on the pavement back there, but pretty frightening all the same. He had a look in his eyes, the expression of one who was shell shocked. It reminded Michael of the way Susan had looked only a few days ago.

Maybe the "crazies" was contagious.

Michael slipped the Glock into the inner pocket of his jacket and sat silent as the pickup truck raced along the empty streets of the outer edge of Dunwich. He felt sick—sick over leaving his car and his things, sick over what he had just witnessed, sick over being forced to trust this strange man. He was not sure he would ever get over the jolt of what just happened. His knees were still knocking together and he placed his open hands on top of them to try to steady himself.

"What the hell were you doing out there?" the man asked.

"I'm looking for someone."

chapter seventeen

Susan did not recognize the room. She was cold and headachy and her arrival in Dunwich was nothing but fragmented moments, much like broken film spliced back together. There was the vague recollection of Devin sweeping her up into his arms and carrying through this dark, sprawling house, up the stairs and into his bedroom. She then slept, aware of his arms around her—big, possessive arms holding her even in sleep as if she might spring from the warmth of the bed and flee.

Devin's room was not what she expected. There is a small fireplace, the remains of a fire, the embers glowering like devil's eyes in the gloom. Books lined the walls, some in rows, others in stacks teetering on the verge of tumbling over. In fact, the number of written pages in this room rivaled a library. And where the walls were visible, maps, yellowed with age and curling at the corners peeked through. Here and there various European cities and villages were circled. The furnishings were an odd mixture of pieces from different eras—rich mahogany and dark fabrics that seemed better suited to when the house was likely constructed in the early nineteenth century. However, here and there were pieces that were simply out of place like the art deco chair with big purple and yellow swirls and chrome legs that sat against the wall in the far corner and the funky framed movie poster of Clint Eastwood in The Good, the Bad and the Ugly on the closet door. There was a curtain over the window, the edges nailed tightly to the window trim, allowing not so much as a sliver of outside light in. A number of burned-down candlesticks stood like war-beaten soldiers all around the room.

The bed where Susan lay formed something of a cocoon and she snuggled farther down into the covers. The place smelled of dust and age, and the covers smelled of Devin, which she already liked very much. A mirror in an ornate frame hung high and slanting on the wall across from the bed. It was somewhat amusing—did Devin admire himself so much that he must be able to watch himself at all times? Could he see himself at all?

Susan fixed her eyes on the silver pool of glass, searching for herself there. The covers shifted over her as she repositioned her legs, but it was like watching one of those cheesy "invisible man" movies. Transfixed, she began to appear there—perhaps her vampire eyes were accommodating her. Maybe she imagined herself there. Nevertheless, she was there, faded like an old photograph. The woman who stared back was she, but also not she. A *vampire* Susan. Wide-eyed, a little stunned, a lot wild.

Then someone spoke, breaking her contemplation. She jumped and scanned the room for the owner of the deep voice. "Awake, finally." Not Devin. The accent was distinctly British, but unlike Devin's—precise, and less raspy.

She forced the surprise and the uneasiness away and slowly sat up. She stretched, cat-like and rubbed her eyes with her fingers before realizing she was wearing only her bra and panties. "Sorry." She pulled the covers up to her neck, blushing deeply.

"No worries," the man reassured her. "You were dead asleep when you arrived. I helped Devin undress you for bed."

"How nice," she muttered. Then she narrowed her eyes at the man. "How did you get in here without my noticing? You're not one of us. I usually can tell."

"One of us." The man chuckled, but he did not share his secret. He stepped closer to the bed and shoved a mug of steaming coffee toward her. She took it, somewhat grateful, yet determined not to show it. Coffee was not exactly her favorite drink lately.

"Devin is preparing to leave for the evening." The man folded his long limbs and sat down in the eyesore of a chair near the bed. Susan squinted at him, her eyes quickly adjusting to the dim light. She allowed her academy-taught observation skills take over.

He was somewhere in his fifties, very tall and well built. Receding hairline, and what was left of his hair had grayed. He wore a moustache and a nicely trimmed beard. Intelligent green eyes that seemed rather too large for his narrow face, framed with a fringe of long lashes. He looked like a professor, and not at all threatening.

Susan nodded, now more surprised that Devin was not in the bed next to her than concerned with this strange man. She wrapped her hands around the mug, warming her them, then brought it to her face. The aroma was incredible and she took a sip, stinging her tongue. How she missed actually enjoying good coffee.

"Now, tell me," she said, "why are you here? Guarding me for Devin?"

"Maybe," the man answered, smiling. "I'm John Moses." He offered his hand.

"Quite a name to live up to," Susan said, taking it. "I'm Susan. Now. Are you guarding me or not?"

"I suppose I am in that I will not allow you to leave here," John said. "But considering the fact you have already changed, I doubt you would want to risk leaving, anyway."

Susan took another drink of her coffee and sat up a little straighter. "If I did decide to take the risk, how do you plan to stop me?"

"You don't want to test that," John answered quietly.

The tone of his voice caught her off guard; perhaps her first impression was mistaken. Still, she only shrugged nonchalantly. "We'll see, I suppose."

"Sometimes the transformation is difficult. Some people do not adjust well," John said. "It's later than you realize and dusk is soon. Get dressed and I'll show you around. I placed your belongings in that vanity, but the clothes in the wardrobe should fit, if you prefer those." He paused at the door then and turned to her. "But don't try to leave, Susan. I don't want to hurt you."

He pulled the door closed behind him, leaving Susan alone, the covers bunched around her waist. She finished off her coffee, somewhat annoyed with John Moses. Who did he think he was speaking to? "I don't want to hurt you," she muttered. Then she hopped out of bed to dress.

Susan half expecting the old wardrobe to be filled with ball gowns or loose jumpers from the flapper era, but was surprised to find, instead, several pairs of undergarments, comfortable cargo pants, t-shirts and sweaters—much the same things in her own closet back in Reading, except everything here was black. But of course, if Devin had been her shadow for so many years, as he claimed, he should have known what she liked to wear. Relieved she did not have to impersonate Zelda Fitzgerald this morning, she pulled out a pair of the cargos, fresh panties, and a stretchy little turtleneck. She also found a pair of tall lace-up boots with a soft, thick sole and exactly her size. They would be much warmer than the old ratty sneakers she had worn to Dunwich.

In the adjacent washroom, Susan relieved herself, then

washing her hands she noticed that Devin had stocked little shelf below the mirror with various toiletries and new cosmetics—amazingly accurate with her colors. Next, she examined Devin's toiletries—his lilac shampoo and expensive cologne that she doubted he ever splashed on—she just could not see that. Deodorant. All stolen, she suspected, keepsakes from his victims. Odd, and a bit sentimental that he did those things. There was a large claw-footed tub, and she considered running a hot bath and soaking for a bit, but it would be much nicer to wait for Devin.

Once she was together, she emerged into the long hallway. There were perhaps a dozen doors along either side of the passage, like a funky 1920s apartment building. At the far end were an ornate banister and a winding set of stairs.

"John?" she called.

Her boots thunked the wood floor, echoing like dull open-handed slaps. John ascended the stairs and waited at the top for her.

"Thought better of trying to escape, I see," he commented, lightly.

"Now is not the right time," Susan answered, trying to conceal a small, sideways smile.

John led her down, his hand resting on the small of her back as if he was indeed poised for any attempt she might make to run. The downstairs was much as she imagined—a sprawling grand room that could have doubled as a hotel lobby, the warm wood floors worn dull with two centuries of boot heels. At the other end of the big room was another fireplace—this one large enough for Susan to step inside if she were to bend a little. The trim work along the tops and bottoms of the walls was wide, carved with minute details. All sorts of odd, surreal art work—oil, pen to paper, photography—decorated the open spaces between furniture and windows. A large H.R. Giger print drew her eyes. How many people back in Reading even knew who Giger was? Even more books were stacked in the corners in precarious towers of dusty pages, much the way Devin's bedroom had been.

The furnishings were elaborate, made of silk, damask and dark, heavy wood, some chrome, some glass. Nothing matched, but all seemed to work well, despite the lack of continuity. Everything had the appearance of age. Lovely was the best word she could come up with to describe look of the place, despite the smell of dust.

"It's chilly out," John said. He pulled open the coat closet nearest the front entrance, found her woolen peacoat and helped her on with it. "We should have something to fit you better than this."

"It's—mine," she said. "I like it."

"Okay. There," he said as he turned the collar up. He buttoned it at the throat for her, as if she were only a small child. From his shirt pocket, he produced a pair of sunglasses with very dark lenses. "These will make it more comfortable for you on the outside. It's not fully dark yet, but at this late hour, the sun will not harm you." Carefully, he placed them on the ridge of her nose. "Eventually, you will become unable to stand any daylight at all. Enjoy the time you have left—it might be a matter of days. We'll take a walk; I assume you are full of questions."

Susan nodded, somewhat amused by his doting and by his thoughts that he was no longer guarding so tightly. His appraisal of her was sweet and flattering and that made her feel good. Plus, his threatening demeanor had vanished. She realized that she was quite comfortable with him and in fact, quite liked him. He put on a rather smart leather jacket and then led her out into the waning sunshine.

John Moses loved the sun. Infinite dark blue and orange smeared the twilit sky and for perhaps the millionth time, he doubted if he would ever decide to make the full transition. Daylight was just too precious. However, he was worried that the sun was still too bright for the woman.

Once out, he caught her looking back at the building, obviously admiring the majestic façade of the old place. It was full of character and reminded him a little of the old places in Europe, where he once lived. Ornate moulding, wide columns and even a couple of hateful, weather-beaten gargoyles loomed over the dirty street below. A long terrace high above overlooked the irate surface of the bay. This was one of the homes tourists often stopped to admire back in the cities heyday, but those days were long gone and many of the buildings now stood empty. Most could be bought for a song and not even a good one. When he "adopted" Devin McCree, he realized that he owed the man as much protection as he could offer. And the best solution, at least that the time—so long ago it was now fogged with time, was to leave England. They were hunted, Devin and his kind, And the hunter was a man John hoped he would never see again.

John knew only what Devin had told him of the woman. But seeing her in front of him, much of what he had heard seemed impossible. He remembered Devin returning home after his first night with her, a wounded pup with a hole in his middle. So distraught he was, John became worried he might never recover.

They started along the sidewalk. It was still early and there were few people out yet. Here and there, cars crawled along the damp street. Streetlamps flickered on—the few that had not been broken out or burned out.

"So, are we just going to stomp around in silence, or are

you going to tell me why I am really here," Susan said, after a while.

"You're here because Devin has always wanted you. You know that."

Even in the graying day, John could see the color touch her cheeks. She looked down.

They strolled around to the courtyard of the building, and he opened a tall iron gate with a key. This niche of nature in the middle of the city stink opened to a lush, unkempt garden area. The foliage was still green, despite the cooler temperatures. The borders running just inside the iron fence were amazing boxwoods, grown thick and a dozen feet tall, that separated them from the concrete world only meters away. The shadows were as deep as inkwells where a stone bench sat, nearly hidden in a tangle of jasmine and thorny rose vines. John pulled away the ropes of vines and thorns pricked his fingers like cat claws. He muttered a few half-hearted curses under his breath.

Susan smiled tightly and he knew she smelled his blood. "Careful," she warned.

When they were able to sit, John glanced at his hand. The thorns drew little dots of scarlet in four or five spots across his fingers and palm. Absently, he placed one bloody fingertip into his mouth and licked away the drop of blood. Susan wet her lips and turned away.

"Now the rest, I don't need to tell you, Susan. Think about what happened the night your brother died. Think about *this.*" He traced the fresh wound at her throat to prove his point and she flinched away.

"I'm only telling you in order to protect you. Perhaps you don't deserve what Devin has put upon you, just as he did not deserve it," he said. "But don't deny the fact that you know what Devin really is. What you have become."

"Sounds like a lot of bullshit to me, John. Maybe I'm here because of Devin wants revenge. Maybe he changed me to hurt me."

John shrugged. Her argument was half-hearted, for the sake of not giving in without a fight. Susan was clearly not a woman who gave into anything easily. To humor her, he decided to play the game.

"Think what you want. But I can tell you Devin is not like that. He's loved you from the shadows for more than twenty years, Susan. If he wanted you to suffer, he wouldn't have intervened when you needed help. And you know it's true."

Susan said nothing else. There was nothing more for her to say.

chapter eighteen

T he guy's name was Kasper Jacobsen and he made
Michael feel exceptionally insignificant, as he stood well
over six feet, with a wide chest and big biceps. His eyes
were the color of a cloudy day and he had a week's worth of
stubble on his cheek, flecked gray. His hair was quite short
and twisted in oily spikes like he had not seen a comb
recently.

Sitting under the dim yellow light at the kitchen table, he
did not appear as deranged as Michael originally thought;
only haunted. Perhaps Michael did not need to worry
whether he would kill him after all. At least not yet.

Michael did not realize how famished he was until
Kasper put a plate in front of him. Spaghetti and tomato
sauce. He muttered a thanks and dug in. The pasta was
undercooked, the sauce microwaved in the jar, but tonight it
was fit for a king.

Kasper then poured two glasses of red wine and pushed
one across the table toward him. "Here. Drink up. And
calm down." He took a drink from his own glass, wiped his
lips with the back of his hand. "What the hell were you
doing out there?"

"I told you," Michael said, between forkfuls of pasta.
"Looking for someone. My girlfriend is missing. I believe
she might be here."

"So you just decided to drive up? In the dark? You've lost your mind, yes?"

Michael shrugged. "I have to find her."

Kasper studied Michael a moment, then leaned closer. "Look at my house, Michael, and tell me, what do you see?"

Michael stopped eating long enough to look around the dark kitchen. After a moment he answered, "You have your windows all boarded up."

"Exactly," Kasper said. "Those things. Those creatures that attacked you, this city is crawling with them."

Michael sat back and shook his head. "Those creatures? They were only men--" he began, but even as he said it, he knew Kasper was right. "Do they all act like that?" he asked.

"No. No, of course not. It's just that . . . some go crazy. Probably the ones who were unstable to begin with."

This made Michael think of Susan. Would she be one of those?

"Besides, they're not men. Not anymore. They might have been men once, but now they are something else." Kasper finished his wine and refilled his glass. "What do you do when you're not trying to get yourself killed?"

"I'm a doctor. I have a family practice over in Reading."

Kasper nodded. "I had you pegged for a doctor. My father was a doctor, also. He was a gentle man. Like him, it's not in your nature to fight. I can tell."

"Physicians' trait." Michael could not decide whether he should feel insulted or not. So he was not exactly the Terminator. Instead, he went on. "Susan's a cop." From his shirt pocket, he removed a dog-eared photo he had taken of her out on the boat docks just behind his house and passed it over to Kasper.

Kasper stared at it a long moment, then his brow furrowed a split second and smoothed out again. He smiled uneasily. "Pretty," he said, "but worth risking your life?"

"Yes," Michael answered without hesitation. The warm,

calming effects of the wine was taking hold and he wanted to go on about what she meant to him, but held his tongue. He could not impose his drunken pity-party on this stranger.

Instead, he said, "Listen, do you know the name Devin? I'm not sure of the last name, but she woke me, talking about him in her sleep. Before you say anything, I realize how ludicrous it sounds, but I know he's behind this. I'm not sure how exactly he's connected to her, but I'm positive he is."

Kasper's eyes narrowed. "Devin McCree, maybe?"

"Could be." Michael helped himself to the wine, filling his glass nearly to the top. There was a pang of excitement, of hope in his belly. Obviously, Kasper knew the man.

However, Kasper's expression was not optimistic. "You must realize, Michael. Devin McCree, he is the vilest creature I have ever seen."

"You know him, then. Can you take me to him?"

"He is the reason my life is what it has become. The reason I am here in this hellhole of a city. But getting to him is not as simple as it sounds or else I would have killed him a long time ago." Kasper raised his glass to his lips and Michael noticed that his hands shook. Only slightly, but this was the first indication that there were indeed cracks in Kasper Jacobsen's steely exterior.

"I've chased that bastard from one end of this earth to the other. If your girl is with this man, it will not end well. She will either be killed or she will end up like him—blood-thirsty and crazy. I cannot tell you which is worse."

Michael pinched the bridge of his nose. A headache was developing behind his eyes, likely from the cheap wine. "Maybe if I had been stronger for her—"

"It's a disease, an addiction," Kasper interrupted. "Love holds no meaning when it comes to this thing, Michael."

chapter nineteen

1891.   A tiny village along the Mosel River, Germany.

It was so cold in the house that Kasper could see his breath, despite the good fire in the hearth. The fire provided light and that was far more precious than warmth this night. It painted the small room a flickering, watery orange and made the round cheeks of his younger brother and sister appear like apples, barely ripe. They huddled closer to the flames, warm, but he could not join them yet.

It was his turn to mind the window, what there was left of a window. He thought a window was to allow in light and to offer a view, but the windows of his home no longer gave anything of a sort. These windows were boarded up, as if against a coming storm. He peered through a small opening he had left between two boards, surveying the front of the little townhouse and the empty street beyond.

Night was what Kasper's family guarded themselves against. They would never again open their doors to the darkness. Two nights ago, their neighbor--a woman of about thirty and with a sickly infant--had come to the front door. She had called for Kasper's father. *Arzt, bitte. Mein baby ist krank.* Doctor. Please! My baby is ill!" Brazen, she pounded on the door. Ingrid, one of the twins and only six, moved to answer and Mother pulled her back.

"No." she hissed.

The pounding and shouting went on for ten minutes, perhaps less, but certainly no more. Then a shrill cry of pain ripped the night, a thud that made the door and the front windowboards rattle, followed then by nothing. After a moment, blood began to seep beneath the door, a slow stain that Mother mopped away with an old towel, wordless. Through the split between the boards, Kasper thought he saw a familiar figure, loping along the shadows, half-mad. *Father.*

He did not mention it.

Darkness was indeed the storm they guarded themselves against. Darkness and Father.

Kasper was tall for his age. At fifteen, he was the very image of his father, but he towered inches above the older man already. Handsome and strong of build. The girls had started noticing him, giving him shy smiles behind their school texts or behind their hands. Not that he had any concern over the fairer sex now that Father was gone, dragged away down the dismal alleyway and into the night three weeks ago.

Kasper had bigger things on his plate now.

People were becoming quite ill, others dying. The population of the village had dwindled. It was popular to speak of illness—a kind of influenza, perhaps, or cholera, better than what they all really suspected, because what they suspected was fodder for penny dreadful novels. Kasper's father, Lars, the only physician for miles, had been called out into darkness. But there had not been an ill neighbor that night; only shapes waiting in the shadows like black ghosts.

Kasper had gone with him. Luckily, he could make himself very small when he needed to, despite his lanky size,. And that night, he did. He fled and then slipped into a big pile of rubbish outside in the back alley of a tavern. The stench was horrible. His eyes watered and he fought the urge to gag. Perhaps it was the rotting odor of the garbage that disguised his own sharp, acrid scent of fear that bled from the pores his skin.

From his cover of trash, he watched creatures that looked like men drag his father away into the darkness. His father's cries were the dialogue that laced his nightmares.

Now, it was his father whom he locked their windows and doors against. It was his own beloved father he waited for, a hunting rifle across his lap and a sharpened stake underneath his bed. He sat at that window and silently, he prayed the moment would never come when he would have to confront the old man.

Kasper was ruined now and that was the only word he could think of to accurately describe his mental state. He did not want his younger brother or sister to end up the same way. They had been fortunate enough to have been spared the sight of the last moments of his father's human life. As far as they knew, he was out hunting monsters and would eventually return, their wretched heads under one arm and a sack of treasure under the other.

Of course, Father did return to them, but it was for *their* heads.

It was easy enough for the creature that had once been their loving parent. He entered through the front door, asked inside by his mother. She threw her arms around him and the smaller children cowered at his knee, hugging his legs tightly to them.

Could they not see the changes in him, or were they so grateful to have him back that it did not matter? His kind face was roughened with a scraggly beard. His clothes were tattered and bloodstained. And his eyes were glazed with madness. He stunk of decay and death; the death of others on his dirty hands.

Kasper did not approach Lars, instead hanging back in the shadow. He grasped one of the shortened wooden stakes behind his back.

"Come here, boy. Have you not missed your father?" Lars Jacobsen grinned over the shoulder of his loving wife, revealing a wondrous set of very white, very sharp fangs.

Kasper moved closer. His mouth was suddenly very dry, but his hands were slick with sweat as he clutched the oak stake. He licked his lips and approached, wary, his knees trembling.

"Father," he whispered, "I can't."

Lars squeezed his wife tighter against his chest.

"Lars, dear one. You're hurting—"she complained, her words muffled against his dirty lapel.

"I don't want to hurt you, Father."

"You can't hurt me, you fucking pup.'

"Lars," Mother began. But in an instant, her words were cut off. Lars brought his hands up to either side of her head, his dirty fingers lost in the yellow curls of her long hair. He twisted and the snap was audible. Audible enough to be the soundtrack of Kasper's nightmares for the rest of his life. Kasper had waited too long to strike and now it was too late. Another thing that would dog his sleep for the rest of this life.

Little Markus and Ingrid at Father's knee continued to paw at his trousers, vying for his attention, as Lars pressed his lips to his dying wife's neck. Kasper heard the wet smack and the greedy sucking—a blood-wet soul kiss.

Lars' eyes rolled backward, blind with ecstasy just as Kasper sprang, wielding the sharpened stake high above his head. He flew across the shadowy little parlor and roughly shoved his tiny siblings aside.

"Hide! Now. It's not Father. It's a monster!"

Lars let the white-faced corpse of his wife fall to the floor in a heap. He glanced at Kasper, his mouth a gore of red from ear to ear like that of a crazed clown, against his complexion of white greasepaint.

Screaming, Kasper plunged the stake into his father's chest. The ferociousness of the attack threw the two back against the front door. Kasper continued to force the weapon deeper into the chest of the thing that had been his father. His hands had become wet with the hot, vicious blood.

The stake exited Lars' back and pierced the door, pinning him there, motionless. His head dropped forward. Kasper stepped back, bloody and breathless. Only then did he realize that Ingrid and Markus were howling in terror. He wondered if their cries would draw others like his father to the house.

"Shh. Be quite now. He cannot hurt you."

Lars raised his head slowly, a grinned spreading across his gaunt face.

"Hide," he cried, realizing the man was still alive.

"Wooden stakes, my boy? Nonsense!" With a wet smack, he pulled himself off the skewer. Slowly, he stalked toward Kasper. His blood had soaked through his clothes, turning his jacket, shirt and trousers crimson. "I am not a creature of myth and old books. I thought I taught you not to believe in faerie tales. I thought I taught you to be a man of science. Of reason. And reason tells us that vampires do not exist." As if he wished to emphasize his point, he flicked his tongue against the sharp points his new canines.

The smaller children scrambled away, behind the old chair that Lars had long ago deemed his reading chair. They clung to each other as if they were one person, their cherubic faces, terrified and glowing orange in the dancing firelight.

Kasper retreated from the filthy grasp of his father. His eyes searched the room for something, anything he might use as a weapon.

"Please, Father. Please do not hurt the little ones."

"Please, Father," Lars mimicked. He then feigned tears and dipped an index finger into the wound in his chest that was now noticeable smaller and more shallow. "Look what you have done to me!" Then he laughed and added, "Tasty morsels, those two. Yours is the tougher flesh. But I shall taste it all. "

"I am sorry, Father," Kasper whispered. Despite his effort not to weep, tears stung his eyes and blurred his vision.

Before he could again move away, Lars snatched him up by the throat. He held him high over his head with one nasty claw. Kasper was much taller than his father was and outweighed him by more than thirty pounds, but Lars movements were effortless.

Lars rushed across the room with Kasper in a hateful vise grip. Kasper felt as though his windpipe was being crushed as Lars slammed him against the wall. Framed pictures and paintings clattered to the floor and their glasses shattered. Kasper saw stars for an instant and as his vision cleared, saw his faces was mere inches from his father's. He could smell his mother's blood on Lars' hot breath.

"My dearest son. I am going to allow you to watch me devour your brother and sister before I kill you."

He hurled Kasper to the floor hard enough to make the thick wood planks splinter. Kasper lay in a gasping bundle, staring up at flickering light and shadow. Then he turned over to his hands and knees and began to climb to his feet.

Laughing like a madman, Lars brought his heavy boot down on the middle of Kasper's spine, driving him back down to the floor. He then pounced on him, bringing his entire weight down onto the pit of Kasper's back. Pain flooded Kasper's body. His open hands grabbed at the floor. Shards and splinter of wood embedded beneath his fingernails. After a couple of excruciating breaths, his legs began to spasm. Blood flowed from his parted lips.

His bladder let go and warm piss wet his clothes. He

twitched a moment more and then fell completely still, unable to move.

In a gruesome triumph for Lars, Kasper's eyes remained open as he lay immobile. Still weeping he watched his father slaughter his smaller brother and sister. He tore their plump limbs from their soft bodies and gorged himself on their blood. And then, in a final insult to their ruined remains, Lars removed his clothes and bathed himself in the gore.

Kasper lay wretchedly helpless as the blood drenched him like torrents of warm spring rain.

He closed his eyes and waited for his own death to arrive.

Perhaps his father still had a heart despite his metamorphosis. He did not dismember his oldest son.

Kasper woke to the stench of death. He opened his swollen eyes to a bright and hateful sun. Slowly he raised his head and looked around. Dear God, the pain. It was like a bullet the brain. He moaned and squinted into the burning blue-white dawn.

It took a moment for realization to dawn. To his horror, he was atop a sea of bodies. There were corpses as far as his watering eyes could see. Corpses of his neighbors. Nearly his entire village had been slaughtered and tossed like so much rubbish into a huge mass grave. Suddenly he began to flail about, horrified and sickened. Some of the bodies were whole; others were only pieces and parts. Here and there, he saw limbs, torsos, heads.

He began to wade through the stinking, rotting flesh. His hands sank into the wet, putrid torso of an old man, headless and without limbs. He wept and pawed at his eyes, smearing gore across his face. He pushed through the mass, to his relief striking solid ground finally. "Please, dear

God," he whispered.

He fell headlong and came face to face with little Ingrid. Her curls fell across the back of his hand, heavy with blood. Her doll's face appeared sleeping. He touched her icy cheek. "Wake up, Ingy," he said, knowing that there was no use. Still he shook her gently.

Ingrid's tiny head rolled to the side and then he realized that it was not attached to anything. He scrambled away, through and over bodies now, shaking his head quickly as if clearing away the image of his dead sister.

Then he was climbing out of the pit of bodies. He sprinted for the woods, leaving his dead village behind him. His clothes were stiff with blood and freezing. He wondered where he would go. He wondered if he would survive the coming night.

chapter twenty

Devin threw back the shower curtain just like Norman Bates. The unfortunate man behind the sheer plastic was blessed with the equally unfortunate name of Wallace. Devin had grown to know him over the past few months, stalking him now and then on the boulevard when he had nothing better to do. It had become a game, to watch this miniature fifty-something gay lothario try to lure boys back to his Lysol and Old Spice-scented motel lair. And that was what helped Devin make his decision to tail this little man— his taste for boys; the younger the better.

Devin often did that, stalk his victims, becoming their shadow, growing to know them, often growing to like them. It added a pang of sadness when he decided to end their lives, but most had nothing to live for, anyway. Devin this did one thing that helped set his mind at ease—he chose people who were not worth the air they breathed.

Devin was not sure how a man like Wallace came to live in this motel. From what he had gathered, the little man was an accountant in his previous life. Closeted, married, a father to a college-aged son. But he had done something terribly wrong and it was only a matter of time before his little victim spilled the beans. So he had vanished while he still could. Wallace knew no one would miss him.

One night, barely two months ago, he brought Devin

back to this little flat. The look on the Wallace's face was one of sheer surprise, like a man who just won the lottery, although Devin was hardly the helpless child Wallace typically preferred. Repeatedly, he told Devin how beautiful he was, until Devin began to feel a bit guilty for planning his death as he held him in the shadowy bedroom.

Finally, just to reaffirm his own dark motives, Devin whispered to Wallace in the darkness as he excitedly removed his clothes, "I saw you with that boy earlier. Do you feel like a sick man?"

Wallace stopped undressing, pulled his baggy underpants back up and frowned.

"No."

"Do you feel like an evil man?" Devin asked. Inside the little man's little brain, thoughts swirled. Devin picked up the image of the boy that had sent Wallace to Dunwich. Guilt seethed inside his mind like waves churning in a storm.

"I can see inside you, Wallace. I can see Bobby Miller's blue, blue eyes, staring at you as you shoved your . . ." He stopped and took a deep breath. He wanted to take Wallace's head off now—but that was not part of the game. Discipline was part of the game and after seventy years, Devin was still a student of patience. "Maybe you should repent," he said after a moment.

Fear seized Wallace's chest and his breathing grew labored. Devin wondered a moment of he might be having a coronary.

"Maybe I should, at that," Wallace croaked.

"Get undressed, you little bastard. Penance will come soon enough," Devin said, laughing.

On the upside, Wallace gave great head.

He had managed to keep Devin on the threshold of orgasm for what seemed like hours. Devin remembered lying back on the bed and taking in the dim room through eyes clouded with bloodlust: the ugly, cheap abstract hotel prints, the dirty shag rug and the rust-colored crack that ran along the ceiling over the bed.

But Wallace looked so different now than he did that night two months ago. Devin suspected illness, but maybe it was loneliness. Perhaps leaving his wife, running from the normal life, and ultimately, guilt, took its toll on poor little Wallace. He deserved it—all of it. Besides, Devin was just putting Wallace out of his misery, doing him a favor.

Under the stream of the shower, Wallace appeared exceptionally small and frail. He screamed like a little girl at the sight of Devin's wicked, smiling face through the rising steam. He brought his hands up to block Devin's fist, but he was much too slow. As if in super-slow motion, Devin saw the little man wince as his knuckles impacted with his head. The old man's skull cracked loudly like an overripe melon and Devin's heart thudded in his chest.

With the second blow, Wallace fell limp and slipped down the funky aqua and coral checkerboard tile. He was still alive; his eyes fluttered back open. But his logic was gone. Devin stepped over into the tub and the hot water soaked him, making his jacket and jeans heavy and uncomfortable. It was sobering, but that was good. Devin wanted to be completely alert for this—nothing was more exhilarating than the hunt. Not drink. Not drugs. The dazed man reached up and grabbed at Devin's coat, but it seemed that his hands no longer worked right.

Wallace's bony, spasming fingers slipped over Devin's crotch and Devin's held Wallace's wrists for a moment before letting his arms fall. He then reached down and snatched Wallace back to his feet by his hair. Baring his fangs, Devin thought he found the faintest look of recognition in Wallace's eyes. Inside Wallace's head, the taint of guilt swirled, mixed with a heavy helping of terror creating colors like a bruise. Wallace knew death was coming.

"Why?" Wallace croaked.

"Why not, you sad little pervert?"

Devin yanked Wallace's head back, exposing the soft skin of his neck. He smelled the subtle scent of some kind of moisturizer—something women used. Beneath the pallid skin, the jumping pulse of Wallace's jugular, lay a line as pale blue as a robin's egg.

Devin sank his teeth into that thrumming blue line, tearing skin and muscle along with it. The blood really began to flow, a wondrous, hot fountain. Salty and metallic, it filled Devin's mouth and he gulped it down like a man dying of thirst.

Wallace clutched at Devin's back, as if holding on to the living might save himself. He moaned softly. In only a few moments, Devin had drained him to the point of death. He was nothing more than a lifeless sack of flesh and bone, barely coherent.

Devin let him fall.

"You're no better than an animal," Wallace mouthed.

The words meant little to Devin. The water turned pink with the remnants of Wallace's blood and it splashed up the sides of the porcelain, up the walls, up Devin's jeans-clad legs, magically dying them not red but black in the harsh light of the bathroom. Devin tilted his head back under the flow of the shower and parted his lips. The water jetted against his teeth and his tongue and he swallowed, letting it scald his throat.

Finally, breathless and close to exhaustion, Devin stood motionless. Through the steam, he caught someone staring at him. Wide, crazy eyes, a grimace of pure horror, blood running down striping the cheeks like war paint.

His heart quickened. *I am in here with a madman!* But he was only seeing his reflection in the mirror, ghostly and little more than a suggestion of himself. He had forgotten to mention that little side effect to Susan. He doubted she was very pleased with it.

He remembered how startled he had been, searching for

his face in the mirror, not finding it there. Eventually, as it faded into view, it had grown so gaunt and sallow Devin thought he must have been dying.

When he first changed, he tried to survive on the blood of animals—dogs, cats, even rats—anything to keep him from harming the flesh of a human. But months of that made him grow as weak as a child. He wondered if he was starving himself to death, death as it was.

He suffered from malnutrition. The bones of his cheeks and the round hollows beneath his eyes so clearly visible, as if he were looking on the stark image of a skull, almost. His hair had become brittle; his lips dried and split. His body, always broad and powerful, wasted away to sinewy, stringy muscles and tendons that flexed beneath his thin skin like writhing snakes. He was never a vain man, but even so, he knew that he had been beautiful.

In a fit, he had smashed the mirror with his fist and sank to floor, then crawled to the darkest corner of the tenement where he rode out the hateful daylight and wept dry and painful sobs.

Devin realized then that for him to live, others would have to die.

The beast in him grew with each kill. Of course, he could have taken just enough blood to quench his immediate thirst, but where would that leave him? Obligated to hoards whose aging process had slowed so dramatically that they would live 200 years or more? Just because of his precious and poisonous bite. No, he could not have that.

He took a series of long, deep breaths and shut off the water. He climbed from the tub, then reached back in and retrieved Wallace's flowery shampoo and conditioner. Next, he went back into Wallace's bedroom, his wet shoes squishing and his wet clothes like heavy blankets, and riffled through old man's belongings, tearing open the closet, pulling the drawers all the way out and dumping the contents on the bed. He searched for anything worth keeping—anything to remind him that he was nothing more than a rotten killer. He needed those reminders around him, in his room, in his house. He needed that dose of guilt.

In the heap were several dog-eared paperback books. One stood out to him for some reason—the cover featured nothing but text in large gothic lettering: *Interview with the Vampire.* He snatched it up, along with an older generation iPod, and left.

Outside, the breeze nearly froze Devin in his wet clothes. He thought of Susan—of what he had shown her already. When he was still able to see inside her mind, he knew she was simultaneously terrified of him and excited by him. Now that she had transformed, he did not know what she thought and that was a little frightening.

What exactly did she think they were? Soon he would need to show her how to hunt and kill. How difficult would it be for her to adjust? Not very, he suspected. Her heart was hard—she was already stronger than he ever had been.

Devin dropped his new loot into the passenger seat of the Rover. He started the engine and cranked the heat all the way up, then tore out of the driveway and into the ghostly tourist-free streets of Dunwich's beach district.

chapter twenty-one

The craving for blood—for Devin's blood—plagued Susan's mind. She was as restless as a drinker in need of a shot of whiskey, pacing the rambling old mansion, stalking the wide expanse of library. She picked up John's thoughts as she passed through the long room and his eyes followed her nervously. He knew what she was doing.

She picked up his fear of her, but rather than the possibility she might spring at his throat any moment, was the concern over whether she might become sick from not feeding. Somewhere in the darkest corners of his mind, he considered offering himself to her. He was attracted to her and the idea quickened his pulse. There was a small twinge in the pit of his stomach when he considered her lips on his throat. When Susan seized this idea, unwelcome excitement warmed her middle, as well.

A fire roared in the huge stone fireplace, straight out of the gothic novels that she spied here and there on the shelves. The warm scent of burning hickory infused the room, making her think of the holidays when she was a girl. She selected a book without noticing the title and sat down heavily in an overstuffed leather reading chair.

John appeared time and again, more now to check on her than to guard her from escaping.

"Everything's all right, yes?"

Finally, after what seemed to be the fifth time of him asking, she slammed the book she was holding (but not reading) closed. "Hell, no. I'm not all right. I'm fucking miserable, John. Why did he do this to me?"

John drew closer, tentative. "Please, Susan. Calm down. Devin will take care of you. He will be back before dawn."

"He left me here like this."

At first, she had been happy when the sun sank low in the sky. The brightness had given her a sickening headache and left her nauseated and shaky. Now she wanted to rave, to vent her frustration on John. She could not understand why she felt so *bad.* She did not have an addictive personality, but the taste of blood had her in its grips. Her mouth watered, thinking of it.

Briefly, she toyed with the idea of actually asking John to come to her, since he had considered it, as well. She was shocked to find herself contemplating sleeping with him only to render him vulnerable enough to tap into his vein. She had not known the man twenty-four hours, yet she was entertaining the idea of having sex with him. Was that what she had fallen to? She was no better than a junkie on the street.

She went onto the terrace and looked down at the moonlit garden below, which was a sharp contrast to the streets and sidewalks beyond the gates, sparsely littered with pedestrians and blowing trash. The chilly nip of autumn touched her skin. She shivered, then crossed her arms to warm herself. The scent of wilted gardenia whiffed up along with the salty, fishy odor that drifted in from the bay just ahead. The musky odor of small wild things scurrying in the shadows had become easily distinguishable, even against the rancid stink of the old city. That was something new and mildly interesting. She even glimpsed the little creatures here and there, mice, birds, an unfriendly cat. It was something, seeing with her vampire eyes. Moving shadows, even against the inky darkness were easy to spot.

Mere colors were now mesmerizing. She found herself more than once staring at Devin's Giger print, at the shades of gray. Before, she had imagined gray was only light or dark, but the spectrum between light and dark were so apparent. The near-sightedness she had lived with since her teens had vanished and good riddance.

However, she had not yet grown used to her heightened sense of hearing. The night sounds deafened her. The sawing of the cicada and crickets, the chirps and belches of frogs. It irritated her until she plugged her index fingers into each ear, hoping to stop the sounds, if only for a moment. It never worked, of course—the thunderous boom of her heart beating in her ears only replaced it.

John approached her from behind and placed his large, warm hands on her shoulders.

"You will be all right, dear," he said.

"I don't want to be like this." She allowed herself to relax to his touch and knew she would not hurt him.

"It will be easier with time."

"We'll see," she said. "We'll see."

"You've kept her waiting too long. She's nearly sick," John snapped when Devin entered the house.

"If you're so worried, why didn't *you* take care of her, Moses?" Devin withdrew his newly confiscated paperback from the inner pocket of his wet coat. He then shrugged out of the coat and tossed it over the back of the sofa.

A touch of redness appeared on John's cheeks. "I'm not a donor, you realize."

"It's too late to pretend to be a gentleman now," Devin laughed. "Besides, I seriously doubt you would have minded very much. Nobody ever does."

"Nevertheless . . ." John did not bother finishing.

Susan stood at the window, paying as little attention to the exchange as she could, and instead focused on the red blossom-shaped stains on Devin's white t-shirt. She smelled the blood there, still wet, still fresh, and clinging to his skin. She flicked her tongue across her bottom lip and inwardly hated herself for being so weak.

Devin grabbed her hand and led her upstairs to his room, leaving John alone. Her knees felt weak, so she held onto to his hand and arm tightly to keep from stumbling. How she hated the sudden dependence she had on this man. On *any* man. It seemed like years instead of only hours that anything other than the other of feeding entered her mind.

Devin put the book on his nightstand atop a stack of other paperbacks and kicked off his Chuckie T's. He flopped on the bed and sank down into the soft down of the quilts. Stretched out and beautiful, he put out his hand. "Come here, Susan," he whispered. "Make me feel human again."

Feeling a pang of despair, Susan moved to him. Did he even realized what he asked. How could she make him feel human when she no longer felt that way herself? Michael and her old life was behind her now. Whatever Devin had done to her had taken hold. She would belong to him as long as she had a thirst for blood.

"It's been a difficult night, hasn't it?" he asked.

Susan moved over the top of him, loving the warmth of his body against hers. "You have no idea."

Devin pulled her to him, cradled her head in his large hands, and offered himself to her. She bit into his throat, as she had before. The wound had already healed completely from the last time. Straddling his waist, Susan accepted Devin's crimson gift and eagerly began to drink.

The heady scent of the blood escaping his vein made her a little dizzy, but at the same time a sense of calm washed over her. The weakness in her limbs vanished and instantly she felt she could do anything. Her mind was as sharp as it had ever been. All was right with her; she had what she needed. She was relaxed, relieved and overwhelmed with positive thoughts.

I really could stay here. I could be happy like this.

Taking another greedy pull from Devin's vein, Susan wondered briefly if she might kill him. If she had fed this much from Michael, she would have surely killed him. But of course, Michael was only a man. Devin was...

She was beginning to believe Devin was really what he claimed to be. A Deathwalker. He called himself and those like him Deathwalkers, but she knew what they really were. Vampires.

Vampires aren't real, stupid.

Then she must have been overtaken by some kind of crazy hypnosis. They all were. Besides, the blood was delightful and that was all that mattered now.

She rose up a moment, her eyes almost closed and she could just make out Devin beneath her, his big hands on her waist. The corners of his lips curled into a slight smile. It was evident he enjoyed this as much as she did. Warmth spread through her body and her mind and she closed her eyes completely, shuttered and bent her head down to his throat again. The throbbing between her thighs beat in time with her heartbeat, with Devin's pulse against her mouth.

Grinning, Devin pulled away and sat up, pulled his shirt over his head, and tossed it to the floor. In the warm, flickering glow of the flame, she was again taken by his beauty. His eyes were no longer menacing, but soft, the flames infinitely reflecting in them.

Susan's hands moved downward, over the ridges of muscles in his chest and stomach. But suddenly she stopped and drew back. There, just below his sternum was the scar she left him with that Halloween night so long ago. He should have died from a wound so violent, but he still had the strength to punish her so severely that it took her weeks before she fully recovered.

Frowning, she traced the wicked valley of that puncture,

as wide as the tip of her finger and more than five inches in length. The skin had grown poorly over it—hairless and smooth, more like a burn than a stab wound.

Devin fell still and allowed her to examine the place a moment. Then he took her face in his hands and kissed her deeply, lapping his own blood from her tongue.

Finally he broke the kiss and whispered, "Do you really have any idea what I am, Susan? What *we* are?"

Devin reached to a stack of battered books that sat on the bedstand. He first found the paperback copy of *Interview with the Vampire* that he had stolen from Wallace's apartment. Picking it up, he casually thumbed through it. After a moment, he threw it against the far wall.

"Rubbish!" he complained. "Who the hell would want to spend eternity wallowing in such self-loathing?"

Next, he retrieved a book that was especially dog-eared. He turned through the yellowed pages a moment and then began to read.

"Check this out. Vampires," he said, "neither ghost nor demon, but who partakes in the natures of both." He paused briefly and wet his lips with a flick of his tongue. "A pretend demon. Said to delight in sucking human blood, and to animate the bodies of dead persons. That's what the books say, at least."

He took Susan's hand and placed it to his chest. Beneath the cage of his ribs and the wrappings of his warm flesh, the puckered skin of the wound she left him with, the strong thump of his heart beat against her palm. "Do I feel dead to you?"

"Hardly," she laughed and leaned in to kiss him. She cared less about what he claimed they were or rather what she had only just become. She only cared for another taste of his sweet and salty blood.

"First, listen," he told her. He flipped over several more pages, his finger running along the text until he came to the passage that he had underlined with a black pen. After a moment, he continued on, quickly as if he knew the passages from memory.

"It was generally supposed that all suicides, after death become vampires, and this was easily extended to those who met any violent or sudden death."

He closed the book and placed it back on the nightstand.

Susan laughed. "Please, Devin." She touched the scar on his chest again. "This obviously was not as bad as it looked."

Devin grabbed her wrist. "This would have killed a mortal man, my dear. "

"Perhaps you were lucky." Though she believed him, she decided she would not let him win so easily.

Devin rose up on his knees and flipped her over and suddenly she stared up at him, unable to squirm free of his weight. But of course, she did not really want to.

"Why won't you believe?" He took both her wrists in one large hand and pinned her arms above her head.

"I don't believe anything until I see it for myself," she challenged.

"Even then, you will try to disbelieve."

"We'll see," she said

"You will see."

chapter twenty-two

The sun sank, painting the sky with a pretty pink glow. It illuminated the lingering clouds and haze as Michael and Kasper crossed Kasper's weed-ridden front lawn and stepped onto the deserted street.

Kasper pulled a pair of dark sunglasses from his coat pocket and slipped them on. "I hate the glare of sunset," he muttered.

Michael ignored him and scanned the old neighborhood in disbelief. As he arrived last night, he not been able to tell the dire situation the place had fallen into. He had slept much of the day away and had not seen much of anything except the inside of Kasper's gloomy old house until now.

This was the north end, the miles of beach that had once been where the families on a budget vacationed. He had the vague memory of playing in the surf along these shores as a very small boy, having been treated to a daytrip by this usually distant father. Rows stilted houses sat abandoned, paint peeling away like strips of dead skin, wood siding gone to rot and breaking off like cancerous flesh. Blackening, rotting boards covered the windows, as if it was the day before a hurricane. The ones that were not covered were broken out. The remaining glass reminded Michael of a Jack o'lantern's jagged grin. Scattered here and there were beachwear shops in dire shape. Street front awnings hung in tatters down onto the streets like torn, filthy flags. As he and Kasper walked by, Michael saw how the front displays were shattered and the shelves emptied. Across the street from the Atlantic, was an old arcade and next to it, a small amusement park where the remains of a broken wooden rollercoaster loomed like a prehistoric creature waiting for its next meal to come along. This was a ghost town like the rest of Dunwich. First the tourist left and then the natives left. And nobody returned, despite the prime beachfront real estate.

To the south, the city waited, buildings dark against a darkening sky.

A few cars lined the street and sat in parking lots, windshields and windows grimy from the salt air. Their doors and trunks had developed patches of rust. It was a horrible, apocalyptic image and one Michael could have just as well done without. It seemed that the owners of these homes, these cars, these business simply left, abandoning the place without a second thought to packing up or taking their things. It spoke of death and decay. Even the stink of abandonment lingered on the chilly early evening breeze. It was as if people had simply given up on the place. Trash blew down the street—pieces of newspaper, plastic supermarket bags, a woman's Sunday hat.

Ahead, Michael spotted a couple rounding the corner and began heading their way. They were the first people he had seen on this end of town. He could not help but watch them—a boy and a girl, no more than seventeen, he guessed, extremely frail and emaciated. Kasper shifted the black duffle he carried from one hand to the other and scrutinized the two. As they trudged passed, the boy boldly met his gaze.

"You'd better get out of here, son," Kasper said. Michael detected a sudden softness to his usually harsh tone. "While you can, make your way back home."

"Butt out, dude," the boy shot back. He slipped his arm

around his girl's waist and pulled her to his side. Beneath her loose sweater and ragged boy's jeans, the girl's belly was large and round.

"For the girl's safety—"

They passed without another word and Kasper only shrugged. "To hell with it, then."

Michael's heart broke for them and the physician in him wanted to take hold. The girl was too pale and sickly; she would surely lose the baby and possibly her own life in the process. It was so strange to allow them to pass without some offering of help. As he watched them lumber away, Kasper nudged his shoulder.

"Let them go. This won't be the last time you see kids like that around here."

Kasper motioned southward. "This way. There are a couple of shops up here. Get you some of the things you need."

"Why don't we just drive out to my car for my bag?" Michael asked.

Kasper laughed. "I'm positive everything in your car has been taken by now. Those creatures are nothing but scavengers. They steal what isn't nailed down."

"Oh." Michael nodded, somewhat saddened by the idea of someone or something rummaging through his things— his clothing, the couple of photos he kept in his jacket. His Blackberry. The iPod he had in the console of the BMW.

A block further, Kasper stopped in front of a men's clothing store. A street bench had been thrown through the front window and now laid half inside and half on the sidewalk.

"Be careful," Kasper warned as he removed his sunglasses and hid them away back into his coat. He stepped up and through the display into the store. "Those things like to hide in dark places."

Michael followed, squinting into the heavy shadows of the old store, his chest tightening with fear. It reminded him of the old Charlton Heston flick, *Omega Man*. At least a dozen mannequins posed, frozen in time, wearing styles from the late 80's and early 90's. Uneasy, he felt as if someone was watching them. Kasper moved through the shadowy place brimming with confidence. He was so far removed from anything resembling fear, it amazed Michael. Perhaps he had become immune to it. Not a bad way to be in the end, Michael reckoned. But the things he must have seen to get to that point.

Kasper opened the leather duffle and removed two modified shotguns with leather straps. He handed one to Michael. "This is a riot gun. You'll need to get used to having it with you at all times."

Tentatively, Michael took it, and hung it over his shoulder. He did not like the gun in the least. He did not care for the ruthless black barrel and the weight of it, but resigned himself to the fact that he would need a gun and would very likely have to use it if he ever wanted to get Susan back.

The place was indeed dark, and smelled heavily of mildew. Behind the walls was the scurry and scuffle of rats running to hide. He hated this, and for a moment, considered again simply letting Susan go. Could he really do this? He sighed and followed Kasper deeper into the thin darkness of the store. Silently, they sorted through what was left of the trousers and jeans and shirts. Nervous, he could not stop looking around, expecting someone to spring from the shadows and rip out his throat. The mannequins made him even more uncomfortable than he normally would have been. They seemed to be watching, waiting. Plus, there were so many of them, thin plastic things with oddly high cheek bones and messy wigs.

"Try and find a jacket, also. The nights get cold," Kasper suggested, moving off to the left, leaving Michael at a rack of cargo pants. Finding his size was a trick—he was of average build. Everything of value had been taken, stolen just as Kasper said, just like what they were doing now. However, Michael managed to pluck out two pairs in his size.

"Okay, I'm good." He threw the clothes over his shoulder, ready to be out of there and back into the less-claustrophobic street.

Then one of the mannequins moved. Just as Michael looked up, the thing screeched, leapt over one display, and upended another, rushing toward him. Michael grabbed his rifle from this back and thumbed the safety off, but it was over before he ever took aim.

Michael dropped his gun and dove behind a display of dress shirts. Kasper removed the Deathwalker's head in a cloud of pinkish gore, then blasted another round through the creature's chest for good measure. Michael remained crouched as the thing's body landed in a heap next to him. Only a man, he realized. Looking at it, it was only a man.

Then he rose to his feet, his heart thudding at an alarming speed. "Shit!"

"Sneaky fuckers," Kasper muttered, frowning. He strode toward Michael, his rifle now at his side. "You need to be on your toes, man. Always, always! If your girl is one of them, do her a favor. In the flash of an eye." He snapped his fingers. "She won't feel a thing." He nudged the dead man's leg with the toe of his boot. "You all right?" he asked without looking up.

"Yeah, I'm okay," Michael answered, trying to keep his voice from shaking. He had serious doubts he would be able to find Susan unless he has this guy's help.

Kasper stifled back a yawn, then grinned. "It's all right. Don't worry." He stepped closer and placed a big hand on Michael's shoulder. "You look scared."

"I am scared," Michael said.

"You can't allow it to control you. They can smell it, Michael. Fear will get you killed."

Michael nodded, but he was not sure what to do about it.

He *was* afraid, for Christ's sake. Afraid of those creatures, of what might have already happened to Susan. He was even still a little afraid of Kasper. He was not sure he had ever met a more unstable person in his life, yet he owed his life to the man, not once, but twice in less than twenty-four hours.

"You have to get mean. You have to get pissed. Everyone who was afraid is either dead now or changed into one of those things." For an uncomfortable moment, he realized Kasper was watching him quite intently. Then he picked up Michael's rifle and shoved it at his chest.

Kasper gestured toward a bald mannequin—an ugly, slouchy shirtless figure, dressed in baggy jeans. The face seemed made up, with large, blood- red lips and too-blue eyes. The waist of its jeans hung too low, revealing a set of sharp hipbones and then the puckered waistband of red polka-dotted boxers.

Michael raised the gun and the site wavered a moment, but he quickly steadied on the forehead of the doll.

"Go on," Kasper prodded. "Imagine Devin McCree's stupid face up there."

Biting his lip, Michael did just that. Involuntarily, he stiffened, prepared for the report and the sound, but neither was as much he expected. It was quite a smooth motion and the mannequin's head vaporized into a small cloud of plastic and dust.

Michael stood there a moment stunned. Before last night on the highway, he had fired a gun a total of twice in his entire life.

"That's it!" Kasper cried. "Now that one!" He motioned toward a preppy figure with Ken Doll hair, dressed for a round of golf.

Michael swung the gun around, more quickly this time. The aim did not waver nervously as it had the first time, and he fired. BAM! Still gripping his three-iron, the golfer became instantly headless. Next, in a span of only a few seconds, Michael cleared out a row of two adults and a little boy dressed for a day at the beach. He decapitated the entire group in a rain of plastic and dust.

Kasper was silent a moment. Then he whispered, "Bloody hell."

Michael turned to him, smiling wickedly. "I think I have it."

"I think you do," Kasper agreed softly.

chapter twenty-three

As the moon crested the night sky, they returned to Kasper's placc. Michael was relieved to be back inside. On the outside, he felt too vulnerable and exposed. He doubted he would ever get back to normal after this, even if he managed to return to Reading with Susan. Having finished a dinner of Ramen noodles, they were now on their second bottle of wine. Michael dizzily wondered if Kasper ever ate anything other than pasta, but decided not to ask. Judging by Kasper's wolfish features, he may not want to hear the answer.

"This town is shit." Kasper growled between gulps of the wine. "Have you ever seen such a place?"

"Why do you stay, then?" Michael asked.

Kasper laughed bitterly. "Revenge, of course. Besides, where am I going to go now? My own country has abandoned me. They drafted me into doing this thing, for this reason, and then they forgot about me." He swirled the wine around in the wide glass, as red as blood.

"Drafted? Were you in the military?" Michael asked. He was becoming too drunk too quickly and felt more than a little queasy. And wine made him too loose with his words. "I hate war. This country loves to fight and I hate it," he said and immediately wished he had not.

"We Germans live for the fight," Kasper said. He

removed   a pack of cigarettes from his shirt pocket and tapped one out. He lit it and took a long draw.   "Now, if your girl is with that scum, she's probably as good as dead, anyway. She might not know it yet, but that's the way it is." Smoke seeped from his nose and the image of a dragon briefly popped into Michael's head.

"The only way to kill one is to remove the head," Kasper rambled on. "They have these amazing restorative powers, you realize. Simply shooting them—even in the head only slows them down for a bit.

"The head *has to be removed.*"

"Susan's strong," Michael whispered. "It won't come to that."

"For your sake, Michael, I hope it doesn't." Kasper stood and stretched. "Tomorrow night, you'll go and look for her. Maybe it isn't too late." He finished his glass of wine, then vanished into the next room, trailing his stinking tobacco smoke behind and leaving Michael alone with the wine and his muddled thoughts.

Michael frowned. He would never harm Susan. He chewed his bottom lip and took another drink of the too-sweet wine. Even if she had become something . . .else, he would never harm her. He would simply leave her instead.

But first, he would warn her about Kasper.

chapter twenty-four

On the other side of the wall, Kasper listened to Michael move about, getting ready for sleep. Just like yesterday, he would listen to the soft whisper his guest's breathing and marvel over how easy it would be to simply...

No. He would not allow himself to consider that right now. The good doctor may prove to be quite a find. Because of his love of a woman who in all likelihood either dead or no longer anything resembling human, Michael may draw Devin McCree out of his cowardly hiding place and finally Kasper would have his opportunity finish him off and set things right.

Would things ever be settled between them, Kasper wondered. Not until they were both dead and mouldering in the dirt. How much loss could two men share? Because of Devin, he had lost everything that mattered and in the end, he lost himself, as well.

Kasper had tried to cling on to what little humanity he had left, but most was stripped away when he watched his own beloved father murder his family. And then there was Lexi. Beautiful, innocent Lexi. Five decades had passed and he still saw her questioning, terrified face behind his eyelids when he tried to fall asleep.

How he hated Devin McCree for making him what into a monster. How he hated Devin's handsome face. He wanted to carve it from his pretty skull and feed it to the wild dogs.

Memories of their last meeting, sometime during the German occupation. Kasper had been recruited by the *Deutsches Reich* because of his experience with the creatures who had boldly named themselves "Deathwalkers." He had come into Northern England in his quest, but his duties had changed. He was no longer an exterminator, but hunter of live specimens.

He tortured those creatures in the name of the Führer and Devin quickly became his favorite toy. With every puncture of his knife into Devin's skin, Kasper felt he was redeeming himself in the eyes of his slaughtered family. He cut the Deathwalker, he burned him, he beat him until his face was a ruined mess, only to heal again and again. He fucked him in the shadowy darkness, driving Devin's face into the dirt, threatening him with daylight if he fought.

When he was finished, Kasper held Devin as he wept.

But it turned out, Devin loved life, as it were, more than he first exhibited.

Convinced that the Deathers were virtually indestructible, the Nazis began sending in their young and their strong. For Devin to give them their fatal kiss. Finally, in the spiral of death, he opened Devin's vein and let the vampire's blood flow like a fountain into the waiting lips of those dying soldiers. He could only imagine how many other creatures his blind following created.

Kasper knew the ones he had made—he had left his mark upon their bodies. He had branded each one with the "black sun," the occult symbol the Reich had adopted as one of their own signs—the circle and the jagged spokes blooming from its center. Kasper remembered giving Devin the brand, the sharp perfume of burnt skin and the tears from Devin's eyes. But the Deather had not cried out. He had not uttered a sound at all.

Finally, Kasper branded himself, a secret connection to the creature he once loved as his battered pup.

In the end, Himmler's ideas of an indestructible army never materialized. Many of the Deathwalkers became wild things, like the ones who attacked the doctor as he rolled into town the other night. They fled into the darkness and were gone forever.

When Devin managed to escape, Kasper felt oddly betrayed. The Deather had, after all, professed his eternal devotion to Kasper. It never occurred to Kasper that it had only been a ploy to get Kasper to lessen his guard. He had grown to felt something like trust for Devin.

When Devin vanished into the night, Kasper thought he had seen the last of the handsome Deathwalker. But Devin sought vengeance for the things Kasper had forced upon him and those he had cared for.

It was in some pathetic English village that Kasper could no longer name or cared to name that he heard Devin call him out. Devin had been there since his escape, as it turned out, living in luxury with a man and woman who only wished for a replacement for their dead son. It was then that he realized that he was no longer the hunter, but the prey. Devin had been watching him, waiting, like the cold-blooded snake he was.

Kasper could hear the man's boot heels on the deserted stone street because McCree wanted him to hear it. He wanted him to be afraid. The moon rose painting the dank little town in something like daylight, but colder and deadlier.

The houses, the flats, shops and taverns had all learned it was best not to be open after dark. No human risked showing his or her face to the moon. The windows were shuttered, as if guarding against a storm. Just as Kasper's little village along the Morsel River had learned to do before the end.

Kasper waited in the damp alleyway behind some dump of a restaurant, his fist clenched until his fingernails cut little half-moon slits in his palms and the sweat smarted like bee stings.. Rats scavenged the spilling trash cans and cats scavenged the rats. The stench of rot and the underlying stink of a burst septic tank made him want to retch. But quickly, the cats fled, hissing at the shadows.

Devin stepped from the darkness, his long coat flapping behind him like wings. "Kasper. I have had enough. You must realize, we are not so different, you and I. I want to just walk away. I want you to do the same. It all ends tonight." His breath rose like small clouds in front of his face, obscuring it a moment.

Kasper removed his rifle from beneath his own long coat. His chest felt as though a weight had been placed upon it. His hands trembled "You're right, Devin. We end this tonight. On my terms."

Devin laughed and stepped closer. The moonlight touched his eyes, casting them silver for an instant. Kasper remembered how, although he was the one who was armed, he was suddenly afraid.

"Get away from me, monster!"

"Monster? Now, do I look like a monster?" Devin asked innocently.

"Looks can be deceiving, Devin. You know that, probably better than anyone." Kasper thumbed the safety off the shotgun. Despite the cold night, his palms were slick with sweat. It ran into his eye, stinging, and he blinked it away. When he wet his lips he tasted salt. Devin moved still closer.

"Why are you doing this? We're on the same side. We could rule this place, if we wanted to." Devin smiled and looked around. "It's more beautiful than you realize, living for the night."

"I don't want your disease."

Kasper leveled the gun at Devin's forehead and the vampire's chilly stare did not waver. The night had become silent save for the soft rush of wind kissing the bony branches of the trees and his blood pumping furiously inside his ears.

He fired and at first, he was positive he had hit Devin. But Devin was quicker than he expected for a man of that height. The shot struck the building behind where Devin had been, destroying the brick along one corner and creating a cloud of clay dust that floated into the air like rusty smoke.

Kasper glanced around stupidly, searching for the vampire. He cursed himself for being so careless as Devin snatched the gun from his slippery grip. With his other hand, he grabbed Kasper's throat and began to squeeze.

Kasper gasped for a breath as Devin lifted him effortless by the neck, his feet leaving the surface of the road. He held Kasper high over his head for a moment, grinning like a madman. He drove Kasper against the wall of a butcher shop and then slammed him back down on the pavement, hard on his back.

The pain was exquisite and for a moment, Kasper blacked out. Bright lights danced behind his eyelids and his stomach recoiled as if he might throw up as his breath was punted from his lungs. He groaned, trying to find air.

Devin then kneeled over him and shoved the nuzzle of the gun under his chin. "Like a newborn," he whispered.

Kasper blinked up at him, trying to focus. Devin's small, pointed fangs glinted in the moonlight.

"Kill me, bastard," Kasper moaned. Thick blood covered his tongue and filled his mouth and he realized he was bleeding internally.

Devin drew his finger around Kasper's lips, an oddly warm gesture, and then licked the blood from his fingertips. "What did you say?"

"Kill me." Kasper tried to pull in another breath, but pain laced his ribs and back. He coughed weakly. "I feel like I'm dying anyway."

Devin pushed the gun deeper into the soft underside of Kasper's chin and smiled tightly. "You fool. You're not dying. You more than anyone should know that." Abruptly, he pulled the gun away and then pulled Kasper's head back, exposing his sweating throat. Then he tore the skin there, but the movement was tender and the pain was brief. Blinking up at the gauzy clouds, at the fat moon, Kasper gasped again. Peace settled over him for a moment, but the sensation was foreign. No matter what Devin had said, he knew he was dying. Finally, Devin drew back and thumbed a drop of blood from his bottom lip. Then he brought his wrist to his mouth and roughly tore it open. "Now. Drink, if you want to live."

Kasper turned his head and the blood fell on his cheek and the side of his neck. "Never. Dying is better than living like you."

"Is it?" Devin asked. He then snatched Kasper's face in his big fingers and forced his gushing wrist to Kasper's mouth.

Kasper struggled, gagging and sputtering, but he was no match to the power of the Deathwalker. He had to choose to drink, if only to breathe.

After what seemed an eternity, Devin let him fall back to the cobblestone street. "I've wasted enough time on you," he muttered, standing up. He punted Kasper hard in the ribs.

Kasper struggled to sit up. Dizzy and sore, he watched Devin stalk away down the alley. Devin then stopped a moment, swung the gun like a cricket bat and smashed it against a brick wall. He then had tossed the busted butt back toward Kasper.

"I won't stop, Devin," Kasper had shouted. "I'll never stop!"

chapter twenty-five

The city spread out before Susan like stains of gray and yellow. Because she had been sleeping, she had not been able to take in the desolation of Dunwich the other night as Devin drove her through the barren streets.

It was shocking, this rundown version of the place she once called home for a short time as she left childhood behind. Businesses had closed—the pizza joint where she had shared too many drinks with a weird girl named Mary Lei. Seeing the little restaurant boarded up, the sign gone to rust and peeling paint brought a pang of sadness to her heart.

The little college she and Peter had attended—Stevens and Brown School of Art and Design—was shut. The campus had been nothing more than several majestic-looking, wide-columned buildings, over two centuries old to begin with. Now all the structures were in various states of decay. Windows had been broken out and appeared to be staring into the night, black-eyed and rather sad. For a moment, Susan imagined running to class, late as usual, the sun warming the top of her head.

The student center where she and Peter had taken art history and portrait drawing (and had both volunteered to pose nude for extra credit) was only partially standing now. Fire had taken down half. All that remained was the blackened framework and charred, crumbling bricks.

A smattering of businesses remained—essential to those who chose to stay in this hellhole or else could not afford to leave. Bars, bodega groceries that seldom received shipments of fresh food, strip clubs. The only redeeming quality the place held was the shore. Mother Nature had regained her glory over the beaches, devoid of tourists stupid with days off and money to waste. Dunes, untouched for at least a decade stood tall with reeds and dune grass. Myrtle trees grew wild, having escaped the sheers of overzealous pruners. Jasmine vines snaked up and over fences and porches, still fragrant even in the midst of autumn. Beyond that, the Atlantic seethed, angry and black, the sound of the waves as harsh as a complaint.

Susan felt invincible, and she supposed to a degree, she was now.

By way of a rusted and creaking fire escape, Devin led her up five stories to the top of the old and rickety Palmetto Hotel. When she looked up, flakes of rust floated down into her eyes, stinging. Cursing softly, she blinked it away. Once on the flat, gravelly roof, their breaths billowed like plumes of smoke from their lips in the chilly night wind. Susan's hair whipped wildly across her eyes and lips and she tried unsuccessfully to smooth it back.

Devin brushed his hand across her ass, then squeezed one cheek hard. He pressed his lips to her ear, warming it nicely and said, "Maybe I'll just throw you down and have you right here."

Susan laughed. "Hands off, darling. You don't get anything from me until I decide."

"As you wish," Devin replied with a quick bow. He planted a soft kiss on the frozen tip of her nose and she shoved him away playfully.

The salty scent of the ocean puckered Susan's lips, but there was something else, something more interesting. She leaned over brick wall that edged the rooftop and looked down. A man strolled along just below them, in the shadows of the alleyway between the hotel and a closed down bookshop. Susan detected the smell of blood, of body odor and recent sex on the man's skin. For a moment, she imaged taking him and opening him up just below the jawbone. She imagined drinking, her mouth filling with hot blood.

She shook her head, as if that would clear away the wretched thought. Just how far from human had she already become?

Quickly, she detected another scent, as well. More delicate—he was trailing a woman. Susan squinted, training her eyes on the man, her mind latching onto his thoughts.

She deserves what she gets. Nobody'll miss that bitch, anyway.

To move her mind from the man below, she turned away from the edge of the building and looked at Devin. "Why did you choose to come to Dunwich?" she asked.

Devin kicked at the tarry gravel with his sneaker. "I don't know, really. Maybe it's because dead cities draw creatures like me. Maybe it's because this place is shit and the people are shit." He laughed, a rough, barking sound. "Really, all I'm doing is clearing the rubbish. Taking out the garbage."

Susan had not heard him sound so cynical before. That was her role. "Every place has its share of shit, Devin. This place is no different."

"It doesn't matter," Devin told her. "I couldn't very easily leave after setting my eyes on you. I needed a reason to go on and you became that reason." He looked away, almost shy now. "Eternity is a long haul, Susan. You have to find your reason, or else you'll go mad."

Susan smiled, touched by his openness. "We're all mad, anyway. Now, come here."

"Make up your mind."

Susan grabbed a fistful of his leather jacket and yanked him to her. She kissed him hard, pulling his bottom lip between her teeth, then bit down sharply.

"Ouch! *Damn,*" *Devin hissed, but Susan kissed* him again, tasting his blood.

She was suddenly, intensely aroused.

"Maybe I will let you have me here," she whispered into his mouth.

His hot, sweet breath caressed her face and he cupped her bottom in his hands, lifting her up, grinding himself against her. "Naughty thing," he said, smiling.

It seemed that all Susan's senses had come awake since taking that first drink of Devin's blood. She could hear a cat padding along the street below; she could hear the thrumming of Devin's blood beneath his skin. The darkness might as well have been daylight, she could see so well and so easily. She wondered naughtily exactly how much her sense of touch had improved, as well.

That, she would find out later. Her eyes bored into Devin's. She grinned and flicked out her tongue to get that last drop of his blood from the corner of her mouth. Until now, he had acted as though he were in charge, that she was his to do with what he wanted. Tonight she would turn the tables on him. She would make him scream her name.

A small, secret smile touched her mouth, thinking of him beneath her, her tongue working him into a frenzy, his head thrown back as she drove him to orgasm.

She almost tasted his sweet, salty taste of his blood.

"Now, listen to me," Devin said, pulling her back into reality. "First things first, sweetheart. You need to know how to hunt."

Devin leaned and peered over the edge of the building. He quickly spotted the male walker below, still teetering along. "That one. I know you've already picked his brain" he said. "Now you just follow what I do and we'll get to him before he gets to that woman." He climbed to the top of the wall, crouched and looked downward.

"What the hell are you doing?" Susan asked, panic unwinding in her gut.

"Shhh. Trust me."

Devin leapt off the top of the building, arms spread-eagle, and into the soft cloud of mist rising from the street. Susan leaned over the edge of the roof, shocked.

"Shit. Shit! What the hell did you just do?" she muttered.

In a breath, she could just make out his bulky form as he settled on the pavement. Despite his size, it was a soft, catlike landing, his knees giving slightly before he straightened back up to his full height. The man went on, unaware he was being watched. Farther up the alley, the woman meandered, singing some old blues song to herself, her mind racing. She had just fixed, having bought the junk from the man who was now stalking her.

Slowly, hesitantly, Susan climbed the low barrier wall herself. Condensation slicked the surface of the bricks and her boots slipped. How she hated heights! Her breath caught in her chest a moment and her leg muscles tensed, then froze.

She glanced down one final time, her eyes watering from the cold, then took another deep breath, chilling the silky lining of her lungs and her throat. She exhaled a balloon of steam.

Closing her eyes, she thrust her legs up and out, away from the rooftop and into nothing.

She was falling.

Falling.

But in an instant, it was over and she landed as light as a dancer, on the balls of her feet. It was a far easier landing than she imagined; her knees and hips flexed just enough to allow her joints to absorb the impact of the sixty-foot leap. Her fingertips scraped the pavement and then she stood up and scanned the fog for Devin.

The heavy mist dampened the sound of the walker's boot heels on the road and she lost track of him.

Then Devin appeared at her side. "Told you to trust me," he said, but his eyes were trained on the man coming along the alleyway, the thud of his boots dully punctuating his steps. As he emerged from the fog, Susan was immediately taken with his beauty. He was of African descent, broad featured. His light eyes appeared startlingly pale as the streetlamps reflect upon them. His dreadlocked hair was like a spider's nest of that fell past his shoulders.

Taking on a predatory stance, Devin moved closer. His eyes narrowed; his fists clenched at his sides. Devin stalked toward the man, but the man made no move to run despite the fact Devin towered over him. In fact, the dark man did not appear frightened at all.

Instead he held his head up, his eyes meeting Devin's. "What the fuck you doin' out in this alley, golden boy?" he snapped as he reached into his coat. "What you doin' out here with that girl?"

Susan tensed and wished she still carried her service revolver at her side.

Devin cut his gaze to her, then he winked and closed in on the man.

"What do you plan to do to that girl up there, Rasta man?" he asked, nodding his head toward the woman who still moved on, happily oblivious. He laughed then reached out and batted the man's dreadlocks playfully with his open hand.

The dark-skinned man drew back, angry and a silver blade flashed to life in his fist. "I ain't doin' nothin'." But concern creased his brow like a kid caught with his fingers in the cookie jar. His throat worked visibly as Devin paced slowly across his path.

Devin leaned closer, seeming to breathe in the scent of the man's fear. "Don't you know that night is when the monsters come out?"

Susan could not take her eyes from what was unfolding. The younger man's scent changed; she now smelled the acrid odor of fear mixed with the adrenaline that seeped from his pores. His heartbeat throbbed inside her ears, quickening. He was ready for a fight and he told Devin so.

"I've dealt with the likes of you before, big man. I'm not afraid." Then he spit, "Fucking *vampire.*"

His voice, even more raspy and rough than Devin's amused her. She liked his lilting faux-islander accent.

Slowly Devin circled the man, enraging him more, enticing him to make the first move. "What are you dressed up for, Rasta Man? A costume party, maybe?" He smiled and wet his lips. "*Rasta Man.* This isn't Kingston."

"Screw you!" Rasta Man could barely contain his anger now and just as Devin anticipated, he made his move. But what Devin did not anticipate was that Rasta Man would go after Susan instead.

The switchblade glistened like a slash of light and before Susan could move, he brought the razor across her breasts, slitting her leather jacket clean through to her sweater and then her flesh.

"Damn!" She staggered backward, looking down in surprise and horror. Hot blood bubbled up like a red fountain and she fell backward onto her bottom, shortly dazed.

"Maybe I'll just take your bitch, then, big man!"

Rasta Man's shadow fell over her and she could not clearly see his face. He swung the blade in a wide arch once again and Susan kicked upward, her boot connecting with his kneecap.

The icy breeze touched the gaping wound like a corpse's kiss and she wondered dimly if vampires could bleed to death.

Rasta Man stumbled, but he did not have a chance to make another move. Devin snatched him back by his long dreadlocks and swung him around, the man's boots leaving the pavement. Effortlessly, Devin threw him into the side of the old hotel, his body striking the bricks with a sickening thud. The knife clanked into the shadows and vanished as the man collapsed into a gasping pile at Devin's feet.

Devin raised one grungy Chucky-T sneaker and pressed it against the man's throat, pinning him to the ground. "You're going to die for that."

"No, Devin!" Susan sprang to her feet and grabbed a handful his coat. She pulled at him, but she could not budge him.

After a long moment, he looked down at her and drew back from the injured man. "You all right, babe?"

Susan stood clasping one hand over the gash. "Yeah. No biggie." But her voice trembled and she hated the sound of it; how weak it made her seem. She wanted to, at the very least, *appear* to have herself under control. She forced a small, weak smile as she trailed her fingers trail over the cut, then glanced down at herself again. She looked as if she had pulled on a single red glove. The entire front of her black sweater was soaked with blood. It splotched the front of her jeans like spilled paint.

The gash was a wide, wicked grin, just above her left breast, perhaps six inches in length, reaching to just beneath her armpit. The chilly air helped the blood cool. Already it was congealing, so she would not bleed to death, after all. That aside, nearly having her boob taken off did not make her happy.

Devin took her sticky hand and wove his fingers between hers. "Don't worry. You're not like you were before." But when he traced his thumb along the wound, even *he* winced a little.

He then marched back over to the Rasta Man, his head down, his breath steaming from his lips. "You see what you did to this young lady?" he growled. "You should apologize." Then he added in a bad attempt at a Jamaican accent. *"Doncha tink?"*

He reached down, took the dreadlocks in his fist again and yanked Rasta Man to his feet. The frightened man grunted some reply and Devin popped him in the nose with the back of his hand.

"I-I'm sorry," the man muttered. Blood streamed from his busted nose, down across his lips.

Devin yanked ropy hair again, pulling Rasta Man's head back, exposing his beautiful brown throat. "You don't sound sorry."

Susan wanted detachment from this. It was survival, after all. This bastard had cut her. He had defended himself and he had lost. As simple as that. Susan inhaled the scent of his blood again, gamey with terror and putrid with on-setting death. Strange how easy it was to distinguish his blood from hers own.

"Come on and do what you must do," he whispered up to Susan. He pushed the trembling man back down to the pavement.

Susan's mouth ran with desire as she dropped to her knees beside Devin. She closed her eyes and leaned over the man. He no longer protested and when she pressed her mouth to his sweaty neck, the pulse throbbed strong against her lips.

The softening, blood-damp kiss of his breath touched the side of her face as she licked his salty skin. With a deep breath, she bit down, hard. Her teeth tore through the skin and slowly she shook her head, unsure of how exactly to proceed. Blood arced into the air, onto her hands and across her waiting mouth and she sealed her lips over the pulsing wound, a lover's kiss, determined not to lose another drop. She drank until she was no longer aware of the gaping cut across her own breast or the ache of her knees on the pavement or even Devin's comforting presence.

When she was satisfied, she fell backward and lied there, staring up at the starless sky between the hulking old hotels.

Devin leaned over her, his own lips smeared with the man's blood. Grinning, he pushed her sticky hair from her brow and cheeks and kissed her deeply.

When he moved back, Susan looked at him, at his beautiful, bloody face. "What have I become, Devin?"

"You have become what everyone wants to be. You are eternal." He got to his feet and then took her hand and pulled her up. "Together, we will watch the end of the world."

"Are we monsters, do you think?"

"I don't know. Maybe we're just survivors."

chapter twenty-six

"**W**hat on earth happened?" John rushed to them as they came through the door. He wrapped his arms around Susan's shoulders and shot Devin a reproachful look. "You allowed her to get hurt?"

"It's nothing, John," Susan reassured him. Although she had known him less than forty-eight hours, she had already come to enjoy the old man's protective manner. Wincing, she removed her jacket and Devin was there to help her. The pain in her breast had reduced to a dull ache; the knife had ripped through the muscle and tissue, but now, it felt like nothing more than a serious exercise injury.

Susan had no idea how quickly she would heal, but either way, she sure as hell did not like being cut open. It was as frightening now as it was before her change.

John led her upstairs to the big washroom adjacent to Devin's bedroom and a moment later Devin joined them, carrying military first aid kit that had seen better days.

John found a cellophane packet, tore the end and removed a pair of rubber surgical gloves. He pulled them on with a snap and then bent a little to get a closer look. He probed the gash gently, but a sharp bolt of pain shot through Susan's chest and arm and she drew back, hissing softly. "Shit."

"So, you're a doctor?" asked Susan, growing more concerned by the moment.

"You may call me doctor." John winked. He squinted deeply and tried unsuccessfully to thread the nylon through then a rather ominous-looking needle he removed from a suture packet.

"That's not very reassuring," Susan said, glancing at Devin. "Can't he see that?"

"Pay no attention to him," Devin answered.

She glanced down at the yawning gash again, he stomach flip-flopping.

"I have a Ph.D. in Psychology. So technically, you *can* call me a doctor."

Devin peered over John's shoulder into the bag of medical goodies. "How old is this shit?" He pulled out something that resembles a pair of scissors, but with dull, clamping ends, and held it up, opening and closing the jaws with thin, metallic snaps. John snatched it away and stashed it back into the bag then tried to thread the needle again. Finally successful, he smiled. "That was the difficult part. Now…" He laid the newly prepared needle on a swatch of sterile cloth he had unfolded on the back of the toilet.

"I don't see how you're qualified to sew me up," Susan protested. She pulled the torn edges of her sweater closed.

"Just relax," Devin said. "He hasn't killed *me* yet."

Sighing, Susan leaned back against the pedestal sink and Devin squeezed her arm gently. "Of course, that's only because we can't die so easily."

"It appears that we will need to remove your sweater," John said. He flexed his long fingers inside the blue gloves.

"Knew that was coming," Susan muttered, and gingerly raised her arms. But John was ready with a pair of silver scissors and cut away the top along the side seam.

Shortly, she was naked to the waist, except for a sheer white bra, covered in drying brown blood. She shivered.

John nodded approvingly. "Well, now."

"Down, old man," Devin growled.

"This is completely awkward," Susan complained.

Devin removed a large towel from the linen basket near the tub, unrolled it and draped it over her shoulders. Then he scooped up her hair and pulled it back.

John drenched several thick squares of soft gauze with antiseptic and cleaned inside and around the cut. "Do you want something for pain?"

"A glass of wine, maybe," Susan replied. "Otherwise, just hurry. I'm freezing."

"I can tell," John commented, leering comically at her breasts. "Okay, let's get started. This will sting a little."

It stung a lot. Susan bit her bottom lip as Devin held her hair back with one hand and squeezed her fingers gently with the other. "You'll be okay," he whispered.

She looked up at him and held his gaze a moment. For the first time since leaving home, she realized she just might.

Devin was convinced he had told Susan the truth when she asked if they were monsters. They were survivors and survivors did what they had to. Still, so many times, he wondered if he were something less than human. What was wrong with his heart? Had his happiness been ripped from him so many times that he had become afraid to feel anything but anger and fear? He questioned all his actions. Even now, calm and dared he think, happy, watching Susan sleeping beside him.

Her face was peaceful, as smooth as the girl he had loved and followed along the shadowy streets of this ancient city twenty years before. He stroked her cheek and she made no move. She was deep in her own dreams; her eyes twitched beneath the silky cover of her eyelids. He traced a finger along the stitched-up gash along her breast. John had done a good job with it. Devin knew the man was attracted to her, but what could he do except ignore it? John had always been his most trusted ally. He would have been long dead if it were not for John.

Devin touched Susan once more and wondered what exactly went on in her mind now that she had transformed. He was locked out and found himself missing the ability to slip inside her thoughts. Over the years she had become very much like he was. Afraid to love. Afraid to care. Buried within both of them lay the desire to be "good." He wondered if he had completely corrupted her instead. She had gone after the man earlier as if she were made to do it. Did she view it as survival or was it more than that? Did she enjoy the thrill of the hunt?

Downstairs, John played the piano. He was human, but had come to embrace the hours of vampires. Over their many decades together, John had taken steps to refine Devin's brash demeanor, to make him more cultured. Beethoven's Piano Sonata number twenty-six, *"Les Adieux."* Devin could quickly name most of the pieces John played. *I can name that tune in two notes—he had heard that phrase on some* stupid television show a long time ago, before he decided to throw a vase through the screen. *He loved movies, but loathed the* triviality of television. The advertisements, the inane *loudness of* it.

Devin rolled onto his back and stared up at the ceiling. It would be light soon, but his mind just refused to shut down, despite the fatigue that had settled into his limbs. Rain again, the sound like a million fingers drumming anxiously on the roof and the windows. A snap of lightning brightened edges of the shaded window. He sighed and memories of Kasper Jacobsen popped into his head, a night inside the little prison when the lightning had brightened the barred windows and Kasper's torture had let up long enough for something even more wretched.

Kasper had dogged him from Scotland's Tayvallich Bay to the bleak polar nights of Norway. He had killed people Devin loved and would do it again, as soon as the opportunity arose. He knew Kasper had finally found his way to Dunwich.

It had been so long, Devin had actually grown comfortable in the idea he had shaken Kasper from his heels, thinking that perhaps he had been killed. Now, he needed to be on his guard with Susan. He slipped his hand under the waistband of his shorts and fingered the raised scar on his lower belly, that ugly spiraling sun. What a joke, to be burdened with a symbol of something he would never again set eyes on. He considered running like the coward he felt he was, but Kasper would keep on coming until one of them was dead.

chapter twenty-seven

Kasper drove Michael over to the nearly deserted beaches of Dunwich, only a couple miles from withered heart of the city as the last of the sun's light faded from the sky. The way the stars twinkled like shards of glass over the black water made Michael nostalgic for home. He played the past two days in his mind, but it always came back to what Kasper had told him.

If she's one of them, she's as good as dead.

There was no way he could allow himself to believe that. Since Susan vanished, time had taken the dull slowness of a nightmare where nothing went as it should and there remained the nagging feeling that things would ultimately end in disappointment.

The wife of a one of his patients who had died of cancer once told Michael that when someone you love died, you felt the pain of their passing in your heart. You knew it even over the miles. She insisted she had felt it when her husband passed. Michael had not felt anything like that yet, only damned scared and plenty pissed.

Kasper turned off the main highway and onto the northern end of Atlantic Avenue. On the surface, this part of town was nothing more than the dead remains of a tacky but once booming resort. The pickup's headlights carved the thickening darkness. Hotels and empty, broken buildings lined the pitted and potholed road.

Kasper had the windows open a little because the windshield fogged up quickly and the defroster did not work. The salty scent of the ocean and a cloying stench of garbage was a bad combination and Michael's stomach clenched uncomfortably. It was either the beginnings of an ulcer or the fact he had not eaten all day. Whichever, he rolled the window closed to be rid of the stink.

"Sorry. The smell—" he began.

"Yeah, the stink of death," Kasper answered. "As a doctor, you're not used to it?"

Michael shrugged. "It's not something I want to be used to."

Kasper did not reply. There were a surprising number of people on the sidewalks. All kinds of people, dressed in all kinds of ways, huddled and slumping beneath flickering streetlamps.

It would not be difficult to locate Susan if she was with McCree. With his golden blond hair and his towering height, Devin McCree would be easy to spot.

Kasper parked in a deserted hotel lot near the center of the boulevard.

"We'll separate for now," he said.

When he climbed from the truck, Michael felt dreadfully awkward with the sawed-off shotgun in his hand. He would rather have left it behind but remembered the insane creatures that had welcomed him to town two nights ago.

In his stolen black coat, he probably looked like a poor imitation of Neo, but hid the gun away beneath it, secured over his shoulder by a leather strap. He was ready now—as ready as he would ever be, anyway.

Would he see Kasper again, or would he have any luck finding Susan? Maybe it was all just a wild goose chase, but Kasper insisted their kind liked to hang around the beaches. Michael took another deep breath, his heart pounding in his chest. He was going to hyperventilate if he did not calm down. He glanced at Kasper.

Kasper did not bother concealing his weapon. Still he was not brazen enough to walk the streets out of the cover of the shadows. The Deathwalkers knew him by now, he said. Apparently, there was a price on Kasper Jacobsen's head, so maybe being with him was a poorer option than prowling the boulevard alone.

"Meet me back here just before sunup. If you're not here, I'll assume . . .well . . ."

"You're extremely reassuring," Michael said, laughing nervously.

"I'm extremely realistic." Kasper threw him a small salute and disappeared into the shadows of an alleyway, leaving Michael alone and unsure of where to head next.

Michael showed Susan's photo in the few taverns and food markets that were open, but nothing came of it. Some people laughed softly when he mentioned the name McCree. Devin was certainly known around here, but most were either unwilling to give up his location of else really did not know.

The streets were much worse than Michael expected. Some grids still had electricity while other blocks were as dark as caves. Scraggly pedestrians wandered here and there, sticking to the light whenever they could. Dirty faces without hope, looking for something Michael certainly could not place. Eyes as vacant as a doll's. Drug use was rampant and nobody bothered with discretion. A frail and feminine boy pushed a needle into the blue rope of vein along his bonethin arm under the darkened Ferris wheel. When Gerald told him Dunwich had become a ghost town, he was not exaggerating.

As a physician, Michael was all about order. His life was

schedules, lists, and structure, but of that had been tossed aside now. There were no sirens, no lights, no restrictions. Freedom could be a frightening thing. Even after what Kasper had told him, it was still difficult to imagine such a lawless state. What if this kind of virus spread beyond the invisible boundaries of this broken town? And perhaps it already had. If he ever saw Kasper again, he would ask him what he had seen in other cities.

Was Susan worth this? What he had seen the past two days had left a stain on his memory he would never erase. But he had already come this far. He was in this now, for better or worse. He just hoped he found her before it was too late. Suddenly he felt he was no longer racing to save her from Devin and the darkness, but Kasper, as well.

chapter twenty-eight

"Stay close to me."

Devin took Susan's hand and led her through the empty amusement park.

"For my protection or yours?" she asked

"What do you think?"

He squeezed her fingers gently and looked around. Always on guard. She wondered who would want to mess with him in the first place. Michael popped into her head. Kind and gentle as a boy, and that was what had attracted her to him at first. And then there was Devin. Beautiful, dangerous Devin. He was a wild thing and now so was she. She welcomed it--the freedom, she could not have imagined that two weeks ago.

Disheveled, discarded figures stood in the streams of pissy light of the streets. Always in the light. Those who still had a trace of humanity in them were drawn to the light like moths. Fear touched their eyes; they had taken a path that they no longer wanted, but were unable to steer clear of. Some appeared crazed. All appeared empty.

Eyes crawled over her, both men and women, and it was not unpleasant. How did she look to them, dressed all in black, her hair clean, her body strong, her expression unafraid? Devin pulled her closer, as if someone might try to steal her away from him.

"Look at these people. Pathetic things. They come here to vanish. Maybe they're sick of their jobs, their families. Looking for something better. They have no idea," he said. Then he nodded toward a group of children. "Check them out."

They were obviously Deathwalkers. There was something in their beauty that separated them from the mortals. Was that how she looked, too?

The ragtag gang sprinted past them, then up a ramp and into the pitch dark House of Horrors where a wicked clown grinned down at them with a blood red mouth and coal black eyes.

"Don't worry about them, Susan. The kids, they have no trouble adjusting to this life."

"But won't they be children forever?" she asked.

"Is that so terrible?"

In a pool of tepid light in front of a crumbling brick city building with wide, mold-stained columns sat a dull-faced girl on a bench that was missing most of the slats on the seat.

"She's here every night," Devin said. "Too wretched to bother with."

Quite. Bent over and weeping softly into the cup of her hands, the girl was a sorrowful thing. Dirty, tangled no-color hair fell in clumps across her round shoulders and when she raised her face to the air, her mascara ran like paint on her pale cheeks. She was heavy and the seams of her thin jacket screamed. At her feet sat a blue laundry basket, the grid of plastic broken and busted on one side. What appeared to be dingy receiving blankets and towels were piled inside, but after a second, Susan noticed that the heap of fabric moved. A muffled whimper and a tiny pink starfish hand slipped from beneath the faded pink and blue blankets, then vanished again.

Susan's stomach thrummed with hunger and she pressed her hand to her belly as if that would quiet it. She tasted the salty thickness on the back of her tongue, coating the inside of her mouth and throat like warm silk and tries to ignore it, but her stomach refused to obey.

Devin placed a feathery kiss on her ear. "Only a moment longer," he whispered.

He knelt beside the crying wretch. "What's wrong?" he asked, his voice gentle. He pushed the girl's stiff hair from her face. "There. Don't cry."

The girl was indeed as worthless as Devin said. She stunk of sweat—it was evident she had not bathed in at least a week. Her runny eyeliner was old and stained into the tiny lines around her eyes.

"Are you them?" Cigarettes and liquor on her breath whiffed up and Susan breathed through her mouth to avoid the odor. Devin pulled a discrete, disgusted face and Susan almost burst out laughing.

Instead she bit it back and watched quietly, until he glanced up at her and nodded. This was her kill.

Susan reached out and took the girl's bloated hand. "Them who?"

"The ones who live forever."

"Maybe," Susan answered.

"Look at me," the girl said. "Just look at me!" She pawed at her running nose with the back of her hand and wiped it on the leg of her ratty jeans, then shoved the basket with the toe of her torn sneaker, nearly flipping it over. "And look at him!"

Susan put her arm around the girl's slumping shoulders. "I *am* looking at you. But you look at *me.*" Susan smiled just enough to flash her neat, perfect little fangs.

The girl turned and gazed longingly at Susan. "Make me

like you. Make me beautiful like you." Then she shot a pleading glance to Devin. "Both of you. So perfect."

The twinge in Susan's gut had grown into a nagging little pain, but calm washed over her. This would be easy, just as it had been that morning outside the church. This was a task, a job and it had to be done efficiently and quickly. Just as Devin said--this was survival.

"I sit out here night after night, dragging this little burden with me," she whispered. "Waiting."

Devin sat down on the bench beside her and the old wood groaned with his weight. "Why would you want to live forever, anyway?" he asked. "Someone like you, would you not prefer to just die and be done with it?"

He touched her brittle bottle-blonde hair again and then looked at his fingers before wiping them on his leg.

"Maybe things could be better. If I could stay here. In the darkness."

Susan straightened up and looked passed the girl to Devin. Devin smiled and shook his head slowly.

"You want the baby? Have him; I don't care anyway."

"And in return you want us to do what?" Susan asked. She played the game now and it was fun seeing the frustration, the desperation cross the girl's piggy face.

"Change me. Change me into something . . . better."

Devin leaned down and removed the blanket from the baby. Pretty boy baby, skin darker than mother's, eyes bright despite the look of hunger on his face. His cheeks were not as round as they should have been. His little hands were bluish with cold.

"Aren't you feeding him?" Devin asked, frowning.

"When I can. I can't breastfeed, not when I'm using."

Devin plucked the child from the basket, rearranged the blankets around him and cradled him gently. "How noble of you," he muttered.

The pig-faced girl ignored him and went on, "I thought I would be something more than this. . ."

"We all carve our own path," Devin answered.

"Do we, Devin?" Susan whispered. She glanced at him a moment, suddenly agitated, thinking of how Devin made her into what she now was. How she had little say in the matter, just as she had so little say in the matter of Peter's death.

Quickly, she dismissed the thought. She was beginning to tremble. Jesus, how much longer? She was addicted, just like a druggie hooked on heroin. This like this girl they looked at with such distain.

Devin stood up, still cradling the baby against his chest. He looked at Susan. "Now, do what she wants you to do."

Susan hesitated.

Can I do this? Can I actually do this thing alone?

Her stomach muscles seized again, almost doubling her over and she had her answer. She put out her hand to the miserable girl. "Come. Let's go into the shadows."

The girl's hand was icy cold, but clammy. Fat and as soft as a baby's tummy. Disgusting, distasteful and for a moment Susan wanted to squeeze the pudgy fingers together until they snapped. In the shadows of the old hotel, they stopped.

"Come here," Susan said, taking the girl's rounded chin in her fingers. She tilted her head back. "What's your name?"

"Cindy. My mom named me after the girl from the Brady Bunch."

Susan laughed. "Well, my mom named my for a character in a children's book."

Cindy's thick lips drew into a frown. "Is this gonna hurt?" Before Susan answered, she added, "It is, isn't it."

Susan flicked her tongue across her lips. "Only for a moment."

She pushed Cindy's straw-hair back to expose her sweat-stinking neck. "Still, now." Her nerves are vibrated beneath her skin, her heart drummed painfully inside her chest. She took the girl's blubbering face in her hands, her fingers denting the supple flesh.

"Wait," the girl said, her words muffled and slurred. But Susan did not wait. It was too late for that now. Her fingers dug into Cindy's fat cheeks.

"Wait," the girl whined again. She tried to shake her head out of Susan's grasp, but Susan yanked the heavy, clumsy body against herself and with a deep, trembling breath she sank her teeth into the sticky flesh of the girl's throat. This time it was easy and the blood started like turn on a faucet.

It fountained warm and sticky into Susan's waiting mouth. Susan closed her eyes, savoring the taste, the silken caress, not unlike a lover's wanton kiss.

The girl struggled again, her hands shoving against Susan's chest. Her fingers snatched wildly, for a moment grazing the wound the Rasta Man had left there. Susan gasped but did not pull away. Instead, her death grip tightened and grew more determined, her fingers carving holes into Cindy's fat face until she felt the girl's wet, uneven teeth against her fingertips and blood ran like ribbons of paint across her palms and down her arms.

Susan fed, vaguely aware of the sound--wet, sucking, greedy.

"Oh, God, help me," Cindy wept, her words garbled through Susan's vice grip.

Susan stopped for a moment and pressed her lips to the girl's grungy ear. "Help you? Isn't that what I'm doing?"

Cindy shrieked.

Giggling, Susan relinquished her hold and stepped back. "Now what? Do you think I'll just let you go?"

"Y-yes." Cindy whimpered. She looked down at herself, at the dark stain spreading over the breast of her grey sweatshirt. "Oh, shit. Look at me."

"Run," Susan screamed at the girl. "Run for your life."

The girl sprinted away into the shadows, but her size made her lumbering. She stumbled and started away again. Her breaths were heavy; her steps were leaden. Susan waited, knowing she would not lose the fat girl. She followed her sound easily. The blood that flowed from her gashed throat created a path of scent.

Susan glanced back at Devin, who had sat back down on the broken bench, still cradling the babe in the tattered blankets. She then scanned the canyon of shadow between the old hotels for Cindy. In the thick, oily darkness, she quickly picked out the girl's herky-jerky movements. She was perhaps two hundred yards away, weeping and panting along, her breaths pluming out like white balloons, already too exhausted to run anymore.

"Run," Susan called. She giggled again, but staggered sideways, her head saddening spinning. Something tainted the bitch's blood, but the effects were not altogether disagreeable. Besides, the brief taste of blood only intensified Susan's hunger and she as now ready for more. "Run, because I'm coming!"

Susan took off, her legs pumping effortlessly, so fast she felt as though she was flying. And maybe she was. Her coat trailed out behind her like wings or maybe Dracula's cape, she imagined. She sprinted and bounded more than a dozen feet up the rough and weathered bricks of the Marksman Hotel then came down like a cat ten yards ahead of the terrified girl.

In the back of her mind lay the needling thought. *What have I become? Do I need to be so cruel?* Silent now, she waited and watched, her vampire eyes seeing what Cindy's eyes could not. The girl plodded on, groping the bricks to find her way. Susan walked along her side, as quiet as a ghost.

Finally, "I'm here."

Cindy froze and through the darkness, Susan watched her throat work nervously. Each swallow brought a new surge of warm, stick blood to the surface of the wound at her neck.

"You promised it wouldn't hurt."

Susan threaded her fingers into the girl's dry, broken hair, entangled them. "It gets worse before it gets better."

Susan pulled Cindy's head back again, and pressed her lips to the sticky wet opening at the girl's throat. She fed, savoring the drugs in the girl's system. As a police officer, Susan never touched the stuff, but that was the old Susan. And how horrible was she now, anyway? She was still cleaning up the streets.

After a few moments, she shoved the girl away, disgusted. Surely there was more inside her than mere survival instinct. The girl fell hard onto her ample backside, confused, horrified.

"Get the hell out of here! Now, before it's too late for you!" Susan said. She wiped her mouth clean and slid down the brick wall, laughing softly. She lay down on her back, stared up at the starless sky between the buildings, and drifted into a light doze as she waited for Devin to come and find her.

There was no way to know how much time passed before he appeared. It felt like hours, but it could not have been more than a few brief moments.

"You awake?" he asked.

Devin still cradled the baby in his arms, but he had tucked him into the warmth of his coat, against him.

"Yeah, I'm awake." Susan answered. Her throat felt like gravel.

"So? What's wrong?"

Susan slowly sat up. "I'm not supposed to be way, Devin. I'm suppose to feel *something*. Right?" She pinched the bridge of her nose, between her eyes. A headache was coming on. Soon it would be a roaring bastard. She took a deep breath.

Devin put out his hand to her and pulled her to her feet. "It's not as if she was a bloody girl scout, you realize."

Susan drew her coat tighter around herself. They walked in the cold away from the hotel district and toward the old residential section, without another word. Her brain felt like it had swollen to a size to large for her skull. What had that girl ingested? And if it made her feel this shitty, why on earth would she do it?

The scent of rain made the air smell clean for a change as they climbed the stairs of the weather-beaten beach house. The impression of life was unmistakable there. Someone had carefully arranged a collection of seashells along the paint-peeled porch railings and the pale glow of a reading lamp filtered through a sheer curtain to the left of the front entrance. It was a warm light and Susan wished they were back in Devin's bed, his long limbs tangled heavily around her, instead of out in the cold, salt-kissed night. A harsh breeze lifted from the Atlantic yards away. Half-dozen wind chimes of varying materials and sizes dangled along the front edge of the porch and they clinked, chimed, and jingled as the wind tickled them.

Devin had returned the baby to the laundry basket his mother left with them. The child slept soundless and snug, one tiny fist balled tightly and pressed against his rosy mouth. Every now and again, he sucked at his knuckles, the sound like a damp kiss.

"Are you sure this is wise?" Susan asked. Her eyes wanted to drift closed and she willed herself to remain awake.

"She'll do what's right. That's why she remains out here, untouched."

He placed the basket in front of the door and pressed the bell. The buzz sounded tired; the bell was broken. Bending down, he placed a small kiss on his first two fingers and then onto the sleeping babe's forehead. Quickly he and Susan moved off the porch and into the shadow, waiting and watching. After a breath, the door squeaked open a sliver. Realizing the package, the door opened wider and a river of whitish-yellow light bled out onto the baby and basket.

A round elfin-faced woman of indeterminate age knelt, grimacing as her knees creaked loudly. Cautiously she pulled the blankets back a bit, then breathed the smallest gasp of surprise. She then took up the basket and vanished back into the warm confines of the house. The rusty tumble of old locks turning followed.

As they started away from the house, Devin slipped his arm around Susan and pulled her close. It began to rain.

As the first light of morning painted the sky orange, they toward the Rover. Arm-in-arm in the pale rain, just as they walked twenty years before, but this time Susan nearly dozed on her feet, she was so woozy from whatever the piggygirl decided to use to pollute her flabby body. She tried to recall what had happened earlier, but everything came in pieces and disjointed fragments. Her back ached and she wondered vaguely what she had done to hurt herself.

"What are we, Devin?" she asked, her tongue as thick as a slab of meat behind her teeth.

Devin was silent a moment, contemplating. Finally, he said, "We are stories without an end."

Susan lolled her head against his bog shoulder. "Any story worth a damn has an ending."

She stumbled and Devin braced her to keep her from falling on her face. "Hang on, now," he told her, chuckling softly. The freezing rain numbed the skin of her face and neck as they made their way inward, away from the deserted beachfront toward the lone vehicle parked among the tall weeds that pushed stubbornly through the broken and cracked pavement. Susan stumbled again, and Devin snatched her off her feet.

"You're gonna fall and smash your face." Like a prince from a fairy tale, he carried her to the truck.

Finally, he sat her back on her feet and pinned her against the passenger's side door with his warm body. Looking up at his beautiful face, she realized she has not even thought of Michael this evening. Maybe she no longer cared—Michael had been everything once, but perhaps that had been because they were alike. No longer. Inside the truck she rested her head on Devin's shoulder, stifled a yawn with her hand. Devin cranked up the heat and then they pulled away, the headlights cutting through the steely, slanting pinpricks of rain.

Susan eased into a light sleep as they crossed the bridge over the saltriver and back into the main part of the city. Devin flipped the radio—some old jazz standard—and rested his hand on her thigh, his wicked fingers slipping between her legs.

After what seemed like only moments, the Rover pulled to a stop.

"Wake up. We're here."

He shook her shoulder lightly and kissed the tip of her nose.

She opened her eyes. "I'm up."

Devin hooked his arm around her, and led her into the warmth of the big house. His home and her home, now, also. If that was what she really wanted.

In the bedroom she sleepily undressed herself, and Devin, ever the gentleman, helped her, tossing her clothes and then his own onto the chilly wood floor. As he pushed her down onto the feather bedding, and thrust into her, she tried to imagine Michael for a moment and found she could not get a clear picture of him. An odd twinge of despair needled her brain, as if mourning the death of a lover instead of the death of a relationship.

Devin's face hung above her, brows knitted in concentration, lips parted slightly. What did those fools back in Reading think happened to her? Did they think she had died, maybe? Well, then they would be right, she supposed. Gone crazy and fled her screwed up, yet humdrum life? Well, maybe was a good assumption, as well. Perhaps they reckoned she had grown tired of Michael but did not have it in her to break it off with him.

What did Michael think? Had he just simply let her go and moved on? Had she hurt him? Did he even really care? Did anyone outside this house care anymore?

chapter twenty-nine

After years of working the E.R., Michael had little trouble altering his waking hours. But this afternoon he lay awake, the white-yellow light of day oozing between the tight opening between the wall and the plywood barriers Kasper had sloppily nailed up.

His mind refused to shut down for more than a few moments at a time. He tired to imagine who might have occupied this room before. Plain white walls, and snatches of tape here and there. Bare mattress—Kasper had given him a stolen blanket to cover up. There was a particleboard bookshelf, empty except for a broken alarm clock. It was impossible to tell how old the owner of this room had been, or the gender. A single tennis shoe lay sole-up in one corner, adult size.

Room. Tomb. Michael shivered.

Maybe the person who had slept in this bed, dreamed in this bed, was now one of those *things*. Transformed? Jesus, he was beginning to think of these things as normal occurrences. Since when was becoming a fucking vampire normal? Maybe he was losing it.

Later he would prowl the streets with a guy who was undoubtedly off his rocker, wearing a damned Matrix costume and a sawed-off shotgun strapped to his ribs. That was a good indication that he was not exactly stable these days himself.

Of course, the standards around these parts were low, judging from the things he had seen so far. Last night as he skulked the district of ratty bars, taverns and porno shops, looking for any indication that Susan and McCree might have been in the area, he saw two men converge on a boy who could have been no more than twenty and beat him down.

The two had obviously of the same species as those creatures that attacked his car coming into town. Catlike, feral, they spotted the young man as what he was—an innocent and a mortal. They pulled him inside the doorway of one of the condemned hotel entrances and proceeded to do God only knew to the kid. The boy's horror-filled screams haunted Michael when he came back and put his head on the pillow. He had done nothing to stop it. Just as Kasper had told him.

"You'll see things here that are like from a horror movie. The only way to survive is to pretend you don't see it," Kasper had said.

As Kasper had advised, Michael slinked through the shadows like some pathetic rat. Uncertainty was the name of this game and hopes of finding Susan came and went with the tide. But right now, all he could do was lie, wait for the sun to begin to grow dim and for Kasper to wake, ready for the night's hunt along the smelly congregation of taverns and headshops and topless bars along the oceanfront.

He closed his eyes and imaged he was kissing Susan's warm mouth. What would he do if he found her? He knew the one thing he would *not* do and that was alert Kasper.

Later, someone was watching him sleep, but Michael swam in the mire of dreams and thoughts that were too thick to allow him to surface. A touch, flittering at the collar of his t-shirt. Could it be a spider? Michael jerked awake, swatting at his neck.

The black twin eyes of a shortened shotgun trained on his face. Behind it, Kasper, scowling.

Michael sat up quickly, his heart pounding.

"Kasper? What are you doing?" His mouth was dry.

"She has you," Kasper snarled. He switched on the bedside lamp.

"What the hell are you talking about?"

Kasper knelt beside the bed and the sour stink of wine filled the cloying air. He reached over and tapped the roughened tip of his finger hard against Michael's temple. "Here. *I know.* I know what's inside that brain."

Michael winced and blinked against the harsh lamplight. He could not answer. There was nothing to say to deny the obvious. Instead, he countered, "Why are you in here?" He squinted to see Kasper's face, lost in the too-bright yellow cast. The man was obviously very drunk and that was never a good sign. Even the most stable person could become mad with drink and Kasper was not exactly stable.

"Maybe I should go ahead and kill you now," Kasper muttered, his words running together crazily.

"Why? What did I do?" Michael asked. His breath caught in her chest. *Shit. Don't snivel, you wimp.*

Kasper cocked the gun. "You know what you plan to do, you weak little bastard. You're gonna try an' warn her."

This was no bluff. Michael knew he needed do some fast talking if he wanted to keep his head. "I haven't changed my mind, you silly fuck!" he shouted.

"It's only a matter of time before you're just like the others," Kasper whispered.

"Listen. She doesn't want me. You hear what I'm saying. Susan doesn't want me. She wants to be with *him.*" The words spilled out and they stung as they played in his ears. "It's over. I'm going back to Reading."

Kasper lowered the gun and nodded. "It's for the best, anyway. Doc. She's as good as dead." He snorted a short, bitter laugh. "You don't want to be here for what she's gonna get."

He left the room then and Michael sucked in a long, deep breath and hoped his heart would not pound through the cage of his ribs.

When he was sure Kasper had fallen back asleep, he grabbed the gun Kasper had given him, the few other things he had, and slipped out into the safety of the blossoming daylight.

chapter thirty

It had been a week since escaping Kasper's drunken accusations and still there had been no sign of neither Susan nor McCree. Michael made his way back down toward the extreme south end of Dunwich Beach, away from the crowds and the dilapidated commercial buildings. He stuck to the shadows, but it had become evident that the Deathwalkers had extremely acute senses of both hearing and smell. They would find him and pounce easily enough, if given the opportunity.

The homeless slept in the caverns of the alleys and unused building entrances, but other than those few transients, the city was deserted out this far. Rows of ramshackle beach houses stood pitch dark and silent in the cutting Atlantic wind. Hotels loomed like bent old men.

Michael was nearly asleep on his feet, having spent the last seven nights in the over-populated area of the shoreline only a few miles back. He had rented a room, stinking, filthy and roach-infested, on the second floor over a porn shop on the boulevard, hardly sleeping for fear of who or what might pay him a visit. He had dozed sitting in a lumpy chair against the corner of the room, drapes drawn tight across the windows to block out the sun and hide him, his gun gripped in his fist. He jumped awake at every little sound. At night, he searched, but no luck. Dread gnawed at him; had Kasper gotten to her? He would not leave Dunwich until he knew for sure.

He could not remember when he had last eaten anything substantial. His limbs were heavy with fatigue. As a physician, he knew better. He had allowed his body to become depleted of nutrients, and somewhat dehydrated.

Earlier that evening, he liberated a knapsack from an abandoned beach store and packed it with granola bars, bottles of water, candy bars and power drinks that he had also stolen when the cashier had turned his back to fetch a pack of cigarette for a customer. He hated that—stealing. But he had nothing now. His wallet was gone with his car and his identification. If he died, nobody would ever know what happened to him.

Out here, the small houses had become shabby long before the fall of the area. The lawns were scrubby, sandy, weed-infested. Weeds popped up through splits in the sidewalks, driveways and the broken pavement of the road. The streetlamps had been broken and on the walks below, the glass caught and reflected the fat, white moon like diamonds. Many were boarded up like a hurricane was swirling just off the coast, and the boards had gone black with rot. Graffiti decorated some of the boards—others were left untouched. Boards, just like Kasper's little beach shack—to keep out intruders or sunlight?

The first house Michael chose had been flooded by a storm at some point. Toxic black mold climbed the walls like an entity from a Japanese horror flick. The odor was overwhelming and he scarcely stepped through the door before backtracking.

The next house had obviously been spared the wrath of the storms, likely because of its proximity to the dunes. Tucked behind a sweeping mound of sand and reeds, it was nearly impossible to even see the ocean from the back deck. Hell of a view, Michael thought grimly.

Entering these houses was a gamble he would have never

entertained under normal circumstances. A few weeks ago, intruding on a bum or a runaway druggie with a gun would have been a great concern, but that was now small potatoes when a stray Deathwalker might be sleeping out the daylight in the cover of shadow.

Stringy, leaning dune grass and weeds laid claim to the front yard. Two of the front windows were broken out, smiling jaggedly at him. White paint had peeled away in sheets in some places. Shingles had blown from the roof and were now laying scattered over the yard. A short length of yellow plastic tape wavered in the breeze—was it crime tape or perhaps the remains of a party streamer? It was too worn and tattered to tell.

Creeping across the lawn, Michael removed his pack from his back. He stopped in the shadows of the overgrown crepe myrtles and knelt, rummaging through his things until he found a flashlight. He straightened up, replaced the pack across his shoulders and headed up the winding stairs of the deck to the side door. The boards groaned under his steps. Judging from the splintered frame, someone had jimmied the door open, but the moisture had swelled it. It was jammed. Michael shouldered it hard to nudge it open enough to enter.

Just as he stepped inside, the sky opened and an angry rain plummeted down. No matter what already resided inside the decrepit place, Michael resigned himself to take care of him, her, or it. Anything was better than wandering around in the dark and the freezing rain.

Inside a smallish kitchen, Michael again unshouldered his pack, sat his flashlight on the counter and checked his gun, although he knew the safety was off and it was loaded and ready. He then picked up the gun in one fist, his light in the other and stood quietly, listening for anything that might indicate he was not alone, and scanned the place.

The house smelled awful, but it was not an odor he was accustomed to—he was a doctor, after all, not a coroner. Rot. Animal droppings. Mold. Death. Second thoughts about staying in the house crept into his head, but the next one might be just as bad, if not worse.

Lightening illuminated the windows for a breath, just enough to see a fat and sassy rat scurry across his boot. He stepped back with a gasp.

He trained the light around the kitchen. The décor was mid-seventies suburban—an avocado refrigerator and range and gold, orange and green wallpaper with a funky pattern straight from the "Bob Newhart Show." The place must have been vacant since Michael was a kid or else a rental owned by extremely cheap property owners. On the refrigerator door, tacked up with magnets shaped like apples, oranges and bunches of grapes were snapshots of a couple of kids—a boy and a girl, about eight or nine. From the little girl's Dorothy Hamill hairstyle and Brady Bunch clothes, he placed them somewhere in mid-decade. Underneath the photo were the names "Joey" and "Jeana" in bold blue and pink lettering.

He moved into the sunken living room and nearly broke his neck, as he overlooked the stepdown. He stumbled, dropped the flashlight and frightened away another hefty rat.

"Shit!" His voice echoed dully. The startled rat squeaked a reply from the deep shadows.

The found the flashlight and spotlighted the furniture which was also green and yellow and then a large stone fireplace and high hearth. Throw pillows were scattered along the rim of the stepdown, creating Japanese-styled seating. At one long wall sat big console television just like the one Michael remembered watching growing up. If the electricity was working, he could almost imagine switching it on and finding an episode of "Six Million Dollar Man" in all his leisure-suited glory. Thick shag carpeting cushioned his steps.

Moving cautiously, he stepped into the narrow hallway. More scurrying and squeaking of rodents followed by something heavier. Heart pounding, Michael raised the nose of his gun slightly and trained the lighted ahead. *Wouldn't I just shit, if I found somebody here?* The smell of decay lay heavier there, but time had erased its potency. Graffiti decorated the door at the far end, and there was another barrier of yellow tape. Crime scene tape, he saw clearly now. Inwardly questioning why, he moved ahead. It was almost like a train wreck—he did not want to look, but something inside drove him onward.

On the door, someone written the legend, "Because I could not stop for Death, He kindly stopped for me." He recognized the quote immediately from college lit, remembering how he had waded through the poems of Emily Dickenson for a semester, unable to make heads nor tails of most of it. It had been the only course he scored less than a "B."

He passed three other doors, all opened on a fraction. After a quick inspection with the swipe of the flashlight, he discovered none was as interesting as the room with the crime tape.

Michael used the end of his riotgun to catch the police tape and tore it down. He twisted the knob. Locked. Stepping back, he kicked in the door sending it crashing back against the wall.

It was the kids' room. Two beds and the room divided into halves for a boy and a girl, one side all stuffed bears and Barbie and Ken and a bed with covers of bold flowers. The other, footballs and baseballs and G.I. Joes, the bed and drapes on that side of NFL, dark green and bright red.

But something was wrong. Although the odor of death had dissipated over the decades, it was there, concentrated in this room. Something awful had happened here. Shining the light around, Michael saw the splatters on the wall, arching upward like a rainbow, gone dark brown against the faded sunshine yellow. At the top of each bed, where small sleeping heads had lain. Horror uncoiled in his stomach— the years did nothing to lessen the impact of knowing that children had obviously died here. Bullets had splintered the girl's cream-colored headboard. Deeply embedded in the old wood was a tooth, milky white against the dark splatters of dried gore.

Shuddering, Michael backed out of the room and pulled the door closed. He leaned back against the hallway wall for a moment and took a deep breath. The trauma physician in him created the scenario in his mind, in all its vivid Technicolor glory. He squeezed his eyes shut tightly as if that would help clear the image from his head. No success.

Not much of a choice, staying in this house of ghosts or going back out into the freezing rain with the crazed Deathwalkers and an even crazier vampire hunter.

Sighing, he moved back to the kitchen and retrieved his pack, then went to the livingroom.

He found a wooden stool that was nearly crumbling sawdust with age. He smashed it with his boot, then stacked the pieces into the hearth. He struck a match and the fire easily stoked to life against the old wood.

Michael shrugged out of his coat and sat down as close as he could stand to the fire. Still, his breath hung at his mouth like vapor coming from ice. His gun across his lap, he rummaged through his pack for a yellow Gatorade—he was old school with the Gatorade—and a pair of granola bars.

Finally growing warm and his hunger somewhat abated, he laid down on the carpet and covered himself with his coat, his gun in his hand. He fell immediately into an exhausted sleep as the world continued to storm outside.

Sometime before sunup, a female Deathwalker entered the house. As quiet as a ghost, she sat and watched the man sleep. She did not move to wake him and had no interest in harming him. The man slept on, blissfully unaware.

As morning touched the grungy glass slider that faced the backs of the dunes that served as a barrier between the row of houses and the Atlantic Ocean, she slipped away, vanishing before the rays of the sun could scorch her skin.

Michael woke sometime after noon, better rested than he had been in days. He sat up slowly, his muscles stiff and achy from sleeping on the floor. Sleep was slow to relinquish its grip. Shivering, he sat rubbing his eyes a moment, disoriented. The fire he had created from a broken rocking chair had died during the night—he would need to find more wood to burn and quickly. He hated the cold. At least it was daylight, and quite sunny, judging how gloriously the light poured through the windows.

He reached into his pack found a can of diet soda and a package of cheese crackers and grimaced as he ate them. He would go out and find some decent food soon—even Kasper's overcooked microwaved pasta was beginning to seem appealing.

He chewed the crackers slowly, little flavorless orange squares of cardboard in his mouth and washed it all down with a big gulp of the soda and belched heartily. Where the hell was Susan? Could he just leave her here to die an ugly, gruesome death at the hands of a maniac? Hell, no. Susan was all he had. He had no family to speak of, only the patients and friends back in Reading. He felt bad about leaving his patients—any decent doctor would—but he was not the only physician in town. As for the friends, what did it really matter? A bunch of talking heads to drink with on Friday evening. He doubted anyone cared he was gone.

Cynical much? He had asked Susan that once, lying in bed together one night and reading the Yahoo headlines on his laptop. A story about the abuse of a puppy somewhere in Florida set her on a tirade over the decline of humanity.

Why did she matter so much, anyway? Was it the companionship? The sex? Having her on his arm, in his bed, in his house? Did it make him appear more a man? They would have been married. She would have been his forever. But the past came back and snatched her away from him. He wanted to see Devin McCree dead nearly as much as he wanted to get Susan back.

Tonight he would move inside the shadows, watching for her just as he had done for the past fifteen nights straight. He would carry his gun and it would be loaded and ready to take anyone's head off that stood in his way.

Susan had changed, but he had changed, also. Incredible circumstances called for incredible measures, as they said. A cliché, but it was very true.

He had nearly six hours until dark. First a look around—this place could become his home for the foreseeable future.

With the light falling through the windows, Michael was able to see the old house better. It was still pretty much the way he had assumed it was when he viewed it through the small, yellow circle of light last night. Seventies suburban. God, would it have killed them to have a wind chime or maybe a few seashells thrown in with the décor? The house did overlook a gorgeous slice of Atlantic coastline, after all.

Killed was probably an unfortunate choice of words.

He still expected Carol Brady to appear next to him any moment.

The place was amazingly clean considering it had been abandoned for perhaps thirty years. Not much dust or cobwebs. Of course, there was the occasional spider or stray rat turd in the corner of a room or along the runner in the hall.

Michael did not go back to the children's room. The feeling of death in there was just too overwhelming. The master bedroom was spotless, the bed made, novels of Harold Robbins and Joseph Wambaugh on the bedstand, beneath the reading lamp, bookmarked and neatly stacked. Inside the closet were men's and women's clothing. Hardly top of the line, but the woman's side appeared to have been rummaged through fairly recently. The man's clothes were for a hefty fellow—forty-two waist, long inseem. Much too large, but Michael would not be caught dead in a Banlon shirt and a pair of green Gabardine golf slacks, anyway.

The master bath was clean enough and Michael managed to get some icy water to run through the faucet at the vanity. It flowed rust brown for nearly five minutes before finally running clear. He found a towel, dusty, but clean in the linen closet, removed his shirt and washed up. He pulled a toothbrush (stolen new) from his bag and brushed using the travel-sized tube of Colgate. Then he stood there, toweling himself dry. Shivering again, he stared into the mirror. He needed a shave and a haircut. There were bruised half-moons underneath his eyes and he had visibly lost weight. The plains of his cheekbones and jawline stood out sharp. His ribs appeared like the bars of a cage.

He tugged his shirt back over his head and went back to the bedroom, rubbing warmth back into this arms. Now that the sun was hitting the big double windows opposite the king-sized bed, he realized that there seemed to be an indention on the comforter and pillow. As if someone had recently lain there. Had he intruded on someone, *something*. There certainly seemed to be some sort of stigma attached to the house—the death that had touch the place. Perhaps it was the circumstances involved. For a moment, he considered sleeping there tonight, under the covers on the big, reasonably comfortable bed. No neck aches or stiffness.

No. He could not bring himself to do it. He was pushing it enough to be under this roof.

He rummaged through the drawer of the bedside table. This made him feel truly like an intruder, spying on the personal, secret items of these long-gone people. He had to assume the police had rifled through everything here, three decades earlier. Anything of value had likely been taken years ago.

A jar of nightcream. A small photo album, with more pictures of little Joey and Jeana, a various stages of their short lives. A shopping list in looping, elegant handwriting—*1 doz. Eggs, Kotex, Blue Bonnet Margarine . . .* At the top of the page was the legend "Don't Forget, Dummy," in big, bold, comic-style letters.

Michael moved to the dresser, a big, heavy nine drawer affair of mahogany wood. He tugged open the stubborn drawers. Fruit of the Looms, socks of all different colors and lengths. Panties that looked to belong to a woman of at least forty-five, of motherly stature. The middle top drawer and now he finally saw the faces that belonged to the brief and panties, posing in a wholesome family portrait with the insignia "Olan Mills" stamped in flaking gold at the bottom right corner. Faded to the point that the would-be bold yellows and oranges were dull and as cloudy as seeing them through dirty water.

The man was indeed very large, unsmiling. His dark eyes serious, but not unhappy. Next to him sat a woman with short, curled auburn hair. Pretty, but indeed motherly. Pert nose, wide-set eyes. The children had their mother's features.

Moving the photo aside, Michael found a small book. He thumbed through the pages, beginning at the back. Blank until he reached about half-way. He scanned through the tight writing—the same hand as the shopping list in the bedstand drawer.

A journal.

Not really knowing why, he kept it. Perhaps he would need something to read later.

chapter thirty-one

Michael was gone, and he had taken the gun with him. Of course, it was indeed best for both of them. Kasper sympathized for him—he really did. He knew what it was to lose a woman, and did not want kill him because of it. Maybe his drunken tirade had scared the doctor enough to scurry back to whatever little piss-ant burg he had come from.

No. Not likely. The man was afraid, but he was also determined.

Things with him were not finished. Michael loved the woman and that was something easy to see, not a random notion picked up from delving into the doctor's head. He would protect the here, even if it killed him. In the process, he would likely succumb to the woman's seduction. Even if she was only using him for blood. They would meet again. And it would be ugly.

But now, Kasper's task was to remove a vermin called Alexander from the world. Kasper had heard his kind were known as rogues. It was a title he quite enjoyed and it fit him well. He fed on others of his kind, rather than humans.

This night, he feigned innocence and told Alexander he did not know how he had gotten there. He needed money. He did not know how to hunt. He had been changed and then abandoned. Just like a child, he said, to which

Alexander replied poor, poor thing and licked his lips like the big bad wolf.

Kasper removed his coat, and the gun together, careful to keep the gun concealed. He placed it on the floor, within easy reach and then sat on the ratty hotel bedspread, pretending nervousness.

Alexander opened a bottle of Amstel and passed it to him.

Drawing this vampire's interest had been easier than Kasper anticipated. Only a shy nod and within the hour they were in this dank, smelly hotel room.

Tonight, Kasper's went by the name Quincy, same as the ally of Professor Van Helsing in Bram Stoker's novel. Often, he chose the names of those characters as his alias. Jonathan, as in Harker, or Abraham as in Van Helsing, the vampire hunter himself. Nobody read anymore. Not the younger ones, anyway. They would never catch on. Perhaps, if he claimed to go by "Buffy" one of these nights, it might give at least one of these fools a sporting chance. Acting came into play quite often. Plus, Kasper could blend in with the others—none of them, aside from that bastard Devin—knew what he looked like.

This doomed Deathwalker was a tall, thin fellow. Short hair, streaked with burgundy and his face smooth, though he was not as young as Kasper originally thought earlier in the tavern. Pretty and androgynous in the same feral way that most of the younger blood drinkers seemed to be. He sat down on the bed beside Kasper.

"Poor, poor Quincy," he said again.

Kasper's skin crawled at his touch. He should have just killed him as soon as they were inside the door. But there was always the chance, no matter how small, that one of these morons might know where to find Devin.

"Who did this to you?"

Kasper took a drink of beer, working to keep from pulling away from the man's hot, foul breath. "His name was Devin. Maybe you know him?"

Alexander smiled. "Yes. I know of Devin McCree."

"Maybe you know where to find him?"

Alexander took the beer from Kasper's hand and put it aside. "I'm not telling you anything just now. A trade maybe?"

"Maybe," he whispered, the shy-act difficult to maintain. Besides, this one was insufferable. He sighed. "Then you know?"

"Relax, Quincy. We'll see." He pushed Kasper back onto the bed and moved on top of him. The repulsive sheets stunk of come and sweat and old blood. Kasper tried to hold his breath. Alexander's hands strayed over his body, slowly, greedily, and one rested lightly at Kasper's groin, stroking him through his jeans. Sweat poured down Kasper's face. His head pounded.

The Deathwalker kissed Kasper's throat, his hand ceaselessly moving, more firmly now, as though he would like to inflict pain rather than pleasure.

Then he rolled off Kasper and abruptly stood up.

"You know, Quincy, this isn't gonna be any fun of you don't fucking relax a little."

He bent forward and slipped his fingers into the waist of Kasper's jeans, pulling him to his feet. Then he dropped to his knees. "Now, maybe this will help."

Wrapping his wiry arms around Kasper's waist, he held him tightly. His fingers fluttered across Kasper's buttocks and he buried his face into Kasper's crotch.

Kasper reached down and took Alexander's face in his hands. "Come here, first," he whispered.

Alexander straightened up and their eyes met for a long moment. This time, he was the one who appeared nervous. Something flashed in his eyes, a seed of fear. Kasper had taken control of the situation. He leaned closer and ran his tongue up the side of Alexander's beard-scruffy throat. He took the man's fine hair in his fingers, yanked his head back and bit into the warm, pale flesh. Hot blood jetted into his mouth. His eyes slipped closed in ecstasy. He pushed Alexander back onto the filth-stiffened sheets.

The man groaned and cradled the back of Kasper's head. "Jesus! That's more like it."

Kasper sucked at the wound greedily, grinding himself against Alexander's sharp, thin body.

After a few moments, Alexander rasped, "Please, Quincy. Stop. I'm going to pass out."

Kasper drew back, his face a lather of crimson. He smiled a wicked gore-red smile and raised up. "Enough?"

"Enough. Now let me have you." Alexander propped up onto his elbows. Drowsy from blood loss, he watched Kasper through heavy lidded eyes.

Kasper wiped at his stained mouth and took a deep breath. As with each time he fed, nausea followed. Stomach cramping, he fought the urge to vomit and squeezed his eyes closed. He hated this. Was it in his head? Was he allergic? That would be one hell of a thing, a vampire allergic to blood.

"Not until you tell me of Devin," Kasper said, stalling until he regained his composure.

Alexander fell back onto the bed. "Devin? I know nothing of Devin. I haven't seen him in years. He might be dead, for all I know."

Rage boiled in Kasper's brain. He clenched his fist. "You said—

"I said what I said to get you here. Would you have come otherwise?"

Control, Kasper. He smiled and shrugged, the innocent boy again. "I suppose not."

"Then come here."

"All right," Kasper said. "But just a moment. I want to show you something." He knelt and reached for his coat.

He removed the shotgun and stood. "Now keep your eyes closed, my dear. I have a surprise for you."

"Should I open my jeans?"

"If you like."

Alexander smiled lazily, his eyes still closed. Slowly, he unbuttoned his jeans and then eased down the fly.

Kasper placed the shortened muzzle of the shotgun just beneath Alexander's smooth chin, but the chill of the steel alerted the vampire and his paperthin eyelids flew open.

His blue eyes met Kasper's, but only for a breath.

Kasper squeezed the trigger, as he has so many nights before, for so many years. Bodies and years—he had lost count of both. Vaguely he imaged the bodies piled into ragged stacks, limbs askew, thick blood and clots of white and gray gore littering the floor all around. The years, he saw as calendars, tattered, pages missing.

Alexander's pretty head opened in a bloody blossom of deep rose petals. Brain matter, like chunks of unsubstantial meat splattered onto the wall over the bed, giving the ugly yellow and apricot abstract a new look. Bone sprayed all over like shards and splinters of a rotted old tree branch. Teeth pierced the wallpaper and embedded the plaster. An eyeball bounced hard against the headboard of the bed like a handball against a wall, finally landing at the toe of Kasper's left boot.

But what came next was what Kasper always hated most of all. The body voided itself. Much worse than a little blood and bone and brain. Kasper placed the gun on the bed beside the motionless body. He snatched up his coat and pulled it on, grimacing at the atrocity of the odor. He flipped up the collar and pulled it across his nose and mouth, a mockery of the Count himself.

Disgusted, he kicked the Deathwalker's jean-clad leg hard. An audible snap, but whatever. He could not feel it now.

"Bloody, smelly bastard," Kasper muttered.

Then grabbed up his gun and stepped out into a spray of green and pink neon light.

chapter thirty-two

Suddenly Michael was looking into Susan's blue eyes. A pang of fear and surprise gripped him and he could not think of what to say next. The bustle of the street, people passing behind her and in front of her, between them.

He fell into her gaze and everything around her dissolved into bits of dust and fragments of memory. McCree was nowhere in sight and Michael was not sure he was glad of this or not. Part of him wished for the confrontation and for once, he was glad to have the weight of the gun at his side. Susan reached up to touch his face, but stopped and glanced back to her escort.

She diverted her eyes from Michael. Above them glowed a sign read the Pirate's Chest—ridiculous name for a titty bar—the hideous neon red painted her face and hair bloody. Tonight the streets were crowded, despite the hellishly cold weather. Behind her, his hand resting possessively against her back, was a very tall, older man who reminded Michael of a professor he had back in med school. He appeared extremely out of place in the likes of this place.

His heart pounding, Michael reached for her, but she drew back. God, he just wanted his hands on her, to have her with him. He wanted rush her back home and put this past month behind them.

The look of surprise on Susan's face transformed into one of complete blankness. Michael fingered the trigger of riotgun beneath his coat and wondered where McCree was. Anger swelled to the surface and before he could stop himself he said, "Don't act like you don't see me!"

In an instant, the tall man planted himself firmly in front of Susan.

"Do you know this gentleman?" he asked her in a proper British accent.

Susan's response was a kick to his gut. "No. I've never seen him." She did not raise her eyes to his again.

"If you value your life, step away," the old man said in a tone that he might have used to mention rain in the air or offer a slice of pie. He then took Susan's hand and led her away.

Michael watched them move on, still fingering the trigger of the gun hidden under his coat. When they were far enough away, he went after them, sticking to the doorways and the shadows of the buildings, out of sight.

After a few moments, McCree jogged by, apparently to catch up. Michael remained hidden, but the sight of McCree—the very man who saved him from a potentially gruesome death only three weeks back--sent a rush of rage through him. Michael sighed, now gratefully aware of the weight of the gun tethered to his side. If he wanted, he could have simply take the big man out in a spray of red, right on the crowded street.

But no. He needed to keep his composure. Drawing attention to himself was not the answer, as Kasper had explained. It was merely a good way to get himself killed. Kasper was batshit crazy, but some of what he had offered was turning out to be very valid.

Besides, could he really do it?

The trio stopped walking for a moment, and McCree leaned, pushed back Susan's hair and whispered something against her ear. She laughed, the sound very far off and like that of a dream of some distant memory. It made Michael's breath catch in his chest. As they began moving again, the older man relinquished his hold on her hand, seemingly reluctant to do so. McCree slipped his arm around her and pulled her closer to his side.

Susan glanced back. Was she looking for him?

They strolled on easily, the patter of conversation rising over the street sounds from time to time. Shortly, they stopped in front of a mammoth old hotel.

The moon passed through a lace of smoky clouds, darkening the streets—there were no working street lamps in front of this place. Most had been broken out with rocks, shells and fragments of glass bottles, as was the faded sign reading "New Dunwich Inn" out front. Michael faded back into the shadows, but closer to Susan and her companions now. The snippets of their exchange rose in the air and became more animated.

"I'm not going in there," the older man said.

McCree winked at Susan. "He's afraid of rats." He walked his fingers playfully up the older man's chest. "And spiders."

"So what?" the older man countered.

It sounded like three kids on a whim of double-dare.

"Well, I'm afraid of rats, too. But I'm still going in. I want to see," Susan said, laughing.

Did she just scan the shadows and sidewalks again before vanishing into the darkness of the building?

"Bloody hell," the old gentleman whispered.

"Find me, if you can," Susan called from the gloom of the building.

The two men climbed the stairs leading onto the wide front porch the New Dunwich Inn, which was about as far from "new" as anything Michael had seen since leaving Reading. The floorboards groaned like a snoring giant under their steps. Michael moved out of the shadows and stood before the hotel, considering whether he wanted to chance finding Susan alone.

Had she issued some kind of veiled invitation? Probably his imagination or else wishful thinking. She had clearly changed. Worse, she appeared happy on McCree's arm.

The white façade of the building peeled away like old skin and the windows stared down upon the street like blank eyes. The two-story inn looked more like a big country home than a beachfront hotel, except for the red and white candy-striped awning that ran the length of the porch and over each window, torn and tattered as a homeless man's coat. The green shingles of the roof had been ripped away in various hurricanes over the decades, leaving raw wood exposed, black and rotten.

After a moment, sure McCree and the old man were well inside, Michael crept onto the porch. He crouched in the thick darkness, waiting, gather his courage. His heart thundered in his chest. This was stupid, but he prepared to go inside, anyway. He pulled the gun around in position to fire, if he actually needed to. He thumbed the safety off and slipped through the front door.

The darkness was as heavy as a blanket and the stink of moldering wood and furniture was strong enough to make him sneeze. He fought the urge and breathed through his mouth instead until he became accustomed to it.

Michael could just make out the inky shape that scurried from behind the front desk before it circled behind him. Fingers wove hard through his hair and another hand clamped over his mouth. Susan. He had no trouble recognizing the touch and sweet smell of her hand, so he was not as startled as he might have been otherwise. Quickly, she guided him into the small office just past the desk area, took away her hand and pushed him back against the wall.

"Shh," and she quietly shut the door, then twisted the lock.

The moon decided to make an appearance and flooded

the small, grungy window with yellow-blue light, illuminating Susan's face. She stood before him, an angel, albeit an angry angel, with blueglow skin and shining eyes. For a moment, Michael could not move, he was so struck by her appearance. She had indeed changed, somehow, but just as the morning sitting at their kitchen table, he could not place his finger on exactly what it was.

Her movement were fluid, catlike. Her face leaner than before, her high cheekbones more pronounced. There was a deadly elegance about her and he was suddenly a little startled, after all.

Susan placed her finger to his lips and "Shh," again. The heavy clonk of one set of footfalls overhead, but McCree was wearing sneakers. Still, the creaking floorboards indicated both men were now upstairs.

"Come out, you wicked thing!" one of them called.

Susan's eyes bore into Michael's. "How did you know where to find me?" she whispered.

"You talk in your sleep."

"Well, you need to go," she said.

"Not without you, I'm not," he answered. He looked at her a long moment. "God, you are so beautiful."

He moved toward her, touched her hand, but she pulled away.

"Don't, Michael."

"Why did you do that to me on the street before?"

"I didn't want you to get hurt," Susan said.

"But you drew me here. I know you did," he countered.

"I did. To tell you that I don't want to leave here. I knew you would just keep turning up, so I wanted to end this tonight."

Michael clenched his jaw. He wanted to cry; he wanted to strike her for hurting him.

"Well, it hasn't ended. Not like this."

"I'm with Devin, now. That's how I want it," Susan whispered. "You need to go back to Reading. Alone."

This was complete nonsense. "How do you decide you no longer love me over night?" Michael snapped. Then he took a deep breath. "I'll fight for you, if that's what I have to do." The words spilled out, and he could not stop them, no matter how ridiculous he sounded.

"Then you'll die for me," Susan said.

"No." Michael held up the shotgun. "At least not alone."

This time, it was Susan who looked afraid. "No, Michael. Please. I don't want to see you get hurt, but I can't allow you to hurt Devin, either."

"So, you do love him."

She dropped her eyes. "Yes. I do."

Michael's anger faded into despair. He lowered the gun and squeezed his eyes closed. "Fuck it, then. Fuck him and fuck you." How petty he sounded, but what did it matter, now?

"Susan?" McCree called. The footfalls were still overhead, and directly above them at the moment.

"I need to go to him," Susan said.

She moved toward the door, but Michael grabbed her hand. "Wait."

He took her face in his hands and kissed her. Turning her around, he pinned her against the wall. She pushed him away, but half-heartedly. Her lips parted and she sucked his tongue inside, greedily tasting him. She moved against him and her mouth trailed down the side of his throat like hot silk. She lapped at his skin, the touch of her tongue maddening him. He pressed against her, his penis instantly like steel. He dropped his head back and closed his eyes.

"Oh, Susan." Her hand slid over his chest and stomach to his groin. Delicious. She massaged him through his pants.

Her mouth lingered against his neck and he was vaguely aware of a sharp sting there. Not that it mattered. All that mattered was her hand on his cock and her firm, feverish body against his.

"Susan? Come on, dear. Where are you?" the older

man's voice now and he sounded as though he was just outside the door.

Susan drew back and wipe her mouth with the back of her hand. "I have to go. Devin will be able to tell."

"Susan, wait." He snatched a dull pencil from the desk. On a crumbling receipt, he jotted the number and street of the house where he was sleeping. He shoved it into the front pocket of her jeans, his fingers lingering desperately.

Susan pulled away and vanished through the door, leaving him in the murk of the dusty hotel office, his heart thundering in his chest, his balls ready to explode. He touched his neck where Susan's exquisite lips had been and felt the warm stickiness there.

Black blood painted his fingers. "Damn."

chapter thirty-three

Two nights later, Susan sat shoulder to shoulder with John Moses on the concrete bench in the side garden. All around, vines of jasmine and honeysuckle, both bare for coming winter, ensnared the bench, a birdbath and a thick live oak. It was difficult to believe the ugliness of an abandoned city lay just beyond the high brick walls.

It was chilly and although the long wool coat was toasty, Susan pulled closer to John to absorb his warmth. Above them, the moon slipped in and out of a lace of wispy cloud. The breeze carried the briny scent from the Atlantic a mile away.

"It's freezing," Susan commented.

"This will keep us warm," John told her, slipping a hand inside his own heavy coat. He brought out a silver flask, unscrewed the top and passed it to her. The flat side of the container caught glints of the moon and then the few remaining streetlamps that rained down sickly snot-colored light on the street just beyond the brick barrier.

Susan took a drink and the cognac burned like gasoline in her throat. "Jesus," she rasped as she quickly passed it back to John.

"But you're warm now," John said, smiling.

"Yes," she agreed.

"*Courvoisier Erte No. 2,*" *he went* on. "It goes for over

three thousand dollars a bottle. Devin found thirteen bottles in the cellar of a mansion over near the salt marshes. Evidentially, the owner had decided to leave and never return." He winked. "We thought of moving over there, but instead brought most of the valuables over here."

"You didn't feel that was wrong?"

"Your police officer is showing, my dear." He passed the flask back to her. "Right and wrong become grayer as the years press on. Besides, it belonged to a politician. A corrupt one at that," he added, dismissing it.

A pair of stern-looking men entered the gate and headed up to house. They nodded to acknowledge John, who offered a hearty toast with his flask. Devin greeted them at the door and they all vanished inside the warmth of the house. Susan did not know exactly why these, or the four or five other Deathers who arrived moments before, were there. John briefly mentioned earlier that other Deathwalkers were seeking Devin's advice regarding the numerous killings of late. She had heard the name Jacobsen mentioned, which was odd—that was also the name she snatched from Michael's thoughts the other night. Apparently, this Jacobsen had been hunting them down and now she, Devin and all like them were in danger.

Frankly, she felt no fear of this so-called vampire hunter. Devin would protect her. If she needed it. Still, it was interesting that one man was creating such a stir.

"So this guy, Jacobsen, you know him?" she asked.

"I know of him. His handiwork was what brought Devin to us."

Susan took a longer, bolder drink of the cognac. She was beginning to feel quite warm indeed, now. Her limbs loosened, her shoulders relaxed slightly. She could not recall being this relaxed since coming to Dunwich, despite the looming threat of someone named Jacobsen.

"When was this?"

"1942. In the midst of the Great War."

She laughed. "'42? How old are you, John?"

"I have no idea, really. Do you? I was fifty-one when I was bitten near the end of that same year. But how do you determine age for someone like me? Or like you were, before? Halfings," he chuckled softly. "Half-way to immortality."

He appeared to have only aged ten or fifteen years since.

"I didn't know I wasn't aging," she said. "I thought I was just lucky. Good skin, you know." She shrugged.

"It was my beloved Lillian who discovered Devin cowering in our barn. He later told her that he had been held and tortured for twenty-eight days. He knew the passing days by the way the sun filtered through the cracks at the doorway of his torture chamber.

"Pitiful thing, he was. A beaten puppy. No human could have endured what he endured and live. His feet had been fractured, pounded with a hammer and worse, the Achilles tendons had been severed almost clean through. I can only imagine how he managed to get away, crawling like a child through the sticky, muddy fields and woods. His body was a rainbow of bruises. He was cut. He had been burned in places. But Lillian loved him from the time she set her eyes on him. She assumed he was an injured soldier and our own son had been killed somewhere in Italy only a year before."

"Didn't that hurt you, your wife being so taken with another man?"

John sighed, pondering this a moment. "I don't know, really. Looking back, I suppose not. He was helpless and he was beautiful. Besides, Lillian had a tender heart. It was not a sexual attraction. At least, not at first. I don't care to dwell on how things progressed.

"Neither of us had any understanding of what exactly Devin was at the time."

John looked at Susan a moment. She picked up a deep pain inside his thoughts. She had determined that slipping into John's thoughts was off-limits, but sometimes the mind reading was an accidental thing.

"You regret it," she whispered.

"Sometimes. But you must understand, Jacobsen then involved with the S.S., so there was no other choice but to fight and protect Devin. The Nazi thinking, strange as it might have been, was to create a squadron of super-human soldiers, thus creating the new ideology of a master race. Deathwalkers, as you realize by now, are close to indestructible and Jacobsen used his vast knowledge as a bargaining tool. He apparently rose quickly in the ranks to become Himmler's right hand man.

"Devin escaped—something Jacobsen could not deal with. He abandoned the Third Reich and finding and killing Devin, and all like him including my dear Lillian, became his purpose for living.

"We came here because we were confident Kasper would not find us. Years, even decades passed and suddenly, a couple of months ago, he showed up. Devin would hear nothing of leaving here until he had you."

Susan glanced at him. "What about now?"

John took a drink. "Now? Who knows?"

chapter thirty-four

1942. The door swung open and poison sunshine spilled in like a tainted river. Devin scrambled deeper into the shadow and plunged his face into the sweet hay. Dear God, he felt so very bad. So sick. He groaned softly and folded his arms across the back of his head.

"Kitty? Come out, Kitty, Kitty." A woman.

Soft padding of footsteps, drawing closer and Devin no longer cared if anyone found him or not. He could not run, so escape was out of the question. He would be better off if someone just killed him. But quickly. Not the torture that Kasper inflicted all in the name of the Fheur.

He groaned and went into a coughing fit that sent spasms of agony through his entire body. He drew his legs up tight and curled into a foetal position.

"Who's in here?" The woman moved closer and seeing him expelled an audible gasp. "Young man? Let me help you."

She placed her hand on his broad back.

"You're injured. You must let me help you."

Devin coughed and squirmed away from her touch, frightened of her. Whom might she tell and what would they do next?

"Oh dear. I'll not hurt you."

He must have been freezing to death in this weather—dressed in only a thin undershirt and undershorts that were stained with dried blood. Enough blood to indicate that either he was gravely injured or he had put someone else in the grave. Lillian could not yet see his face.

"Dear, oh, dear!" she muttered to herself. She was frightened, yet energized. She had always been that kind of person—one who wanted to help others. She was a nurse, what seemed like a hundred years ago. Now, she took in strays of all sorts—dogs, cats, even a runway child or two. Now, a pitiful man.

Mindful of her arthritic knees and of the pretty, flowing sarong John had bought her on a trip to India several years ago, she kneeled beside the wounded man and touched him again. Gently, so gently, she stroked his soft, fair hair. He flinched away—even her most tender touch pained him.

"No more," he moaned, his face pressed into the straw-scattered barn floor. "Please."

"Poor, poor thing. So hurt and cold. Let me get my husband and get you into the house."

"No. Please. The sun. I can't bare it," he said.

"I won't let anything harm you," she assured him.

She ran as fast as her stiff knees would allow her, back to the house to fetch John, her long dress bunched into her fists to keep from tripping on the hem. By the time they returned to the barn, the blond stranger had managed to hide himself again. But the trail of blood he left behind was an easy give-away. They quickly discovered him behind the trough of oats and hay that their elderly cow fed from on especially rainy or cool days when she could not venture into the pasture.

John was not handy with firearms and never hunted, but

notion of "there should be gun in every cottage" had not been lost on him. He had placed his Webley .38 in the waist of his trousers, out of sight under his field coat. Still, it was against Lillian's wishes—the poor man in the barn could scarcely stand, let alone fight.

"He could be one of them," John reasoned, meaning, she was quite positive a German.

"No. He spoke perfect English," she answered.

"Still, We cannot be sure yet. Until we are, we carry the gun at all times."

Getting the man into the house was no easy task. Quickly, though, his weak and spastic struggles and raspy pleas convinced John and Lillian that the only way to handle it was to humor him. He was photosensitive, or at least thought he was, so John gently hooded him in the heavy wool horse blanket that had belonged to their long-deceased mare, Agnes.

John carried him as best he could, but the man was quite large, standing slightly taller than John's impressive 6'4". He was big boned, but frighteningly emaciated.

John complained later of an aching back, but in his typical kind nature and dry wit, often suggesting to Lillian that she had been the cause—to have gone as far as to demand he carry another man into their home, into one of their beds. Of course, she had giggled, but how far from the truth was he?

Just as they stepped out of the barn and into the crisp light of the autumn sun, the man whispered against her ear, "Thank you. My name is Devin."

Days passed and Devin's body slowly mended. However, his need for blood went unsatisfied. He did not know how to tell them what he needed. John and Lillian were saints, caring for him wonderfully. In morning, Lillian came in quietly and drew the heavy drapes and then the thick brown blanket John had nailed across the bedroom's single window. At dusk, she opened the fabric and tacked it back, to allow the night to pour in. They saved him. Now was he to simply say, "I must have blood to live?" They would think him an animal. Some kind of demon.

Still, he was starving. He was wasting away despite Lillian's sweet insistence that he take the food she made. Wonderful peasant food, much like the food Evie used to prepare for him and the children, singing sweet songs in their cramped kitchen.

He knew what he must have looked like—wasted to the bone, his pale skin stretched over the framework of his skeleton like rubber, his blond hair brittle and faded to no-color.

Finally, one night about a month into his recovery in the Moses home, he could not take it any longer. Night bled through the small window. The fat, high moon rained glorious white-yellow light in across his bed and illuminated the rest of the small room. Lillian had pulled a leather reading chair to his bedside and the book she had been reading to him was lying open across the arm. It was an espionage novel—John's—called *The Dark Frontier* by Eric Ambler. He did not much like it, but he did enjoy Lillian's lilting voice and her warmth.

Bandages tightly bound his injured feet. Lillian claimed with a smile that once a nurse, a nurse for life, not just until retirement. She cleaned and dressed his wounds daily, marveling at how quickly he healed. The tendons at his heals were knitting back to together nicely. His crushed feet were no longer plum-colored, but dull jaundiced yellow. And the swelling had decreased greatly.

Wincing with pain, Devin swung his legs round. Dizzy, he sat a long moment on the edge of the bed. The legs sticking out beneath the borrowed nightshirt were unrecognizable as his own. So thin, they were little more than twigs covered with flesh the color of a fish's belly. Below, his feet were so heavily bandaged that they seem huge and cartoonish, without shape.

He pushed himself up, biting back a cry of pain. His feet felt they were being torn from his legs. He collapsed into a weeping heap beside the bed, biting into his palm to quiet himself. On hands and knees, he crawled to the open bedroom door and out into the dark hallway. With his vampire eyes he had no need for a lamp—the darkness was as easy to navigate as daylight. A long hall and floorboards that spit splinters into his palms and into his knees. Big Tudor-style home, cluttered and lived-in, full of the eccentric spirit and strange interests of John and Lillian and their lost son, Cillian, who lurked in every corner of the place like a disincorporated wraith. It smelled of lilacs, fresh and dried, and of Lillian's powder and of cooking and some chemicals that John had experimented with.

The silence made him feel a bit ill. Though he slept much of the daylight hours, he grew to love the evenings. It was the deep night silences of the house he had quickly grown to despise since coming here. The times when John and Lillian slept and their silly, dry banter did not ring in every rafter and the radio was shut off. No news of war and death, no tinny jazz filtering its way up the stairs and into his room. The night cut them off from one another and the rest of England, and the world for that matter.

Moving in silence was an animalistic skill he found he had gained once becoming a Deathwalker, but without the use of his feet, he knew he was moving awkwardly, loudly. He felt as if he were betraying his surrogate family, slipping along their corridors in secret, in darkness, his mouth running with hunger for blood. He hated himself for being what he was—if he had been mortal, none of this torture, this dreadful loneliness, would have been heaped upon him. Downstairs, however he managed to get down the stairs would yield something. The blood of a pathetic mouse scurrying along the baseboards. One of Lillian's beloved stray cats, perhaps, Devin thought, disgusted.

At the landing, he lay on his belly, his nightshirt twisted around him like a villain's arms, his legs against the cold floor, he stared down into the darkness. A long, wide flight of treads. He would surely break his neck, and a broken neck was a long recovery he was quite positive, immortal or not.

Just as he rolled onto his back and swung his legs around, ready to maneuver downward on his ass, the dim and flickering wall sconce hummed to life. Above him stood Lillian, her eyes bleary with sleep.

"Whatever are you doing, dear?"

She was as beautiful as an angel in the soft lampglow. Her hair, which he had seen loose only once before fell onto her shoulders, reaching the top of her breasts. Nearly black, but a black that had gone soft with years, paling to ash grey. Her white cotton gown was like the cloak of a seraph. Devin wondered a moment if he might be delirious, seeing angels and saints everywhere. Was he close to death and if so, he was quite sure it was demons he would encounter on the otherside. Was he not a demon himself, anyway?

He tried to answer, but the words just would not come out. What could he tell her now? That he was going down to the pantry to murder and devour a few mice? "I-I—"

She knelt and slipped her arm under his head. "Shhh. Let's not wake John, now." He smelled her, the warm flesh of her throat above the lace of her gown, perfumed with rose -scented soap. Her breasts pressed his shoulder and his chest. He sighed and turned his face away.

"Let's get you back into bed. I'll bring you whatever you need."

She raised him to sitting, her body still pressed to him, lifting, strong nurse's back working the way she knew would work. Now he pressed his face into the curve of her neck. He wept.

"Lillian. I—I'm so sorry."

She stroked his hair as if he were her child. "There, now. You're going to be all right, you realize."

"No. I'm not," he breathed against her ear.

His fingers wove into the silken ropes of her hair and he held her tightly.

Surprised, she gasped his name.

His teeth sank into her flesh and thick, metallic liquid flooded his mouth. He rocked her back and forth against himself, his cock swelling and pushing against the pillow of her stomach. Tears spilled down his cheeks and he hated himself for the beast he had become. Lillian gripped his hair. Instead of fighting him, she pulled more tightly to him. Her heart beat like the frantic struggles of an injured bird through the cage of her bones. Her mind raced and he absorbed every thought—the fear, the excitement. She wanted this. She wanted him. He rolled over and she was beneath him, his weight, as much as it was at that point, pinning her to the floor. She did not cry out.

Moments passed. Devin was nearly unconscious with the ecstasy of finally gaining sustenance. But he forced his awareness back to the shadowed hallway of the Moses home and the woman who was already dying against his body. He rocked his hips against her again, now aware that he had come and hot semen flooded from him onto the flat of her stomach.

He pulled away, shaking, but new strength filling his limbs and chest. Lillian stared up at him, her eyes wide. Was she seeing him or was she too far gone? He dipped into her mind once again, like slipping into an icy pond. Did he want to see death from that side again? Cautiously he entered her thoughts and found no fear there.

Sobbing, he pressed his face to her breast. "I'm sorry," he whispered. "Oh, Lillian."

What to do now? Should he flee into the night? And

how could he, anyway, hobbled as he was? John would surely kill him once he discovered Lillian.

He should crawl like the vermin he was out of the house and into the field beyond and wait for the retribution of the morning sun.

Instead, he tore his wrist with his teeth, just as he had watched Judy do through his own dying eyes. Blood welled there and then spilled down his arm, blotched his nightshirt and Lillian's white gown even more with red circles. Drops like tears. He pressed the running wound to Lillian's lips.

"Drink, Lillian. Drink fast and live."

For once horrible moment, it appeared he was indeed too late. She lay there, unmoving. Finally, he felt the sweet, quivering movement of her lips against his skin. Her tongue working, her teeth tearing the gash wider. She pulled at his vein until sheering pain uncoiled up his arm and across his chest. He sucked oxygen through his clenched teeth and tears of despair became tears of agony. Was this what a coronary felt like? Would John wake to find him dead and Lillian covered with blood instead of vice versa?

After a moment, he yanked his arm from her gasp and scrambled away, holding his bleeding wrist against his chest.

Lillian climbed to her feet, and her movements were easier than he had ever seen them. The stiffness, the constant ache of her knees that made her limb like an old lady before her time, was gone. She drew the back of her hand across her lips, wiping away the blood, smearing it like a mad woman's lipstick and stepped to him.

Teary-eyed, she smiled down at him. "Devin? What did you do?"

chapter thirty-five

Susan sat in the in the grand room by the fireplace, pretending to flip through the "lifestyle" section of the local paper that was over two months old. Instead, she listened as they wrapped things up in the parlor. She followed their conversation perfectly well through the closed door. Her hearing was incredibly keen now, but it was no longer as disconcerting as it had been at first. She did not care to be caught eavesdropping on their meeting like some kind of nosy girlfriend, but she needed to know what was going on. Devin could be closed to her at times, so unlike Michael, who had willingly shared everything. His day, his dreams, his fantasies, his plans for the future—Michael had been an open book. Getting Devin to open up was akin to excising shrapnel from an artillery wound.

There were five other Deathwalkers in there, three of which she had never seen before tonight. The fourth was her friend from college a lifetime ago, the strange Mary Lei. Mary nodded to Susan and smiled a knowing smile and Susan was positive it must have been Devin who had turned her, as well. A pang of unwarranted jealousy prodded at her heart. She did not speak to Mary Lei and Mary did not speak to her.

The other woman was about Susan's mortal age, stunning, lean and wild-looking, with skin like coal. She sported a large afro. Next was a man who appeared to have some Native American in his lineage. He made Susan's heart skip a beat when she first saw him, he was so beautiful. His crow-black hair and hawkish, haughty profile made her blush a little when he nodded to her as he entered the garden gate. The other two were not as notable, one a scrawny Kurt Cobain look-alike and an older fellow, balding and grumpy-looking, with an odd accent she could not quite place who carried a military air about him. By the sound of it, all were both angry and confounded by Devin's indifference toward them and the fact that so many of their kind had been taken down by Jacobsen. Some of them had thrived there for many decades before Devin came to the states, but they evidentially looked to him as a leader.

Stories of him circulated among those who had always been there and among the fledglings. Perhaps it was his choice to hunt only the dregs of society served as inspiration to the few who wished to maintain some semblance of humanity, or maybe it was his cunning ability to never get caught. Either way, most considered Devin McCree the strongest and most human of their kind in Dunwich.

Despite the Deathwalkers' immortality, most of them were not living very long after making the change, lately. Leader or not, they blamed him for drawing Jacobsen to the city and to the shoreline.

Finally, the voices on the other side of the door quieted. Susan waited and read, paying no attention to the printed words. The parlor door opened and they filed out, unhappy, not speaking.

Passing through, each of them nodded to her as they headed for the door, showing themselves out. She waited until they were well gone before going in to confront Devin.

When she walked in, he was pouring himself a tall glass of scotch from the decanter.

"Want one?" he asked, not looking up.

"No." She was still a bit loopy from John's expensive,

high-octane cognac.

Devin sat down at the big mahogany desk and stroked the stubble on his chin, lost in thought. If there was any time he ever looked out of place to her, it was now, behind a desk, worry creasing his forehead.

"John told me why they came here. What are you? Some sort of king?"

Devin shrugged. "I suppose I am *assumed* to be in charge. It makes no sense to me. I never asked for it, nor do I want it. Either way, I'm responsible for Kasper. I am his maker, after all."

Susan nodded, pulling a face. "Nice move," she said. "John told me about *him.*"

Devin looked uncomfortable. "Everything?"

She sensed a slight change in his tone. Maybe it was overly sensitive police-woman bullshit, but she stepped closer searched his face and whispered, "Everything that he knows."

"Why don't we just leave here?" she asked.

"Because this is my home, that's why. I'll not allow Kasper Jacobsen to drive me away until I'm ready to leave." He took a sip of his drink and then sat it aside. "Come here," he said.

She straddled his lap, hung her arms around his neck and kissed him.

"You should have killed him when you had the opportunity," she said. "He's not going to stop until you do." Seeing Devin's concern, she felt ill thinking of someone prowling the streets looking for them. The things he had done to Devin; the horrible torture. She wondered why Devin had ever allowed him to go. She would have killed the bastard. She would not have questioned it, she would have shot him in a breath.

"I'll have another chance," Devin said.

Susan led Devin upstairs, the front of his linen shirt wadded in her fist, pulling him along playfully. She coaxed him with small, wicked kisses, her tongue slipping across his mouth briefly and then away, like the touch of a butterfly. Ascending the winding staircase, she guided one of his open hands over her breasts and her nipples hardened and stood out through her thin t-shirt.

"Wild thing," he muttered, clearly surprised. "What is this, anyway?"

"This is me pulling you out of the funk those people pulled you into."

He laughed softly. *"People?* When will you learn the difference?"

"I know the difference, Devin. I just can't get used to the terms."

At the top of the stairs, Susan kissed him once more and then she jumped up, hooking her arms around his neck, wrapping her legs tightly around his waists. She loved warmth of his tongue, the malty sweetness of scotch inside his mouth. Effortlessly, he carried her to their room, his big hands cupping her ass, his mouth never leaving hers. He kicked the door closed behind them.

Together, they fell across the bed. For a moment, she buried her face in his hair. How she loved the tickle of his soft hair against her face, the smell of ginger shampoo and a faint hint of oakwood smoke from the fireplace.

They undressed each other, their lips exploring each other's throat and chest, greedy.

Devin nudged Susan's thighs apart and entered her slowly, as if savoring every moment, every movement, every incredible, excruciating thrust. He slipped his hand between them, his fingers stroking her just like she wanted to be touched. Her orgasm grew instantly and for a moment she thought she might faint if she did not come soon. He drew his wet tongue up from the cleft of her breast, over the front of her neck and then her chin, ending again at her mouth. He was huge, his cock like hot stone and Susan pressed her face into the crook his shoulder to stifle the cry she felt building behind her lips.

She closed her eyes and for a moment, she imagined the coppery, salty scent of his blood thrumming beneath his skin. It was maddening and she flicked her tongue out to taste him.

He drove into harder, more quickly, his fingers stroking her clitoris in time with his movements. With her teeth, Susan punctured his flesh, drawing a small, pained groan from him. With a slight turn of her head, she opened the wound just enough and his blood began to flow across her waiting lips.

She drank from his vein, then arching her back against his sweat-slick body, she came. After only a moment or two, Devin exploded into her, his eyes closed, his face beautiful in the moment. Then he bent and kissed his own blood from her lips.

They drifted to sleep together, a tangle of limbs and covers, Devin cradling her protectively against him.

"I love you, you know," he whispered against her ear.

"Then never leave me."

Susan slipped down the sweet spiral of slumber. Sometime during the early moments as sleep was only beginning to hold her in its grip, she thought she heard Devin whisper, "I'll be back."

She wanted to respond, and even thought she had, but only sighed and turned onto her side.

A few minutes later, John's voice drifted to her, annoyed.

"The others need a leader or else Kasper is going to kill them all. You know that. They blame you, but they also look to you."

Devin's reply was clipped, annoyed. "I'm no leader. I want to be left alone. I want Susan to be left alone. I don't care what happens to any of them. *She's* all that matters, now."

Drawers opening and the faint sound of clothes shuffled around. Then, "And since when did you decide to become the voice of my conscious, anyway, John?"

"Someone needs to be."

She was faintly aware of the sweet brush of Devin's lips across hers, the tickle of his warm breath on her face and he was gone.

Sleep grew denser, heavier and she dreamed she reached out for Devin, but no—not Devin, but Peter. She wanted to laugh over the fact that he had fallen asleep beside her.

However, it was not Peter because even in the storybook of her dream, she knew he was dead. Instead, it was Michael, snuggled warm and easy to her side. Sunshine floated through the window in dusty, soft rays. How she missed the warm kiss of sun on her face. The heat on her bare shoulders as she ran through the park and along the bay back in Reading. Michael looked at her, hair wrecked from sleep, the sun touching the blue of his eyes and turning them the pale blue-white of a ten a.m. sky.

He laughed and kissed her and for a moment, she wanted to cry.

Susan woke, her face stained with tears. The covers wrapped around her like a fist and she kicked at them to get free. The room was too muggy and cool sweat layered her skin.

Devin was gone. Thinking of things that might have been dreams or not, she knew that Devin was searching for Kasper Jacobsen. She wondered if Michael had actually taken her advice and left. She doubted it. He was a man, after all—stubborn and pigheaded. If he had stayed, was he still alive? She thought of the scrap of paper he had slipped into her pocket, the one he had jotted an address on. She had saved it in the depths of her coat pocket, where Devin would not find it. She would need to send Michael on his way before something terrible happened to him.

She climbed from the bed, grabbed the robe that Devin left for her and she had never worn, pulled it on and cinched the robe about her waist, then went downstairs to find John.

John was down in the library, dressed in his pajamas and a red silk robe that made him look especially debonair. He had graduated from the cognac to scotch and a lot of it by the looks of the decanter, which was nearly empty. The fire had died to glowing embers. Basie and Holiday at the Savoy played softly on the small digital stereo that sat atop the middle shelf among the books and various trinkets. Susan was willing to bet that somewhere in the house he had the vinyl 78 stored away, immaculate and scratch-free.

"Hi," she said, rapping on the open door and entering at the same time. "Don't you ever sleep?"

John stood wearily. "Hello, my dear. And no, not lately, anyway."

He motioned to his chair, waited for her to be seated, but she took the ottoman opposite. He then sat back down.

"Where are my manners? A drink?" He picked up the decanter from his reading table and swirled around the dregs at the bottom.

"No, thanks."

He shrugged, then poured the amber liquid into his glass and then drank it down.

"So, Devin's gone to find Jacobsen, hasn't he?"

"Yes."

"How long until sunup?"

John glanced at his watch. He laughed and shook his head slowly. "It's only a quarter of three."

"What happens if he doesn't come back?" Susan sighed. "Look at me, John. I would have never chosen this kind of existence if he were not for him. He can't leave me like this."

"I seriously doubt that's his intention. He only wants to make things safe for you. Safe for the two of you to live together."

"I wish we could just leave," she whispered. Thoughts of Michael popped into her mind again. She made her decision when she allowed Devin to drink her blood. When she decided to drink from him, not that she had an option, really. Again, she wondered if Michael had returned home as she had asked.

What would he say when people asked after her?

"Jacobsen managed to find us here. He won't give up." John stifled a cough with the back of his hand. "Besides, I want to see that bastard dead after all he's done. He deserves to suffer."

"Maybe we all do," Susan said.

"Perhaps so, but some more than others." John looked at her a moment, then leaned forward and took her hand in his and squeezed her fingers gently. "Don't worry." He stood and pulled her to her feet.

She rested her head on his chest and he slipped his arms around her. Slowly, they began to sway to the music. "Lillian and I used to dance to this very same music."

"In your pajamas?"

John chuckled softly and stroked her hair. "Sometimes."

After she left John and returned to bed, Susan was

resolved that sleep was not in the forecast—not with Devin spending most of the night looking to confront a mad vampire hunter and was not yet home despite the coming daylight. Yet she was dead asleep when her head hit the pillow. Perhaps she owed it to the fact that she had finally given in and drank a half-bottle of wine with John, or perhaps it was the slow dancing and the mellow music. Nevertheless, sleep fell and it was as heavy as boulders. Unfortunately, nightmares were still the order of the morning.

Morning—even in dreams, the dawning sky bled in around the heavy shield of the drapes.

Where the hell was Devin?

Although he was not in the bed next to her, he was certainly inside her head, but the space was small and crowded since Michael lingered there from her earlier dream.

Some shabby, dank room where others have died. Devin stood over Michael, just as he had done the night they left Reading.

Then he raised one blocky fist high over his head.

Susan opened her mouth to scream. To warn Michael to wake up, but no sound came. She grabbed at Devin's arms, but he cut through her as if she were nothing but vapor.

Devin's fist plunged into Michael's chest, to the wrist. Michael's eyes fluttered open and the smallest gasp slipped from his lips. His eyes met Susan's, for a fleeting moment.

There was a wet, sucking squelch as Devin yanked Michael's still-beating heart from his chest.

Blood flowed as if it had been twisted on like a faucet, the metallic, salty scent filling Susan's nostrils.

She jumped awake just as the dream-Susan leaned over Michael's dying form to drink her fill from the chasm of his chest.

She sat up in the bed, her legs twisted into the sheets. Next to her was Devin, warm and sleeping beside her.

"Okay?" he asked sleepily.

"I'm just glad you're home," she answered. She snuggled against his warm side and stroked his hair, silently cursing herself for her dreams. The residue of those images would stain her thoughts for hours and sleep would come again that day.

chapter thirty-six

Downstairs, John stoked the fire inside the stone hearth and brought the dying embers back to life. He tossed in another slab of oak and then straightened up, his back complaining as it did most days lately. Volumes line every wall from floor to ceiling. Many were left from the original homeowners and as old as the house itself. The others, his books on psychology—by Jung, Freud, Skinner and subjects such as behaviorism, humanism, existentialism sat along tattered horror tales, legends, myths and folklore. Vampires. Werewolves. Demons. Most he had read and re-read a dozen times over.

He had been a professor of Behavioral Science at Imperial College in the late 1920s, but had gotten enough by '35. Later he took a position at a horrid, nightmare of an asylum called Knowle Mental Hospital. But it was not long before the patients began creeping into his nightmares. The conditions and the treatments plagued his waking hours. He battled the supervisors constantly the year he was there, finally throwing his hands up and retiring with Lillian to their country house. Blissfully poor, despite the luxury of the old home itself, farming, writing. Taking in the stray vampire or two. He snorted a bitter laugh and pinched the bridge of his nose. A headache was building behind his eyes.

He sat down in his leather reading chair and considered finishing off the cognac from the flask that now sat on the side table, but decided not to. The alcohol had helped put him into this foul mood.

Devin had returned and he felt an odd mixture of relief and disappointment. John had little doubt the time would soon come that Devin did not come back. Devin was no killer and frankly, not much of a hunter, either. Jacobsen was both.

In the beginning, John allowed Devin to remain under his roof because he viewed him as merely another case study. He had assumed the man insane from the day he found him cowering like a wounded animal in their barn. A vampire? More like a psychotically depressed individual. Hallucinations. He indeed thought Devin to be dangerous, just as he told Lillian. Perhaps not a Nazi, but certainly delusional. Nevertheless. . .delusional or not, he deserved protection from a fiend like Kasper Jacobsen.

Talking to Susan of Lillian brought old heartaches to the surface again. Thoughts and memories of his dear wife dogged him like a ghost in the corner of the room, reminding of the things he could not change.

Then Lillian transformed and it felt like a dirty secret. The few acquaintances they had, they visited in the depths of night under the excuse of that she had developed a rare allergy to the sun. They ventured out to a pub from time to time, the two of them for a pint. Later, she would leave him and run the shadows with Devin. John loved Lillian and came to love Devin, as well, but he hated what they were. However immortal, John felt they lived on borrowed time. Kasper would not relent. Devin mentioned he had seen him skulking around the village. It was only a matter of time before he found them.

John considered turning Devin over to Kasper, a bargaining tool for peace, but in the end, found he could not. He loved the man as much as a son. A replacement son for their sweet Cillian. Almost.

Suddenly, it seemed Lillian regained her youth. Her movements were fluid, as graceful as they had been twenty years before. She still appeared a woman of fifty-one, but it was now a fit and lively, somewhat dangerous fifty-one. No longer the woman she had been, beaten down with arthritis. He remained a middle-aged man, unflinchingly, frustratingly unaltered. Of course, there were benefits. She was insatiable in bed, which made him wonder if she was sleeping with Devin, as well. Part of him doubted it. They were obviously inseparable, but he felt that neither of them would consider hurting him. Still, did she see Devin's face in the darkness above her instead of his? For more than two years, it was a marriage of three or was it four, with the three of them always searching the shadows for Kasper Jacobsen?

If memories of Lillian lingered like a ghost, it was the last moments he saw her alive, as it was, that laced his nightmares.

Kasper managed to spy her alone, just outside the barn, feeding her kitties. Dusk was just setting, heavy-handed and quick in the English autumn. He set her afire, somehow drenched her slender form in petrol and then a match on her as if she were so much rubbish. The barn went up around her, along with the decrepit cow and the cats that moved too slowly to escape. The smoke was like lethal gas, pinpricks to John's eyes and claws to his throat. It rose like a tornado in reverse, ghostly fingers reaching for the purple and orange streaked sky.

They decided to let the barn go—what could they do? Instead, they drowned Lillian's writhing body in icy water from the pump. Fourteen buckets before she grew still, smoldering at John's feet.

She tried to scream but her lips had been fused by the kiss of the flames. A horrid thing; a blackened malformed shape of a woman. Her beautiful hair gone to ash, her eyes lidless, staring but unseeing.

John never forgot the smell of her those last moments, that putrid stench of charred flesh. He screamed for her, maybe because she could not and sank to his knees at her side, wanting to hold her and knowing he could not. What pain might a simple caress bring?

What she was, a Deathwalker, meant she would remain like that forever. Purgatory on earth—straddling the line between life and death.

Devin snatched up a shovel.

"You don't need to see this," he told John, raising it up in both hands.

John opened his mouth to speak. And for what? To plead to Devin to allow her to live, to remain indefinitely as she was? John moved to Lillian on hands and knees, pressed his lips to her brittle and cracked cheek.

"I'll always love you," he whispered. Then he turned away, unable to look anymore.

The sick, dull *thunk* as Devin brought the shovel down and removed her head because that was the only way. Only a little blood, but still the smell of it like old copper pots. John buried his face in the cold, damp grass and wailed into the ground, oblivious to the agonized brays of the cow as it cooked alive inside the flaming skeleton of the old barn.

He remembered how he begged Devin to kill him after that, but Devin only held him and wept silently against John's shoulder.

John never saw Kasper, but he knew. Bloody fucking coward, slinking in the darkness like a rat. Over the course of their years pursuing and being pursued, he knew realized that Kasper had been changed, as well. The embrace of bloodlust was now his.

It was cannibalistic.

He worried that Susan would suffer the same fate as Lillian. Or worse. He heard the talk of the modified shotgun Kasper used to "retire" Deathwalkers. How it removed the head in a rain of blood and brains, leaving nothing above the shoulders. The thought of Susan meeting up with this maniac sickened him to the heart, his mind and his stomach, because he already loved her.

Devin had not been able to save Lillian. What would make Susan any different?

chapter thirty-seven

It began to sleet as Devin and Susan crossed the broken parking area of the old amusement park. The hulking wooden coaster sat in the darkness like a mammoth snake or perhaps a prehistoric creature, coiled, waiting. Without the garish but joyous lights marking the spokes neon green and pink, the Ferris wheel sat bleak and dead.

Just as every night, the hunger hit Susan like a punch in the guts. Her nerves ached, seeming to reach for the surface of her skin. Her awareness was far too keen. Her brain throbbed inside her skull. The inside of her mouth tasted like sand.

Across the street and into the piss-smelling hallway of an old cinderblock motel, Devin vanished into a groundfloor apartment like a thief. His mark was a man, thirty-something, olive complexion. Black hair done up like a mafia movie reject. He was as tall as Devin, but wider. Probably a highschool linebacker gone to fat in his impending middle age.

Susan had wanted to try and hunt alone, but Devin had become overly cautious because of Jacobsen. Life had suddenly become nothing more slinking in the shadows and feeding for survival.

There was no sport in this—waiting for "her man" to serve her.

Susan shivered in her damp trousers and coat. At first, she had hoped one of the advantages of becoming undead was losing the little annoying discomforts that accompanied living. She hated being cold more than almost anything else.

She certainly had not considered paranoia becoming a problem, especially after death.

Overhead in the hotel breezeway, a light hung by a frayed black cord, swaying slightly in the breeze. Every now and again, a gust would blow the freezing rain into her face.

The hunger was maddening. She had never been a big user of drugs, but this had to be what addiction was like.

She looked down the hallway at the bare wall, white paint peeling away and exposing the gray concrete beneath. The open corridor emptied onto the beach. One a narrow stepping stone path, overtaken with dune grass and reeds now, curved between the high dunes. The ocean sang its low, gritty, constant song. Far away music played, tinny and as thin as crystal. No sounds came from the hotel room.

For a moment, she was overcome with the urge to simply run away into the night. She could return to Reading and curl against Michael's warm body, deep inside the covers of their bed and pretend she was normal. But there was no going back from this and besides, had she ever really been "normal," anyway? Something had broken inside her twenty years and maybe she had only been pretending since.

The door opened and Devin stepped out. In his hand was a plastic hotel cup overflowing with thick blood.

"This will make things better, yes?" He offered it to her and she accepted it greedily, downing it in a long drink.

"Come. He'll be dead in a moment and spoiled."

Inside the room, the lamp casting a jaundiced glow on everything. Like all the other rooms in Dunwich, this one was decorated in 1970s tacky-chic. Green shag carpeting, now becoming saturated and brownish with the big man's blood beneath where he lay at the end of the bed. He lay face down, unmoving, the only sign of life was the pump of blood from the gash at the side of his neck. The room was unbearably warm after being in out in the crisp evening and Susan shrugged out of her coat. She fell to her knees at the man's side, bent low and pressed her lips to the yawning flaps of fat and flesh beneath the lobe of his ear.

Devin watched her feed. There was some morbid fascination he held with witnessing her drink. He had admitted that it turned him on. In the back of her mind, aware of this, she became aroused, as well. He sat on the end of the bed quietly, patiently.

Almost wanting put on a show, she took the dying man's hair in her fist and yanked his head over. The snap of bone, the gash grinned wider. She groaned softly and shoved her tongue deeper, lapping like a cat.

After what was too short a time, she realized she could no longer feel the faint, soft pulse of blood rising to meet her lips. The man was dead.

With a sigh, she sat back on her knees, wiped her mouth with her wrist. Her hair had gotten into the blood and now the ends were gummy with the stuff as it congealed.

She wondered about tonight's quarry. Why had Devin chosen him? Not that it mattered very much. The need for blood had been stronger than the reigns of her compassion. And she trusted Devin—he would not prey on an innocent. He was no mindless killer—whatever this man had been, he had not been good.

Almost sensing her question about the men, Devin said, "A killer of women, that one." He nudged the body with the toe of his sneaker.

"How do you know?" Susan asked.

"Followed him," he whispered, then leveled his eyes on hers. "Besides, a man can recognize his own kind."

Susan stood up and regarded him a moment. He did look the part, with the blood staining the front of his white cotton shirt, and running in rivulets down his sweaty neck and along his hairline, into his right eye. But upon closer inspection, the blood that ran into his eye did not belong to the dead man. It was his own. The big Italian had put up a good fight. There was a deep gash along Devin's eyebrow, made from a sharp punch or the heel of a boot.

Susan pushed Devin back onto the bed, her mouth first on his mouth and then licking away the blood from his throat, sucking at the wound above his eye as greedy as a nursing child. It was no longer hunger that drove her, but lust. Devin's erection was sudden and huge, pushing hard against her belly.

His mouth found the ticklish area of her neck, beneath her ear. He bit her there, the sting as sharp as the kiss of a blade.

"You'd better stop me, Susan," he groaned into her hair.

She ignored him and grinded her hips against him. Devin moved his hand down, caressing her buttocks through her trousers. Susan kissed his eyelids, her tongue flicking at the lashes, tasting his saltiness.

"I don't want to hurt you," Devin warned again.

"You can't hurt me now."

"We'll see," he whispered.

He slipped one hand between them, roughly kneading her crotch through the coarse denim. She covered his hand with hers and guided his fingers to her aching sex. Her orgasm was a hot, pulsing burst of electricity and she rocked against his hand, gasping. She pulled his hair harder than she meant to.

Breathless and trembling, she opened his pants and pulled his feverish member free. Roughly she massaged him and he thrust into her sweat-slick fist quickly. He bit into her throat, drawing blood, drawing a cry from her as he came into her hand. He grunted hard twice, a sound that was almost like that of a man in pain.

Afterward, they lay together, breaths slowing, heartbeats growing calm again.

Susan was almost dozing, her head resting in Devin's chest, his heavy arm across her and cradling her against him.

"We should get back," he told her.

She rose up, bleary-eyed. "Okay," she whispered.

Michael's pulse quickened when he set eyes on her. She was about one hundred feet away, emerging from the gloomy breezeway of an old motel, dressed in an oversized leather coat that he did not recognize. When she turned his way and her eyes met his a moment. He saw that the front of her shirt and jeans were stained dark and she glanced down and then closed up her coat. Blood. Devin McCree loomed behind her. She reached back and he took her hand and they started toward the amusement park.

Michael moved parallel with them, hanging in the shadows. He checked the shotgun as he walked, his steps as silent as he could make them. He eased the safety back. He was going to kill this sonofabitch tonight and then he was going to drag Susan back home, even if she kicked and screamed.

He moved closer now, biting his bottom lip hard. They picked up their pace and he realized that Susan was leading McCree. Running now and faintly, he heard McCree ask, "What's gotten into you?"

"Just come on," she said. "I'm ready to get you home."

But Michael was quicker and cut around ahead of them. He stepped from the shadows and raised his gun, ready.

But they were not there. Vanished into thin air, it seemed. He stood for a moment, breathing hard, his eyes watering in the cold wind. He blinked hard and listened.

He could still hear their footfalls, now it sounded a thousand miles away.

"Fuck!" he screamed.

Susan and McCree's laughter echoed across the empty parking lot, seemingly mocking him.

Michael returned to the beach house frustrated and angry. He remained on the boulevard for more than an hour, prowling the trash strewn streets and sidewalks, treading upon derelicts who smelled like the bottom of garbage bins and in fact wrapped or burrowed in trash and layers of clothes to shield themselves from cold. They appeared shapeless lumps left over from some silly science fiction flick or maybe a Lovecraft tale. Michael half-expected one to sprout tentacles quite suddenly, capture him in a death-embrace and devour him like a drumstick.

There was no way possible Susan and Devin could have vanished so easily—unless they were something more than human. He was not sure how they did it, but he was simply unable to pinpoint their whereabouts, even as they were within yards of him. Susan had spotted him and that was all. *She was the one who decided to run.* Devin never knew. If was as if he had lost of sense of direction as their laughter rose up into the cold, damp air and echoed down the alleyways and across the grass-scattered flats of abandoned parking areas.

He yanked off his coat and flung it to the sofa. Next, came the gun, strap over his head, but carefully propped against the high step of the sunken living room.

He sank down on the hearth and cradled his head in his hands a moment. "Fuck," he said aloud, "what am I doing?"

Tomorrow he should just head away from the beaches and back out town, then call someone to come for him. Gerald perhaps. In daylight, he would be relatively safe—from vampires, at least.

Of course, he could not do that. He had to see Susan one

more time. He had to appeal to whatever was left of her human self. Surely, she would listen. He would tie her up and force her to hear him, if he had to.

Yeah, right.

He made a fire and considered eating. He had two granola bars left and a can of Beenie Weenies. Not very appealing, so he decided on a beer. He pried the top off against the edge of the hearth and drank greedily. The best thing about huddling inside an unheated house was that the beer stayed cold.

After two bottles, things began to appear a bit more positive. At least she was still alive. That question was now answered. There was always another opportunity.

He sat down on the dusty sofa with a sigh. From his coat pocket, he removed the little journal he had found in the bedroom. It was a smallish booklet, faded hot pink with a cartoon of an abnormally slender woman holding an abnormally long cigarette on the cardboard cover. On the insider flap bore the title "This journal belongs to: and written in that same elegant, loopy hand as the "do to" lists on the refrigerator was the legend *Sandra Harp.* Inside, lineless pages, yellowed and brittle with the passing years was nothing more than the daily journal of a woman bored with her life. A husband, whom she still loved, apparently, but who paid her little attention. Children she adored, lived for, but who remained ultimately ungrateful. Sandra evidentially did not care for the beach and how the kids brought sand into the house on their feet. She was unhappy with her mother's meddling. She was unhappy that the woman next door had evidentially gotten a boob job. Recipes from *Good Housekeeping* for some sort of roasted chicken casserole. A recipe for peppermint bark.

Michael thumbed further through the pages and realized that he did not like this woman very much. He would, however, had love to have a big hunk of that peppermint bark, which the woman had deemed a hit with her kids in large letters and an exclamation point.

It had become set in his mind that the husband was the one who did it—murdered the family and then perhaps himself. If she complained as much aloud as she did in her diary, it was little wonder, he thought odiously, then felt rather loathsome for it.

He paged onward, no longer really reading, but skimming for some indication that something as ominous as what had occurred here was on the horizon.

September 13, 1973 was the date that drew his attention, because on that day, she encountered a man by the name Devin McCree at an antique dealer just outside Dunwich.

Tall, blond and handsome, he looked just like someone from an old movie. I haven't blushed looking at Jerry in ten years, but this man made me blush like a teenager. What's more, he saw me. He smiled and I could not even remember why had gone into that shop in the first place.

A glorious English accent, but his voice was rough—older than his face.

He claimed he was new in town and for some reason I volunteered to give him a lift back to his hotel.

I left with him—God knows why—I left with this man and went to a hotel that was so seedy that there was little chance of anyone spotting me going inside with him.

In my entire life, I had never done anything like that. Of course, a man like Devin McCree had never taken an interest in me.

Thoughts of dinner and the kids popped into my mind—would they even notice I was not there, in front of the stove?

Devin removed my clothes. It was like something from one of my romance novels.

I had never felt the way he made me feel.

I died.

I died, but I am not dead.

I am more than I was.

Devin wept when he was done and over again whispered he was sorry into my hair. I held him and told him I was happy it happened.

He told me I would not be happy for long.

October 21, 1973

I do not know what to do. Something grips my heart and my stomach. Devin McCree—that bastard—I've not seen him again.

I lapped the bloody run-off of the hamburger I was thawing for dinner from the bowl it rested in. Like a nasty animal.

Jerry knows something is wrong. He wonders why I keep the drapes pulled all day—I tell him the sunshine is causing migraines.

I'd like to rip his throat out. I smell the blood of my babies through their skin and my mouth waters. I feel dirty.

The children. I cannot allow them to become what I have become. Worse, I cannot allow myself make them that.

Sometimes I wonder if I can survive this way. If Devin was right, do I want to? Do I really want to?

October 31, 1973

I stopped it for them, but it never stops for me. I cannot die. I used all of Jerry's bullets—my head is a goddamn mess, but still I am not dead. I am ruined, but I am not dead.

I will live with this until the end of the world.

It's what I get.

There was nothing more after that. Nausea uncoiled in Michael's stomach. Did Susan experience these feelings? Was she now an animal, just as Kasper had said? Was there any hope of making her human again? Susan. Somehow, she had known he had been near, watching.

chapter thirty-eight

Killing the man, as horrid a man as he was, had been no easy task for Devin. Knowing it strengthened Susan's love for him. Finally, she saw the man, not the vampire. Devin was softhearted and seeing that made Susan wonder even more about how or what had happened to her somewhere along the way of her life. And afterlife. She had spent too much time fearing and hating a man who had done nothing but defend himself. She had allowed Peter's death, and then the baby's death to consume her. She had shut herself off from those who wanted to love her. Michael. Poor Michael. He never deserved what she did to him.

But enough of the self-pity. There was always redemption.

It was a new night and there was a new piece of vile garbage that needed to be removed. They had watched this bastard most of the evening, peering from the shadows of a back corner booth and drinking shots of tequila and sucking limes that tasted old, as he made his play for an extremely young girl. He plied her with drinks that she should not have had for another six or seven years, legally. She drank like an old pro.

The child should have been watching Hannah Montana and reading books about babysitters and their crushes or maybe shimmering vampires who enjoyed daylight. Young enough to wonder what it would be like to move into the ninth grade and kiss a boy for the first time.

But she had done all of that already because things were messed up in her world and in the world in general.

The man, a greasy middle-aged nasty, draped an arm across the girl's tiny shoulder, in control like a demented parent with his hand grazing the buds of her breasts as they left the tavern. Susan glanced at Devin. Was he thinking of his own long and lost daughter? Susan's hunger rose and ebbed like the tide. Slowly she had learned she could control it rather than have it control her.

Into the alley and the big man's gentle caress morphed into the rough and abrupt handling of property he did not especially care about keeping for very long. His fat fingers bit into the soft meat of the girl's bicep, through the thin cloth of her pink jacket.

Susan and Devin trailed behind, their trick of levitation a gift, their feet grazing the pavement like a kiss and leaving no echoing boot claps on the silent street.

The fat man sang sweet nothings at the small girl. He would make her love him. He would buy her a new coat if she would allow him what he wanted. He asked if he was her first and she giggled so softly and so knowingly that it broke Susan's heart. Devin scowled in the shadows. This man would not make it inside to confines of his apartment.

The light rain dampened the streets as if the night itself were weeping. The apartment building loomed, art deco chrome and aqua, both faded and peeling like disease had taken hold of the façade. The man fumbled with his keys— a big ring of dozens of them, to open the glass doors to the lobby. It was apparent his was the only occupied flat in the place now, the others having come to their senses and fled, or died, long ago.

The girl swayed on her stick-pin legs, clad in tights with holes and boots that needed to be laced, but had no laces. She shivered and waited, stifling a yawn with the back of her hand. Her were eyes as glassy as marbles.

"I'll get it," the fat man told her, and sweat beaded on his cherry-red swollen upper lip although it was near freezing outside. He kissed the girl quickly and when he turned his attentions back to the stubborn lock, she wiped her mouth with the black of her hand. Susan's mouth watered, but was it was from the prospect of feeding or the notion of tearing this bastard apart?

I am not good. We are saving this child, but I am not good.

Devin winked at her, but he did not appear happy. In the next instant, he appeared between the fat man and the door. He snatched the keys from the man's sausage-sized fingers.

"Let me help you with those," he said,.

He barred his teeth and something entirely erotic twisted in Susan's middle. He was not aware of the incredible specimen he was. Above animal. Above human. They were superhuman. The food chain had not considered them. Evolution had not considered them. But here they were. Like gods, deciding who lived and who died.

The young girl screamed and Susan wrapped her arms around her, pinning her.

"This is not for her to see," Devin said and his voice rasped like a wild creature attempting to form words that were unfamiliar.

Susan pressed her lips to the girl's pink seashell ear, breathing in the smell of cheap shampoo, last used days ago, and cherry lipbalm. "Go on, now. Go and find your way home to your parents. Or you'll end up dead. Like me." She let go of the girl. The girl stumbled away, losing her unlaced boot. She did not stop. In a moment, she had vanished into the night.

"What the hell?" the man said. "You know what you just did?"

"Actually, I do," Devin said.

"You owe me for the drinks. And who are you, anyway?

Her father? Some kind of super-fucking-hero?"

Susan laughed loudly, unsure why it was funny to her. Perhaps it was the liquor. No matter—the man's terror was comical. This disgusting creature was frightened of dying—frightened of the very same thing that he had burrowed in the back of his stupid and shallow mind for the girl. He would have killed her and he would have violated her corpse until she became too deteriorated to keep. The detective in Susan knew the profile. And perhaps it took a monster to know one. But some monsters were worse than others.

Devin vanished and reappeared behind the man, a wondrous trick that Deathwalkers came by easily enough, like the levitating. He threaded his fingers through the man's thick hair and shoved him, a motion that appeared fluid and easy. The man sailed through the plate glass, shattering the entrance of the grand hotel until it appeared a gigantic spiderweb. The man landed in a broken heap in front of the front darkened lobby, moaning. Blood ran from him, an expanding pool of black ink in the darkness.

Glancing back at Devin, he reached up and grabbed the top edge of the front desk. Sobbing, slobbering, groaning, he dragged himself up.

Devin stepped through the shattered entrance and Susan followed him. The man had shat himself—she smelled him now like a dozen soiled baby diapers.

"What do you want from me, motherfucker?" he screamed. Blood bubbled from his lips and his nostrils.

Susan felt the adrenaline kick in. She tried Devin's little vanishing and reappearing trick, but she was still an baby when it came to those ancient ways and her form wavered a moment before she found herself before the trembling man. She lacked Devin's concentration when the hunt was on. She was impatient.

She put her hand up before her.

"Here. Don't be frightened. Maybe I'll save you from him," she said sweetly.

"Please," the man whispered. He placed his hand against hers, the warm blood sealing their touch for an incredibly intimate moment. "Sweet Jesus, please," he pleaded again.

Blood pumped too hard and too rapidly in Susan's brain. It thrummed inside the hollows of her ears like a bass drum. It throbbed deep inside her groin and made her nipples harden.

She smiled demurely and slipped her hand around the man's meaty forefinger and snapped it back before he could pull away. The man howled and she twisted the digit around, the bones like twigs underfoot, and then free of stringy meat.

"Oh motherfucker! Shit, kill me now." He held maimed hand in front of his face, the blood creating a shiny crimson glove.

Susan bit off the fleshy pad at the tip and spat it back into the man's anguished face. Blood trickled from both ends, thickening to a syrupy, gluey consistency. The muscles contracted once, *come here, and then relaxed and grew limp*.

Reasoning was beyond her now. The creature, this perverted animal deserved whatever horrible thing they delivered him. She allowed the shackles of her humanity to slip away like an old coat.

She laughed, then slipped the dismembered finger into her mouth. The man's blood was sour and she knew immediately he carried disease inside him. Cancer, perhaps or maybe something that may have been contagious to mere mortals.

No matter, she could not stop now. The horror on the man's face drew it out of her, playing the devil. She drew the bloodied tip end along the line of her lips, creating a madwoman's grin and then tossed the finger casually back to its owner.

"Here. You have it."

It bounced off the front of his coat and dropped to the

floor. He again put his ruined hand up, looked at it and gasped.

"I need a doctor, you bitch," he wailed.

"You need an undertaker, you fuck," Susan answered.

Devin snatched the man's face, his fingers sinking deep into the flabby jowls until that disappeared into the depth of fat. Blood ran. The man screamed again, muffled, comical, pathetic. Devin lifted him as if he were the weight of a rag doll and tossed him behind the front counter.

Like a cat, he sprang onto the counter and from up there, he glared down at the fat man. "How do you like being scared?"

"I-I don't like it," the man blubbered. "Listen. I've learned. I'll never touch another one."

"Another what? You don't even know what you are doing wrong. Say it!" Devin yelled.

"A child. A little girl. Never again."

Susan could not see the man now, but she could imagine him lying in a soft heap on the floor among papers and file cabinets. She leapt onto the counter next to Devin.

"Peedos never stop," she said. "I used to be a cop, so I know."

Devin dropped to the floor soundlessly and loomed over the broken, bloody man. He reached down and lifted the creep by his collar and draped him backward over the counter. Susan kneeled over him and showed him her fangs.

"Jesus, don't."

Devin yanked his head back and exposed the thick neck, offered the vein to Susan. She kissed the man's bleeding lips, first licking away the dark blood.

"In your heart, you know you deserve it," she told him. Then she tore out his throat like a rabid wolf.

He did deserve it.

Still, when Susan saw her reflection peering back at her through the shattered glass of the hotel portico, she felt sick. The man's rancid blood threatened to come up and she placed her hand to her mouth. The thousand-faced ghost in the glass did the same. Blood in her hair, blood on her cheeks like a child with an ice cream sundae, her clothes stains black in the weak blue lights what bled back there from the streets.

What was she? She sobbed, a foreign sound coming from her lips.

Devin moved slowly toward her, concerned. He wiped at thin line of dark blood at the corner of his lips with his thumb.

"Susan?"

She fled through the yawning hole in the glass and out into the chill of the winter night. Down the breezeway alley between two hotels and toward the beach. Her breath up and up like speech balloons in a comic book, heart beating too fast for a dead woman.

Her eyes teared and she could not stop rubbing them. At the lapping edge of the water she collapsed and vomited until her stomach was as empty as her soul.

Breathless, she then washed her hands and face in the icy tide. It numbed her hands and fingers immediately, but she loved the feel of it, the soft foam like lace across the backs of her knuckles, the crash of the waves against her knees as she sank down into the sand.

She felt so bad. So tired. She fell back on her ass in the cold water. Could not get the little girl out of her head. And why was that? She had seen that shit over and again and she had never felt anything more than a passing indifference. What had changed tonight?

Devin? Devin picturing his own child in that situation, perhaps? Herself and her lost child?

It was *someone's* child, after all. Part of her wished she could take down every single perverted lowlife in this world like the one they had drained tonight, but how much of herself would lose in the process?

Devin appeared beside her and warm. He took her hand

and pulled her to her feet and up the beach, onto dry sand. From the pocket of his big coat, he produced a half empty bottle of the tequila they had started in the bar. He plopped down on the beach and pulled her down onto his lap and kissed her, then offered the bottle. She took it greedily.

"What's going on, Susan?"

She wiped her mouth with her wrist and passed the bottle back. "I don't know, Devin."

He narrowed his eyes and looked at her sideways. "You're not growing a conscious, are you?"

She laughed. "Never."

He smiled, gorgeous in the moonlight. "Maybe you should. I know it's in there somewhere."

She laid back on the sand. "How much good is a conscious to a killer, Devin?"

"You'd be surprised."

The sound of the waves grew hypnotic very quick and the salty scent of the ocean reminded her of beach trips when she was a kid with Peter and her parents. Above them, the stars glimmered like diamonds on a windshield.

They remained quiet on the beach for a while, drinking, and her mind meandered, dull from drink and feeding. She wondered if it was Christmas yet and she asked Devin.

"Christmas? I love Christmas." He laughed. "You'll know when it's Christmas, believe me. Anyway, John is like Father Christmas. Lights. Wine. Gifts. He's just an oversized boy."

Last year's Christmas with Michael, they had stayed awake most of the night talking, giggling and for a while, she felt like she had a long time ago—before Peter's death. He held her and they watched a cheesy kid's holiday show—and Elvis played on the radio, soft as snowflakes.

She shrugged. "I miss the sunshine, Devin. I missed the warmth on my face. I miss it coming through the window early in the morning."

Devin took another drink. "So do I, Susan," he said, "but

you must learn to hold onto to things that can drive you on."

"Like what? Killing?"

"Like removing the ones who don't deserve to be here."

Susan took the bottle. The liquor stung her throat, but it was pleasant, salty, a bit sour. Another swallow and back to Devin. "Sometimes I feel like none of them belong. They're worse than we are, you know. They call us monsters, but humans are the monsters." She laughed bitterly.

"It's the darklands. That's what John called it."

"The darklands? What the hell is that?"

"What you're going through . This period of uncertainty. Of despair. You don't know what you are, what you should feel. Whether you even have any *right* to feel. It is hypocritical to murder in the name of saving another? Or saving yourself? I went through the same thing, but John got me through it."

"I don't need anyone to 'get me through' anything, Devin. I'll work it out for myself."

Devin sighed, then leaned over and kissed her temple. "You don't have to pretend to have no feelings."

"It's not pretend. I just don't know any other way to be. Why feel anything? It only leads to pain in the end."

"Not always," Devin whispered.

She turned to him and smiled. "Of course not always. I know what I feel about you. Right now, that's all I need."

But she did feel, and telling Devin those things created a little stab of guilt in her gut. It was almost as if Michael had never been a part of her life. She had always been here in Dunwich with Devin McCree. She had never lived the life of a cop, never lost a child, never lost a brother. Never had parents who wished she had died instead of their beloved son. She felt her old life again slipping away, awareness of who she once was, was lost like the shedding of skin.

For a moment, she tried to imagine what eternity really meant, but the idea was so vast it was impossible for her to get her drunken mind around it.

Devin offered the bottle to her one last time. She shook her head and he finished the last of the tequila off, then set the empty aside. He leaned back on his elbows and ran his fingers through his hair. From the street, the music rose and fell like the surf.

"Devin?" she whispered after a while. "I want to feel again."

He turned to her and touched her face. "You're not lost, Susan."

He played with the top button of her blouse. Blood had dried on it, as thick as paint and he scraped a flaked away with his thumbnail.

"The man's blood was spoiled. You need to cleanse your pallet, I think." He pressed the inside of his wrist to her lips and she was surprised by how warm he was. How could anyone think them dead?. They were far warmer than any human.

"No," she said. She lay motionless for a moment, feeling his blood move through his veins, throbbing as slight as a bird's breaths against her lips.

"Nonsense. You are what you are, Susan. Now, drink."

Sighing, she gripped his arm with both hands and bit down on the inside of his wrist furiously. He cursed at the sudden and unexpected fury of it, and she laughed at him deep in her throat. His blood spilled into her mouth and she latched on savagely. She rolled over on top of him and immediately she was one with him, her heart in time with his. Salty blood washed between her teeth and dribbled down her chin. She pressed against him like an animal, filled with bloodlust and eager for release and sucked at wound until she began to feel slow and sleepy.

Suddenly she was pulled back by her hair. Devin had broken her clinging hold and she straddled his waist, staring coolly down at him. He was already growing pale.

"Enough," he said, breathless. "Damn!"

Susan giggled and kissed him hard on the mouth. His blood covered her lips and smeared slick and sticky against. He lapped it from her tongue and down over her chin. She nuzzled his throat, licked the coarse stubble of beard on his jaw, then ripped the buttons of his shirt and tore it open, exposing his chest to freezing air.

His nipples hardened and she bit one and then the other until tiny drops of blood beaded against her lips. She moved against him, striving selfishly for her own pleasure. His penis was an iron rod in his pants.

Frantic, Devin opened her jeans and yanked them and her panties down over her hips and passed her knees. She kicked out of them without hesitation. Roughly, he rolled her onto her back. She tore at his jeans and freed him, then stroked him a moment, wetting her fingers in her mouth and then drawing them along the underside of his cock slowly, teasing the pulsing head, until she knew he could no longer wait. He pinned her beneath him and pushed into her quickly. She stared at the sky a moment, at the stars, the clouds passing across the face of the moon, the closed her eyes. Devin pounded against her—she would be sore tomorrow—and she climbed the crest of her orgasm almost immediately. In the distance, she thought she heard a baby crying and it chilled her to the bone.

The sand cut and scraped her naked bottom until she felt raw, but she could not stop moving. Above, Devin was as beautiful as an angel in the yellow-blue glow of the moon. He kissed her mouth, then bit her bottom lip, drawing her blood this time. She smelled it, then ran her tongue out to taste it.

When she climaxed a second time, she locked her ankles around his hips and shuttered against him, calling his name again and again. Devin slammed into her, faster, immersed in his pleasure now.

When it was over, he stroked her hair and planted a kiss on the end of her nose.

"It's freezing," he said. "Let's go home."

As she dressed, Susan smiled a little to herself. Home had a good ring to it.

chapter thirty-nine

"**J**oey? Is that you?"

Voice garbled, wet and words as loose as sand through open fingers. Michael sprang to his feet, frightened out of a light sleep. Lying by the fire, he was as warm as a cat in the sunshine, and now, having drunk more beer than he should have on an empty stomach, he was lethargic and dull.

"It's me, Joey. It's your mamma."

Michael determined the owner of the voice was indeed a woman. He picked up his rifle, thumbed back the safety, but did not raise it.

"Sandra?" He recalled the photos on the refrigerator— Joey and Jenna.

"Sandra," the dampened voice repeated, as if the name was an alien thing. She sounded like a person trying to speak under water might sound. No determinable gender or age. Only this wet thick sound—syrup coating the tongue and throat. Michael had heard those kinds of voices from cancer patients after nicotine corroded their esophagus or jaws and tongue.

"Yes. Sandra Harp," she repeated, sounding now as though the name suddenly triggered something inside her memories.

She moved toward the firelight, but the movement was

odd, surreal. She was an imposing creature, looming taller than most women. But closer, Michael was startled to realize that she hovered about six or eight inches from the floor. He had not yet seen this trick of the Deathwalkers. And Sandra Harp was indeed imposing, despite the levitation. She was large-boned, but slumped at the waist like a woman browbeaten and tired. Shoulders rounded as though a stone had been placed upon them. Jesus, in his head, Michael had conjured the image of Carol Brady's 1970s perkiness gone awry, not some Amazon figure dressed in a faded green polyester skirt and blouse with funky green, white and black do-dads. She matched the kitchen wallpaper, Michael thought, buzzed, but right now he hardly felt like laughing.

"Sandra." He swallowed. "I'm not Joey."

"Not Joey." Dejected. A pause and she stared at him a moment. "Michael."

"How do you know? Never mind." He wanted to wet his lips, but his tongue was as dry as sandpaper.

"Why are you still here, Michael? She told you to go."

Michael frowned. "Wait—how do you--?"

"A perk that goes with being undead, the mind reading." She stopped the spooky levitating shit and came to rest on the carpeted floor, but that did not make her appear any less frightening. She took a halting step forward, and he could now see her face clearly.

She was the stuff of nightmares, this undead housewife from hell. On the left side of her face, she appeared as he had imagined—almost. Short, brown hair, styled into what was left of a choppy shag. It was as if she had taken a kitchen knife to it herself. Her face on that side was attractive, although a little harsh. As pale as flour.

The right was a monstrosity rivaling any Saturday "Shock Theatre" B-movie flick he might have caught on late night television as a boy. There was no way to comprehend the mess—the misshaped mass where skull and hair and flesh should have been. Craters in bone, chunks missing and skin grown over in pitted and scarred patches like that of a burn victim. Worse, however, was her jaw on that side, which was missing. Her tongue moved inside like a writhing creature, exposed and then hiding as her words formed.

Her eye on that side was lidless, staring and dry.

Michael had seen all sorts of horrors come through the E.R. doors, but this was enough to make him want to retch. He turned away and drew a long, shaking breath.

Immediately, he wished he had not. Now he smelled her, also. The cloying, stifling odor of rose sachet, filth and decay emanated from her.

"May I sit?" she asked.

"Of course. I mean, this is your home, not mine." He stepped aside and motioned toward the sofa. She chose the big, overstuffed reading chair instead.

"You sit," she said, smiling as well as she could. "I'm not going to hurt you, so don't be so antsy. I've watched you sleep, so if I wanted to harm you, I would have drained you the first night you slept here."

Hesitantly, Michael sat back down on the sofa, but he did not relinquish his grip on the gun just yet.

"The woman, Susan, told you to go," she said again. "You don't belong."

"I'll leave—I didn't know someone still lived—"

She waved him off. "No one does, Michael. Besides, I mean in you don't belong in Dunwich, not in this house."

"Susan doesn't belong, either," Michael said.

"Is Susan still human?" She leveled her gaze at him. "Or is she like I am?"

This last statement threw him. Like her? Could Susan ever become like this creature? He wanted to ask her why she looked as she did. Was she tortured? Maybe Kasper had gotten to her at some point. "She has . . . changed."

"We call it transforming. Do you know who brought it on her?"

Michael nodded. He felt strange saying it, after reading Sandra's journal, but after a pause, he said, "His name is Devin."

"I see," she replied. "Must get around, that one."

Michael smiled, uneasy, but slowly warming up to this odd woman. "I suppose."

"Would you be uncomfortable if I straightened the house a bit?"

"No. I probably should go, anyway. Been thinking about returning home. Maybe it would be best to leave Susan at this—whatever it is."

Sandra stood. "No. Don't go. I just try to tidy up from time to time. Makes me feel like I did when I was alive. When Joey and Jenna were alive. Stay. Stay and talk to me."

She moved to the open kitchen and removed a towel from the handle of the oven. She then began to wipe at the counter, the heavy darkness of the area seemingly unnoticed. Michael got another beer and tended the fire. He tossed the remains of the chair he had broken onto the flames. "Sorry about the chair."

"It doesn't matter. Nobody likes to be cold."

Michael found her easier to talk with once her face had faded back into the shadow. From where he sat, only her silhouette was visible. She scrubbed hard at the range, her back to him.

"Would you like a beer?" he asked.

"Never was a big drinker," she told him. Then realizing what she had said, she laughed, watery and nearly choking.

As dawn spread its running orange paint across the purple sky, Sandra Harp left her home to sleep the day away in the cluttered and pitch dark garage belonging to a neighbor she had never liked in life. She confessed this in a not-so-subtle trade-off—you leave me alone and I'll do the same.

Michael added the spindly wooden legs of a bar stool to the fire, at Sandra's urging. "I never like the things, anyway. Joey fell off one and split his chin. Burn them all."

Sleep found him quickly, but it was as thin as gossamer and riddled with nightmares.

In the most vivid of the bunch, Susan trailed a cool finger around his ear, that little trick she used on him time and again because she knew it drove him crazy. She then drew her naughty fingers across his lips and he kissed the tip of each one.

Next, she worked her way lower, through the coarse hairs of his chest. She scratched one nipple sharply with her nail, and then followed it with an incredibly tantalizing nip with her sharp little fangs. He grew hard. But then her sweet touches became rougher, feverish . . . *twitching*. A putrid odor filled his nostrils.

Inside his dreamworld, Michael opened his eyes.

Standing above him, her face just visible in the moon's flat silvery glow was Sandra Harp, except the ruined half of her face was alive—writhing with maggots. They slipped into her gaping jaw, between the broken tombstones of her teeth, up into the wide space where her nose used to be. She bent and brought her rotting, torn lips to his.

A fat, slow-moving roach fell from her hair and onto the pillow beside Michael's head. Her dry and wrinkled hand fell to the front of his pants.

He woke screaming Susan's name.

A rat, roughly the size of a puppy crawled lumpish and awkward across his groin. It paused at the top of one trembling thigh, turned and threw him a disapproving stare, daring him to swat it away.

With a disgusted groan, Michael reached for his gun, but the flabby creature had already faded down the hallway, into the darkness.

His heart thudded like a flat tire and he wanted so much to just go home.

But he could not go alone.

He had seen Susan and she was alive. Still, in just the hours since, her image had taken on the fuzzy quality of a dream itself.

Through the salt crusted slider that faced the Atlantic, the sky gave him the vague indication that the sun would be up soon and very bright, almost like spring. No matter how terrible the dreams became, he could count on sunrise putting an end to the night. Sunrise used to work for the dreams, as well, but that was all over now. Nightmares had become a constant thing and did not end just because the night faded to light.

He lay awake, staring upward, at the ceiling growing lighter by the moment. He would not sleep again anytime soon. He lit one of Sandra's fat white candles, but the vanilla scent had long faded. He then found the journal from beneath the cushions of the sofa where he had shoved it when he realized Sandra had visited. He did not want her to see he had read her diary, but she probably already knew.

He read and reread it until he dozed in the safety of the sunlit morning.

chapter forty

"**D**o you know why I look this way?"

Michael prodded the fire and nodded his head. Of course, he only had his suspicions, and what he had imagined was far-fetched, even when he compared it to all he had already seen in Dunwich. He did not look at her. Even after four nights of her visits, her appearance chilled him. A woman missing half her face was not an easy thing to grow used to.

"I suppose it's obvious," she said.

"Does it," he hesitated, searching for a tactful way of putting things, "hinder your feeding?"

Sandra sipped the cheap wine he had purchased earlier from the dank all-night supermarket—the only one that stayed open after dark.

"Sometimes I have to do things . . . things that no person—no *mother—should have to do.*"

Michael could not stop thinking of Susan. Did she hate the thing she had become? At times, she appeared as emotionless as a machine. He remembered Philip, one of Susan's colleagues at the police department, referring to her as the "Terminator," one day early in their relationship when he had come to meet her for lunch.

"So, you're taking out the Terminator?" he had asked.

Taken aback, Michael asked, "Pardon?"

"The Terminator. You know—that amazing lack of feeling. Surely, you're not expecting to have a good time."

It had pissed Michael off, but he only shrugged good-naturedly and replied, "I hope we do."

Philip slapped him heartily on the back. "Good luck, man."

There was certainly a darkness in her—he had felt that on their first date. It was nothing directed toward him, but it was there. A part of her, just like her blue eyes or her dead brother. To love her was to love everything about her—the good and the bad. And he had done just that.

To have given so much did not leave the option of letting her go without a fight.

He came back to the present and Sandra was still describing the horrors of the hunt and the despair that came with the thirst for blood. It sounded like an addict recounting the sick craving for drugs and that wicked hold that it had over them.

"So many times I tried to end this," she told him, her poor mouth malformed and gnarled with scar tissue. Wet voice like a drowning woman. Michael had found himself, more than once, hearing that hideous voice in that fugue of consciousness as sleep was just taking over. He always woke startled and unable to fall back to sleep.

"Did you know that it is impossible for those like me to die, Michael? We're doomed to this world, no matter what." The wine had made her sound melodramatic. "Demons. Or maybe ghosts with unfinished business that still resides in a physical form."

Perhaps the wine had affected him just as oddly, but before he realized what he was telling her, Michael said, "I know how you die."

Sandra placed her glass on the coffee table and raised her eyes to his. The firelight touched the ruined side of her face and created deep, harsh shadows in the craters of her skull.

"You know how we can die?"

Michael shifted his gazed. He saw where this was leading and attempted to divert her attention from him. "What about sunlight, Sandra?"

"It doesn't work. At least now quickly enough. It's agonizing. Plus, it is not foolproof. Sometimes it takes so long, the sun sets and you're still living, left to heal overnight. You're left in pain. It's like burning. No vampire wants to be burned. It's a true living hell, and I've seen it. I've seen it—at the hands of some madman on the boulevard. He strung a boy Deathwalker up on the tombstone sign outside the haunted mansion—that old tourist trap—and doused him in gasoline. Then he lit him on fire. Left him there for days. No one would help the poor thing. The flesh burned away to the bone, black as a chicken left on the grill too long.

"The sun cooked him even more, and in the cool of the night, he would heal. But just enough to continue living. He stared. How he stared—his eyelids had melted away. He screamed all the time. For nearly a week, these hoarse and whispery screams, because he no longer had much of a throat and his tongue was molded to his lips.

"Children hit him and yelled for him to be quiet. The adults ridiculed him, but nobody came to help him.

"And then one night, I realized the screaming had stopped. When I got to that corner, the boy was gone."

She stopped and looked at Michael.

"If you know what it takes to stop this, you need to tell me," she whispered. *"Michael."*

"You *know*," Michael answered. "Nothing can go on without brain function. The head needs to be removed."

Sandra collapsed back into her chair. "Yeah, that. Of course." She laughed, soft and weak, like a balloon losing air. "You must realize—removing one's own head can be a tricky proposition."

"I can imagine," Michael agreed.

"At first I thought a gunshot would be enough. The pain—it was as if my brain had caught fire. I could not see, could not move. Inside this very house. But I came back. Slowly. I remember touching the side of my head and realized that part of it was missing. I felt for sure I would die from it, but no. No such luck—I never had much luck, anyway—one time I won a contest at a Tuperware party and got a free snack bowl. Anyway. . . "

Michael did not know what to say. How the hell do you respond to that? *Sorry your suicide attempt didn't work out. Maybe I can help out next time. At least you won a Tupperware bowl.*

Like she had read his mind, she said, "Help me, Michael. You know what to do."

Michael stood and moved over toward the fire. Still, he felt chilled to the bone and his stomach hurt. "Sandra . . ."

"You know what to do."

"Listen to me. I've never killed anyone. Even as a physician—I've never helped anyone die."

"I'm already dead, Michael."

He took a deep breath. "Sandra . . . " he whispered. But when he turned and caught her hideous face in the orange firelight, he knew he would do whatever she asked him to.

chapter forty-one

Against Devin's better judgment, they left the house to feed. It had been nearly a week since they had last gone out. Their last kill had been the would-be child molester at the high-rise hotel. Since then, word was out that two more Deathwalkers had been killed—one burned alive and left. Devin was positive it was the work of Jacobsen. Because of that, he and Susan had been relegated to feed on each other. Neither of them was completely satiated, but it was enough to keep them going and somewhat clear-minded.

Susan needed an excuse to break away from Devin's and John's watchful eyes and go to the address Michael had scribbled on the torn receipt back at the New Dunwich Inn weeks ago. She plucked Kasper Jacobsen's name from his thoughts. He knew something. She could not entertain the thoughts of creeping around, scared like some kind of pathetic animals on the count of some lunatic.

Repeatedly, she felt in her coat for the little slip of paper although she knew it was no longer there. Had she dropped it, or had Devin or John discovered it? If it had been John, she would have picked up that stray little thought. Although it was an unsaid rule that John's mind was off-limits, she still pried into his head from time to time.

No matter. She had memorized the street. If Michael was around, she could pick up his brain waves just as easily as she could John's.

They moved along the litter-strewn streets of Dunwich, their feet never really touching the pavement, only grazing it, soundlessly as cats. The night was clear, which was a nice change—Susan had become accustomed to the perpetual drizzle of the shore. There was a tavern—the one where they had found the john and his tiny prostitute before. A band played for some time, old New Wave songs and the only one Susan recognized was the one by Blondie. The tempo of "Dreaming" was obscenely slow-paced and the male singer had a much higher voice than Debbie Harry.

She knew what Devin was up to—paranoid creature he had become—he anticipated making her too drunk to hunt and then he would take her back home where they would exchange enough blood to live yet another night.

"Come on, Devin," she whispered, squeeze his arm. "I need to feed."

"Let's have another round first, all right?" He motioned to a waitress who looked like a strung-out porno star and smelled like two dollar perfume that made Susan's nose itch. Shortly, she sat two more glasses of horrid red wine in front of them. Susan's sloshed over the rim of her glass and the waitress fished a wrinkled paper napkin from her sagging apron and tossed it on Susan's lap.

"Sorry," she muttered.

"I'm sure." Susan picked up the edge of the paper and placed it carefully on the other side of the table. Then she turned to Devin again.

"You made me like this, you know. Now, you need to live with it."

He sighed, threw a wad of bills on the table and led her by the arm through the crowd. She could tell by his walk he had made him angry. She did not care.

Outside, Devin pushed her back into the doorway of a shutdown donut store, out of what little red and blue neon light and sick yellow streetlamp glow that threatened to touch them and give their whereabouts away to someone with a big gun.

"I don't see why you want to do this. You know how dangerous it is, with Kasper out here." He glowered at her. "This not a game, Susan. It is about survival."

She grabbed the front of his coat and yanked him hard to her. She kissed him long, her tongue probing into his mouth, tasting him. He pressed himself against her and pinned her against the wall. She loved the hot crush of his body on hers and bit his lip, drawing a drop of blood. She then licked it away slowly.

"Shhh. It's better than draining each other night after night."

"I can't let you . . ."

She kissed him again and he smiled slowly.

"I always share," Devin protested. "Besides, I don't enjoy the thought of you with another man."

"How do you know I even prefer men? Women are easier to catch."

"Are they, now?" He laughed. "That's sort of hot. How about I follow. Just to watch?"

Susan shook her head. "I need to learn. You said so."

"Tonight is not a good time."

"No," she said. "I know what I'm doing, Devin." It occurred to her to simply tell him the truth, but she could not determine how much danger that might place Michael in.

Devin drew back slowly. "Alright. Okay, go. But meet me at the pier before light."

"I'll be there." She started away and then looked back. "And don't try to follow."

"Of course not."

"I can see it in your face, Devin," she said.

"Okay. Okay! Here, I'm going back inside, to listen to that shitty band and drink more of that shitty wine.

Instinct is to help when a human hears the cry of a child. That had not changed very much for Susan since the transformation, so when she thought she heard the sob of a young boy, she had to search it out. Devin had disappeared back into the tavern, but she wondered if she should get him before following the sound.

She spotted the source of the weeping quickly. A pretty little thing, a boy child of nine or ten years of age. Down the boulevard, he wove between a bum on one side and an aged hooker on the other. He glanced over his shoulder toward Susan, tears on his face shining like wet silver. Blond—summertime hair and he wore jeans and a t-shirt without sleeves in the cold. No shoes. He would freeze before morning if he remained outside.

Susan followed, zigzagging between the bum, the hooker and several other unsavory-looking characters and wondering who exactly smelled the worst.

"Wait," she called. She would give the child her coat, she might even bring him home for food and a warm night's stay. Neither she nor Devin would feed from a child.

Maybe she was growing a conscience, as Devin put it. Whatever—she had always had a place in her heart for children. The image of the Grinch and the old holiday cartoon popped into her head—his heart growing until the little frame around it burst.

The child rounded the corner of a boarded-up arcade, the front nothing by dense, heavy darkness. His feet slapped the uneven sidewalk and Susan closed in. Nearby, the jangle of calliope music rang out loudly, but out of tune.

The boy turned back to her once more, eyes wide and wet, and then slipped between two high rise hotels.

"Wait, kid," she called again.

She was close enough to snatch the back of his shirt, and

she had him. He was a fast kid—as fast as a Deathwalker—but it was too late to reason that now.

"Why are you—" Her words died on her lips when he turned to her again.

Teeth bared, she saw that face, that wild look in his eye.

He smiled at her, small, milk-white fangs protruded from his top jaw. A thin line of bloody drool unwound from his plump, cherry-red bottom lip.

"Oh, hell," Susan muttered, his stomach falling.

She turned, too slow. The butt of a rifle connected with her temple and she was out.

chapter forty-two

She woke to see the little boy's face hovering before her. He smiled, beautiful and terrible, revealing his baby-white teeth.

He ran to a tall man. "She's waking up. Look," he said, tugging on edge of the man's shirt.

Susan ached all over. There was a stereo playing somewhere--Charlie Mingus, she thought, but she wasn't sure. Unable to move her neck, she felt as stiff as a case of whiplash. Her lips stung and jaws and teeth hurt where a leather strap gagged her, tearing sharply at the corners of her mouth. A chain bound her wrists, pulled high up above her head. Her toes barely brushed the concrete floor.

Some kind of strange warehouse, it seemed. Massive with a high, arching metal roof and tall windows, all covered with layers of tin foil, applied so carefully no light from the outside could penetrate. All sorts of oddities that seemed to be cast-offs from the beach's tacky tourist trap heyday cluttered the place—carnival horses, Technicolor monsters covered in a blanket of dust from the house of horrors, props and displays that evidentially came from the wax museum. George Washington still stood in command aboard the little wooden boat, but the Potomac had become a trash-strewn floor. Blackbeard stood in another corner, devilish and wild with a cutlass in one fist and a disembodied head in the other. There was what first appeared to be an upright coffin with a black lacquer finish and a silver pentagram painted on the front, but she quickly realized it was some kind of magician's box.

It smelled of dried blood, decay and stale popcorn—an extremely foul combination.

Through the clearing fog, she tried to recall what had happened. How did she end up there?

"You're awake. Finally."

A heavy German accent. A tremor of fear raced up her spine. Kasper Jacobsen, the so-called vampire killer. She struggled against her restraints, as his steps grew closer.

She tasted blood on the back of her tongue. Kasper moved in front of her and now she could finally see him. Big, broad-shouldered, powerful. He wore a tight black t-shirt that showed off the muscles of his chest. He could have been intimidating if she were the same woman she was a month ago. Amazingly, she smelled fear on *him.*

She smiled behind the rough leather strap.

"Michael was certainly right about you," he said. He eyed her up and down as if she were some sort of prize, and then disappeared behind her. *How did Michael know this animal?* Susan twisted around, not wanting to let him out of her sight, but he grabbed a handful of her long hair and held her steady.

Kasper's hot breath tickled the back of her neck making her shiver. He reached around her, slipped his warm hand under her shirt and rested it on her stomach and nuzzled the side of her neck with his mouth, the stubble on his chin scratching wickedly. Susan struggled, but the binds held her tightly. She took the opportunity to look up at the chain that held her so tightly in place. The cuffs at her wrists were thrown over a big, industrial-sized hook. It was not impossible to escape, if she could only get up high enough to slip the chain free. If she had been feeding properly, she might have been able to leap that high. Malnutrition had made her physicality almost…mortal.

Kasper pulled her closer to him; she could feel the heat radiating from him in waves. The little boy took a seat on the back of one of the carnival horses, a winged Pegasus, but the tips of the wings were sadly chipped away. He watched intently, but said nothing.

"Now, I am going to remove the gag," Kasper told her, "provided that you will not try and bite me."

He untied the leather belt and pulled the gag away— sweet relief. She flicked out her tongue and licked away the blood that was drying at the corners of her mouth. He moved back in front of her and touched her bruised lips with his fingers, a surprisingly gentle gesture.

"I'm sorry," he whispered. "You don't deserve this. Michael didn't deserve this. That kid. None of us deserves this shit."

He moved to the black magician's box and flipped a latch on the side The narrow door opened slowly and revealed a horrified woman inside. She blinked at the sudden light and then apprehensively stepped out.

In the stark and shadowy warehouse lighting, Susan saw that the woman was thin and hard—and obviously a prostitute. Nobody would miss her. She might have been pretty under other, better circumstances. As it was, life had worn her down and worn her out. She wore her long, brittle hair piled up high on the top of her head. It was dyed the color of blood and maybe that was what caught Kasper's attention in the first place. Her make-up was too heavy; eyeliner had settled into the fine lines around her eyes, making her appear even more tired than she probably was and her lipstick looked a hell of a lot like a brownish oil slick.

Her leopard-print tights had holes. Her shirt was too low-cut for the weather.

"She's gonna be extra," she told Kasper, throwing a quick glance to Susan. Her accent was mountain flat.

Kasper smiled as shy as a child. Susan knew that trick; she and Devin had used that many times, themselves. "No. No—she just wants to watch."

"Oh? Then What about the boy?"

"I don't think so."

The whore grabbed the front of Kasper's shirt. "Just need 'im to learn something, then?"

"You said you'd pay me for getting her to follow," the boy said. He hopped off the horse's back and moved to Kasper. He tugged at the big man's shirt again. "You said you'd let me feed—"

Kasper shoved the boy back, sending to the floor on his skinny ass. "Behave, little thing, or you'll pay sooner than later."

The whore watched this, eyes wide, but she only said, "Okay. What'cha want?"

Because of the chains, Susan could not avoid seeing what was happening. She felt dirty and wrong and exhilarated all at the same time. A notion wriggled inside the depths of her mind like fingers picking a scab—what was she doing? What horrible thing had she become? Again, the answer came—*I was never normal in the first place.*

They were animals, the woman and Kasper and their movements were rough, callous and wild. It was purely a physical act, by two beings who appeared to loathe each another. The woman kneeled between Kasper and a brigade of paint-peeled carousel horses. Kasper slipped into her mouth and she took his entire length effortlessly, expertly. He pushed against her, easily at first. From the boulevard, music rose—the Stones—mingled with the jazz and created some weird mélange of sounds. He sang along softly and very out of tune.

Susan's eyes were riveted to his movements, his lean buttocks and how his thrusts quickened. The muscles flexed. He lost the rhythm of the song. All around them, the stench of wet garbage hung low like a noxious cloud. The whore's breathing became labored.

Susan glanced to the boy, who was now back in his seat on the horse. His eyes huge, his hand moving quickly inside his tattered jeans, his sharp little fangs protruding over his rosy bottom lip.

Kasper slammed harder into the woman, his hands gripping huge snatches of her hair, pulling it down and ruining it. Then there was a dull THUD as her head smashed against the side of one of the horses, upending it. It tumbled and the others followed like a group of multicolored dominoes. He pulled her toward him against, and she gagged loudly. Susan no longer wanted to see this, but she could not stop herself. Kasper shoved the whore's head back, still grasping her hair, nearly flinging her away from him.

Finally, one hand in her hair, the other behind her head, he pulled her against him once more and held her fast. She was choking, struggling, but she was going nowhere until Kasper decided.

Kasper grunted as he came into her mouth. When he was finished, he shoved the woman backward and sent her tumbling onto her bottom and then back onto the horses. He then glanced back at Susan and zipped up.

The woman struggled to sit up, dazed and blinking slowly, stupidly. She touched her bleeding mouth— Kasper's zipper had slashed her bottom lip. She ran her tongue out and licked a drop of blood away. Kasper stepped closer to her. "Come," he said, putting out his hand. "I didn't mean to hurt you."

The whore—Susan never knew her name—cowered and tried scramble away on her ass, but the carousel horses blocked her movements. "Get away, you animal. You *monster."*

Susan found her voice, but it was not because she felt for the woman. Kasper and his oafish ways disgusted her.

"Get away from her, you self-righteous prick!"

He turned to Susan, his eyebrows raised. Smirking, he stalked toward her, his fists clenched. "You think I asked for this?"

"Did any of us ask for it?" Susan countered.

He wanted to hit her; Susan could read it in his eyes and she braced herself for it. Instead, he turned his attentions back to the whore.

"You. Do vampires frighten you?" he asked the woman.

"Y-yes."

He snatched her up by her hair and she screamed. "Why the fuck are you here, then?" he cried.

"I didn't know. At first, I-I didn't know you were one. I couldn't tell."

He pulled her face to his. "Can you tell, now?"

She shrieked and he loosened his hold on her hair. "Shhh." He traced his finger around her lips, rubbing away the thickening blood there. "Shhh," he told her again, his voice instantly soft, his gestures transformed into those of a lover again. "Be a nice girl and I'll let you leave."

She kissed the tips of his fingers, licked her own blood away from them. Slowly, he slipped his index finger across her lips, past her teeth, then the middle fingers.

"That's the way," he cooed.

Susan could no longer see—Kasper's wide back blocked her view. Suddenly, there was a hideous wet, ripping noise, followed by a loud snap—the sound of bony joints becoming dislocated.

No scream this time, only an odd, nightmarish gurgling. Susan squeezed her eyes shut and buried her head against her arm.

When she looked again, Kasper was coming toward her. In one hand, he held the prostitute's head, unhinged from her lower jaw and body. Her eyes blinked once, twice, before staring as blank as those of a doll.

"Look, you bitch. Look and see what's coming." With the other hand, he took Susan's face in his fingers, squeezing her cheeks until she tasted blood and tears ran from the corners of her eyes.

Impulsively Susan tried to back away, but her tethers held fast. The cuffs bit into her wrists and blood began to run up her arms, warm, sticky.

Kasper thrust the bleeding edges of the whore's torn jaw at Susan, pushed it against her mouth as she struggled to turn away. She had seen so many horrors, but nothing compared to this. She felt her stomach contract and loosen. She wretched, dry, painful.

The blood touched her mouth and for the first time since her transformation, she found it repulsive—the scent was sickening, the metallic taste horrid. She spat into Kasper's face and he wiped it away with a wicked smile.

"Fucking hypocrite," she said, snarling.

"Fucking bitch," Kasper replied casually. Then he held the head above his upturned face and allowed the slow stream of blood to flow into his waiting mouth.

chapter forty-three

The old man emerged from the shadowy hallway just as Michael entered the house.

"I had hoped she would be here with you," he said. "Then, at least I would know she's safe."

Michael jumped and instinctively raised the gun. "What do you want? How did you—"

The man held up the slip of paper with the house number scrawled on it in Michael's handwriting. "I didn't come here to hurt you, Michael," he said. "I'm John, by the way."

When he moved out of the darkness, Michael could see him better—the look of worry, of sleeplessness on his face. He was weary and finally seeing the man up close, Michael realized he was no monster, only an man. He lowered the gun and tossed it to the sofa, but he could not ease the tension the man's presence created.

"She hasn't been here," Michael told him. "I assumed she must have changed her mind." He moved away from the bigger man. "Or else, was detained."

"I wouldn't hold her captive, if that's what you're indicating."

"She came to Dunwich of own free will, then?" Michael asked.

"You must realize, Michael, she was never happy with you." John smiled. "Only tolerant."

John's eyes drilled into his and he looked away. "You know Kasper Jacobsen. Do you have any idea where he might be keeping her?"

"No." Michael sank down onto the sofa and pressed his face into his hands. "You think Kasper has her?"

"She's not with Devin. She's not here. Things don't look very promising, do they?" John said, his tone softening as if he was searching for some reassurance.

"No. No! She must have found a way to escape. Must have. She's way sharper than you could imagine. Jacobsen is an ass."

"He is that," the man agreed. He walked around the room slowly, his eyes not leaving Michael. "Look at you. You're over your head here. You're shell shocked; I've seen that look before. I ought to kill you for this, this stupidity of thinking she would even want you again after the change."

Michael shook his head, suddenly furious. He started to say something—probably something pointless and stupid, but it did not matter. The older man rushed at him. He grabbed the back of Michael's shirt and yanked him off his feet. In an unexpected ferocity, John drove him backward against the brick hearth. Michael's head thudded hard, sending stars dancing before his eyes.

"I ought to drag you out onto the streets and let *them* take care of you in any manner they see fit."

The man was amazingly strong for his age. He wrapped his long fingers around Michael's throat and squeezed, cutting off Michael's breathing.

"It wouldn't be pretty, Michael."

He slammed Michael back against the bricks once more and then let him go. Michael doubled over, hands braced on his knees, gasping for sweet air, as John backed away.

"You listen to me, Michael. I'm only letting you go because you love her and maybe you can help find her. So, get to work."

Susan was not aware of how much time had passed. There was no way of determining if it was day or night, because the windows were blacked out. The boy had gotten his payment and had feed on the hooker's leftovers. Enthusiastically, he had gone at the heavy breasts and had torn away the rosy nipples from the graying, cooling body. He drank until he sank to the floor beside the decapitated corpse and slept like an infant, curled into a small ball.

Kasper stalked around like an angry cat, fists clenching and unclenching. He stood in front of Susan for a moment and whispered, "Do you think he will come for you?"

"Is that what you really want, Kasper?"

"Yes."

"Then you want to die."

Kasper laughed. "Perhaps."

Sometime later, an explosion startled Susan from a paper-thin doze. She screamed, hated herself immediately for being so weak, and jerked her head around to find Kasper holding the stubbed shotgun.

The boy lay on the floor, but something was not right with him. At the angle in which he lay, she could no longer see his pretty head.

Could no longer . . .

Sickness, despair overwhelmed her and if she were not bound, she might have collapsed.

"What have you done, Kasper?" Her voice sounded as if the wind had been kicked out of her.

"Only what I am supposed to do, Susan."

"He was a child," she whispered.

Kasper stepped around the sprawled body, treading through the expanding pool of blood, leaving red boot-shaped stamps on the concrete. Above his head, a naked lightbulb swung back and forth lazily, thick blood splatters cooking on the hot glass, reeking like spoiled meat.

"What gives you the right to do these things?" Susan asked.

Kasper frowned deeply. "What gives *you* the right? You're no better, you know."

Susan sighed and rocked her head from side to side. Her neck and shoulders were felt as though molten lead had been injected into her muscles. She glanced up at the chain binding her wrists. If she only had a way to get her higher, closer to that fucking hook.

"Devin and I are better. What we do is rid the world of the dregs. The scum that have no business living, anyway." Then smiling, she added, "Like you."

Kasper closed in and raised the gun and pressed the barrel against her cheek. It sizzled against her skin, still hot from the shot and she drew back, her teeth gritted. The odor of charred skin filled her nostrils.

"So, you're doing God's work." He pulled the gun back slightly and Susan sighed, relieved. "Just as you said, we are only doing what we are supposed to do."

"So am I, sweetheart. Death should not mean new life as some kind of fucking *animal*. You—we--are abominations. God never meant—"

"Enough!" Susan cried. "Don't lay a load of religion on me. I don't need to hear it."

"No?"

And without warning, Kasper raised the gun and he shot her.

chapter forty-four

"**D**on't cry, tough girl," Kasper whispered, hot against Susan's ear.   Slowly, consciousness returned, unwelcomed. Her feverish eyes were swollen with tears and a searing agony had settled like an illness in the muscled curve of her waist.

Still suspended from the ceiling, her hands remained bound tightly above her head.

"You bastard," she croaked.

"Yes?" He grinned and she noticed blood rimming his mouth. Hers?

"How long was I out?"

"Long enough." He made a show of dabbing at the corner of his lips with a thumb and winked at her.

"What the hell is wrong with you?" she asked.   She wanted to throw up. She smelled her own blood, heavy, gamey. It coated her legs, cooling and as sticky as syrup. Glancing down at the ragged, gaping hole in her side, her knees buckled from the horror of it. She would have collapsed had she not been chained. Her mind play a stupid game of time with her—was this now or was it a dream? The heat of the Sunday morning outside a little white church in Reading flashed through her mind.

Kasper had removed her clothing and she wore nothing

now but her panties and bra. Her arms and legs puckered into gooseflesh and her teeth chattered, from pain and cold.

"It's not like I *killed* you, Susan. Your beloved Devin has already done that. Of course, I could have finished you off. One shot and it could have all been over." Kasper touched her hair. "But not yet. Your little head is much too pretty to vaporize. I can see why Devin chose you."

He pressed his hard body to hers and instead of pulling away, Susan flexed her ass against his groin. Kasper was aroused and although it disgusted her, it was probably a good thing. It bought her more time. Time to heal, to regain her composure. Plus, it meant she had at least some control over him. As long as he was attracted to her, he would be easier to distract.

Their eyes met a for a long moment and she saw that he was more haunted than hate filled. What had he gone through, to make him the vile creature he was?

"You're not going to bite me, are you?" he asked. His voice became hoarse.

"Don't flatter yourself," she answered.

"I know you would like to feed. To heal."

"I'd rather die."

"Don't worry. You will. Eventually. When I am finished with you."

Kasper reached up and traced the back of her arm with his fingertips, sending a shiver through her. Susan swallowed and clenched her jaw against the agony in her side.

She smelled his sweat and his blood rushing beneath his skin. No matter what she told him, how she would love to taste it. How she would love to suck mouthful upon mouthful down her throat and feel that wondrous mending begin to take place. If she could feed, the bleeding would slow. The pain would dull. Her mind would sharpen.

Susan craned her neck, turning her face upward to his. "I'll do what you want, Kasper. Just don't hurt me again."

Now he seemed taken off guard. He dropped his eyes from hers and she kissed him softly. He opened his mouth slightly, his tongue moving to meet hers. He slipped his arms around her and held her to him, giving the ache that had set into her arms a reprieve, but sending new waves of pain through her middle. He dipped his fingers into the yawning gunshot wound and she groaned into his mouth.

Kasper's breathing quickened. This was working. Susan leaned closer again, wanting to remain in constant contact with his body.

He was putty in her hands now. She would find an opening and escape soon enough.

Then he abruptly drew back, smiling. "I'm calling your bluff, sweetheart."

He fumbled his fly open and removed his enflamed cock from his trousers. She got a glimpse of the white flesh of his lower belly, of the raised scar there—the black sun. The same mark Devin bared.

Kasper yanked her bra from her body, breaking the straps free and tossing it aside. Next, he ripped away her lace panties. She writhed on the end of her chain, but he only wrapped his arms around her and held her against him.

"Monster," he whispered.

"Do I look like a monster, Kasper?"

"I've heard that line of shit before," he growled. He shoved his leg between hers and forced her thighs apart. "We're both monsters." He then grabbed her hips in his big hands and moved her onto him. Susan gasped as he slammed deeper inside her. She felt impaled, as though she was being torn apart from the inside out; she was not ready for him and his cock felt as if it were made of sandpaper. She bit her bottom lip to keep from crying out.

She watched Kasper's face, lost in the swirl of sex, his eyes nearly closed, his stubbly jaw clenching and then loosening, his hard mouth becoming softer. After a moment, the movement became easier. She had started to bleed.

Kasper's movements were fast and brutal, his hands digging into the soft muscles of her ass, her hips, into the hole in her side. Susan closed her eyes and forced her mind away from there. There were moments when death was better. What kind of curse was this, this never-ending life?

Shortly, his thrusts slowed and with a low groan, he came. He clung tightly to her as he breathing settled, then opened his eyes and looked at her for a long moment. Her gaze drilled into his and he lowered his eyes first, as if he were suddenly ashamed. Turning away from her, he closed up his pants.

"Maybe I'll keep you around for a while," he whispered, more to himself.

"Don't do me any favors. You shit," Susan said.

Grinning, she took a stepped backward as far has her shackles would allow. Then in one incredibly smooth motion, she flipped her legs upward and hooked them tight around Kasper's neck. Kasper gasped, taken completely by surprise. His fingers dug into his ass, into the back of her thighs. She hooked one leg over the other and squeezed, her crotch pressing against his face. She gritted her teeth, wishing at once she had the strength to snap his neck.

Kasper dropped to one knee. "This really doesn't bother me," he remarked, his sarcasm muffled against the cushion of her crotch. The blood and semen mixture that leaked from her smeared his face.

She looked up, waiting for the right moment. Kasper struggled back to his feet, his fingers grabbing at her arms, at her hair and anything else he could get his hands on. Almost. She shifted her legs, making him stumble to the left. The chain moved up higher on the tip of the meat hook. She stretched up, as far as she could reach, tearing the wound in her side open even wider, sending a new gout of blood down over her hip, onto the side of Kasper's face. The pain was sublime and she nearly fainted, but in the next moment, she was free.

Clasping both fists together, she brought down hard on the bridge of Kasper's nose, at the same time releasing her leglock on his head. She rolled headlong to the floor, as Kasper fell backward on his ass. He scrambled after her on his knees, blood pouring from his nose. He wiped at it with his sleeve, but it continued to flow, over his chin and down the front of his shirt.

Despite the pain and the hunger, Susan was quick, --it was something new in her that she loved completely. She had always been athletic and light on her feet, but this was incredible. Like a cat, she was on her feet and standing over Kasper. She landed a snapping succession of sharp kicks to his ribs. But Kasper was still quicker. He grabbed her leg and snatched her other foot from under her. The back of her head struck the floor hard and consciousness drifted away for a breath.

He yanked her to him, his breaths coming in wet, shallow gasps. "Fucking bitch! I didn't want to hurt you like this. I was going to keep you around long enough for you to say goodbye to Michael."

He collapsed on top of her. He began to swing his fists furiously and somehow she instinctively blocked each punch he threw. A dozen times, right, left, right, her wrists up and deflecting his big fists.

"Fuck!" he screamed, frustrated. Barely able to breathe through his broken nose, he sprayed her face with his blood. She ran her tongue out, tasting the saltiness of it. She laughed out loud.

This infuriated him even more. He grabbed her by the throat and lifted her up and then slammed her back onto the concrete in a football-style takedown. Stars reappeared before her eyes—she was beginning to become quite familiar with them now—a half dozen smeary white lights dancing before her face. New wetness now on the back of her head, tickling the back of her neck like warm, silky fingertips.

"Fuck yourself," she offered, drowzily.

He took a handful of her hair and in return, she reached up, hands still bound together, and gripped his. But his hold was a lot better and he jerked her head to one side. The tendons screamed and she bit her lip from the sudden agony. Pain exploded and traveled upward into the base of her skull, downward the length of her spine. He pulled again, driving her head all the way down, her right ear brushing her right shoulder. A dull, but audible snap and Susan blacked out, more from the shock of the injury than from the pain. Was her neck broken, perhaps? She felt like a drowning woman, trying to find her way back to the surface of awareness. Was this something from which she could recover? Or would she be stuck, immobile, as he finished her off?

However, no more than a moment passed before she regained some awareness. Still unable to move, she remained pinned beneath Kasper. He punched her again. Blood flooded her mouth. She spit it up into his face.

He punched her in the side and bolts of agony quaked through her body like currents of electricity. She lay motionless, unable to take in a breath.

Kasper sat back on his knees, gasping. Finally, he climbed to his feet and then moved out of her sight for a moment. When he reappeared, he was carrying the shortened shotgun. He grinned down at her, his teeth stained red, and prodded her hip with the toe of his shoe. He gave sent a sharp, vicious kick to her wounded side.

Susan found her breath, but she remained dangerously close to passing out again. She rolled onto her side and curled up, making herself as small as possible, hoping to protect her torn side. She wept loudly, as much as she wanted to hold it in. She did not want Kasper Jacobsen to know he was winning. But he *was* winning. He kneeled down, sat the gun aside and snatched her up by her hair. She stood, her legs trembling, her neck screaming, her body in agony.

He touched her lips with the pads of his fingers. Then he pulled her face to his and kissed her deeply, his tongue searching her mouth, greedy for the hot blood there.

When he pulled back, she drove her forehead into his face.

Kasper staggered backward, fresh blood streaming from his nose and busted lips. He shook his head and then laughed.

"You won't stop, will you?"

She fell to one knee, her weakened legs refusing to work just right. "Not until you kill me."

"It won't be long," Kasper said. He grabbed her hair again and slung her across the floor. He then snatched up the gun and stalked after her.

"You put up a good fight, didn't you?" he whispered.

With a cry, Susan rolled over and stared up at Kasper as he cocked the gun and leveled it at her head. She watched his finger dance on the trigger, allowing nothing to register on her face.

"There's no getting out this time."

Just as she saw his finger move, she kicked both feet straight up and out. Both heels connected with Kasper's groin. The gun discharged like an explosion and Susan moved just enough to miss having her head blown away. Buckshot and bits of concrete tore at her cheek and shoulder.

Kasper fell to his knees and the gun clanked to the floor. At the same time, Susan managed back to her knees, and then her feet. She wobbled on her heels a moment, fighting to stay awake.

She scrambled after the gun, but Kasper wrapped his fist around the barrel just before Susan could get it. He kneeled at her feet, holding his hurting crotch. He turned his face up to hers, grinned and cocked the gun again.

Just as Kasper raised the barrel, Susan drove her heel into

his temple and sent him reeling backward. She fled toward the door without looking back, treading through the sticky mess of the little boy's leftovers—brain matter, gluey, tacky blood, bone splinters that dug into the pads of her feet painfully.

She battled with the heavy industrial loading dock door, her body so weak she was positive she would never manage to budge it.

Light headed, sick to her stomach, short of breath. She had no energy and was still bleeding profusely, from the gun shot, from her shattered skull, from the battering at Kasper's hands. She threw her shoulder against the cold metal and pushed upward with a hoarse cry. The door lifted, two feet, and then ground to a halt.

"Shit!" She glanced back, expecting Kasper to be upon her, but he was moving slowly, in pain.

She dropped to the floor and rolled beneath the door and into the freezing December night. She ran as fast as her battered body could take her.

chapter forty-five

Susan emerged into the night and looked around, at first unsure of where she was. But just to her right the old wooden coaster rose up against the gray sky like a sleeping dinosaur. The other way was the parking area and further beyond that, the street, a row of buildings and then the ocean side.

She sprinted toward the parking lot, toward the buildings. She would have an easier time finding a place to hide there.

Hide. She was not one to hide, but now that was all she could do. Just like some useless animal.

Her feet pounded the gritty pavement, tearing sharply at the arches and digging at the tougher flesh of her heels. The cold air was like a million needles stabbing at her naked skin and her breath wafted upward from her lips like smoke.

The docking bay door screeched as it rumbled open and Kasper stumbled out, scowling and scanning the area for a sign of her. Amazingly, he did not seem to see her.

"Don't make it worse for you, bitch!" he called.

Susan sprinted to the row of businesses along the beach and shrank into the pool of shadow until she was sure she was out of sight. Up the inky alleyway next to the tavern where she had last been with Devin, she glanced up. The ladder of a fire escape sat high above her head and out of reach.

She leapt for it, missed hugely and landed hard, coming down as on one knee awkward as a child. Straightening up, stiff, trembling from cold, she began to weep again. Weak bitch, she scolded herself and with a deep breath, she jumped for the bottom rung once again. This time, success and she wrapped her fingers around it. She swung there a moment, naked, freezing, her tears and blood becoming thick and nearly ice in the cool of the morning. Fleetingly, she wondered if she would be able to pull herself up. Her side felt as if it was splitting wider with every move she made.

"Come on, come on," she muttered. She tried to wet her lips, but tasted only dried salt.

She kicked her legs out hard and the momentum propelled her just enough to plant her feet on the brick wall beside the ladder. With that extra bracing, she managed to find the next rung of the ladder. Fingers aching, arms shaking with fatigue, she climbed until she had her feet on the ladder, as well. From there, it was an easier go.

Finally, she made to the platform and collapsed, the icy metal like a blade to her skin. From up there, she could see Kasper stumbling along the parking area, a little bent at the waist, the stubbed riotgun at his side. He did not look in her direction and she remained motionless until he turned and headed back toward the rollercoaster, tilt-a-whirl and the rest of the abandoned rides.

Once positive he would not look her way again, Susan got to her feet and leapt to snag the brick overhang. Using her feet to help her climb the wall, she hoisted herself onto the roof of the building. With an exhausted sigh, she collapsed onto her back and lay there, two stories from the ground, above the tavern and a floor of decrepit apartment flats. She gasped for air but her lungs refused to expand. She wondered if she could indeed die, or would she just lie there miserable until someone took pity on her and finished her off.

The odor of garbage and oil from fried fish, mixed with the briny scent of the Atlantic danced upward, sickening her. She chocked back the urge to retch.

Dear God, I am so cold.

She lay on top of the building, the gravel surface clawing into her back, buttocks and legs like jagged fingernails. The wind was like death's tongue caressing her shredded flesh. Her tears froze on the ends of her eyelashes, the rims of her eyes like sand. The bleeding had stopped and her tongue grew thick from thirst. She could not dampen her lips.

The sky faded to denim. The sun began to rise and her time grew shorter. By now, Kasper must have shrank back into the shadows. She could imagine him inside a dank and moldy coffin like some silly B-movie vamp, hands folded over his chest. He would sleep with his gun, weary of some modern-day Van Helsing, as twisted as he was.

The light had more strength than she realized. Even that sweet taste of orange that bled across the denim began to sear her skin. She thought of Devin. Of Michael. Of Peter.

Finally, of Kasper Jacobsen.

All of them broken in some way or another, just as she was.

She wondered how terrible it would be to just remain there, to allow the sunshine, the thing that was always the sweetest part of childhood, erode her flesh like battery acid. She wished to feel the flood of heat on her skin as she did when she was a girl, soaking up the rays as if she was absorbing its power.

The sky turned the color of a bruise and then streaked like a child's paint set, brewing, moving. Her flesh grew tighter, losing all elasticity. Smoke rose in lacey wisps from her. It stung her nostrils, acrid and prickly.

She rolled onto her belly and slithered her way back to the edge and in one jerky motion, threw herself from the roof. The fire escape platform caught her in its steely embrace and pain surged through her left leg as her ankle caught the guardrail and snapped back like kindling across a knee. She had landed facedown and the flesh of her back, buttocks and legs seared as the first rays of dawn caressed it like an uncaring lover. She must get moving and quick if she wanted to keep any of her skin. Somewhere in her memory was something about burns becoming irreversible, if too severe. Her body was a molten mass of agony.

Despite the abuse from above, she was safe from Kasper's rage now—he would never risk his hide the sunlight, even to get his slimy hands on her.

She imagined blood on her mouth, raining from above her like red rain.

She lay very still, gasping like a dying mermaid, searching for the strength to live, to move again, to flee the sunlight like a wretched insect. Finally, she pushed herself up to her knees, then to her feet, wobbly, drunken with frailty, all her weight on her right leg, her left turned inward at an impossible angle.

The cold thrashed at her violated body, as the every brightening sun scorched it. With a breathless cry, she closed her eyes and allowed herself to tumble backward, pinwheeling like a leaf in the wind to the litter-strewn alley below.

For a while, she knew nothing else.

"What the hell?"

The crash jarred Seth Watkins from his daydreaming, and it was probably too early for daydreams anyway, or else too late, depending on how he wanted to look at it. He had been at the tavern since midnight. All of the scum and weirdos and vampires had cleared out a couple of hours ago and he was left to clean up and close up. The girl he had hired to help had already given up the ghost, so to speak—he found her two nights ago, bled as dry as a dead rose in the ladies' room.

Fuckers—especially the new ones. Before, with the old ones, it was an unspoken rule that his staff were off-limits. Things had changed, the young vampires had no dignity. Shit, they were becoming more and more human by the night.

And here was one lying naked in his discarded boxes, nest to his perpetually overflowing dumpster. The trash trucks seldom made a pass along the boulevard anymore— he paid the driver off once a month to get him to come by and clear away the rubbish enough to allow people to move up and down the alley.

The woman lay in a broken heap, half buried in torn cardboard, nude, as bloodstained as a warrior. Her hair hung in heavy ropes, gummed together like dreadlocks with congealed blood. Smoke rose from her flesh where the sun touched it.

A Deathwalker.

Seth stepped closer and then glanced upward. Had she been thrown or had she jumped? It seemed a desperate thing and reeked of one trying to escape, considering her condition.

"What the fuck?" he muttered again, kneeling beside the broken girl. It was difficult to make out her features, she was so bloody and beaten. He pushed the cords of her hair back and fished a handkerchief from his pocket. A quick check and when he was satisfied it was relatively free of anything too disgusting, he gently dabbed at the woman's face.

"You poor thing," he whispered. "Can you hear me?"

As much as he disliked the fledgling vampires, they all kept food on his table. He served them and in return they left him and his old lady alone. His staff, obviously not so much, lately. But still, he had a soft spot for some of them.

He touched her face again and she whimpered like a

small child.

"Got to get you out of this sun, girl. Is there anyone I can call?"

Her mouth moved, but he did not hear anything. "I'm sorry. I couldn't make that out. Who can I call?" He bent so low, his ear brushed her swollen lips.

"John," she rasped. "Moses."

Inside, with the girl wrapped up snug inside his coat and lying on his ratty sofa in his office, he dialed the number from memory. He knew the name well. John Moses was very much like him, obliged to the vampires. Plus, he had gone to Moses and Devin McCree a few times in the past, for protection from the most brutish Deathers.

"Moses? Seth Watkins, here. I think I've found one of your vampires."

chapter forty-six

John carried Susan through the doors and into the foyer, cradled in a thick wool blanket to hide her tender flesh from the sting of daylight.

Devin sprinted down the stairs, bleary-eyed, hair twisted in spikes. He had not slept and it showed plainly on his face. Deep pockets had settled beneath his eyes like bruises and he had not fed enough. He appeared gaunt and too pale.

"Here, let me have her," he told John, effortlessly sweeping Susan's limp form from the older man's arms. John was hesitant to give her over, having been the one to first set eyes on her after this ordeal—he felt she was safer in his charge, at this point.

Devin pushed the cover from her face and looked down at her for a long moment. John watched his expression alter from relief to anguish and felt his heart break right along with the Deathwalker.

"Oh, no. Susan, it's all right, now. You're safe. You're safe, now," he whispered. He kissed her bloody face and pressed his forehead to hers.

Devin's broad shoulders shook and John realized he was crying. He placed his hand on Devin's back and stroked him as gently as a father might his son. He did not know what else to do and what could he do, anyway? What could he do, now, but make her well?

"Let's get her upstairs, Devin. We have a lot of work to do."

Devin placed Susan on his bed so carefully she might have been made of glass. He then brought his wrist to his mouth, making ready to bite into it, but John grabbed his arm and stopped him.

"Don't. You're not in any condition for that. You must feed before you are any good to her."

Devin slouched back, reluctant but without protest. After Watkins called, John told Devin to anticipate Susan's dire condition and had him set out his first aid supplies—antiseptic, gauze and bandages, a scalpel and a suture kit. John was not much of a nurse—most of what he knew, he had learned either from Lillian's tender bedside care or the years of patching up Devin's battered body himself. Vampires, he had come to know, were autonomous creatures. Susan would live, no matter if he stepped in or not. How long she might live in her dreadful state was the question.

John doused his wrist with alcohol, and then snatched up the scalpel. The silver blade glinted in the white overhead lighting before he sank it into the soft flesh of his inner wrist. He hissed dryly through his clenched teeth. He hated this part. Still, he had done it before and knew what to expect—the nausea, the sick dizziness. He had always been a bit squeamish, even after all he had seen.

The blood welled as if surfacing to the light, fast and dark. It splattered on Susan's chest and neck in great splotches.

None to waste. He sat heavily on the bed next to her broken body and leaned close, offering his bleeding wrist to her. With the other hand, he stroked her tangled hair gently, aware of Devin's eyes on the both of them.

"Here, now, Susan," he said softly, "you need to drink. To heal, you must take this."

He pressed the dripping wound to her slack mouth. "Come, now, Susan." His voice had taken on a pleading tone and he supposed he was pleading her to come around, to drink from him. She did not respond.

Blood smeared her mouth into a crimson frown and John cursed himself for becoming discouraged so quickly. He cursed Devin for allowing Kasper to live; he cursed Michael for asking her to come to him, placing her squarely in danger. He glanced at Devin, wondering if he had picked those thoughts from his brain. He would not be able to conceal Michael's presence much longer.

Devin picked up only his dismay. He bit his bottom lip, thinking and began, "What if she doesn't—"

"She will," John interrupted him, sweat beading on his forehead.

Devin moved to the other side of the bed and lay down beside Susan's still body. He pressed his lips to her ear and whispered to her, coaxing, gentle words that John could not quite make out. It did not matter. It worked.

The movement of her soft mouth was nearly imperceptible, but it sent a chill through John's body. Her tongue, still cool and a roughened from dehydration, pressed against the wound, pushed passed the loose flaps of skin and she began to drink from him.

He glanced at Devin and Devin smiled, tears in his eyes.

Susan drew the blood from his vein until he began to feel lightheaded and dull, but took a deep breath and fought the dizziness for another few moments. Finally, it was Susan who pushed his arm away.

Then she took a deep, chocking breath, the blood spraying from her cracked lips and whispered, "Devin?"

Only one word and she again fell unconscious. John took his bleeding wrist from her limp mouth and pressed a thick square of gauze to the wound to staunch the blood flow.

Devin had not fed in three nights—since Susan first disappeared and now the smell of the blood made him nearly inebriated with hunger. He wet his lips and centered his focus on Susan, stroking her cool forehead. He fingered a smear of crimson from the side of her mouth and resisted tasting it. John's thoughts bombarded him, needling, questioning.

Why did you let Kasper live?
Why will he not just let you go?
Why are you hiding what lies between you two?
Why did you bring Susan here in the first place?
Why and why and why

He sighed and wished he could tell the old man to just shut the hell up, but he should not have been in John's head in the first place. He would regret it later. They had been friends, companions for far too long. Seventy years was a lifetime. Devin was positive he did not want to know everything John thought of him.

John slipped out of the room. When he returned, he had bandaged his wrist and was carrying a basin of water and several white hand towels.

"Here," he said, giving Devin one of the towels. "Help me clean her up. She'll rest more comfortably."

Devin dabbed at Susan's battered and swollen face, careful not to hurt her. In silence, it was nearly a ritualistic process, cleansing away the filth, the blood, the scent of Kasper Jacobsen.

It was John who discovered the trickle of blood between Susan's thighs.

"God damn it," he muttered. He parted her legs slightly.

"Here, look."

The flow was slow, but the color was dark and heavy, as if she had been injured deep inside. And worse, Kasper had apparently fed on her at some point. Deep angry bite marks stood out like slashes of red paint against her now clean inner thigh.

The world swirled in front of Devin's eyes and his legs became rubbery. He pressed the back of his hand to his mouth and squeezed his eyes closed. John grabbed him by the shoulders and shook him roughly.

"Are you going to allow him to get away with this? Devin?"

Devin had only heard this much anger in John's voice once before, on the night Lillian died. But that was not all—John's thoughts assaulted him like a fist to the skull. He could not stop himself from hearing them.

Your fucking fault
Did you love him?
I should take her away from here
She would have been better off with Michael

And how did John know Michael, anyway? He did not ask. What was the point? He clenched his fists again wanted instead to strike out his oldest friend and pound him into a bloody pulp. Michael was nothing—scarcely a glimmer in Susan's past.

"I-it's not my fault."

"That's enough. You didn't kill Kasper when you had the opportunity—Christ—*opportunities*. And now, look.

"Does she deserve this?"

"Do any of us deserve this pathetic excuse for life, John? I'll handle this. She doesn't belong to you."

John turned away and bathed the lower part of Susan's legs. "Take her away from here, Devin. I'll take care of Kasper, if that is what's needed. I should have done it after Lillian, anyway. He's taken enough from both of us. I'll do it, since you can't."

"You're being irrational, John."

"You're not?"

Devin ignored him and concentrated on washing the grime away from Susan's torso and breasts. Even with the advantage of being a day-dweller, John stood little chance against a creature like Kasper. "Let me handle it. Don't do anything."

"Bloody fantastic job you've done, so far."

Devin turned to return some cutting remark, but the look of despair on John's face stopped him. Instead, he wanted to run from the room. To be the reason for so much pain was too much to bear.

He knew John's feelings for Susan—that sad, unrequited love. John hid it as well as he could, but Devin did not need mind tricks to come across this knowledge. It came off John in waves, broadcasted, not whispered.

"I don't know what is between you and Kasper, but she should not have to suffer because of it," John said. There. It was out, inviting some inane response.

John cleaned the gaping gunshot wound in Susan's side and then covered it with a heavy layer of gauze and tape. Then he pulled the covers over her and dimmed the lamp. Devin knelt and kissed her soft, cool lips, then stepped out into the hall.

John was waiting for him, unrolling his sleeves, refastening them.

"It's complicated, this thing with Kasper," he began. Then the words began to pour from him. "There's no other way I can describe it. "I share a mark with Kasper—his mark. Like cattle, we were branded to signify to which tormentor we belonged.

"I never loved him. I never even liked him, but I wanted to live and the only way I could figure to do that was to pretend that I did. I was like his little dog. A cowed, kicked dog, but at least he pulled his blows a little for me."

"Is he still pulling his blows, Devin? Tell me. Look at

Susan and tell me."

chapter forty-seven

No longer starving, she felt proper rest finally enfolding her. Even in her hazy, semi-conscious state, she knew something amazing was happening. The shattered bones, the torn nerves, the shredded tendons and muscles of her neck *itched*. The bullet wound felt tighter, as if the skin became dry, tight.

Random thoughts raced through her mind. Smeared impressions of faces appeared, the plains pale and the valleys like spilled ink. Devin. Michael. John. Even Kasper.

Michael spoke to her, a moment frozen in time, a memory she would carry until the end of the world, if she made it that long.

"I know about the baby."

Bullet wounds. The new one in almost the same spot as the one that had ended the life of her child six months ago.

The flash of skin, Devin's lower belly and the raised scar there, the symbol of what was referred to as the "black sun" a symbol of the Third Reich, just above the coarse patch of ginger pubic hair. The same as Kasper.

She thrashes outward, not seeing, and struck a firm, cotton clad body. A whisper, "It's all right now, Susan. It's all right, now darling. It's John. Only John." Cool palm on her forehead and a warmer tickle of soft whiskers prickling against her skin.

She groaned, but insider her head, words formed and she questioned the twin black suns.

A week later.

"Do you want to talk about what happened?"

"I'm not looking for a session, John," Susan said. She stepped out on the veranda and he followed, a glass of the coveted Cognac in his hand to warm him. The moon hit the shore of her face and the long curve of her neck where the robe had fallen away. Only days before, it seemed she was on the verge of actually dying, as much as it would have been for a creature that was already dead.

John followed her, amazed at the ease of her movements. The marks Kasper left had faded to pale yellow. The nasty gunshot had drawn closed. All that was left was a puckered circle of scar tissue at the crest of her hip—a place he had seen and committed to memories that he recalled more often than he knew he should. Except in his mind, he planted light kisses there and allowed his lips to linger on her warm skin.

Susan turned and looked at him a moment, her head tilted slightly. John was well aware that she read his thoughts—she no longer tried to avoid it as Devin did. He blushed and offered a sheepish grin.

"I was asking as a friend, not a psychologist," he answered.

"Either way." She shrugged and turned to him. "Listen. It was horrible, but so what? There are people who have been through worse." She laughed bitterly and took his class from him, drank a sip and handed the glass back. "Besides, we're not even *people,* Kasper and I."

John hated to see her act so disparaging. "Don't say

that—"

"Why not? It's true. And it's not such a bad thing. What are people, anyway, but shit?"

"Not all of us," John offered, not sure if he should be offended or not.

They stood in silence for a while, watching the lights of some distant freighter glimmer like devil's eyes on the black -glass water of the Atlantic beyond the city.

"I feel like Devin lied to us, John. I saw that mark and then I knew why. That's why Kasper is still alive," she said.

"Do you want to go back home with Michael?" He did not want to ask, but he had to know. As long as Susan was with Devin, that was enough for him. Just having her near was enough. It was sad, but it was better than not having her at all.

She shook her head slowly. "No. No. It's impossible now. I could never go back. I wouldn't want to."

John took a deep breath and taking her soft hand, warmed it between his palms. "What then, Susan? I'll do what I have to. I only want you to be happy."

"I love Devin. And John, I love you. I can't leave. Besides, my life no longer can include Michael."

A single tear escaped the corner of her eye and John wiped it away with the side of this thumb. He then traced his finger along the silky bud of her bottom lip, hesitant to take his hand away. She stared up at him a moment.

Again, she was reading his mind, but she did not attempt to turn away. To his surprise, she instead stood on her tiptoes and kissed him.

As gently as a butterfly lighting on the back of his hand, but it took his breath away and his heart quickened.

Then she did pull back, suddenly as shy as a girl. She giggled softly and placed her hand on his chest.

"What?" he asked, struggling to stop his voice from wavering.

"You. Your thoughts—they were just racing."

"That was the blood leaving my brain."

She became serious. "Let me bring you, John. You know you're no longer safe."

John laughed, turning away from her. Reality was back and he hated it. "Do you honestly think I would wish to spend eternity in the body of an old man?"

"It's better than the alternative, isn't it?"

"I'm not so sure. I can't give up what little I have. The sunshine on my face. Knowing I can die, if I ever really want out."

"Don't be silly," Susan said, frowning.

"It's not being silly. Would you give up Devin for me?" He immediately felt like a fool. "Never mind. Forget I said that."

"Age has nothing to do with my choosing Devin," she whispered. "Think about it. Please."

"I already have. A million times."

chapter forty-eight

The music was a thousand hammers inside Devin's head, shattering glass against his eardrum, intensifying the headache he had developed from the hunger. He was familiar with this ill feeling—this deprivation of sustenance. He wished there could be another way.

His craving was a mania, barely controlled. His hands shook, his back spasmed and he breathed deep and long to curb the torture of muscle cramps. If anyone saw him now, they would assume he was a meth addict. When he passed the glass store and restaurant facades, the reflection was of a man he did not know. His face was too pale, shiny with perspiration. He huddled deeper into the warmth of his coat, but he could not get warm enough.

There was a woman standing outside a forgotten wax museum with a bony skeleton hand resting on the shoulders of a girl. The girl might have been twelve, no more, but dirty faced and emaciated, she appeared younger.

As Devin moved closer, the woman shoved the girl toward him. "Twenty-five for the hour, handsome. I'll throw in the girl for ten more." Her sandpaper voice faded in and out with the bass beat of the music.

Devin smelled the both of them, sweat, filth, chemicals, but the odor of sickness radiated from the child. Cancer. Poisoned blood. Not that diseases of the blood would harm him. He was doing himself more harm by not taking her right then and there.

"I'll pay for both. But I want only you," he managed. He shoved his hands deep into the pockets of his coat and found several bills rolled up. He passed the child a twenty, aware of the woman's eyes on the cash, on the child. Obedient, the little girl turned and offered the money to the woman.

"Here, mom."

But Devin took her small, cool fist inside his hand and folded the twiglike fingers around the money. "No. Not mum's. Yours. Go to that pub there and get something to eat."

"Mister, you ain't—" the woman began. But her eyes met Devin's and her mouth snapped closed. "Go on," she said. "You 'eard 'im."

The girl sprinted away down the sidewalk, clumsy, shoes too large for her and sliding on the pavement, tattered coat, too small to allow her arms to move the right way. She would be better off without a piece-of-shit-pimp for a mother.

"A'right. Time is money and you are using up yours. Want to go back to my hotel?"

Devin felt his stomach clench. His mouth watered and he wet his lips again. "Here."

"Here? On the sidewalk?"

He wanted to punch her for being so stupid. "No. Inside there."

"A weird one, ah? Too weird and it'll cost you extra. You're good-looking, but nobody's *that good-looking.*"

Red-haired and at one time she might have been pretty, but now the woman reminded Devin of the woman who had initiated him into the world of night and how she had sent her own tiny daughter out to seduce Devin with her feeble phony tears.

Of course he had come to love the both of them—his surrogate family, scarcely able to replace his beloved Evie,

Anna and David. They had adopted him and he had in turn adopted them.

But it was not meant to last. Before Susan, he wondered if God had placed him on earth just to watch him suffer.

Kasper Jacobsen, that bastard! He tortured the three of them and so many others like them, in the name of the Fuehrer. They called them superhuman—*übermenschlich; they were* experimented with. How much did it take to kill one? The Nazi forces could be indestructible on the ground. They all bore the mark of the Black Sun.

The day had come when Kasper had determined it was worthwhile to kill little Sara. This was his bargaining tool. Kill the child and Devin would agree to whatever he wanted—even turning traitor to his own country—in order to save Judith.

He had paraded the child's head high on the handle of a broom, terror still distorting her small face. How he had laughed.

Devin begged him to let Judy go. He could not bear her tears and wails. But in the end, he burned the woman, first drenching her entire body in kerosene and then setting her alight. He allowed the vampire to suffer more than a week, lying in pain on the concrete floor of a warehouse somewhere outside of Coventry and knowing she should be dead, yet unable to die. Finally, he buried her alive.

Inside the warehouse, Devin hung from a chain, the earth -muffled woman's screams invading his conscience and unconscious mind until he managed to escape.

He still had nightmares of being buried alive, lying beneath the cold earth, living but not alive. Had she been aware? Jesus, he hoped not.

Was she still there in that prison? Was that her eternity?

He still remembered the stench of burned flesh and kerosene. Kasper had assumed that Devin had been the child's father and Judy's husband, so he forced him to watch it all, and saved his torture for last.

The moon poured into the place in random gray streams, not quite lighting the corners, but making it a little less than pitch. Of course, Devin could have cared less—his night vision was as keen as a cat's. The woman, however, stumbled over the prone bodies of the wax inhabitants, crying out in her sandpaper voice one bit of profanity or another each time.

The place smelled of mold, wet must and mildew. At the end of one narrow corridor, a lone "exit" sign glowed red, somehow still illuminated after all this time. The crimson touched the woman's face, casting hateful shadows at the hollows of her cheeks and the places there at the temples that sank too deep. Her eyes appeared pitted black in the unflattering light.

On one side of the corridor was the "House of Horrors" display. Jack the Ripper stood, stark-faced and staring in his Victorian top hat and his woolen frock coat, a huge, bloody knife raised menacingly over his head. Some old Catherine Wheel song that Devin recognized from a CD he had stolen a dozen years ago echoed through the walls from the club next door. Often he found modern music distracting, but he could scarcely think of anything but tearing this woman's jugular open and allowing the warm blood to jetting into his waiting mouth.

He swallowed and his throat clicked dry as a bone. "What's your name?"

"Rain."

"Rain," he repeated. Too pretty a name for such a woman. "Rain, why do you whore out your child?"

Rain turned to him and laughed. "Don't ask me that, beautiful. And don't assume you know the kind of life I lead. We survive. That's all we can do, now."

She sat down at the end of the hallway, beneath the red exit light. Devin followed. Rain shrugged her oversized shoulder bag down her trembling, skeletal arm. "I have to fix, darlin'." She gave him a sideways look. "You look like you could use a tweak, too, you know? I'm not selfish."

She pulled out a small pink plastic framed hand mirror, a filthy razor blade and a tiny plastic bag of white powder. Without looking up at him, she began to cut her meth.

"N-no. I'm not into that."

"Looks like ya are," she commented. She pulled out a vial of water, a spoon and a syringe. "Only be a moment. S'down." She patted the dirty red carpet next to her and Devin sat down with a sigh.

He rested his pounding head back against the wall and watched the woman. She was as drab as a mop and normally he would not have chosen one so used up. She tied off, pulling one end of the elastic with her dirty teeth until some ghost of a collapsed vein appeared beneath her pocked inner arm.

She slid the needle in and Devin smelled her blood. It was only the faintest drops that pooled around the shaft of the needle. He wet his lips as the blood rushed into the already cloudy barrel and then flushed back away. Rain pushed her no-color hair from her bony face and glanced at him. "Sure? I've more." She closed her eyes. "A little more."

Her lips pressed together until they appeared pale. Then she removed the needle from her arm, snapped the elastic free and collapsed back against Devin's side. She was rushing and he did not like the feeling of taking someone who was toxic very much. At least not with meth. The Germans had plied soldiers with the drug back in the war. Feeding from one who was polluted always made him queasy. He should have killed her before she shot up.

But he was in no position to worry about that now.

"Ya a believer?" she whispered.

"I don't know." He was not sure what she meant. "Are you?"

The syringe fell from her limp fingers. "Used to be."

"Why not now?" His head throbbed in time with his heartbeat. His stomach clenched. He thought of Susan. He needed to find Kasper and finish things finally, but Jesus, he was having a difficult enough time finding the stomach to finish off this useless creature next to him.

"Things change, y' know? People change. People go away. Soon there's a hole too big to climb out of and ya learn to make that hole a home."

He laughed. "I know exactly what you mean."

"Do ya, really?"

"Yes." Devin took the woman's sharp face in his hands and kissed her clammy forehead. Her hair smelled like sweat and cigarettes and he wanted to pull away.

"I'm sorry, Rain," he whispered.

Her big red rimmed eyes met his a moment and he saw inside her mind, something he had avoided since finding her. She knew. She knew and she wanted it to happen.

"You're one of them, ain't you?"

"Yes." He laced his fingers through her greasy hair and pulled her head back, exposing her skinny throat to him. She closed her eyes and he read happiness in her mind. Some stupid song from the 1970s and he almost laughed.

He tore out her jugular with his teeth.

A hot fountain of sticky blood spewed up, onto his neck and his chin and he clamped his mouth over the wound, greedy for every single drop. He could spare nothing now. He held her so tightly to his body that her neck snapped backward. He was acutely aware of the moment when her thoughts stopped.

Devin pressed his engorged member against Rain's sharp hip, rocked against her as he sucked at her throat. Her fix affected him much quicker than he anticipated. He felt as powerful as a god and suddenly nothing mattered. Things were not so bad—he was something better than human, he needed to act as so. He laughed deep in his throat as he ripped at the Rain's faded blouse, tearing it wide and exposing a sagging pair of uneven breasts. He raised his head, glanced at his wicked audience of Jack the Ripper, Lizzy Borden and Blackbeard, all wearing even less blood on their hands and clothes than he. His reflection, like an apparition inside a wicked family portrait. Even in this House of Horrors, he was the real monster. He bent his face to Rain's cool chest and bit down hard on one coffee-colored nipped. He shook his head from side to side and tore it away. He spit that morsel of flesh aside and lapped at the fatty tissue there until he felt satisfied.

When Devin was done, he rolled off of Rain's motionless body. She stared upward, wide-eyed and almost pretty, her lips parted and paled to a flowery pink. His head no longer ached and the shakes from hunger were gone. The only thing that remained was the residue of Rain's euphoric high, which did not last. He sat back and wiped his mouth on the back of his coat sleeve.

The child, Rain's child crossed his mind. Surely she would be better off, but who would she have, now? A child alone. Maybe a vile mother was better than no mother at all. His own beautiful children played inside his head, David and Anna running along a bombed out street, seemingly ignorant to the destruction around them, so small and as fair as the ghost they would soon become. The sun shone on their hair.

Despair hit him like a load of bricks and he brought his hands to his face. Would he be with them now? If he had only given in, would he be with them now instead of living only in darkness, a monster? He pulled his legs up and pressed his face to his knees. Stupid sounds, the sobs exploded from his chest rather than his lips. He wept for himself and his lost family. He wept for Susan and what she might have been, had she not met him.

chapter forty-nine

Sandra led Michael over the rickety boardwalk that took them between the dunes and over the dune grass to the beach. Her wore-out loafers barely brushed the old wood, but the slats groaned beneath Michael's weight. He stepped as lightly as he could, his breath stuck in his chest, afraid he might fall through any moment. The drop would not be a long one, but it would be incredibly painful all the same. The idea of impaling himself through the thigh or the abdomen with a splintered pylon was not especially appealing.

"Don't worry, Michael. It'll hold," Sandra rasped over her shoulder to him.

Michael laughed nervously. "You're telling *me* not to worry. Jesus."

He left his flashlight behind on order to avoid attracting unwanted attention from anyone prowling around, be they alive or dead or undead. The moon floated ghostfaced through the gauze of clouds, stingy with its light.

Shortly they descended an unsteady set of stairs to the sand. Where the flats used to reach the dunes, the beach had eroded from the passing of time and the onslaught of stormy weather. It dropped off sharply.

"Be careful here," Sandra warned, motherly. She leapt down the yard high embankment as deftly as a cat. It was surprisingly graceful move for a woman who, in life, had been a stationary middle-aged housewife. Michael followed, fancying himself equally as agile, but knowing he probably was not even close.

They started down the beach, Sandra's fluid stride quicker than Michael's. In the distance, a fire danced erratically beneath the pier, and a thin mist of rain sprayed into Michael's face, so cold his cheeks his lips become numb immediately and his eyes watered. He took a swipe at them with the sleeve of his coat and blinked hard.

His gun hung heavy on his shoulder, cool against his side, as close as love or death.

"Talk to me, Michael," Sandra said. She sounded as if she was crying.

"I don't know what to say." The fact was he had plenty to say, but most of it was too awkward or maybe even too sentimental, to say aloud. His stomach clenched with anxiety.

"Your voice is shaking," Sandra commented.

"I'm freezing," Michael answered. "Why are you walking so fast?"

"I'm not having second thoughts, if that's what you mean. I just . . . I want to be out of the view of my home. Ghosts linger there. I don't want them to see this. They may haunt you when you return."

Michael pondered this a moment. Normally, the idea of ghosts was about as likely as Santa Claus, but then again, so were vampires. *Normally*. What a laughable idea. There was no "normal" anymore.

Sandra slowed her pace and allowed Michael to catch up. Her face was cast in shadow, the gnarled scars of her cheek and head hidden from view. Michael almost wished that was not the case. What he was about to do would be easier if he could see the monstrous side of this vampire. From this side, her face was homely, almost attractive.

"They hold no animosity for what you did?" Michael

300

asked.

"The love of a child is unconditional, my dear. You know that."

Michael frowned. "How would I—"

"You do. Weren't you a child once?"

He shrugged.

Sandra went on. "You're a good man, Michael. Too good to have seen what you have seen. Too good to do what you are about to do. But it is that same goodness that drives you to do what you are about to. There will be a time when you will have to do it again."

Michael was not so sure how good he was. Lately, he felt like a shit most of the time. He was happy Sandra was rambling on. It would make things easier.

"You will carry the scars forever, you realize. You'll never be normal again." There was that word again. He was beginning to wonder if there was even a reason to strive for such a tepid life. *Nice and normal.* How drab and boring he must have appeared to Susan. And to everyone else in Reading. No wonder she left.

He bit his lip and reached under his coat. He lifted the gun at his waist, thumbed back the safety. He could not mess this up—Sandra Harp deserved to go quickly. Despite what she had done before. In the end, it was an act of selflessness, not evil.

"I can read your mind, Michael. Make it quick. Make it—"

In a crimson explosion it was over. Sandra collapsed in a heap. Where her head had been was nothing but a plume of steam rising into the cloud laced sky.

"Oh, shit," Michael whispered. The riotgun fell from his hands and swung on its tether at his side. The world shifted and swirled and he struggled not to pass out. He had seen as bad in the E.R.

But not by my own hands.

He tasted blood on his tongue. He had bitten a nasty little

gash into his bottom lip.

The waves, always constant, now washed over Sandra Harp's lifeless body. She would become food for the creatures, quickly picked clean to the bone.

"I'm sorry, Sandra," Michael said. He thought again about Susan. He could not do this to her. He did not think he could do this to anyone else. He yanked the gun from the end of the strap and flung it into the dark ocean. Later, he would realize it was a stupid move, he was positive of that, but he was not that kind of man. He was no killer, even if the things he should kill were no longer human.

Slowly, he walked back up to the woman's house where he would search the shadows for the ghosts of her family. Perhaps her ghost might appear there, as well.

The stench hit Kasper before he reached the corner of the next hotel. With his acute sense of smell, he was like a shark and could pinpoint when only a drop or two reached the surface of the skin. But this was not just a few drops or even an open wound. This was something *huge—the stink of a* slaughterhouse, the gamey metallic fragrance that filled the air when he was around and doing his job properly. Instinctively, he removed his gun from the confines of his bulky overcoat and peered cautiously around the corner.

Lying on the weed strewn parking between two dilapidated hotels was what Kasper first thought was a man, lying naked and curled into a tight foetal position, his face away and into the shadow. However, moving closer, Kasper found he could not find the sharp edges of his thoughts. The naked creature was not a man, but a Deathwalker.

He lay in a pool of shiny-slick congealed blood that stretched from his shoulders to his ankles. The reek of regurgitated plasma and bile lingered all around him. There was a sick realization as Kasper stepped closer—he had never seen this before, but knew it was not out of the realm of possibility. This foul creature was devouring himself.

"You ain't one of *them, are you?* I can't see in," the Deather rattled without attempting to turn toward Kasper.

"No. I'm not one of them. But neither am I one of *you.*"

The Deather rolled onto his back and Kasper saw that his belly had been torn open at some point. The bloodied edges of the gaping wound were dried dark brown and as stiff as old leather. Inside, blood had jellied, as black and thick as tar. Intestine looped out over the ribs, onto the sandy pavement, shriveled and blue-white like dead eels. Looking more closely, Kasper saw the man was not simply lying in a twisted position. The lower half of his body was actually facing opposite of the upper half.

Kasper moved back, not wanting to have the nasty flesh touch his boots. The end of the Deather's shrunken penis had been ripped off, leaving only a crusty stump. The meaty parts of his thighs and buttocks bore grooves and finger-gouges. Dried muscle and in some places, bone, lay exposed to the cool night.

"Wait until you get to this point," the man hissed up to Kasper. His teeth were stained with old blood, his mouth as dry as a hole in sand. His eyes rolled up toward the dark sky, not focusing on Kasper, or anything else for long.

"How long have you been here?" Kasper asked. He stepped around the man's sharp, ragged body, surveying the self-induced damage. Could he ever become so wretched? No. No, he had his gun. As long as he retained an ounce of sanity, he would end things before he coveted his own flesh and blood.

"How long?" the Deather asked, his voice so weightless, it was like a balloon with a tiny puncture. "How long has the sun shone? How long has the moon rained silver? How long have men craved a taste of blood just to get through the night?"

"You haven't been here forever." Kasper chuckled.

"No. But it feels as though I have, you know. Hit by a trash truck. It was warmer then."

Kasper licked his lips. He was surprised by the length of time this creature thought he had been here, between the line of death and whatever the hell he was right now. "Warmer? Summer?"

"Yes. I have been lucky, if you can call it that. To lie in the shadow of these buildings. The sun never quite kisses my skin. And the rats are sweet, I've learned." He rose up on the twigs of his arms and grinned at Kasper. "How sweet are you, my dear?"

"Not very, I assure you," Kasper snarled. He shoved the disgusting Deather backward with the toe of his boot. The man rolled clumsily like so much dried kindling, his brittle bones splintering. The bastard smelled awful. Putrid as death. Kasper breathed through his nose to avoid the odor.

"It's an atrocity to outlive your usefulness," the Deather said, pushing himself back up onto one elbow. His scrawny, pitted ass lay exposed, filthy, raw.

"I'm sure," Kasper agreed.

The Deather plunged his hand into the cavern of his belly and brought out a length of ropy, dry intestine. He tore into it with his teeth and chewed slowly, noisily. "Eating your own flesh gets old, you know."

Suddenly, like a fish too far from a river, he lunged. He locked his bony fingers around the ankle of Kasper's boot. "*You're* what I need!"

He grinned like a skull, exposing all of his foul teeth. Kasper jumped back, his heart leaping almost painfully against the housing of his ribs. Shaking, he removed his gun from his coat and pressed the barrel against the man's forehead.

"You monster," he whispered as he squeezed the trigger and sprayed brains all over the empty, weeded lot.

Devin's hands were cold and shoving them down deep into the pockets of his coat did not help. Around the corner was Kasper, torturing some poor bastard and Devin was not even out looking for him anyway, despite his claims of setting out to stop him. Going through the motions, that was what he was doing. He looked bad to everyone now—John, the other Deathwalkers, Susan. Sure, she thought she was hiding it from him and at least she tried to. The rest—to hell with them. Maybe she understood. He was afraid.

With Kasper only a dozen feet away, all he felt was sick. He could not kill the tormentor. Right now he was too afraid to move. He clenched his cold-numb fingers into fists inside his jacket. Had he always been so weak?

He wanted to go back home and climb into the bed and press himself against Susan's warm back and bury the two of them in the safety of the covers. They could wait for the world to end.

Last night he dreamed of the sun on the back of his neck.

But the night was cold yet he was sweating. For an instant he imagined simply stepping around the corner and presenting himself to Kasper, his arms outstretched at his sides and his head back. It would be done and maybe that would be the best thing for anyone involved.

Too fucking afraid of that, too.

Devin closed his eyes and he was back in '41, Kasper arms wrapped tight around his waist, his breath hot on the side of his face. Devin had been so afraid. So afraid. Finally, he pretended to love Kasper and maybe that was the worst thing he could have done. That and transforming him. There was nothing he could do to make up for the things he had done. Betrayal cut deeper than anything he could think of.

The sharp clap of a gunshot startled him from his thoughts and he almost cried out. He clamped his hand over his mouth and chanced a glance around the building. Kasper stood over the remains of the nude, broken man, his gun relaxed at his side, pointed down toward the ground. Smoke rose from the barrel like wisps of gray breath. The smell of gunpowder and blood filled the cold air.

How did Susan manage to escape this fiend?

Devin turned away from the horrible scene and rested his head against the brick wall. His hand shook and his knees trembled. He clenched his jaw to stop the chattering of his teeth.

Susan, her face blue with bruises. The blood on her thighs. Could he allow Kasper to get away with it? Could he? He took a deep breath and blew it out through his gritted teeth. It would be better if they just left Dunwich. He was no match for Kasper. He and John could return to Europe; Susan had already suggested leaving, so convincing her would not be an issue.

Despite what he had told her before, he would chose to run away again, just as he always had.

chapter fifty

1946. People were wise to board the windows against creatures like him. Loathsome things, humans. And Kasper? Just as loathsome, he supposed, with his pronounced incisors and a hunger for warm blood as big as the world.

There were those like him who in ran packs like wolves, but Kasper preferred being alone. He hated the Deathwalkers—maybe even more now that he had transformed.

Of course, he was not the only creature the country folk hid from. In the months following the end of the second Great War, there were also thieves and marauders to worry about. Little food. Little work. Little money. Those were the things that turned good people bad.

However, there were still decent people to be found. Sympathetic, neighborly souls who would do kind deeds even when it landed them in the grave. So when Kasper beat on the door of the little farm house just as dusk spread its black cape across the countryside, he knew he would draw an answer and a kindly nod, followed by an invitation to come inside where the fire was warm and the food was scant, but readily shared.

Although he was new to it, Kasper knew the game well

enough. Besides, rumors of prowling things thirsty for blood along the dead brown winter hills had spread like polio. He dirtied his cheeks and clothing with mud, mused his hair and pulled a terrified face when the bolt of the door grinded back and a wary eye peered through a small opening in the door.

"Please. They're after me." It was only a breath before the door opened wider, revealing a ruddy-faced middle-aged man.

"Sir. Something has been trailing me for over a mile. I fear it is one of the creatures that has taken some of the others out this far. I fled it, but I cannot go on," Kasper rasped.

The man stepped aside, his round stomach leaving little room in the doorway. "Come inside. Quickly."

He led Kasper through to the dining room, which was quite small, but tidy, and gestured toward an open chair at the table. A fire roared and crackled brightly.

The ruddy-face man, who introduced himself as Arthur, asked, "So, did they see which way you headed? Have you led them here?"

"N-no. They did not see. I doubled back. They may have lost my scent, but I am too exhausted to go on." Kasper spoke slowly, in an effort to thoroughly disguise his German accent. Germans were not exactly welcome visitors in respectable homes, after all.

There was a scant table set for supper—a steaming bowl of greens, a small bird (charred on the tips of the wings), pale mash. A woman, just as ruddy and plump as Arthur, stood, her brow creased with concern. She patted Kasper's shoulder tenderly.

"Eat. Then rest until light. We have the room."

Kasper shook his head. "I cannot impose."

"No imposition," Arthur insisted. He nodded to his wife and she disappeared into the kitchen, then returned shortly with another plate. Trailing behind her was a willowy beauty with a halo of flaming curls.

Arthur sat down at the head of the wobbly butcher block table. "My wife, Ruthie and our daughter Lexi. Lexi is deaf and dumb, as they say." The man's face brightened when he looked at the girl until he was almost handsome. "But she's not dumb. Can't talk, but she understands—reads lips some. Can write. See that board on the table there? That's her way of talking."

Kasper smiled. Of his newly acquired vampire powers, he had discovered that he could pick up on others thoughts quite easily. Of course, this took his complete concentration and he and not yet had the opportunity to rest with these people. The time would soon come and pretty Lexi would become an open book to him, despite her infirmity.

The place smelled of burning oak and roasted pork. How Kasper missed enjoying real food, but he forced himself to taste it and made a good showing of hunger when Ruthie placed the steaming plate in front of him.

After what seemed a long supper of food he could not eat and substandard wine that made his stomach churn, Kasper was asked to join the family in the parlor to smoke. The place was as cozy as granny's house from a fairy tale. Doilies placed beneath lamps that were not used—"'lectricity's been off since before the war ended" Ruthie explained. She admitted she quite liked the candles, but for the difficulty it created when she did her sewing. Kasper smiled and nodded as kindly as he could muster.

Neither Arthur nor Ruthie could stop yammering long enough to allow him to climb into their minds. Not that there would be a lot there. What poured forth from their lips was usually bullshit, he determined long ago. Within the abyss of the mind was truth.

Now, sitting before the fire basking in Ruthie's genuine hospitality and Arthur's showing of generosity that was growing less and less ostentatious as the minutes passed. Smoking the man's pathetic hand rolled cigarettes and drinking the remnants of his brandy that was much better than his wine, Kasper finally glimpsed inside their dull minds.

Ruthie was simple enough. Done fluttering about, doting on Kasper's every request, she now settled on the end of the couch with a tattered pair of Arthur's trousers. "I don't know how you wear these things out so quickly," she muttered, not unkindly. Kasper was in her head quickly, thoughts that were as fickle as a baby's—*were those monsters still out on the hillside? Had Lexi taken notice of the handsome stranger and what would it matter because she could not hear? Would there be enough eggs if their guest stayed for another meal?*

It became boring quickly enough and Kasper then focused on Arthur. Getting inside the man's head was a little more tricky. It was a dark place. Arthur furrowed his brow tightly, as if he *felt* something as Kasper zeroed in, as if he actually sensed Kasper entering his thoughts. Of course, that was impossible. Nevertheless, Arthur glowered at him through the swirling gray smoke.

The man was not happy about him being there, that was clear. The fat man's thoughts were clouded with jealousy, possessiveness. Hate, even. But none of this was over Ruthie's actions. Instead, he was worried over his pretty daughter. It had not escaped his notice that Lexi had watched Kasper all through dinner. He did not care for the looks that came through the hood of raven lashes of his silent child.

It had not escaped Arthur's notice, also, that Kasper had not attempted to hide his interest in her.

Uglier images then surfaced—Arthur's hands on his daughter's slim waist. His breath in her hair. He liked that she could not scream or cry out. He went to her bed several times a week and he planned to do so tonight. If he could only get that panhandling stranger out of his hair and out of his house.

Lexi was fortunate not to have to hear the carnage that wailed down the hollow, echoing hallway as Kasper devoured Arthur and Ruthie. Maybe it was the pleasure of killing the two without the need to quiet them. Perhaps it was the screams that pushed him on. But even in the pleasure of Ruthie's pleading cries and Arthur's curses, he finally ripped open their stout, sweaty throats in the end, to cut the screams and to bathe in the fount of blood from a breached internal jugular that he had come to quickly love.

Ruthie passed quickly and without very much struggle. Her eyes grew wide with fright, but it was mixed with a kind of resignation. "Don't hurt my child," she mouthed through a gout of blood.

Arthur was too ignorant to realize he was indeed dead. He stumbled around their bedroom, his air hissing from his neck like a punctured tire. He sprayed hot blood onto the dingy beige walls until his body was truly spent of breath and blood. Finally, he collapsed on the floor, the tattered hand woven carpet absorbing his blood and piss like a sponge. His head fell into the fireplace, across the smoldering embers, sending up a tiny storm of fiery ash.

Shortly the bedroom smelled not only of charred pork, just as the kitchen had downstairs, but also shit and warm, heavy *das Herzblut—heart's blood.*

Kasper moved to Lexi's bedroom. There he stood over her and watched in her peace as she slept. Her flaming curls spread out onto her pillows like waves of coppery silk.

He contemplated killing her, but found he could not bring himself to do it. The girl was simply too lovely. He would keep her instead.

Like a ghoul bathed in the blood of her parents, Kasper remained motionless in the wide path of silvery moonlight that came through the window. On her night table, she had an electric lamp, useless, but there was also a short, fat candle, almost melted away. Beneath the edge of her covers, where one small, pale hand rested, was a well-loved volume—Lawrence's *Lady Chatterley's Lover. Without delving into Lexi's mind, Kasper* knew these pages were forbidden and a secret pleasure of the young woman hidden from the prudish eyes of her hypocritical father.

Kasper returned to the other bedroom. He cleaned up Arthur's and Ruthie's remains and deposed of them in a far smattering of woods at the edge of a field overtaken with brambles and vines, along with the bloodcaked carpets, bedcovers and drapes and whatever else he found that could not be wiped clean of blood. Then he cleaned the blood from the floor and walls as best he could. He did not want to expose the girl to the horror. She did not deserve to have her thoughts plagued with such things.

Face and hands clean, he returned to the girl's room before the sun touched the sky and drew her drapes tightly across the window. Then he climbed into her bed, naked, and snuggled to her, the warmth radiating from her through her thin cotton gown. She stirred, her brow furrowing and then rising. She expected her father and was surprised to find Kasper.

She did not protest his presence.

For three days and nights, he gently fed from Lexi's throat. They made love. Kasper delighted in her abandon and the fact that there was something like relief in her face and in her thoughts when he explained that her mother and father were no longer alive. She showed no remorse.

When she found she no longer needed the burden of her slate and chalk to communicate, she blossomed. Her thoughts opened to Kasper. He had found one who would not abandon him as Devin had. Lexi could not profess her love and then leave him. She could not lie. For this reason, he made her his.

Kasper declined to transform her. To do this would close her mind to him and she would become locked to him.

He was fully aware of the effects of a Deathwalker's bite. The more he feed from Lexi's blood, the slower her aging process became. She could essentially remain young and beautiful forever.

Once the word spread that something had murdered her family, some wild thing, Kasper helped Lexi gather the things she wished to keep. In her old man's ramshackle truck, they vanished into the night.

Lexi never questioned what he was.

Years later, she would lament over the lack of a child. He gave her a stolen boy baby as a gift and she was as whole as any mother would be.

They were as whole as any family could be. All that separated them from normal, human families was his determination to find creatures like Devin McCree and rid the world of them. He was an exterminator of pest and vermin. He provided a service to man. Liberating the world of contemptible beasts like McCree was the most important thing he could ever do.

chapter fifty-one

"**M**ichael."

Susan had approached him as silently as a ghost as he was making a fire from the last of the old barstool pieces and a couple of branches of driftwood he discovered on the beach earlier. He started and straightened up.

"Jesus, you scared the hell out of me," he whispered, but seeing her, his face lit up.

They sank into each other's arms and Susan allowed it. Familiar feelings flooded back suddenly, before the pregnancy, before Devin's return, before she stopped being human. For this moment, it seemed right. It felt good. Safe. Of course, that sense of safety never lasted more than a few moments.

He pressed his face into the curve of her shoulder and sighed and she stroked his soft hair.

"I can't believe you're here," he said.

"I can't believe you're *still* here," she answered. "I told you to go home."

He snatched up one of the tattered quilts from his makeshift bed on the sofa and spread it out on the dusty carpet in front of the fireplace. The fire had caught nicely and the room was already becoming warmer. "Here, sit. I know how cold-natured you are."

"Not so much anymore," she told him, even as she shivered beneath her coat, unsure if it was from anxiety or the chilly house. She had not been out alone since her meeting with Kasper. She folded her legs under her and sat down. Michael pulled off his coat, tossed it to the sofa and plopped down next to her.

"Your friend, John paid me a visit. That's how I found out you were missing. I thought the old bugger was going to kill me." Michael chuckled nervously. "You've made quite an impression on him, apparently."

Are you sleeping with him, too?

Susan extracted the thought from the back of Michael's mind and bristled, but said nothing. With men, it always came down to petty jealousy. Even when the issues were enormous, it all ended up with some sort of prehistoric competition.

"Sorry," she muttered.

"Sorry? Why are you sorry? I thought you had been killed." He looked at her, the glow of the fire making him appear warm but a little haunted. "I couldn't leave here until I knew. Then I heard some talk—that you had managed to get away."

"Never underestimate the power of a woman," Susan joked. She did not know what else to say and things were already becoming too heavy. She had come to say good-bye, nothing more. She needed to see Michael and end things before he ended up as some Deather's next meal. He was not cut from the cloth of those who survived in Dunwich. He was too soft. He was going to end up damaged, if he survived. He would never be the same man after the things he had witnessed since coming there.

Michael already looked different and it was not just the fact that he needed a trim and a shave. Susan could count the few times she had seen Michael looking less than perfect—most times he appeared ready for rounds at the hospital. Now he was unkempt, wild-eyed. He had lost weight and his cheekbones and the hollows of his eyes cast deep shadows.

More than once, Susan picked up on the name Sandra floating around the vortex of his brain. Blood. A despair that had something to do with not only the strange woman, but her, as well. As if Michael had drawn some kind of connection between the two of them. She wanted to ask, but thought better of it. Susan did not like imposing into Michael's head—she felt like a voyeur, but there were too many strange things going on in there not to stay for a while and take a look. Kasper and a dark road between on the edge of the city. Michael wondering about Kasper even now—was he a vampire?

What Kasper had done to her. Had he raped her?

"To answer your questions, Michael, yes, Kasper is a vampire. I believe he let you live because he picked up on the chance that you might somehow lead him to Devin, through me." Finally, she added, "And yes."

Michael stared straight ahead, into the fire, his jaw clenched tightly. He fetched a couple of beers from a sack on the floor near them, twisted away the tops and handed Susan one.

"Can you still drink beer?" he asked.

"Of course," she told him, although she did not have the taste for it she once had. She did not want to appear completely foreign to him.

They did not speak for a time and Susan continued to prowl around his thoughts, which became increasingly darker and agitated, although outwardly he remained calm. After a while, he reached out and took her hand in his, brought it to his lips and kissed her fingers.

"No, you cannot go and try to kill Kasper."

"Stay out of my head, will you?"

Susan laughed and pecked his cheek with a kiss. "But it's so entertaining."

"I'm glad you have not always been able to read minds."

Michael smiled, but his eyes were wet. "You would have slapped me on our first date."

"I don't know. I might have found it flattering. Besides I didn't need to be a mind reader to know what you were thinking."

"I'm that obvious?"

"You have no idea."

"Then I suppose you know what I am thinking now," Michael challenged.

Susan placed her fingertips to her temples and feigned deep concentration. *Are you coming home? Do you even love me anymore? Are you going to drink my blood? Do you even have any control over it? Where's McCree?* Susan finally forced herself to block him out, as if placing her hands up to stifle a speaking mouth. She sighed, pulled him to her and kissed him hard.

"You're good," he whispered. He brought his hands to the front of her shirt and began to unbutton.

Susan leaned back onto her elbows, tossed her hair back from her face and regarded him as he did this. "Didn't anyone ever tell you not to play with dead things?"

He stopped, frowning deeply. "Don't say that, Susan." He cupped her face in his cold hands and kissed her. "See? You're warm." Pushing open her shirt, Michael kissed neck and then lower. His lips lingered on the place over her heart. " I feel your heart beating. No dead thing has a heartbeat."

"You'd be surprised by what dead things can do, Michael."

"Show me, then," he dared.

Loving the challenge, she aggressively kissed him again, her damp lips crushing against his, her tongue invading his mouth, tasting him. She dipped into his head again, but things had already become hazier, distracted by the prospect of sex, the prospect of taking her back home.

Maybe things can be the way they were.

Susan broke the kiss long enough to mutter against his cheek, "It can't ever be the way it was, Michael. Just live in the moment for once. Okay?"

"Okay," he agreed. She knew he could not, however. Michael was a thinker and a planner.

Frantically, they stripped away each other's clothes. Michael ran his hands over the sharp angles of her ribs and across her taunt belly. Susan lapped at his face, at the salty perspiration sheening his skin and found it almost as delightful as the taste of his blood, but not quite. Her hunger swelled so quickly, even she was surprised. She bit his nipples, tugged at the hair there with her teeth.

She suckled at his throat, bringing his blood to the surface. She tasted him through the soft barrier of his skin. Her teeth scratched his neck and she pulled back. She could end this tonight. She could finish Michael off and return to Devin's bed. Nobody would ever know. Her guilt, her fear over Michael's well-being and the constant questions—all of it could be over in a quick bite and twist of her head. She could hold him against her and feel his dying spasms grow weaker and weaker, his heart tiring, until there was nothing left of him but a sack made of flesh and filled with bone.

When he entered her she could hold back no longer. She bit into his throat and his blood flooded her mouth, like hot oil, it spilled over her lips and onto her chin. Careful not to take too much, she drew away and his mouth fell on hers, drinking his own blood from her lips.

Too quickly, his movements became rapid as he chased his orgasm. Susan hooked her legs tight around his waist and maneuvered herself on top of him. She wanted to be in control. She locked her mouth over the bleeding gash in Michael's neck, continuing to rock against him.

Susan sat up and watched Michael's face as he came, his eyes fluttering closed, his mouth softening. He arched his back and drove as deep as he could into her. This sent her over the edge, and she collapsed on top of him in a breathless heap.

"What is it like?" Michael asked suddenly.

Susan started. "What?" She thought he was dozing.

"You know. The vampire whole thing. What's it like?"

She considered it a moment and then said, "I miss the sunshine."

Michael nodded. "Maybe we can find a cure. I have access to any equipment we would need."

Susan sat up and pulled away from him. "Cure? This isn't a fucking illness, Michael. It's a gift." She stood up began snatching up her clothes. She quickly began to dress. "I knew I should have never bothered with this," she muttered.

Michael got up and pulled in his jeans and then tugged his sweater over his head. "Tell me how you can think this is a gift? You cower away from the sun. You murder."

"I live forever." She turned to him and almost smiled despite her anger. He looked like a little boy, wide-eyed, hair in funky little spikes.

Michael laughed bitterly. "Why would anyone want that?"

"Cynical much?" she laughed, relishing what she was about to tell him. "With that one little bite, do you know what I did to you?"

Michael's eyes widened and he touched his throat, his fingers smearing a thin trail of blood across his neck. Absently, he wiped his hand on the ass of his jeans. "What? What did you do?"

"Look at me. I have scarcely aged in twenty years. Since the time Devin first drank my blood."

Michael said nothing.

"When you're eighty, you'll hardly be any different than

you are tonight."

She seized his high frequency thought. *Oh, this is bullshit.*

"I—" he began.

"It's not bullshit, Michael," she interrupted. "Consider it one of the little perks of fucking a dead woman."

He winced both inwardly and outwardly at this and Susan smiled. "Now, I need to get back before the sun comes up, unless you'd like to sweep up my ashes and carry those back with you."

"Susan, please—" he took her arm. "Don't go back to him."

"Devin is what I am. Go home, Michael. Please, before you get killed." She kissed him, her lips lingering on his a moment longer than she should have. "Your mind is already fucked up. Get out before it gets worse."

She had parked the Rover in the carport beneath the house, well-hidden behind the overgrowth of shrubs and weeds and now she started it and backed out, holding back a flood of tears. She sped away from the shoreline, back towards home and Devin.

Overhead, the early morning sky became a patchwork of orange and purple. As she turned onto Magazine Street , she saw the lights brightening the windows of the lower offices. John waited for her.

She parked and sprinted up the side porch and into the foyer, where he indeed hovered by the door.

"Where the hell were you?"

"Don't, John. I'm tired." She brushed passed him and up the stairs, John lumbering at her heels like a suspicious father.

"Well, I'm tired, too."

She turned back to him and laughed. "No one asked you to wait up."

"You must realize—"

I was scared out of my wits.

Susan stopped a moment, touched by his thoughts. She stepped back down the stairs toward him. Standing on tiptoes, she planted a soft kiss on his cheek. "Thanks."

"Just don't do it again." He touched her shoulder, this time speaking to her with his mind, rather than his lips. *Is it over?*

"It's over," she assured him.

John sighed. "Good. I'm not sure I could hide it from Devin any longer."

Soon after she had drifted away to sleep, she felt Devin climb under the covers beside her. He snuggled close against her back and snaked his big arms around her. Relief flooded her mind and instantly she was fully awake again. Had he seen Kasper or was he merely biding his time, pretending to search for him?

"I want us to leave here, Susan," he whispered.

"Good." Susan turned and kissed him. "I'm ready."

"I am, too."

chapter fifty-two

Kasper could not believe his good fortune. John Moses strolled along Benjamin Avenue. Devin and that little bitch were nowhere in sight.

At first, he was not quite sure it was even the same man—the last time he set eyes on him was sometime around the time he decided to burn up Moses' Deathwalking bitch of a wife. He had not changed that much—he had accepted the vampire's kiss, obviously. Never had the balls to go all the way, however. Still, the old man had gotten the best of the passing time rather than the other way around. Distinguished in his long camel coat, he was wide-shouldered and walked very erect. A trimmed beard showed flecks of grey. The lines that touched the corners of his eyes were faint. He did not appear to be somewhere around one hundred and twenty years old.

He was as vulnerable as a babe in arms.

Moses rounded the corner onto Bates Avenue where ancient brick facades lined a narrow two-lane avenue. Most of the shops and businesses had closed long ago. The ones that remained, remained because they drew a strange and eclectic clientele and that was about all that was left in Dunwich.

He slipped inside Tillie's Attic, an antique dealer to regular patrons and a voodoo shop in the rear for those who preferred the darker arts. Kasper knew the place well enough. Old trunks and cabinets and art deco chairs cluttered the front section of the place, but the fragrance of clove or patchouli incense floated through the doors empting to the back area. A woman could not make a living pushing antiques—it was good to have a sideline in a city such as this one.

Tillie was an obese woman of sixty, if Kasper guessed conservatively. Of African-American heritage, but her complexion was as pale as a newt's belly. She had claimed to have a remedy for blood addiction, which had turned out to be bullshit. Kasper should have drained her when he woke up and found he was still thirsty for blood.

He did not know why he allowed her to live. Perhaps it was reading her brain, which was a cluttered with muddled notions as her little store, and he knew she sincerely wanted to help. He let he be and told her to keep working on it.

Kasper lingered just outside and peered through a dusty window. It was drizzling now and he pulled his hood up over his head and cast his face into shadows. He pressed his gun to his beneath his coat like an old lover.

John Moses was not interested in the dark arts, as it turned out. He did not vanish into one of the mysterious backrooms, instead browsing the main part of the shop. Tillie waddled over to him, pecked both cheeks.

They moved to a glass counter that houses all sorts of trinkets, necklaces and bracelets. Kasper had once purchased a pair of emerald earrings for his beloved Lexi at that same counter. She was wearing them when she killed herself.

Tillie squeezed behind the counter. She laughed robustly but Kasper did not bother to try and listen in. Trivial chit-chat. She then spread out a square of black cloth, brought out several pieces of jewelry and displayed them against the black. Moses bent over them a moment and then picked up a bracelet.

Kasper grew tired of watching and turned back toward the street. He waited for John Moses.

Twenty minutes later, Moses emerged from the shop, a small pouch in hand. He shoved it into the pocket of his coat then flipped up his collar against the cold. He heard north on the sparsely crowded sidewalk. Kasper fell in behind him at a safe distance of about a dozen feet. Even from there, he could probe inside Moses thoughts like flipping through pages of a book Gritting his teeth, he squeezed the gun through the pocket of his coat.

Susan. Will she like the bracelet? Will it make Devin angry? I don't really care at this point.

Kasper smiled tightly. There was some tension among the comrades. He picked up his pace a little, but began to levitate above the pavement an inch or so, careful not to allow the snap of his boots on the sidewalk alert the old man.

These thoughts were petty—it seemed a waste of resources. But he would get more. At the moment, he had gotten plenty. Time was short. They were planning to flee. He could not allow that to happen. He might lose track of Devin forever. Vengeance was a good catalyst for living. Their little game made eternity less boring.

Moses was not thinking of much now, a flash of Susan. Had she kissed him? The cold. He wanted to hurry and find a bit of warmth and a glass of scotch. He loved the woman, but he loved her in silence. He would not challenge Devin. He was resigned to simply be near her. Kasper marveled at this. A meek existence, not worth anything.

Moses shoved his hands deeper into his coat pockets and wove through a gathering of about five or six scraggly young people loitering outside a dank beer pub and eatery.

Kasper snatched a thought of going inside for that coveted drink, but instead continued on.

Kasper smirked beneath his hood at the old man with a bad case of puppy love. But if there was any compassion left inside him, he had saved it for the old man. He had, after all, burned his beloved wife alive.

Alive, as it was.

He closed—only arm's length from the man's wide back now. His heart thudded with anticipation, his breath hanging at his lips in the cold air. Would Moses lead him to Devin? Would killing him on the street for all to see bring Devin from hiding? Would he finally unleash the wrath he had so desired when he had tortured Susan? He had never pegged Devin for the coward he had come to be.

Perhaps Moses would lead him to their home. What an incredible secret that had been all these years! He would burn it to the ground.

The number of bodies thinned and quickly they were alone on the street, it appeared. Kasper allowed himself to return to the pavement and his boot heels clacked hard, echoing like a gunshot.

The old man bristled—it nearly imperceptible, but there all the same. Dull dread clouded his mind. He walked on. He did not turn around, but he knew. This part of the game was nearly over.

"Moses?" Kasper called. He stopped, waited.

Moses' shoulders, so squared before, slumped as if a weight had been leveled onto his back. "Yes, Kasper?" He turned slowly.

Seeing Kasper alighted something in the old man and his hatred radiated from him in waves. Lillian and then Susan. All the pain he had caused them. All the pain he had caused *him.*

"It's been a long time," Moses said.

"Forever for most," Kasper answered.

"For most," Moses agreed.

Kasper threw open his coat and removed his riot gun. Moses did not move. "This was bound to happen, eventually." He stepped closer. "It's not going to be quick, however. One way or another, I will get what I want out of you."

Moses raised his eyebrows and a smug little grin touched his mouth. "Really, now?"

"Really," Kasper snarled. "No man can control their dying thoughts. There's simply no way to cloak everything. I mention Devin and you see him in your mind. I mention *her," he said, "and what do I see?* You will lead me right to them."

Kasper did not anticipate John Moses lunging for him first. The old man was surprisingly quick. Briefly, he wondered if the old man had indeed turned—that Susan's presence had provoked him to finally leave the daylight. An awkward rugby tackled and together they crashed through the plate glass front of a shutdown coffee shop. Glass rained like shards of dust jewels. Kasper was aware of things scurrying deeper into the shadows of the old place at the sudden intrusion. The gun clattered to the floor and slid, coming to rest against the rusted pedestal base of a counter stool.

Kasper knew exactly what the old man was after and he was not about to let that happen. He wanted Kasper to lose control and kill him quickly, before he could steal any more thoughts from his brain.

"Fuck!" he shouted, then grabbed the old man's lapels. He slammed his forehead against Moses' face and instantly his vision exploded into splotches of red. Moses collapsed and Kasper shoved him away. Blood ran along Kasper's cheeks like hot tears.

He stood up, grimacing at his pounding head and stumbled to Moses, who was on his knees, attempting to climb to his feet. Blood painted his face in thin, blackish ribbons. Kasper kicked him in the ribs "You fuck! You can't trick me. I'm not a bloody moron."

Moses doubled over in agony, coughing weakly. "Sure, you are, Kasper" he wheezed.

Kasper snatched his gun from the floor and in one fluid motion he swung the butt of it around like a cricket bat. It connected this Moses' temple with a crack like the snap of old wood. Moses buckled and then fell, limp. Kasper was quite sure the old man had gotten what he wanted, after all.

"Oh. Oh, shit," he muttered. He scrambled to Moses. The blood flowed at a shocking rate, from the grinning opening in the side of Moses' skull and from his nose, mouth and ears. The rich, coppery perfume of it filled the air, now, replacing the stink of rat shit and dust and bitter, ancient coffee grounds.

Kasper placed his hands on the old man's skull, his fingers slipping into the wound, becoming wet with hot blood. He closed his eyes and searched for something, a glimmer of thought. And it was there, faint at first and then brightening. Susan's blue eyes, her lips on his lips, his hands on her shoulders, the warmth of her.

Kasper hung onto those images and waited. He stared into Moses' face, into his unfocused eyes in the gloom of the dusty dinner. More thoughts came, like stones hidden inside mounds of clay and Kasper now had to dig inside and sort them through. Susan again. Then something else and how it glimmered, as if it were presented to him like the glint of a shell in the wash of seafoam. He snatched it up before it vanished again.

Susan did not feel at all herself. It was so cold and she leaned into Devin to keep upright. Tongue like a slab of meat in her mouth and her head whirled in the lazy spinning motion of a woman who has had too much wine on an empty stomach. She tasted a sick mixture of bile and vomit and some mannish chick's blood burning in the back of her throat. Heavy-headed and ill-tempered, she found she did not currently like Devin very much for being so high and happy. The pot the girl had smoked just was not doing to her what she had hoped.

They had separated from John some blocks back. She was hesitant and Devin assured her that "Old Moses is a big boy. He'll be fine."

Still, she had a gnawing feeling that things were not fine. It was a mistake to become messed up when Kasper could be lurking around any corner.

A few moments later, he announced, "Let's go to the pier. One last time."

"Let's not, okay?"

"No. The cool air will help sober you up." He swallowed her up in his arms and practically carried her toward the hulking shadowy skeleton of the old Forty-Sixth Avenue pier.

"Cool?" She muttered, shivering.

The pier groaned and complained against the struggle of the tide and push of the wind, but neither she nor Devin placed their full weight upon the old boards. Above, the sky was a blanket, a diamond-studded veil that would not be lifted for hours yet. There were no longer any lights lining the pier; all had been broken out at some point long ago. Just ahead, the beer shack that sat near the end of the boardwalk appeared quite haunted and leaning in the gloom.

They found the end of the old dinosaur rather abruptly and Susan almost stumbled off into the void, but Devin held fast to her wrist. "Watch, now!" he said. The last twenty of the pier had been sheered away in one of the many passing hurricanes in the past couple of decades.

Susan's heart wanted to explode from the confines of her body and she reached up, wrapped her arms around his neck and clung to him, out of fear and in search for more warmth.

Together they looked down, toes hanging over the edge of the splinted planks. Out there the water appeared miles deep and as viscous as oil. Or blood. For the first time, it occurred to her that the water appeared like blood in the darkness, the waves gray ghosts moving about, vanishing and reappearing, teasingly. Directly below, the broken pilings that once were the hulking legs of the pier, remained like decayed fangs, sharp and extremely sinister in the bleakness. There was no signs of the life out there. The sounds of music, traffic, crowds of the boulevard no longer audible over the rush of the water. The air smelled of brine and nothing more—the stink of human life washed away with the waves.

"Well, are we going in?" Devin asked. He dragged Susan back a few steps and then plopped down on his ass and began removing his sneakers, then socks.

"Going in?" Susan asked, incredulous. "Hell, no. I'm not 'going in.'"

Devin stood back up, shrugged out of his coat, tugged his sweater over his head and then unbuttoned his jeans. He stepped out and kicked them and the rest of his clothes into a small heap on top of his shoes. "It's not like it's going to kill us."

"I'd rather not take any chances. You know the whole stake through the heart thing. Those pilings down there aren't much more than enormous stakes, you realize."

"You think too much," Devin said. He pulled at the collar of her coat. "C'mon."

Wearing only a pair of cotton briefs, he trembled against the frigid temperature.

"Well, as enticing as it is—" Susan answered, laughed. Devin's teeth chattered loudly.

He leaped up onto the remaining railing, which bowed beneath his weight, but did not splinter apart just yet.

"You're going to get—" Susan began but caught herself. "Never mind."

For someone as medicated as Devin evidentially was, he was strangely graceful as he walked the creaking old wood rail, like a tightrope walker. Still, Susan was positive he would fall before he was ready to make his jump.

His body appeared carved from marble in the moonlight. The muscles of his thighs and calves flexed as he worked to keep his balance.

He walked about a half-dozen steps, then turned and walked back to where he started, just above Susan. He looked down, wearing a rather smug expression. Susan ran her hands up his legs, over the gooseflesh that had formed on his thighs. She pressed her mouth to the bulge in the front of his shorts and he grew hard instantly. She then looked up at him. "Don't jump. Let's go home?" she asked.

"Jump with me, Susan. Do it because we can."

Susan sighed. "You're exhausting to be with," she told him as she quickly undressed. "I see no point in this."

"The point is I asked you to," Devin said. He put out his hand and pulled her up onto the railing.

"The damned railing is going to snap," she commented. Wearing only her bra and panties, she trembled uncontrollably in the frigid wind. "I hate to be cold."

"A dead girl who hates to be cold," Devin whispered, amused.

They faced each other a moment, and then he kissed her hard, his cold lips pressing to hers, his warm tongue slipping inside. Then he winked and sprang backward, his body arching backward, a slash of white in the night. She turned to face the nothingness of the ocean, but had already lost sight of him. After a moment, heard a splash as he broke the surface of the water.

She peered down into the darkness, searching for Devin, but it was as if she were staring down into a well. Worry creased her brow and her mouth grew dry. "Devin?"

Then he was there, just below her, his upturned face only a pale smudge against the inky waters.

"Coming?" he called.

"If you insist!" she answered. She leapt, feet-first, her body as arrow-straight as she could make it before she could change her mind.

An hour later, Susan climbed between the cool sheets and watched Devin undress in the flickering light of the fireplace. Her mind drifted to his time with Kasper and pondered if there was anything left of that, but she closed the door on those thoughts as quickly as they had come. None of that mattered now. All that mattered was leaving Dunwich. Even if it was running, it was better than waiting around to be killed.

Devin's appetite for her enormous and he entered her hastily. Susan followed the line of his beard-roughened jaw with her mouth, tasting the residue of the salty Atlantic still on his skin. She felt on fire everywhere he touched her. That agonizing burning was something she did not want to end. She arched her body against his, wanting all he had to give her. He exposed his pale throat to her, only for a sweet moment and she was overcome with the desire to open him up, to taste him. She pressed her mouth against him, his pulse nearly humming like electricity beneath his skin. Maybe it was the leftover effects of the drugs that poisoned the blood they had drank earlier.

"I'm going to devour you," she whispered.

Devin laughed. "Do it, then, wild girl."

She did, a nip to tear the flesh. Devin winced, but did not stop thrusting, did not pull away. She felt as though she were on a tiny ship, tossed by the waves, down into the valleys between and then up and over the crests, each one higher than the one before.

When she reached the finally peak, she dug her nails into

Devin's buttocks and pulled him to her with all her strength. She cried out his name.

She was coming down now, her mind calming, the drunkenness and cobwebs dissolving. She placed her hand on Devin's chest and felt the steady, languid pump of his heart. An immortal heart, she thought, and then pressed her other hand to her own chest. This heart would never grow diseased or tired. It would keep on and on, even when her mind became too fed up to move on. Where was the mystery in that? Of course, Kasper Jacobsen provided a touch of mystery—unwelcome as it was.

Kasper.

The house was oddly, chillingly silent. John should have been puttering around downstairs, his jazz playing. He had not been home when they returned earlier. She should have voiced her concerns to Devin, but they were too caught up in their selfish moment.

She sat up and looked toward the window. The drapes, drawn tightly, as always, showed no light escaping in around the edges. It was still a while until dawn.

Careful not to wake Devin, Susan slid out of the bed and quickly dressed. Suddenly she was very ill-at-ease. She left the bedroom and went down the hallway to John's room. The bed was untouched, the fire in the hearth dead.

Worry grew. She went downstairs and discovered nothing. He had not been back. *Maybe he found someone.* No. Seeing inside his mind, that was unlikely. She pulled on her shoes and coat, snatched up the keys to the Rover and left

chapter fifty-three

The streets were desolate this time of morning. The sky had taken on a bruised purple hue, the low clouds lending a touch of paleness but toward above the ocean, there were hints of pink. It smelled of winter rain— cold and as sharp as antiseptic. Susan guessed she did not have but two hours before dawn. She had parked the Rover on a side street not very far from the district where she and Devin had hunted earlier—smelly taverns, mostly empty except for the stays and the orphans who had nobody to share their nights.

Well, John was no orphan, nor was he a stray. Susan was as silent as a cat and her mind scanned those few around her—drunken, stupid thoughts pushed their way into her head, like the ramblings of people who did not have a lot to say but could not stop talking. Nearer the amusement park, the hulking skeletons of those rides throwing grids of shadow onto the parking area and the sidewalk beyond. The warehouse where Kasper had taken her and had done his dirty deeds loomed and the tiny hairs on the back of her arms prickled.

Within, she caught the glimmer of something. Something so familiar because she had grown to know it. She had dipped into John's head enough to recognize his mental voice. Something she should not have done—it was too much like spying on someone as they dressed, but she loved being in his head. It had been a comfortable place. Before.

Now it was chaotic. And very close.

Tense and ready for a confrontation with Kasper, she kicked open the narrow sidedoor to the warehouse. Inside were the same ugly carousel horses, the same stupid leftovers from the park that now resided both here and in her nightmares. She wet her lips pushed deeper into the darkness of the sprawling, cluttered building. From the ceiling, fluorescent lights cast a faint white haze on everything. Here and there, the bulbs buzzed loudly and the light fluttered, threatening to go out.

The first thing that struck her was the smell of blood, foul and frightening, and in great amounts. The building was distressingly warm. This was something that triggered memory of her torture here that she had managed to forget.

Again, that glimmer of John's presence, but picking up his thoughts told her he was still alive. Coughing, weak and raspy coming from one corner and following the sounds, Susan found him.

It seemed her eyes were playing tricks on her at first sight. Maybe the strange drugs she had consumed earlier were still having some effect on her mind. John had been crucified on a cross made of what appeared to be the spokes of one of the smaller Ferris wheels.

Slowly, Susan approached. She did not want to see this, but knew she needed to do something and quickly.

John wore beige trousers and a white sweater she had especially liked him in, but now the sweater was ripped up the front and almost totally crimson, as were the trousers, soaked through with his blood. Along with the sweater, his middle had been splayed open from the base of his neck to the top of his pubic bone. The skin and the underlying flesh and muscle pulled away from the cage of his ribs, affixed by hooks, a half-dozen on either side, to keep him open just as a child might pin back the flesh of a toad in order to dissect it.

His feet were bare and blood dripped from his toes. The

little splashes that it created when it fell to the puddle on the floor below seemed deafening.

She reached up and touched his leg, just below the knee. Her heart broke. "Oh, no. John."

To her astonishment, he responded. "He's not here, but he'll return soon. It's not long until—"

"Don't worry about that, John. I need to get you down."

John's face was the color of chalk. Even his eyes had lost their shimmer. He did not have long. Close by, there was a platform of some kind. On the front of the base were cartoonish characters—a spindly bird with a great pink plumage and a couple of cartoon kids who appeared to be Pinocchio's forgotten relatives. A marionette stage. She shoved it to where John was and leapt on top. Levitating was not an option; she was far too shaky.

How she wished she had brought Devin. She was not sure she could face the death of someone she loved again. Choking back a sob, she reached up and placed her hands on John's face.

"Hi," she whispered.

John's eyes closed a moment. "Hello, love," he breathed.

From this view, Susan watched his lungs spasm and contract within the cage of his ribs with each shallow breath he took.

"Listen. I'm going to get you down. I'm going to get you home and you're going to be all right."

"Home," he said. "I didn't lead him to you, understand?"

Susan frowned, suddenly frightened for Devin. "What do you mean, John?"

"He tried to steal my thoughts, all right. But he's an ass. I sent him to—" He turned his head slightly and placed a small kiss on her palm.

Susan saw it immediately—the house on the south end. Michael.

"I'm sorry, Susan. I had to protect you."

"Shh," she said. "Don't talk." She stepped back and

looked at the elaborate scaffolding Kasper had constructed. He loved torture and this was quite a piece of work. The metal Ferris wheel spokes held John's wrists tightly, bound by wire that had cut through to the bone. At his ankles, the same. The wires had sliced through the Achilles' tendons on both feet. Worse were the wire and hooks that spread open the flesh of his torso, stretched open like the wings of some gruesome moth, colored in dull reds and milky pinks of flesh, muscle and stringy tendons. There was no way to free him without injuring him more.

"Listen. Let me turn you. You'll heal. You'll be with us—"

"No. I never wanted that." John paused. Then, "You know what I need you to do."

Susan shook her head slowly. "I can't do that. I can't." She caressed his face again and pressed her forehead to his, tearing pouring over the rims of her eyes. "You'll make it if you only."

"Do it."

Susan leapt from the table and quickly found a large flathead screwdriver on the dusty floor nearby. She returned to John, gripping the handles on her shaking fist. Her eyes blurred with hot tears and she pawed at them with her other hand. "This sucks," she whispered.

"It does," John agreed softly. "Do it. Now.

"Your sweet face is already seems so far from me."

Susan bit her lip and raised the pointed cutters. She screamed as she drove them into his chest, splintering the bones that protected his heart. She knew she had found her target as the blood painted her hands, thick and nearly black. John's head fell back and he cried out, breathless.

"Goddamn it!" she hissed, driving the tool further home. John's thoughts flooded her mind—a woman's pretty face above his—Lillian; Devin across a chess board; then John holding her as they slow danced in the parlor. He sensed her intrusion and whispered, "Don't look, Susan. Don't be pulled down into the abyss.

"I'm afraid . . ."

She tugged her mind from its connection with his and stroked his cheek with her blood-covered hands. He was gone.

Susan hung her head, weeping great, gasping sobs. After a moment, she gathered herself. She ripped off her bloodstained coat, roughly wiped the blood from her hands onto it and tossed it aside. She leapt down and raced to the Rover. She had to get to Michael before Kasper did. She only hoped she was not already too late.

She tried to convince herself that Michael had finally given up on her and left Dunwich, but as she turned onto Atlantic Avenue, it was apparent he, or someone, was there in the house. Smoke curled up from the chimney like breaths on a winter's night. There was the inviting orange glow illuminating the front windows that indicated life and a warm body inside.

She screeched the truck to a halt and sprinted to the door. As quite as a wraith, she slipped inside the little beach house and moved into the livingroom, her feet barely brushing the surface of the matted carpeting. Silently, she approached Michael, who was curled up under a green Army blanket, sleeping.

She kneeled, watching him a moment. She missed him, although he looked very little like the man she had loved. Beard-roughened cheeks and hair in greasy spikes, he appeared almost deranged, homeless. She had caused this. He did not smell especially fresh, either—the tang of perspiration clung to his skin.

She reached out and touched his shoulder. "Michael?"

Michael started awake, his eyes instantly wide, afraid.

"It's me, Michael. It's Susan."

Michael sat up and shoved the blanket aside. He snatched up his glasses from the floor beside him and slid them on with a shaking hand. "Hi." A small smile touched his lips. "Hey. What are you doing here?"

"Listen to me. You need to get out of here. Kasper is coming. He knows where you are and he thinks you've been protecting me here. He'll kill you."

Michael scrubbed his hand through his hair, confused. After a moment, "How does he even know where I am?"

"It doesn't matter." She looked around. "Where's your gun?"

"Lost it," Michael said.

She allowed that to pass without question. There was not enough time for it. She shook him. "We need to go. Gather what you need. Now."

Michael stood, stumbled around and grabbed his shoes and tugged them on without untying them, balancing like a goofy stork on one leg and then the other.

"Come on," Susan said.

"I'm trying to." He grabbed his coat and pulled it on. "Okay," he said, pushing his glasses up on his nose.

She grabbed him by the sleeve of his coat to hustle him up. "We need to—"

It was too late. The back slider imploded in a rain of glass shrapnel and Kasper stepped through, his gun leveled on the two of them, a huge, insane grin on his face.

"Surprise!" Kasper said.

Unsure of what to do now, Susan stepped backward, still gripping Michael's coat, pulling him back with her. But he shrugged away and placed himself between her and Kasper.

"Don't, Michael—"

"No. It's all right."

Kasper barked short laugh. "All right, Michael? It's not all right. Not by a fucking long shot."

"Devin's not here."

"So?" Kasper stepped closer. He kicked the ottoman out of his path as if it weighed only a few ounces.

Susan watched him, hating herself for standing behind Michael. Michael was so completely powerless and yet he was protecting her. Susan reached behind her, for something—anything—to use as a weapon. She felt out of synch, unsure of exactly where she was in the room. She risked a glance behind her, toward the fireplace. There, at the near end of the brick hearth was the tool set—a wrought iron poker, sweeper, shovel and pointed tongs on a rack. She and Michael hid them from Kasper's view.

"A shame you didn't just leave when you had the opportunity," Kasper told Michael.

"That's what I keep hearing."

"Believe it, now, I'll bet."

"I'm beginning to, yes," Michael said.

She slipped inside Michael's brain for an instant. He was afraid, did not know what to do next other than try and reason with a madman, determined she was not going to get hurt. Touched, she reached out and placed a reassuring hand on his back.

She knew that Kasper was at least as quick as she was, so the only thing she could hope was catching him off-guard. She swung around and snatched up the first fireplace tool she could put her hands on and hoped like hell it was not the sweeper. The poker—perfect. Throwing Michael out of her way, she lunged forward. She swung the poker with all she had and she was right—Kasper did not have the time or the reflexes to react as he would have liked. Knowing instinct would make him duck his head out of the way, she zeroed in lower and the spurred side of the tool embedded deep in his upper thigh.

He doubled over and snatched the poker from Susan's grip, never relinquishing his hold on the gun. "You little bitch! I'll—"

She grabbed Kasper's head in her hands and drove her knee into his nose. It was some remains of her police training, and it worked just as she needed. Kasper sank to his knees, blood pouring.

"Run, Michael!"

She turned and fled after him, down the narrow hallway toward the bedroom that had once belonged to a little girl. Kasper fired after them and the shot tore a hole in wall the size of a basketball, sending splinters of cheap paneling and old drywall into the air like thin smoke.

Michael latched the door. "That's going to hold him for about a half a second," he muttered. But Susan was already up on the bed and kicking out the window that overlooked the front lawn. She ripped down the drapes—Holly Hobby to match the bedspread and pillows.

"Come on," she said, putting out her hand. Kasper blew the thin wooden door completely off its hinges just as Michael dove through the window after Susan.

He landed poorly—the jump was from what would have been two stories as the house rested on pylons as most of the beach houses did, to accommodate the high tides that came with storms. He rolled, his breath leaving him in a soft *humph*.

Susan helped him to his feet and they sprinted to the Rover. She turned the ignition and the engine rumbled, as if she had woken it from a heavy sleep.

Then it died again.

"Shit!" Susan cried. Kasper, pierced leg or not, burst through the front door, and cleared the porch stairs in a wild leap. The Rover wheezed to life just as he reached his pickup.

"This is fucking great. Just fucking great!" Michael said. "How did he find out where I was? I'll be it was that old man. He wanted me dead, anyway."

"Just shut the fuck up, Michael." Susan glanced in the rearview mirror. Kasper was only ten car lengths behind and gaining. But old beach roads outside the business district were fairly straight and unencumbered with abandoned vehicles and she was able to floor it.

Susan glanced over at him, his lips a straight line—the expression that she had come to know as the "pouting look."

"Enough of the sulking. John's dead," Susan said. "Put on your fucking seatbelt."

"Oh," Michael muttered, buckling up. He turned and looked behind them. "He's catching us."

"We'll see." Susan yanked the wheel to the right and the Rover veered in that direction hard, jumping the sidewalk and tearing through a lawn overgrown with tall stands of dandelion. The fuzz drifted in front of the headlights like tiny snowflakes.

Michael grabbed the handle over the door and held on with both hands. "Looks like I'm getting killed one way or another tonight."

The Rover ate up skeletal shrubs, the bare limbs and branches gouging at the undercarriage like a cat scraping at a door to be let out. The pickup stayed in their tracks, still closing.

"Hold on," Susan screamed, ripping the wheel back around to the left this time. The tires carved a donut on the next ragged lawn and they were now facing Kasper's blinding headlights and heading straight for him.

"Ohhh, shit!" Michael screamed. He reached for the wheel and Susan smacked his hand.

"Don't!"

341

She swerved at the last moment—she had to because Kasper was not going to. They were Deathwalkers and it was likely either of them would have walked away—none the worse for wear—from a head-on collision. But Michael—she could not chance it.

They headed back toward town now. Ahead the sky sported a hazy orange halo that enveloped the buildings like a cloud of toxic gas.

"Is he still there?" Susan asked.

Michael looked back. "Yeah, but I think you bought us a little more time." He laughed nervously. "Where'd you learn to drive like that?"

"Are you kidding? Being a cop in Reading—I was a regular Angie Dickinson in *Police Woman.*"

She punched the accelerator and the needle hovered near 110. They quickly approached slow-moving traffic and vehicles parked along the sides of the streets. Susan deftly wove the bulky jeep between cars and trucks that crept sluggishly along.

She noticed the smell of exhaust had become more powerful and she wondered if she had damaged something in the engine when she drove over the shrubs. She pressed the button and opened the driver and passenger windows a little. Behind them, Kasper closed in again.

Susan reached inside her coat and found her cell phone. Driving with one hand, she thumbed Devin's number. It went straight to voicemail. "Devin. Please. I think I'm in trouble. Somewhere around Fifth Street."

"*Think* you're in trouble?" Michael asked. "When exactly do you know?"

"Pretty soon, I imagine."

She took the sidewalk to avoid the traffic at the stoplight, laying on the horn to clear the drunken pedestrians. Michael closed his eyes. Passed the light, she jumped back onto the street.

Kasper, however, plowed through a group of scraggly

onlookers who had been sharing a joint. Blood sprayed upward, painting the front of his pickup and the front of the buildings and glass storefronts. Susan glanced in the rearview, at the mess they were leaving in their wake. Kasper had switched on his wipers and blood smeared his windshield as thick as paint.

Michael turned to see the carnage. "Jesus! We need to stop this."

Just ahead, traffic was not only backed up, but all lanes were halted and blocked. Susan slowed, scanning for another opening on the sidewalk. "It looks like we're about to."

She waited for a lull in the foot traffic, banging the horn again. Nobody seemed especially concerned and she started coming anyway.

"Susan—" Michael began.

"Screw them! You want to die?"

It was too late. They had paused a moment too long. Kasper crashed into their rear with so much force the back of the Rover left the pavement. Bodies scattered across the front of the jeep like broken dolls tossed from a child's toychest. They fell beneath the tires, the crunch of their limbs and torsos giving under the weight of the vehicle, disgusting. But the bodies did nothing to slow things down and they smashed head-on into the brick façade of an old, closed up hotel.

The airbags deployed on both sides as Susan and Michael were thrown forward.

Susan unbuckled her seatbelt and then Michael's. "You okay?"

His glasses were gone and he looked too wide-eyed, on the verge of shock. She shook him hard. "Don't peter out on me, now."

Shoving the airbag down, Susan threw her feet up and kicked out the windshield with both heels. "Come on. Quickly!"

They scrambled through and over the blood-slick hood of the Rover, their shoes slipping in the mess. Kasper threw open the door of his truck and climbed out, still walking slower than normal. The leg of his jeans was brown with his blood. The riot gun swung easily at his side.

Susan took Michael's sweaty hand and they began to run.

They cut down a trash strewn alleyway between a topless bar and a fish restaurant. The stink of rotting fish, empties oyster shells and vile, rancid frying oil made Susan's eyes water. If Michael had not been along, she would have taken to the higher places, first snagging a fire escape access and then upward, to the building tops. Of course, Kasper might have followed—a punctured thigh was not going to slow him down much—but the navigation would have been easier.

Of course, Michael was only human. And not exactly an athletic one. She tugged him along by the hand, and he stumbled trying to keep up.

"Damn, Susan. I can't—"

"You can! Now come on!"

The moon passed behind a cloud and all was in complete darkness. Susan's eyes adjusted quickly—the inky forms of plump rats wobbling the walls and weaving through the garbage cans, cats as thin as whippets hiding. She could see the evanescent glow of their eyes, like the eyes of extraterrestrials or wraiths.

She no longer heard Kasper's boots behind them. She was not sure if that was a good sign or a very bad one. He had either gotten wise and was levitating—it was a little quicker—or else he was above, peering down at them. She was positive he had not given up on them—not this quickly.

Worried about Michael, she slowed and then stopped

completely.   Michael dropped her hand and bent over, gasping for breath.

"Damn," he wheezed.   His breath billowed out like speech balloon in a comic strip. "Why don't you go on? I can hide."

"He'll find you in a heartbeat, Michael." She tapped his sweaty temple with her finger. "Remember. He can hear what's going on in there."

Michael straightened up. "What about you?"

"Deathwalkers can't hear each other's thoughts."

He sucked in another gulp of air. "Then I'm only making things worse for you. Go."

"I'm not leaving you." She took his hand in hers again. His fingers felt like shards of ice against hers. "If we can get enough distance between him and us, he can't pick your brain."

She looked all around, and then up, searching for a thin silhouette on top of one of the buildings. "We need to keep moving." She pulled him on into the darkness.

"I can't see a thing, you know. My glasses—"

"Don't worry. I can."

An old department store loomed ahead, where the alley widened enough to allow delivery trucks.   It had closed sometime in the last decade, after the last big hurricane, but had been a rundown ruin long before the storm, as had most of the city.   They climbed onto the loading platform and Susan tried to budge the roll-up door, but it was latched.

She glanced at Michael. "Check this out," she said. Then kneeling, she gave the handle a mighty pull upward. The metal handle screeched and began to separate from the door, but it did move up—first only a few inches, then a foot, two feet, before the handle gave up the ghost and came off in her hand. She tossed it aside and lay down on her stomach.

"Come on," she whispered. She caught a flash of his apprehension. *Rats. Hobos.* She almost giggled at the prospects of hobos, but instead shimmied under the door, glanced around and then thrust her hand back out to Michael. "It's cool. Come on."

"Great," Michael muttered, but slipped through. Once back on his feet, he tugged the door closed and then groped for her hand in the darkness.

The warehouse section of the store smelled of mold and rat shit. Like most of the abandoned businesses around Dunwich, the only lights were pale red emergency lights. They had been perpetually on since the place had closed and it was amazing that they even came on at all. Here and there, EXIT signs glowed, as weak as a flashlight on a drained battery. They hummed like flies buzzing the face of a corpse.

The place was creepy to say the least. Mannequins lurked the corners of the sprawling room, all in various states of undress and in poses that were somewhat sexually explicit. Someone had left them that way as a joke, but in the blood stain light, it was bizarre.

Down a long corridor and they were out in the showroom. Again, lighted by only the red EXIT signs, most of the store was as black as a dungeon. Metal gates had been lowered across the front display windows and now no lights bled inside or escaped out.

Susan stopped and reached for her phone again. She patted her jacket pockets, then her jeans and felt nothing, then went through the whole routine again, more frantically. It was not there. It must have fallen out when they crashed. "Shit!"

She was keenly aware of the soft rustle of vermin in the old store and could imagine them peering at the two of them with their red little devil's eyes, sizing them up for their next meal. She squeezed Michael's hand a little tighter.

The bottom floor of the store had been flooded and the walls were laced with dark mildew almost to the tiled ceiling. They passed through the kids department and miniature mannequins stood like the ghosts of dead children, wearing blackened faces, blackened clothes. The stink was stronger in here and Susan's throat itched. Michael sneezed softly against the crook of his elbow.

He looked around, clearly anxious. "Maybe we lost him, do you think?"

They stopped walking and turned slowly, searching the darkness. "I don't know. Maybe." Susan would have given almost anything to have her phone—the light and the clock would have especially been nice just now, the contact with Devin notwithstanding. "I wonder how long it is until dawn. Kasper will hide just like these rats when he sees the sunrise."

Michael did not respond and she could not resist the opportunity to probe and pry. She caught an image of Kasper across a dinner table in shitty lighting. Lying through his pointed teeth.

They stood in the musty, dark abyss of the department store a moment. How she wished Devin had picked up the first time she called. Her thoughts wanted to dwell on John, his pain. The fact she was the one to end his long life. She wanted to throw up suddenly, but squeezed Michael's fingers in her hand tightly and breathed deeply.

Poor, sweet John. What kind of monster could do those things to him?

After a few moments of just standing and listening, Michael whispered, "Susan. I want you to be with me at the end. Okay?"

Those words intensified the queasiness in Susan's stomach. "Please don't say that, Michael."

"Really. If we don't make it out of here." He took her head in his hands and kissed her long and hard. Susan was instantly excited—she could scarcely remember Michael showing her such passion. He had always been such a gentle and passive man, she sometimes forgot his needs when they were together.

Somewhere from the edges of his mind, Susan heard him, desperate, afraid--*This is the last time I'll ever do this.* He pulled away, his eyes glistening. She rested her forehead against his a moment, caressed the stubble-scruff of his cheek. "Don't give up, Michael. Kasper is stupid. We'll—"

"Not that stupid." Kasper materialized from the darkness, his gun trained on Susan's head, his face stained red in the light of the signs. "What a pathetic show of emotions. I'm glad I was here to witness it." His nose still tricked blood and his chin and cheeks were smeared with it. He shoe squelched wetly when he stepped forward, filled with blood from this punctured thigh.

Still holding the gun on them, he pulled Susan's cell from his coat pocket, thumbed up a number and sent it to speaker.

It rang only a couple of times before an answer. "Susan?" Devin, sounding sleepy and somewhat anxious.

"Susan's with me, Devin," Kasper said.

There was a pause, a sigh, then, "Kasper. What have you done?"

"I win, Devin."

"Put Susan on the phone." Devin's voice rose slightly, but he quickly regained control of it. "I need to hear her."

Kasper thrust the phone toward Susan. "Say something, little bitch."

Susan realized she did not have any spit in her mouth. She swallowed hard, her throat clicking loud in her ears. "I'm okay, Devin. I can handle this ass."

Michael squeezed her fingers tight enough to hurt.

"Don't do anything, Kasper. Don't hurt her. Just tell me where you are and I'll come. You can have me. Just don't hurt Susan."

"*Have* you? I've had you, Devin. At this point, making you miserable is more fun. I want to take away all you've had. Just like you did me."

He hung up, then dropped the phone to the floor and

crushed it under the heel of his boot. "I hate these fucking things, anyway," he muttered. Then he focused his attention on Michael. "You. I warned you when you first came here, how things would eventually go down. And now here we are."

Kasper dabbed at his bloody nose with the sleeve of his coat. He stalked even closer and Michael pulled Susan more tightly to him. Kasper towered over them as if they were just small children. He appeared hellish in the cherry Kool-Aid lighting, with his busted nose, the blackening hollows beneath his eyes, the blood smears, the lunatic grin. Susan watched every move he made, every rise and fall of his chest, waiting, hoping for an opening.

Not completely unexpected, but too quickly for her to react, he brought the butt of the gun down against the right side of her skull, hard enough to snap her teeth together and make her ears ring. Susan dropped to her knees, black spots screwing up her vision for a moment. Consciousness threatened to slip and she could not allow that. Through a haze, Michael lunged at Kasper and Kasper drove him back as if he were swatting a fly.

Blood, hot and as sticky as syrup wet the side of her face and neck. Kasper grabbed her long hair in one hand and yanked her head backward. He placed the icy gun barrel under her chin and pressed it hard into the soft flesh there. Susan closed her eyes and Kasper laughed.

"Are you afraid, Susan?" he asked.

Susan had several times found herself imagining her life ending in some painful, hideous way, but she forced herself to giggle. "Are you?"

"I have nothing left to lose. Therefore, I have nothing to fear," Kasper answered.

"You will when Devin finds you."

"Devin has had his chance to finish me off. He's a hell of a lot weaker than he's led you to believe. Devin McCree's no killer. He's a coward."

He glanced at Michael again. "As for you. You get to watch this bitch die. Then I'm going to take you, chain you up and drain you slowly."

Laughing, Kasper cocked the trigger of the gun.

Michael sprang then and forced himself between the gun and Susan, sending Susan reeling backward and crashing into a pile of disassembled child-sized mannequins. The gun went off, deafening, accompanied by a soft gasp, as if someone had the wind knocked from them. Without thinking, Susan behind her and snatched up the first thing she could put her hands on, which turned out to be the short, thin leg of a little boy mannequin.

Kasper stood looming over Michael's writhing form. He casually put his hand into the pocket of his coat, fished out two more shells, and proceeded to reload the riot gun. But Susan was quicker this time and brought the plastic doll's limb around and across the gun, ripping it from his hands. It clattered into the shadows, out of sight and even with her vampire eyes, she could not pinpoint where it had landed. She only hoped Kasper would have as much trouble finding it, buying her and Michael a little time.

The choice was there now, to try and go after the gun or to get Michael and haul him out of there and away from Kasper as quickly as she could.

She kneeled, hooked her arm around Michael's middle and dragged him to his feet. His knees buckled and his head lolled back as if it was attached to a hinge. It was bad and she did not have a lot of time.

chapter fifty-four

Susan pulled Michael back the way they had come, toward the loading area and through the box and mannequin-cluttered docking bay.

"Damn it," she muttered. "Sit tight a second." She eased Michael to the floor and tugged at the roll-up door. It did not want to budge at first. Outside, she heard the metallic patter of sleet and realized the door might have frozen. Even with the strength she now had, it was not going to be easy. She heaved upward once again and felt the muscles and ligaments in the small of her back tear. She went to one knee with a gasp and then gave it everything she had and the door rattled up—a foot then two feet, then it screeched to a dead stop.

"Fuck!" She scrambled to Michael and helped him over to the door. "Just lie still. I'll go first and then pull you through."

"Just go on, Susan," Michael whispered.

His coat and the shadows concealed most of his body and she could not yet determine exactly how bad things were, but she smelled the blood on the air, rich and heavy, from deep inside and felt the thick wetness of it when she touched Michael.

She slid under the gate and then reached in and pulled

Michael through. When she helped him to his feet, he wobbled, but managed to stay somewhat upright. He bent at the waist, holding his middle.

It was sleeting hard and it was not until the tears on her cheeks and eyelashes began to freeze did Susan realize she was crying. Behind then, Kasper footsteps echoed in the warehouse. He was ranting at her, cursing.

She pulled Michael's limp body against her and began to run with him as best as she could. The pavement was slick with ice and he went down once, taking her with her.

"Sorry. I'm sorry. Please leave me." She did not risk a look inside his mind now. She did not want to see what was there—she had seen enough with John and that was as close to death as she ever wanted to get again.

"You need to just stop talking, Michael and start walking," she said.

Michael rested his head against her shoulder. "It that a song?"

"Think of it as a mantra. Start walking, Michael, or I will carry you."

They left the semi-sheltered canyon of the alley behind the store and found themselves on the street. Michael left a wide trail of blood behind in the ice—Kasper would have no trouble following them, but she imagined he could trace them with scent alone, anyway. He was as wolf-like as any man she had seen.

"You're dragging me around like you think I'll make it through this," Michael said. "I'm a doctor. I know when someone is dying—especially when that someone is me."

"Shut up, please," Susan said. Her feet slipped again, but she regained purchase before she lost her balance completely. "We just need to get out of the cold. I hate the fucking cold."

Her face and hands were numb. Behind, Kasper was just now scrambling under the docking gate.

"Shit," Susan hissed. "You're going to have to pick it up,

Michael. You hear me? I'm not leaving you, so are you going to let him kill me?"

She knew that would get Michael's feet moving, no matter how badly injured he was. She smiled and gave him a quick peck on the icy cheek. "That's it." Under the light of the streetlamps, she could see him better. His face was pasty and his lips trembled in the cold. Blood seeped from his mouth, painting his chin red—a startling contrast to the bluish color his lips had become. It congealed quickly in the chill air.

They round the corner and followed the sidewalk, Susan's eyes scanning for anywhere that looked dark and cluttered enough for them to get lost for a little while. The few people that remained on the streets at this hour moved aside quickly and let them pass.

"Let get to the trains. Okay?" We'll lose him if we can make it to the trains."

"Okay," Michael agreed. Susan knew she have suggested anything at that point and Michael would have agreed.

But his body was not cooperating with his mind anymore. His knees unbuckled and he fell again, pulling Susan down on top of him. Her face was stiff with frozen tears and snot.

"Sorry," he wheezed.

"Don't worry." There was a movie theatre ahead, one of the grand old places before the multiplexes took over. The front entrance was boarded up and the marquee sported *Bram Stoker's Dracula or at a few letters of it, beneath a broken out neon sign that let* the world know this place was the Uptown Theatre. The lobby posters were ripped away and graffiti decorated the walls instead, crude statements of what the city had become.

She tugged away one bottom corner of the plywood barrier, and luckily the glass door behind it was shattered. Susan plopped on her bottom and kicked it out with her the soles of her boots. Then she slid out of the way and looked up at Michael.

"Now. Just a little more and then we can rest. Just a little farther, Michael."

Michael's response was a weak, wet cough and he sort of wilted to his knees in front of the opening.

"Go on, baby," Susan said. She placed her hand on his back, stroking him. "For me."

Grunting, Michael wriggled through the opening. Susan followed him through and then turned, removed her coat and rubbed hard at the blood he had left in his wake. It was still there, smeared, but hopefully not noticeable to anyone passing by. She readjusted the plywood cover and then crawled over to where Michael lay on his belly, gasping.

She pulled him to his feet and they made their way through the thick darkness. There were no glowing red EXIT signs here to light the way, but Susan's vampire vision could make out all she needed to see and most things she as just as soon not seen—rats, mostly. She hated rats.

Dried animal waste, ancient popcorn and dust hung in the air. Here and there, muted moonglow peeked between the boards and against the intense darkness it glowed like bars of sunlight in the lobby. The glass display of concessions counter had been broken out. Candy wrappers littered the carpeted floors. The popcorn machine had been tossed over the counter and onto the floor. Petrified kernels made walking treacherous.

Susan now carried Michael and he was as limp as a rag doll in her arms. She found a wide corridor. A velvet rope lay discarded on the floor coiled like a sleeping snake. She glanced from side to side, looking for the door that led to the projection room.

Finally, she came to a door that bore no disclaimer and she took her chances. A narrow winding stairwell into another realm of darkness and they were then looking over the massive auditorium. Susan gently lowered Michael to the floor and risked a look over the balcony, half afraid she might spy yet another squatter looking for shelter from the cold night.

It was not so dark in there—the ornate ceiling was completely gone in spots and gray light spilled down onto a tattered and torn screen. Seat cushions bled stuffing. Rats scurried here and there and she felt a shiver up her spine. Rats, but nothing or no *one* else. She kneeled next to him and touched his face. He was so cold. His eyes opened slowly and tried to focus on her. She could not let this happen again. Not again tonight. Not again in her life. She could not lose someone she loved and try to pretend that she was all right to move on without them, without knowing they were somewhere alive on this earth.

She pulled apart the flaps of his coat. The cloth was like a soaked blanket. Michael's middle was nothing but a hole, large enough for Susan to thrust both her fists inside, if she wanted to. In the darkness, it appeared a mile deep.

"Don't leave me, Susan," Michael whispered. He sounded like he was under water.

She kissed his icy forehead. "Don't *you leave me,*" she said.

She pulled back her sleeve and exposed her wrist. "Now listen to me, Michael. I want you to do what I tell you and we're going to be okay." She brought her arm to her mouth and bit down hard, drawing tears to her eyes and her own blood began to flow thickly.

She held the pumping gash just above Michael's slack lips. "Drink, Michael."

He opened his mouth slightly. A small flick of his tongue. Then he turned his face away. "No. I can't."

"You can, Michael." Susan got to her knees and pressed her gushing wrist more urgently to his mouth. After a few breaths, she felt his soft lips working gently against the sensitive skin there. Her heart quickened and she leaned over him and stroked his hair back from his forehead with her free hand. "That's it. Don't stop. Don't stop, Michael."

His thirst grew more burning. He wrapped both hands

around her hand and wrist and sucked at the wound greedily. His chest vibrated against her as he growled deep in the back of his throat. She had never turned anyone and was unsure of when to make him stop. She felt dizzy with blood loss and she could not allow that—if she did, the both of them might be screwed. After another impatient moment, she yanked her arm away from Michael, but he snatched it back. He was now surprisingly strong. She took her arm away again and replaced it with her lips. She gave him a long, lingering kiss, her tongue dipping inside his hot mouth, tasting her own blood. Then she sat up.

"That's enough," she whispered. She ripped the bottom of her blouse and tied it around her arm to staunch the bleeding.

Michael lay perfectly still for a while and she wondered if she had waited too long. Maybe she did not know what she was doing and nothing would happen. She pressed her fingers to his neck and felt a strong pulse, however. She waited, listening to his breathing and for the sound of Kasper bursting into the theater.

With her mind, she pressed against the door of Michael's thoughts. There was a cloud of worry there, that same fear he had felt early, but not as intense. Not as hopeless. Then suddenly, it was as if the door was slammed closed. She jumped back, surprised and then laughed softly to herself.

She sat back against the wall and dozed.

chapter fifty-five

"**S**usan? What did you do?" Michael looked down at himself and probed his belly.

Susan straightened up, rubbing her eyes. She had no idea how long she had slept. "I wasn't going to watch you die."

Michael stood up. He kicked at some a stack of film tins and sent them scattering loudly. "Just what the hell am I supposed to do now? I can't go home like this. *You* don't want me." He raked his hands hard through his hair. "Plus, *Fheur* Kasper wants to kill me."

He turned away from her, his shoulders slumped, his head hanging. "I want to go home. All I wanted was for us to go back home. To have our lives back."

Susan jumped to her feet and shoved him hard, suddenly seething. More than anything, she wanted to punch him as hard as she could. "This is just fucking great! This is your life now, Michael. Like it or not. And you'd better like it. It's better than being dead. No matter what you think, it is."

"Some life." Michael clenched his jaw and shook his head. "What the hell am I suppose to do," he asked again. "Reopen my practice and seen my patients only at night? Rob a blood bank? Maybe they'll give me an account—I am a doctor, after all."

Susan laughed. "Don't be so weak," she snarled. "You

know what? Devin is the same. And so is Kasper. Maybe it's a man thing. Embrace what you've become. You cannot change once it's started, so embrace it.

"Shut the hell up," Michael told her.

"Screw you, Michael. Go back to Reading. Survive on chickens and stray dogs."

Michael swiped at his eyes and she realized he was crying.

"Small towns are the worst," she went on. "Strangeness is like a disease. Talk gets around and the next thing you realize your house is burning down around you. There's no anonymity in a small town. No 'fitting' in."

"But I have nowhere else to go, Susan." He went to her and pulled her into his arms. He cried silently against her shoulder and she relented. She could not help herself. She slipped her arms around him and held him as tenderly as she could, remembering for a moment how it was to be human.

"We need to get out of here," Susan said. They backtracked the same way they had come in. The scent of Michael's blood was still strong, at least to Susan and now to Michael, as well. A human would not have even noticed it. The going was easier now—not only because Michael was healing, but because he could see in the darkness. Susan reached for his hand and he pulled away from her. She felt stung. He had never rejected her before. He had become sullen, quiet and she now felt very alone, unable to reach him with words or slip into his mind.

At the entrance Susan knelt to crawl back through and Michael stopped her. "I'm not crawling like some kind of frightened animal," he muttered, then kicked the wooden barricade hard enough to send it away from the entrance in splintered pieces.

Susan followed him through and back out into the night. It felt strange, him leading her, but suddenly he was someone else—no longer afraid, no longer her lapdog. She wondered if she had done the right thing in changing him, but the alternative was still far worse.

"Where are you going, Michael?"

"What does it matter? Just so long as I'm not out in the daylight?" He shoved his hands deep into the pockets of his blood drenched coat and began walking down the empty sidewalk. He did not turn to her. "Go back to Devin. Go now!"

She stood watching him, wanting to cry again. Somewhere nearby boot heels snapped against the pavement, deliberately loud, echoing and signaling an approach. At the end of the block, a figure stepped out of an alley.

"Run, Susan," Michael said.

The figure stepped under the haze of the streetlamp and allowed the light to fall on him. He raised his gun.

"No, Michael—"

"Just go. Now," he hissed. He walked quickly toward the Kasper Jacobsen, his hands outstretched at his sides.

She fled without looking back, her tears blowing backward into her hair and into her ears like icy kisses.

Before she entered the subway tunnel, the crack of gunfire pierced the night.

epilogue

The fragile light of dawn was beginning to bleed into the sky when Susan awoke. She rubbed her eyes and adjusted the seat upright. Outside the window lay great expanses of nothing—scrub plants, a tall, spindly silhouette of a water tower. Farther in the distance, oil wells loomed like prehistoric creatures against the purple canvas of the horizon.

"Where are we?" she asked.

"Somewhere outside Austin," Devin said without taking his eyes from road. "We'll need to stop soon. The sun's almost up."

Donna Burgess lives with her husband, daughter, son, many cats and one goofy Golden Retriever in Pawleys Island, South Carolina. When she is not writing, she can be found on her longboard or behind a good book. She is also the president of Naked Snake Press.

http://donnaburgess.com
http://nakedsnakepress.net

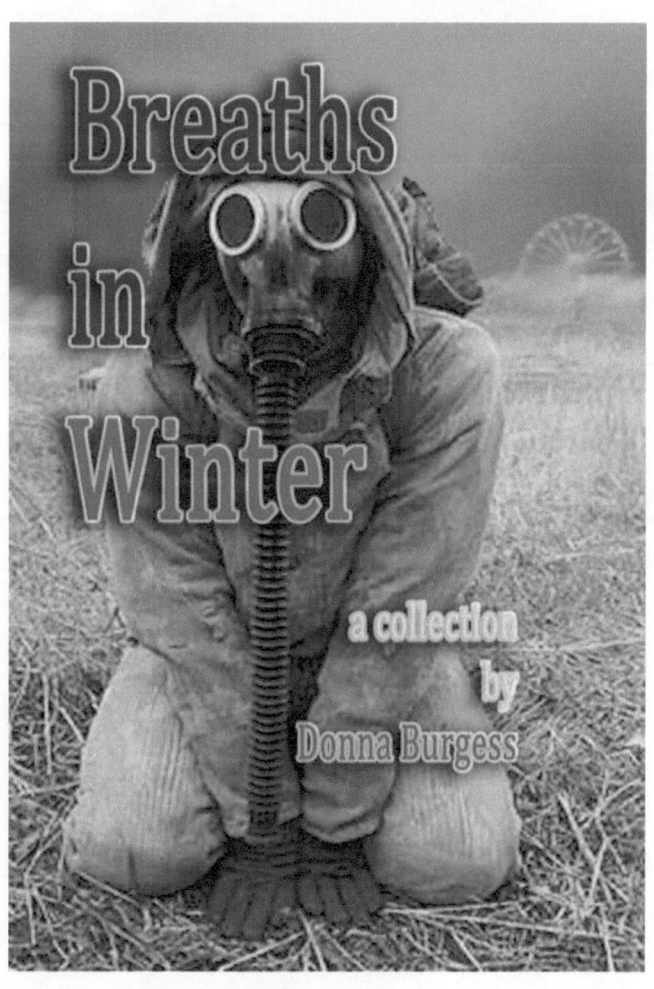

www.ingramcontent.com/pod-product-compliance
Lightning Source LLC
Chambersburg PA
CBHW020221180626
46810CB00006B/2011